The Cabernet Legacy

THE CHARLEMAGNE CHALLENGE

BOOK THREE

NICHOLAS HUNTLEY

"There are days when I look at the whole of existence with the fear that some agony may break out in it and cause it to scream, so great is my terror of the abuse which the body, in so many things, wreaks on the soul, which has peace in the animals and safety only in the angels."

– Rainer M. Rilke

Act 1, Prologue

There is no place in Europe that is more humble to one's existence than the French countryside. This region, completely removed from the proud cities, reveals an honest picture known of Europe since the start of the common era. In every region of France does this humility expose itself by the autumn breeze in late summer, brushing past the trees as one sits atop of a hill, or the gentle row of one's vessel down a crystal clear stream in spring. Even her people, so simple of desire; an exposé of the human heart that is foreign to the cosmopolitan concerned with the wider world. In the French countryside, there are no concerns of the wider world, but of this world. The Vals de Loire, for example, has not changed in the past two-thousand years. For miles upon miles on either horizon, her flat lands stretched out, rugged by deciduous trees, and smooth and organized by vineyards and other farmland. This bocage, delineated by roads and at occasion pointed towards a town of several houses, is heritage to the people of France. One such village is in the commune of Azay-le-Ferron, whose small village surround the Chateau d'Azay-le-Ferron, a small castle with a short, wide and round tower with a coned roof. Her walls consist of marble brick, and her windows of white frames and the rest of the rooftops of triangular peaked roofs. In the garden there is a hedge maze, very short in height and surrounded by shrubs cut into coned shapes and gravel paths. Not too far from the castle, in a field a part of a farmstead, are stone walls, parts of which have fallen over, remnant of more than a thousand year times. This region like many in France consists of history in its very landscape, enriching it so much more to be a place that it will always be, the country of France amid mother Europa.

Charlemagne Phillipe Cabernet lay on his back as he looked up to the light blue skies above him, hands behind his back and his right ankle crossed with his left. He wore tweed trousers, brown leather brogue shoes that matched his likewise brown leather belt. He also wore a light grey collared shirt with faint tattersall crossed patterns that was tucked in and buttoned up to the right before the top button. Charlemagne, a young child, had fair and smooth skin with blue eyes that naturally reflected the color of the sky. His blonde hair was medium length, smooth as well, and silk-like in sheen. His right foot moved back and forth upon his ankle as he hummed a classical tune, Vivaldi's Concerto No. 3, 'Autumn,' and continued to stare up at the many white cumulus clouds like cotton or wool in their abstract shapes and sizes. The sun shined down with fair warmth from the toll it made others pay in the passing summertime. He lay upon a hill not too far from a stream in the midst of the French countryside. Around him were grass fields, bordered with deciduous trees, and beyond them vineyards and farms. At the base of the hill that Charlemagne was on was a primitive bicycle. He stared up to the sky with a pensive appearance, eyes shifting focus from one cloud to another. Charlemagne continued to look up at the sky for another few minutes until his eyes and humming stopped with the screech of the brakes of another bicycle. He froze in place as his ear twitched, and before long, Charlemagne was met with the glance over him of a young lass.

"What are you doing here?" the young girl spoke in a Parisian French accent.

Charlemagne glared at her, sat up, and kept his left arm extended behind him as he propped himself up. He looked at this young girl, around the same age as Charlemagne at this moment. Charlemagne was seven years old, and this young girl just turned six years old. She had fair skin, although with a bit of warmth compared to this young boy. Her hair was thick and wavy in a medium-brown hue almost reddish in the sunlight. Her hair was cut short for an average female, reaching to her shoulders, although it was dense. This young girl wore a sleeveless navy blue dress, although underneath the dress she wore a long-sleeved white blouse. She also wore a short tie. She wore black flat shoes and white socks that came up to her knees.

"I've been looking everywhere for you," the young girl remarked. "Where did you go?"

"If you've had a hard time to find me," Charlemagne replied in his East Anglian accent, "then it's likely because I didn't want to be found. Go away."

"You promised me that you'd play with me," the young girl expressed. "I'm bored."

"That's not my problem," Charlemagne said, slightly scowling at her as he stood up. He held his head up as he walked past her. "I'm not one to engage in such folly, so you'll just have to find someone else."

"What do you mean? You always play with me, so what's changed?"

Charlemagne paused and turned around to look at her. "My papa said so. He said I needed to be focused like him, thinking about what's important, and I to not think that such childish games are of any concern to me."

The young girl held a plain expression as she looked at him, slightly so that she appeared as though she was on the verge of tears. "How could you do that to me? I thought I was your friend."

Charlemagne's expression slightly dropped as she turned her head and then walked downhill by herself. As she was a few yards away, Charlemagne's expression lowered further and he sighed. He then walked downhill after her as she went to her bike, lying half between the grass and the other half between the dirt path.

"Manon!" Charlemagne stated aloud.

Manon picked up her bicycle and brought it onto its wheels as she was about to leave. Charlemagne hurried up and placed his hands at the front of the bicycle.

"I'm sorry," Charlemagne expressed, looking at the sullen face of Manon. "Please don't hate me."

"You're awful," Manon remarked. "You're an awful person."

"I said I'm sorry," Charlemagne repeated. "What more do you want from me?" He slowly released his grip from the front of Manon's bicycle. His grip had been tight.

"How could anyone like someone like you, Charlemagne."

Charlemagne raised a sheepish smile at her as he sort of shrugged. Manon blushed and raised a timid smile. Manon steered her bike away from Charlemagne and stopped at his side.

"In French, we have a phrase for someone like you," Manon expressed. "*Tu te crois.*"

"*Je crois in quoi?*" Charlemagne repeated. "What do I believe in?"

"Not what you believe in," Manon replied. "It's that you believe… I do not know how else to explain – you have to be French to understand."

"Papa tells me that I am French," Charlemagne refuted. "My last name is *de la Cabernet.*"

"If you believe," Manon teased, raising herself onto her bike seat. "*Si tu le crois!*" she repeated in French, cycling forward and then turning around to pass him. "All I hear though is the voice of an Englishman." She then sped off down the path.

"Hey!" Charlemagne shouted. "I'm not an Englishman!" He then growled, turned around, and picked up his bicycle to pursue her. "Come back here!"

Charlemagne peddled forth and began to pursue Manon as she went off along the path. She travelled along a dirt path that came up to a fence on the left and had some trees on either side. They travelled along the short path before they came out to a clearing on the left side and further trees on the right. Manon continued to speed away from Charlemagne as she went up a hill and then past some more trees on either side before coming to a left turn, and then a downhill slope. On the left, the pair passed a farm with a large square-like field. The path passed this field and came around to merge with the road at a stone bridge that went over a stream. After the bridge, they continued along the road before they crossed further ahead and carried on along a path. On the left again, facing east this time rather than north, there was another larger rectangular farm. They traversed down the perimeter of this farm along a dirt path and then came around to a corner to go further east. Charlemagne peddled hard along the straight path, but the coarse dirt made it difficult to finally catch up with her.

As Charlemagne caught up with Manon, he stuck his tongue out at her, and she sort of braked to allow him to safely pass. She then shouted, "Watch out!" He turned his head forward and saw a branch less than a few yards to his face. He quickly ducked and avoided the thorns. He then raised his head again and gave a nervous chuckle as he evaded the branch. Manon shook her head from behind, but Charlemagne continued forward as he sped along.

The path continued forth and began to traverse uphill. On the left, the farm from earlier continued at the side; this farm was large. To the right, tall deciduous trees on the other side of a creek could be seen. Charlemagne peddled up to a dirt road that he crossed, and then continued forward past another farm, and then up to another small field on his left with trees at his right. At a fork in the path, the path split into two ways, and Charlemagne went left and into a narrower pathway with shrubs and trees closer to one's skin. The path continued straight although narrow, and Charlemagne looked behind him as he traversed, slowing down and then stopping at a side path.

Manon was not too far away, and she travelled down the same path, alone, looking ahead of her with a squint as she did not see Charlemagne in sight. At another fork ahead, Manon slowed down and stopped.

"*Charles!*" Manon shouted. "*Charles!*"

"Who do you call a dirty Englishman?" Charlemagne questioned.

Manon turned and looked over to see Charlemagne atop a cliff side on her left. He was approximately ten feet over her with his bike behind him.

"*Charles*, get down from there," Manon complained. "You are going to get 'urt."

Charlemagne scoffed and responded, "You don't understand, do you. My papa tells me that my ancestors came to Canada from France a hundred years ago. He said we likely fled because we were a noble class – do you know what noble means? It means that we were rich, famous, and had lots of power – just like the Cabernet family does now. Who are you? Dumas? Who has ever heard of that name? My papa tells me that I am going to be an important man someday. He insists that I will serve the Cabernet family name well."

"*Charles*, get down," Manon insisted.

"You still don't understand," Charlemagne refuted. "My name is not *Charles* – it's Charlemagne, like the great and mighty king who ruled all of France. My grandfather did not name me Charles, or Charlie – it's Charlemagne!" he elaborated. "*Charles-le-Magne*, if you so speak French, it means Charles the Great – not just Charles, but Charles the Great, because I am great! You were not named *Manon-le-Magne*, and never has there ever been known a Manon who was ever great."

"My mother says that Manon is short for *Marie*…"

"*Marie?*" Charlemagne responded with a scoff stepping forward. "What a stupid name… I've never heard of aaaahh!"

Charlemagne took another step too far and fell face first over the cliff, sliding down its side, tumbling and rolling, and fell onto the dirt path below. Manon shrieked and immediately came towards him as he rested on his side and groaned.

"*Charles! Charles*, are you okay!" Manon questioned.

Charlemagne did not respond and continued to groan.

"I'll get your papa, *Charles*," Manon insisted, backing away. "I'll get your papa!"

Charlemagne stayed put in the exact same position he had landed. After a while when Manon had left, he eventually began to move his lower legs and upper torso. He pulled himself onto his back. His eyes were tearful, his face cut with scratches, and his cotton shirt and pants nicked and dirty. Charlemagne stayed in this position as he waited, staying still for more than a few minutes.

Suddenly, as Charlemagne waited, looking up, he noticed a dark black bird on a perch above him. The bird gave a strong black caw before it took off and fluttered its wings to fly away. Next, Charlemagne heard the sound of hooves galloping towards him.

"Oh, Charlemagne," a deep masculine voice spoke in an East Anglian accent, approaching him.

"There he is," another deep masculine voice spoke in a Orlean French accent.

Charlemagne looked up as he caught sight of a man looking down upon him. The sun pierced through the branches and leaves above, blinding him to the sight of who loomed, but then this man came down on one knee and he could see – the man was his grandfather, Derby Cabernet. Derby had greyish hair at medium length, and he was dressed in a canvas shirt tucked into trousers with boots. He held a compassionate look upon his face as he looked at his grandson. Charlemagne looked back at him with loving eyes.

"What hurts, my dear boy," Derby questioned. "Are you able to move?"

Derby began to examine him as he did not speak, placed a hand on his forehead, and then checked his torso and limbs. When Derby figured that all was mostly well with him, he picked Charlemagne up into his arms and then carried him towards the horse he rode on.

"Charlemagne will be alright," Derby expressed to a man who was with him.

Charlemagne looked towards the man. He was dressed in a striped collared shirt and grey trousers. He was a slim man with light brown hair and glasses. He had been speaking to Manon, who rode behind him on the same horse, in French. Manon placed her hands around his waist.

"If you could, Jean, take my horse with you back to the stables," Derby requested. "I'll take Charlemagne with me back on foot.

"Yes, Mr. Cabernet," Jean-Baptiste responded, fetching the lead for the horse and then going off.

Derby carried Charlemagne in his arms, going down the path and then reaching a side path on the left that went uphill and then around. The path went through some shrubs and then came out to a vineyard on the other side. Charlemagne looked as he saw the many rows of vines. Further ahead, Charlemagne saw a large estate on the plot of land with its stables and barns behind.

"You've had a minor fall," Derby expressed as they walked through the field, "but it's nothing – nothing like what your father had once. You'll be fine, just don't let it get you while your spirit is down too, that's what I told him."

Charlemagne didn't respond, but he continued to look up to his grandfather with wide, loving eyes, simply staring back at the man who raised him.

Eventually, after a few minutes, Derby reached the end of the row and came out to a large gravel lot where he went around towards the barn. From around the paths, Jean-Baptiste arrived not too soon later with the horses. Charlemagne was placed on a cot inside where Derby looked at him more closely in the light.

"Fetch me some water and a towel, Jean," Derby requested. "I'll try to clean up the wounds, but he ought to just take a bath. I just want to be sure there's no serious wounds."

"Of course, Mr. Cabernet."

Jean-Baptiste left and then returned with a bowl of water and a towel. He began to clean Charlemagne's wounds, removing his shirt and seeing that there were no major injuries, nor minor or major cuts.

"*Manon, sors d'ici!*" Jean-Baptiste complained in the background. Charlemagne looked over and could see Manon poking out from around the corner.

"Just as I thought," Derby expressed, standing up as he was on his knees. "He'll be fine – I'll take him inside and run a bath. I'm sure you've learned your lesson, hm Charlemagne?"

Charlemagne looked back at him and slowly nodded. "Yes, papa…"

"Good," Derby affirmed, "now on your feet, soldier. You're good enough to walk, so let's go get you cleaned up."

Charlemagne pivoted around, planted his feet, and then stood up. He looked over and could see Manon avert his gaze as she hid around the corner. He held a plain expression and looked down at the ground. With Derby's help, Charlemagne took his grandfather's hand, and began to walk inside the house to cleanse himself from the accident he had outside.

Act 1, Scene 1

There was as much silence as a human being could anticipate in their own being. The external ambience was muffled so much so that all that could be heard was the beats of one's own heart, pumping the very same blood that made its way around the body. There was as much as one could see in pitch darkness, less than what could be seen if one shuts their eyes for this perception was of complete solitude and darkness. At one's skin, there was tightness on the body and a pressure upon oneself of one's body heat in contrast to the crispness around. As a whole, one drifted, being pulled down into the depths head first, going down into the unknown.

Charlemagne turned on the spotlight lantern he held in his hand and revealed a beam of light ahead of him that showed the murky water he was in. He was dressed in full-suit scuba diving gear, including a wet suit that came around his head, a scuba mask, and oxygen tank behind him. He had a belt with numerous items and at his feet were flippers. Even as he provided himself with a bit of light in the dark waters he swam in, there was still a clear void around him as he drifted in the midst of the body of water alone. Eventually, Charlemagne came to the bottom where he shined his light upon a steel barrel submerged into the sand, encrusted with barnacles, and surrounded by greyish-green kelp. He shined his light around his location and found a few large boulders stuck into the ground as well as additional kelp. From his current location, Charlemagne looked at a compass at his wrist to get a sense of which direction he faced. The surroundings around him were very much the same. He was approximate a bed of seagrass with a variety of patches of nothing more than loose sand. Charlemagne turned to face east and then proceeded to swim forward.

The sea did not have much variety to the environment. He passed some yellowish-brown algae plants, and then came past a school of fish near the ground that were dormant and jumped into action to swim away. The overall surface of the seabed was consistently clearings of sand met with the occasional rock or large boulder sticking out from under. Eventually, Charlemagne came towards a clearing of sand that only occasionally had patches of seagrass that poked out. He continued forward through this clearing as he continued to swim in the darkness. After a moment in which he wandered around in the dark, he eventually found himself facing the pointed bow of a vessel made of steel.

This vessel was tall, but it was no mere nor ordinary boat; this vessel was a sunken submarine. The steel exterior of the submarine was corroded and now a rugged terracotta reddish-brown. Although partially submerged into the seafloor, the vessel was not particularly tall compared to most warships. The vessel appeared to be little more than ten yards, or ten meters in height with a quarter of its height sunken into the sand. The vessel was wide though, arching out to a beam, or width, of close to seven yards. Charlemagne followed the side of the submarine, looking up about halfway as he swam forty yards to reach the conning tower. There were no visible marks on the side of the submarine that could be seen. Charlemagne swam up to the top of the tower and found a watertight hatch. He grasped the valve and attempted to open it, but it would not budge. He looked around the tower and then began to swam down to the portside of the submarine. He swam down the length of the ship as he shined his light upon the outer hull of the ship, as though scanning it with the beam of visible light. The stern of the vessel had a sharpness to it. From either side, horizontal stabilizers poked out horizontally from the vessel, lying flat on the sand, and these objects were like fins. Directly between each fin was the propeller of the ship. He continued down the starboard side of the vessel, returning to the bow. He looked at three sets of nooks on either side of the bow from where torpedoes would fire, and then went back around as he came to last section. As Charlemagne swam to the portside of the vessel, he noticed a rupture in both layers of the hull. He quickly swam towards the rupture and began to examine the damage. The damage was severe and left a large hole big enough for one to swim through, and without hesitation, Charlemagne went through and found himself inside the submarine, specifically a cargo hold by the appearance of wrecked cargo crates and debris. The space was nearly devoid of any objects, but Charlemagne persisted through. He came around to a space with a washroom at the side, and then carried on forward to a mess hall by the appearance of five tables and booth-like seats at the side. Behind the mess hall was a kitchen, and then a mechanical room by the sight of pipes and valves. This room followed with the engine room, where on both the left and right, the pumps of each engine could be seen, gathering rust. A ladder on Charlemagne's left provided sight to a way up in what was otherwise a dead end. He took hold of the valve and began to turn it, not using much force to open the valve with ease, but not without a large object to flow downwards.

Charlemagne was pushed backwards by the object, dropping his spotlight and floating away in the darkness. He quickly grabbed the spotlight as it shined to a water tank at the back of the engine room, and then looked around at what had swum towards him. He then saw a skeleton directly in front of him, looking straight across to him. He stared back at the face of death and then continued upwards to a room that contained air flasks. He reached another watertight door and began to turn the valves to open it, moving aside in case any object rushed at him, but none came. He found the dormitories and then the command room where various consoles and gauges were found. He looked upwards to the other side of the valve from the conning tower, and then carried on forward into another section of the command room where there were some communication devices upon desks, and then the officer quarters. Charlemagne searched the officer quarters thoroughly, going from bedroom to bedroom to pull drawers and cupboards. There was seldom to be found in the vessel. He reached the end of the vessel from this deck where there were torpedoes in storage, and then backtracked as he found the captain's quarters. He searched this room thoroughly and pulled a drawer beneath the bed where he found a wooden box. Charlemagne was quick to open the box, removing shreds of wood from the within to remove a large, egg-shaped yellow diamond.

The diamond glistened in the light from Charlemagne's spotlight. He brought it up so it was a few inches from his goggles, directly in front of his eyes. The diamond was finely cut. He looked at the diamond for another moment before he placed it in a pouch in his vest. He then proceeded to leave, returning to the command room. He swam up to the conning tower and began to attempt to open the hatch from the other side. Although he had to put up a struggle, the hatch opened this time and he was able to escape through the conning tower outwards into the depths of the sea again. Charlemagne swam upwards, going past the seafloor and above it by many feet. He stopped after a while and began to look around. He checked his direction and then began to swim westbound for a few minutes until he stopped again, looking around and then turning off the beam of his spotlight. He looked around again and then continued to swim upwards, stopping once more as he looked about in the darkness. He then caught sight of a reddish light in the distance, which prompted him to swim towards it. The red light blinked in the water, guiding him back towards the surface where eventually he was able to catch sight of the moonlight above that filtered through the water. He continued in the direction of the red light, seeing it flash from the top of an anchor that kept a small boat above in place. Charlemagne swam towards the stern of the boat, surfacing directly behind and looking about. He was in the midst of a sea not too far from a coast a hundred or so yards away. The coastline consisted of cliffs and rugged beaches with tall boulders and such. A lighthouse could be seen not too far, as well as habitats along the coastline with lights turned on. The moonlight poured fourth around and provided ample light to see with the naked eye. Charlemagne swam aboard the stern of the ship, sat down and began to remove his gear. He removed his goggles, oxygen tank, and then pulled the hood of his wetsuit back to expose his light blonde hair. Charlemagne appeared young at this moment, his face covered not with a moustache, but a thin blonde beard. His eyes were in their similar sky-blue color and his skin was otherwise fair. He placed his gear at his side, retrieving the diamond from a pouch within to get a closer look at it. He raised it up towards the moonlight to examine it more closely. The diamond shined in the moonlight, revealing its dark yellow glow.

"At last," Charlemagne muttered to himself, standing up and turning around only to stop. "Oh, blast…"

Charlemagne stopped as he saw that he was in the presence of three Middle Eastern fellows who glared upon him.

"A pleasure for you to join us, Mr. Cabernet," the man in the centre stated with a sort of French accent. This man wore a pinstripe dark suit with a collared shirt underneath. He also wore a wool overcoat. He had tanned skin, and a minor beard and medium length hair. At his right side was a man in a grey suit with a brownish turtleneck. He had a large stature and was bald. On the left side of the man in centre was a slimmer man who wore a turtleneck and cargo pants. He had a full beard and also wore a skullcap. "If you could be so kind, we don't want to cause any trouble."

Charlemagne growled, stepped forward to meet with the man and provided him with the diamond.

"You should have known we would be right on your behind, Mr. Cabernet," the man in the centre spoke. "Even when you think you've won, we will outmaneuver you because our client always gets what he wants."

"I've had about enough of you and your client, Le Havre," Charlemagne replied. "You're nothing more than hired muscle for your client, a man of no principle and no desire."

"I am a man of plenty of desire and one principle, the desire of which is my money and the principle of which is to get the job done. I live a simple life..."

"For a simple man..."

Le Havre growled at him, swiped the diamond from his hand and then looked at it with his eye. "Is this it?" he questioned.

"Of course, that's it, you git," Charlemagne responded.

"I wasn't talking to you," Le Havre replied, passing the diamond to the colleague on his left. This colleague produced a loupe and looked at the diamond more closely.

"Whether it is the diamond in question, it is a real diamond," the associate claimed. "A diamond like this is one in a million, likely worth millions..."

"Give it back here then," Le Havre said, taking it into his hands. He pocketed it into his suit jacket and then turned to face Charlemagne. "We appreciate doing business with you..."

"Wait," Charlemagne said, "if it's money you want..."

"We have a job to see through, Mr. Cabernet," Le Havre stated. "I hope you can understand..." he said as the others boarded a neighboring vessel. "I'll be honest with you, Mr. Cabernet, working alone... you should have seen something like this happen. The world is not a safe place, especially for a little man like you..." he then laughed and left. "Let's go."

Charlemagne stepped forward and watched the neighboring vessel roar to life. A cable used to keep the boats attached was released, and the boat shot off forward.

"Little..." Charlemagne muttered, squeezing a fist. "Hmph..." he set forward to the steering wheel of his own ship, retrieved his anchor, and ignited the engine. He then set the boat to move forward, reaching top speeds as he pursued the boat of the gangsters. "I'll show them…"

The boat began to gather speed as it approached its target. Charlemagne saw Le Havre sat with the other crewmember at the stern of the ship while the other crewmember steered the boat. As Charlemagne approached, the crewmember sat down noticed and pointed him out to the others. Le Havre stood up and looked, but before he could command anyone, Charlemagne steered the boat into the rear of the other causing them to fall over. The boat immediately steered left and broke off from its path. Charlemagne continued to pursue from behind as he caught up with the larger vessel, ramming his into the side of the other vessel. The boat began to shake with every hit, causing the others to remain unsteady on their feet.

Eventually, before one of the crewmembers could react as the boat sped forward, Charlemagne barged into the boat again and caused them to fall overboard. Le Havre quickly went to the other crewmember to pull them off the steering wheel and divert their attention to Charlemagne. Charlemagne continued to pursue the boat while the other struggled to stand on his feet. Eventually, he took a firearm out from his jacket and began to open fire at Charlemagne.

"Blimey!" Charlemagne remarked, ducking. "What a madman!"

Charlemagne stayed low as the bullets missed him and the boat, only one causing the glass to slightly shatter while others flew past. The man stopped to reload, prompting Charlemagne to hit the vessel. When he was finished reloading, Charlemagne could hear Le Havre shout, "Don't just stand there – do something! Jump aboard and get him!" Charlemagne hit the boat as they continued to swerve around in the ocean. He looked over and saw the crewmate attempt to hold on. Charlemagne stayed close and began to come around for another swipe, but this time they rammed the side of their boat into Charlemagne's.

"Grrr...." Charlemagne growled as he forced his boat into theirs as well.

The grunt on the other side attempted to aim his firearm as he continued to unleash another cartridge of rounds. He ducked and they missed. When that failed, the grunt moored the two boats together and tightened them. He then jumped overboard. Charlemagne turned around as he saw him, taking a moment to reload.

Charlemagne relinquished the wheel and turned to face him. The cartridge fell to the ground. The boat continued to travel at full speed. He quickly rushed towards the man, but he swatted him with his hand and knocked him back. The man attempted to kick Charlemagne, but he rolled out of the way and then came around to release the anchor. The anchor released and as it landed on the seafloor below, the boat lurched backwards but then continued to move forward tearing at the seafloor below. The grunt fell backwards, prompting Charlemagne to stand up and quickly jump to the other boat. He released the ties between each boat and the other boat fell back. Upon sight of Charlemagne on his boat, Le Havre relinquished the wheel and turned around to now face him.

"Aren't you quite bothersome, Mr. Cabernet," Le Havre remarked.

"I want that diamond back," Charlemagne simply stated.

"You can go to hell!" Le Havre responded, marching forward and taking swing at him.

Charlemagne dodged out of the way, causing Le Havre to fall forward with the velocity of the boat. He then quickly picked himself up, while Charlemagne looked ahead at the direction of the boat and steered it to the right slightly. Le Havre then took another swing at him, but Charlemagne caught his arm and pushed him back. The two men proceeded to fight as Le Havre grabbed Charlemagne and then threw him onto the ground.

Charlemagne dodged a kick as he rolled over and then staggered backwards.

"You know, we typically charge a bit more when we are required to kill someone, and our client was not willing to pay extra for that service, but I'm in a generous mood tonight, Mr. Cabernet," Le Havre stated, producing a switchblade. "I think I may just kill you for free."

Charlemagne looked at him with a bit of fright, but then noticed the path of the boat. He slowly stood up and held on as the yacht went aground at full velocity, gaining air for a brief moment before it crashed onto the beachhead. Charlemagne held tightly at the boat crashed, while Le Havre, unsuspecting to the crash, fell to his side and hit his head against the side of the boat railing. The boat continued to move forward another inch before it slowed down and came to a complete halt. Once all was calm, Charlemagne slowly stood up and looked around at the beach they had landed beneath the cliffs. He then looked out as he saw the other boat in pursuit not too far. He went over to Le Havre and checked up on him. He was breathing, but knocked out. Charlemagne retrieved the diamond from the pocket it was stored in, and then quickly jumped out of the boat. He rushed down the beach as he proceeded to evade the last grunt not too far away. He proceeded to climb up a pathway that went to the top of the cliffs, and then continued forward to a parking lot where he stopped at payphone and dialed emergency services. Charlemagne looked at his side as he yelled out for help in German, providing his location, and then hanging up.

The last gangster was not too far from behind, but Charlemagne rushed forward down another pathway as he made his escape. He went along a pathway that ran along the top of the cliffs with a steep slope covered in vegetation to the beach and water below. He ran for a few minutes, slowing down to catch his breath and then continuing forth with a sense of urgency. He eventually came to a fork in the path and looked both ways before choosing one that went away from the cliffside. He went up the path and came around to a dead-end where there was a bench. He then looked down and saw that there was a steep decline to the bottom. He had reached the end of the park and the beach was much narrower with properties stretched forth otherwise along the shore. The gangster eventually showed up as Charlemagne attempted to climb down, being pulled over and then given a single punch.

"Stop, please!" Charlemagne pleaded, backing away. "I'll give in, please just stop!"

"No, no more waiting," the man remarked as Charlemagne stood up. The sound of police sirens could be heard not too far. The grunt took out his firearm and pointed it directly at him. Charlemagne stared down the barrel of the gun, less than an inch from his face. He could see the grooves inside.

"What are you going to do? You're going to kill me? The police are not too far away. Is it worth however much you're being paid? I have money…"

"I want the diamond," the grunt asserted.

"Well," Charlemagne spoke, "you'll have to go get it. I threw it over there," he said, pointing over the beach. "It's just down there…"

"You idiot of a man," the grunt remarked. "I ought to kill you right now!"

Charlemagne and the grunt both heard the voices of policeman shouting in German from nearby.

"If you run now, you may just find it and return to your boss…" Charlemagne expressed. "Run…"

The grunt growled at him and then slowly retreated backwards. He then disappeared, leaving Charlemagne in place. He gave a sigh of relief, sat down, and then opened his pouch to take out the diamond.

"Gullible fool," Charlemagne muttered to himself, laughing. He then stood up and looked down towards the beach as he saw the grunt searching for the diamond in the sand. He crossed over the fence and came around to a rock so that he could stand high above him. "Sorry, did I say that I threw the rock, actually I've got it right here, but I do believe it's too late! How's that for you?! You see – that's what you get when you lot mess with Charlemagne!"

Le Havre caught up from behind and shouted out towards his colleague in a foreign language. The grunt was about to withdraw his handgun once more, but was told to stand down as he retreated with the other. Charlemagne continued to wave towards them from above the rock. He then chuckled to himself.

"Pillocks," Charlemagne cursed, "bloody fools." He then pivoted at his leg, catching the edge of the boulder he was stood upon and slipping. "Oh damn…!"

Charlemagne fell overboard again, falling over and tumbling down the side of the cliff to land on the sands below. He grunted as he landed and then attempted to move, but cursed out in pain and gave in. He placed a hand at his side and stayed put, eventually being assisted by emergency responders who appeared and attended to him. Charlemagne was raised up onto a stretcher and was then promptly wheeled away from the scene.

Act 1, Scene 2

A few days later, Charlemagne sat up in bed, pillow behind him as he rested in a hospital bed. He was dressed in a patient gown, the top shirt unbuttoned and his mid-section of his torso wrapped with bandages. He sat at the end of a multi-patient room, shared with three other patients, two of whom were across from him and one next to him. Charlemagne's bed was closest to the window. Each bed was divided by curtains, some of which were pulled across while others were open wide. Charlemagne sat secluded behind his curtains with a bit of light pouring through the window on his left. He was on the fourteenth floor that looked out towards the city skyline to the east, the most notable landmark that direction of which was a tall, slim tower with a reflective globe two-thirds up before a tall antennae poked out from above another few yards. This tower aside, there were very few tall buildings and most buildings were old, the most four stories tall, and with reddish rooftops and facades. The skies were grey at this time, stale, and although the windows were closed, a chill came into the room. Charlemagne's patient room was quiet, but from outside there was chatter in German between doctors, nurses, and patients. Charlemagne sat in his bed admiring the diamond that he held in his hand as he looked at it in daylight.

Suddenly, Charlemagne could hear some arguments outside. He quickly hid the diamond beneath his covers as he raised an ear to overhear, but then he heard steps come towards him followed by the front-most curtain being rushed open.

"Ah, there he is!" a rumbunctious man remarked in his deep voice and Orlean accent. "*Danke, danke,*" he spoke to the nurse, turning to her and then coming forth to Charlemagne. "Here is my boy. I've found you."

"So you have," Charlemagne replied with a smile, looking over to his mentor who placed a hand at his wrist. "It's good to see, Dr. Dumas."

Dr. Dumas at this day and age had a thick grey beard and likewise grey hair combed to the side. He wore a brown plaid three-piece suit with a vest and collared shirt underneath. The shirt was bluish-white with a plaid pattern. At his side he had a messenger bag and his other hand a tweed cap. Dr. Dumas was in his mid-fifties at this time, apparent by the crow's feet at the side of eyes and the formation of wrinkles beneath his eyes, if his grey hair did not suggest otherwise. Dr. Dumas held a wide, loving smile as he looked at Charlemagne with a joyous and hearted appearance.

"It's good to see you too, my boy. It's good to see you too. I'm sorry I was not here sooner, but I assure you I came as soon as I could," Dr. Dumas insisted, "but let me tell you, you were not easy to find. We went to Rostock where they found you, but by the time we arrived, you were gone. They told me that they could not tell me where you went, so we checked all the hospitals we could. At any rate, we got your phone call and came as fast as we could here."

"We?" Charlemagne questioned.

"Yes, of course. We," Dr. Dumas replied. "I… *Où est cette fille?*" he asked as he looked over to where the nurse had been. "*Mon amour, où es-tu?*"

Charlemagne looked directly ahead of him as a woman stepped forward and then stopped at the foot of Charlemagne's bed.

"Manon," Charlemagne noted.

Manon looked back at him from the other side of the bed. She was young and youthful still, always a year below Charlemagne. Her skin was fair with a slight tan, and her eyes medium blue. Her hair, medium brown, stayed brown and was cut short up to her shoulders and still dense with a little wave to it. She wore rouge at her cheeks, and lipstick at her lips. She wore eyeliner at her eyes, and her eyebrows were fine, pointing towards the bridge of her nose. She had bony cheeks and a slim figure. She wore a black beret that matched her dark denim trousers and contrasted her white short-sleeved shirt. She held a small beige purse at her side, its strap no less than a foot in length. Her trousers ran short, exposing her ankles, while her shirt sleeves went right up to her elbows. Manon held a plain expression as she looked at Charlemagne until suddenly flinging her purse down and hitting Charlemagne's lower legs.

"What is wrong with you?" Manon spoke in her Parisian accent. "Have you gone completely insane?" she questioned, hitting him again. "Why do you do this, Charlemagne?"

"Ow, Manon, please," Charlemagne expressed. "What on earth are you talking about?"

"*Manon, ma cherie…*" Dr. Dumas replied, reaching over to stop her. "Enough, my dear."

Manon growled and took her purse back. She then pointed towards Charlemagne and said, "*Vous savez à quoi ressemble cet homme fou.*"

"*C'est assez, Manon.*"

"*Oui, c'est assez,*" Charlemagne affirmed. "*Tu ne sais rien de ce que j'ai fait.*"

"I know plenty of what you've been up to, Charlemagne. I spoke to Cisco who told me everything…"

"Bah," Charlemagne dismissed, "Cisco knows nought."

"And what about the Turkish bandits? The ones that have been after you through Germany?" Manon questioned. "He said that ever since you were in Spain with him they had been on your tail."

"That bloody loose lipped…"

"You were putting yourself in danger, weren't you, I knew it," Manon remarked, bringing her purse down and hitting him again.

"Alright, alright, stop," Charlemagne fessed. "I'll come clean. I may have been having a bit of an adventure alone…"

"Is it true, Charlemagne?" Dr. Dumas questioned with a stern look. "Did you find it?"

Charlemagne raised a smile to his mentor and nodded. "Of course it's true." He took the yellow diamond out from beneath his covers and showed it to Dr. Dumas. His elderly eyes lit up and he received the diamond into his hand and raised it up, turning around towards the window to get a better view of it in the daylight.

"Ah, isn't she a beauty," Dr. Dumas remarked. "Thought to have been lost until my brilliant boy here discovered its location. Where was it, Charlemagne? Why Rostock?"

"Not Rostock, but off the coast of Pomerania," Charlemagne explained. "You'll never guess, but it was in the possession of a sea captain, of the Kriegsmarine, in his quarters of his sunken submarine. I had to dive for it to find it right where it was said to have been… at least what my sources told me."

Dr. Dumas turned around and looked over to Charlemagne. He remarked, "You are a treasure to the efforts of historical research, my good boy. Oh, what a proud man your father would have been – what a proud man I am, to know that although you are not my own, I've done all I could for you."

"Papa, what are you doing?" Manon questioned. "This is not the time to be encouraging this man's wicked behaviors. He could have been killed…"

"Oh, Manon, please…" Dr. Dumas pleaded. "What are you on about?"

"Go on, tell him," Manon remarked. "Tell him how you risked your life, for this silly rock."

"Silly rock?" Charlemagne refuted. "Well, that's pretty low, even for you – don't lecture me, Manon. For little more than five years we journeyed together in search of artefacts like this one just the same."

"Just the same? We never had gangsters come after us, or ever had to risk our life. Where do you meet such people to come after you?"

"What can I say?" Charlemagne expressed with a proud smile as he placed his hands behind his head. "I'm just a desirable fella – everybody wants a piece of me. I'm renowned, you know, at least by these lot, as a treasure hunter, so naturally, a bit of pushback is expected."

"And you take pride in this…" Manon questioned.

"What good adventurer doesn't have his rivals? It just tells me that I'm doing my legwork, and also makes it a tad bit more difficult – a challenge I can love."

Manon shook her head and replied, "Ever since you disbanded the team, you have been like this. Please, papa, you need to understand that he is unwell and getting himself into danger, willingly."

Dr. Dumas looked at Manon, and then down to the diamond, and then over to Charlemagne. He cleared his throat and then said, "You say you found this underwater? How did this silly thing get in there?"

"Isn't it curious?" Charlemagne replied, both ignoring Manon as he brought his hands out. He received the diamond back and began to explain. "I had to start where we last thought the diamond was, naturally. The rumors that circulated were that the diamond either went to South America or the United States, but then I found a better lead while travelling in Spain. I was told that the diamond had never left the continent, but was assumed to have been taken when Charles the First went into exile in Switzerland. This rumor suggested that the diamond was stolen and sold to a mechant who took it back to Austria. After following up on these leads in both Switzerland and Austria, and confirming a bill of receipts to a Mr. Seuss, I learned that this aristocrat had the diamond taken from him shortly after the Anschluss of Austria."

"Really?" Dr. Dumas questioned, sitting down.

"Yes," Charlemagne asserted, "which confirmed the rumors that it was stolen, and also pointed towards where it had landed. Another man came close twenty or so years ago on the same path, but fell short and his research was never published because he had no definite pathway nor confirmation. I picked up on that work and since the reunification of Germany, I thought I may have access to archives that were otherwise kept hidden in East Germany. The task from that point was not easy; I had to travel to a lot of archives across the country because papers had been shuffled around. You'll never guess, but the diamond eventually made its way back into the hands of Adolf Hitler."

"Really?" Dr. Dumas questioned in a different tone.

"Yes, really," Charlemagne confirmed. "According to documents I had found, Hitler, although opposed to the Austrian-Hungarian monarchy, still respected the former king and delighted to have received the stone. It was in his private collection in East Prussia until the Soviet advance towards the region when it was moved alongside some personal items. The most difficult trick in all this was finding which submarine it had been in, which took me more time until I determined: U-1260, which I located off the coast of Rostock, was a couple of kilometers from the port it was set to have docked at. According to official documents, the submarine had sunk and the entire crew was written off as deceased (this was before I determined where it was sunk). I was at a loss but couldn't help but be struck as these details as being odd compared to other submarines, especially for a boat not too far from the coast of Germany. I did some research on the crew, and it turns out that most of them actually survived; a few returned to Germany, some didn't make it through the post-war, but one that did mentioned to me in person that the crew was rescued by a Swedish coast guard ship and those who wanted to return to Germany were allowed to (although not immediately), and those who did not want to return to Germany stayed. Their captain stayed in Sweden out of fear of being court martialed and never returned to Germany. I met with him, in Sweden, at the age of ninety-two, still alive, and he told me all that happened in detail and it led me there... to the submarine where sure enough, the diamond was in his quarters."

"*Tres bien*, Charlemagne," Dr. Dumas commended. "You've done quite well – you have always been gifted in your capabilities as a historian. We are lucky to have a man as bold and intelligent as you."

Manon frowned at those words.

"What will you do now with the diamond? We need to document and cite all your sources to have located this diamond," Dr. Dumas remarked. "I will help you with that, no doubt."

"Thank you, Dr. Dumas, but as for this beauty, I have no use for it – I'm not any sort of collector, and at any rate, as my grandfather once told me, and you reinforced, something like this gem ought to be in a museum."

"Yes, that it should, but which do you think?"

"I'm not sure," Charlemagne confessed. "I've not known Germany all that well..."

"And?" Manon questioned.

"Yes?" Charlemagne replied.

"And what of these wounds? You tell me you were injured while diving to a submarine?" Manon asked. "How did your hurt yourself?"

"Well, occupational hazards are due to come... you remember what happened to me in Peru."

"I remember what nearly happened to you in Peru..."

"I still did my ankle in," Charlemagne assured her.

"But you had your team to assist you, and Gudrun to care for your wound."

"I can care for my own wounds now."

"So why are you in hospital?"

"I… well, if you insist to know…

"I do insist," Manon interrupted, "but please, do tell – and be honest."

"Manon…" Dr. Dumas scolded.

"I had a bit of a tumble…" Charlemagne answered. "I admit, I got a bit careless, and I fell… simple as that."

"You fell?"

"Yes."

"And what were you doing before?"

"I had just obtained the gem from the submarine."

"And the Turks? They didn't push you, did they?"

"No, of course not," Charlemagne remarked. "I was atop of a rock on the beach, had a slip of the foot, and fell overboard – that's all."

"So why did the police find your boat wrecked at the beach? Why did they say they were sure you were somehow in conflict with someone because they had received a call of such?"

"My boat… oh, damn… my boat," Charlemagne stated. "Oh dear…"

"Manon, what are you saying, my flower?" Dr. Dumas remarked. "Why do you lambast Charlemagne so? He's made a great discovery…!"

"I lambast because your protégé nearly cost himself his life to find this stupid discovery," Manon answered. "It's only gotten worse, but killers too?"

"Not killers, just competitors."

"The police say that you said killers…" Manon refuted, "and still, this man lies to my face, and your face. *Incroyable…*" she remarked, leaving in her frustration.

"I'm so sorry, I don't know what's gotten into her. She was concerned, that's all I can say. Very concerned when she picked up the phone to learn that you were injured. I'm sorry, she was staying with me at the time."

"No, it's quite alright," Charlemagne replied, looking over to his mentor who continued to sit next to him. "It's annoying to say the least, but manageable. Honestly don't know where she understands it to be her business to worry about me like that."

"Ah, but she's just like her mother," Dr. Dumas insisted. "*Ma petite cherie* would do the same for her man whenever I would go out on expeditions. Perhaps a bit of her mother is getting to her..."

"Yes, I suppose so..." Charlemagne said, looking back to Dr. Dumas. "As for the diamond, I want you to take it from this place. I don't trust anyone here, and I don't want it to be stolen. I'll be discharged soon; the doctor's say I broke my ribs from the fall I had, but will be good as new by next week. I need you to do me a favor though. I need you to get into contact with Cabernet Industries and inform my people where I am, and what I want done – we're going to donate that gem to a worthwhile institution and so we'll need to celebrate the occasion in style."

"I think I know just where to send this little precious stone," Dr. Dumas said. "A museum not too far from here, best to get it off our hands before the authorities catch up to us. They can be a particular way about lost items, especially from before the war. We'll need to ensure it is kept in Germany, I'm afraid, but don't worry, I know where it shall go."

Act 1, Scene 3

A few weeks later, not too far from the hospital that Charlemagne had stayed in, he rode in a black limousine that took him through the streets of Berlin in the evening, down a major two lane road through the eastern part of the city. He passed numerous apartment buildings on his left and right, as well as some large, densely forested parks. The apartments varied in style, although most of them were all the same, likely from the same era. They had flat exterior walls that varied from light blue to greyish-green, to a faint orange. They all had white windows and many of them had the same pattern to these tall rectangular windows; a simple cross, like a Christian cross. They were all about the same height, five stories tall plus attics. The rooftops were not visible from the ground, but they were red and low-sloped. The road the limousine drove on was an avenue with likewise two rail lines in the middle. The same tower, *Fernsehturm Berlin*, that Charlemagne could see from his patient bedroom, he could see ahead as the car reached a large intersection. The limousine drove towards the tower as it continued down the road. As the car drove into central Berlin, the buildings outside became larger and newly built in the last ten years. Charlemagne rode comfortably as he looked out the window, dressed in tuxedo and with a small glass of a clear liquid inside with ice.

"To think, almost ten years ago, all this was behind the oppression of a communist government," Charlemagne remarked, sipping his drink. "I've longed to see this part of the city for years now."

The limousine came to a stop at an intersection just ahead of the Fernsehturm where there was a church and plaza at the southeast street corner and the *Rotes Rathaus*, Berlin City Hall, with its red bricks, arched windows, and clocktower. The flag of Berlin, two red stripes separated by a thick wide center with a bear on its two feet in the center, waved in the wind. The limousine continued forward as they continued to drive through *Mitte*, the center of the city. To the left was a large plaza park with trees that had lost all their leaves. Afterwards, as they drove over the Spree River, was a large four-story tall and square building known as *Humboldt Forum* that was plain, brutalist, and constructed of white marble. In contrast on the right there was a grand dome church constructed in renaissance and baroque architecture. The *Berliner Dom* was a large former cathedral with two side towers with turquoise domes, and then the central partition with a large turquoise dome. The exterior façade of the church consisted of tanned brick, and the front entrance of pillars with large rectangular doors. The front plaza had a minor bit of shrubbery, but like the park, barren trees. The limousine turned at the street corner where the Berliner Dom was and continued north. On the left was another park, this one with clearings of grass and a fountain in the center. The park was in front of another structure, the façade of which consisted of tall pillars above wide steps at the front. At either side of the steps were statues of horsemen. The limousine turned and came towards the front of the steps where there were crowds of people. A series of banners that drooped from the top of the building denoted 'Return of the Tuscany Diamond' with a visual representation of the gem. The limousine came to a stop in front of the museum steps

"Alright then," Charlemagne expressed, placing his drink aside. He fixed his tuxedo bowtie and then moved towards the exit, "Charlemagne, it is showtime."

The chauffer opened the door for Charlemagne, and he stepped out and proceeded to greet the crowd with waves. In addition to the crowd of onlookers, there were also television cameras and media reporters in the nearby area. The flashes of photographers nearly blinded him as he continued to wave, unfazed, and then continued up the steps to the main entrance of the museum.

"*Herr Cabernet,*" a man in a suit greeted from the top of the steps, but before the main entrance, "a pleasure to meet you."

"*Danke,*" Charlemagne responded, "*freut mich.*" He proceeded to shake his hands with several other persons before meeting the last one. He was then guided through into the museum past two security personnel where he was led through the main atrium.

The main atrium was a large circular space with two levels, a top floor and a bottom floor. The top floor was supported by composite pillars. Between each gap among the pillars were marble statues of figures, male and female, some of whom were dressed in robes, and at least two of whom were nude for twelve in total. The atrium floor was white with black round small circles towards the center. In the center of the atrium was a display case that held the Tuscany Diamond on a velvet pillow. There were numerous people inside already, all of whom were dressed in formal clothes. On the floor above, there were nooks within the marble walls with additional marble statues, and then the ceiling likewise, domed, had nooks that consisted of depictions of angels in the first row, and then animals and cherubim in the second row, and finally shells in the last two rows before a round glass top. The door left and right were closed with velvet barriers in front of them. The only door available to go through was further ahead which led into a rectangular room where refreshments and food could be found. The main atrium was the center of the party and so Charlemagne met with further people on his left as he was greeted.

"Welcome, Mr. Cabernet," a familiar figure stated to him.

"Thank you, Mr. Adlington," Charlemagne responded. "And thank you for organizing all this."

"Not just me, Mr. Cabernet, but Ms. Summers and the rest of the Cabernet Foundation sends their regards."

Mr. Adlington appeared much as he did nearly ten years ago. He was dressed in a dark suit with a golden tie and white collared shirt. His greyish-white hair was combed back, and his skin was wrinkled with flabby cheeks. He was a tall man with fair skin and blue eyes.

Charlemagne moved aside and met with a few more people.

"An impressive piece of history," a man stated to Charlemagne. He spoke in a Russian accent. He was a fair-skinned man with a goatee and dark hair. He wore a pinstripe dark suit and held a martini glass. "How does a man like you find such treasures?"

"By a good sense of research and investigative skills," Charlemagne simply stated. "Thank you for attending."

Charlemagne then looked to the woman who was next to him. He stopped for a moment as his eyes came upon her. She had smooth fair skin, a round face, and brown eyes. She had a tall nose and dark hair tied in a braid. She had fine eyebrows that were slightly arched, and eyeshadow in a purplish hue. She was slender, a few inches shorter than Charlemagne, and she wore a silver-colored necklace and around her upper arms were two silver arm cuffs. She wore a robe-like dress with white stole around her neck. Charlemagne looked at her face closely and held a plain expression.

"Hello, my dear," Charlemagne finally stated. "A very special welcome to you," he said, offering his hand.

"Thank you, Mr. Cabernet," the woman responded in an Eastern European accent, offering her hand to him as she looked at him intently. "It's been an honor to meet you."

Charlemagne took her hand, looking at the silver ring at her index finger where a purple sapphire was encrusted. He brought her hand to his lips as he leaned over. He then gently kissed and stood up the straight.

"The honor is all mine," Charlemagne responded, looking to a statue of a Greek goddess on his left. "I can see now why the

Greeks would want to encapsulate a woman as beautiful as yourself into marble. You are right at home," he said, motioning to the statue next to him, "with beauty and art."

The woman lightly laughed as she retracted her hand and brought it to her chest with flattery. She replied, "Aren't you quite the charmer? I didn't realize the illustrious Mr. Cabernet was so coy."

"Yes," the man next to her replied, "well, it's been a pleasure nonetheless," he said, linking arms with her. "All the best, Mr. Cabernet."

The couple then left. Charlemagne continued to meet with a few others, stepping forth and meeting with a man in a long-sleeved white robe that came around their entire body. A thin brown veil or cloak then covered the rest of the body outwards, both of which came down to the feet. The man's hair was covered by a white head covering, and at his feet were sandles. He was an older male, although at least fifteen years older than Charlemagne.

"How are you doing, my boy?" the man spoke in perfect English. He spoke in a deep voice too. He took Charlemagne's hand and brought it in for an embrace. He also patted Charlemagne on the back. "What an impressive task you've done. I'm so proud of you."

"Thank you, Mr. Al-Suli," Charlemagne replied. "I'm very happy you could join us."

"Not a problem at all," Al-Suli responded, continuing to shake his head. "You are like a son to me, Charlemagne. What you have done for me and my family is tremendous, and we hope that this bridge between us that you and I have built can carry forward for generations. For as long as we do, great fortune will exist between us."

"Yes, of course," Charlemagne remarked as they released hands. He then looked next to Al-Suli where there was a young male, a few years younger than Charlemagne, slim and with a ruffle of dark hair. He did not wear a robe or cloak, but instead wore a suit. He had similar tanned skin, although a bit lighter and he also had a taller head and no beard. "Hello, Ali."

"Hello, Charles," Ali simply responded.

"How's Le Havre doing? I hope he isn't too upset ever since he had his little accident a few weeks ago."

Ali didn't reply. He instead made a growling noise as he repressed his words and then left. Charlemagne smirked at him and then looked back at Al-Suli.

"Don't worry about him," Al-Suli remarked. "I don't know what's gotten into him. Tell me though, when will you come back to Qatar to visit us? I told you – you don't need an invitation, my house is open to you, and Yasmin would like to see you. You know, she hasn't seen you in some time, and she always asks me, dad, when will you see Charlemagne again. She misses you."

"Ah, yes, Yasmin…" Charlemagne responded. "I haven't forgotten about her, or the time we spent in Dubai… Last I heard from her, she told me she had something to tell me, but alas, I've been busy, travelling around the world and such."

"Yes, you have been busy, and you've been doing a great job," Al-Suli commended. "What a great guy."

Charlemagne continued to converse with Al-Suli until he felt a hand on his shoulder. He jumped and turned around as he was met with Dr. Jean-Baptiste Dumas. He wore a fine tweed three-piece suit.

"Ah, there you are, my boy," Dr. Dumas said with a laugh. "I regret again that I am late, this time to your party."

"Not a worry, Dr. Dumas – doctor, I would like to introduce to you my good friend and a valued business partner with Cabernet Industries, Mr. Harun Al-Suli, of the Al-Suli family in the Gulf states."

"How'd you do," Dr. Dumas greeted. "I've heard much about you."

"Nice to meet you," Al-Suli responded. "At any rate, thank you for inviting me, Charlemagne. I look forward to seeing you come to Qatar one day – remember, no invitation, come any time."

"Absolutely, Mr. Al-Suli, let's get together some time," Charlemagne encouraged, toasting as he raised his glass. He then turned to Dr. Dumas. "Blimey, I thought you wouldn't show. What took you so long?"

"Ah, women, you know how it is," Dr. Dumas replied.

"Women?" Charlemagne questioned, looking past Dr. Dumas. As Charlemagne glanced, he saw Manon enter into the atrium through the main entrance. Lamps shined down from where she stood as he looked around, enhancing the view of her and causing Charlemagne to fixate on her. Her medium brown hair flowed from behind, and her skin was smooth and fair. Her blue eyes encircled by a dark red eyeliner. Her lips painted in the same hue and cheeks ruddy. She wore a dark blue dress that came down to just below her knees. The dress consisted of a velvet fabric and was like a toga as it tied around her right shoulder. The dress went over, or was attached to a black long-sleeved shirt. She also wore a pearl necklace and dark high heels. After a moment of looking about, Manon looked over to where her father and Charlemagne were. "Yes, Manon…"

"Ah, there she is," Dr. Dumas remarked as she joined them. "My beautiful girl." He gave Manon a kiss on the cheek."

"Sorry we were late," Manon remarked, "how has the party been?"

"It's been a party for sure," Charlemagne expressed. "I should have opted to make a speech. Seems to me like most people are her for the social aspect than the historical moment. I've had to endure relentless questions of people believing the stone to be Italian because it's been called the Tuscany Diamond, or what the significance of such a gem proved. At the same time, the crowd is not entirely what I expected, and this venue is small and cramped."

"We are all here to celebrate your success in this moment, *Charles*," Manon remarked. "What more can you expect?"

"I just wished it could be larger, grander; a party like the sort that could be celebrated in the Royal Harlech Museum, if not in a large ball room of any five-star hotel. I want to draw all sorts of historians and avid freethinkers into the same room to announce and pay respect to the donation of a valuable artefact for the admiration of the public."

Manon gave a mild laugh and replied, "What a childish fantasy... You truly have no exposure to the universities, do you. Nobody expects a select few people care about history to the extent that we do, *Charles*. The socialites who happen to be in Berlin, or otherwise were invited from afar, will be the best that you can hope to find."

"This feels no different than the average Cabernet Foundation event..." Charlemagne expressed.

"What does a crowd have to do with the celebration?" Dr. Dumas interrupted. "A crowd is a crowd, but the people, you, me, and Manon, should be what matter in these times to make a toast to your accomplishment. Speaking of a toast, where do I find myself a drink?"

"There's a bar in the back room," Charlemagne remarked. "An open bar."

"Excuse me, I'll be right back," Dr. Dumas replied, leaving. Charlemagne looked as Dr. Dumas left and then back to Manon.

"Well, you certainly look... well dressed for tonight," Charlemagne expressed. "I suppose you have the advantage of all things desirable for the female being in Paris."

"Actually, I bought this here in Berlin a few days ago," Manon confessed. "It's not a designer dress either."

"Oh…" Charlemagne replied, crossing his arms as he looked aside. "Well, thanks for coming. Sorry it's been a bit of a downer of a party."

"Why downer? I've just come here, and you already saying it is over or that you are leaving?"

"Hm? No, no, it's just…" he said with a sigh, "it's not what I came to expect or want. I mean, you're a historian, Manon, so you tell me. I thought the Florentine Diamond to have been an exquisite find, an item thought to have been lost at the start of the century, and here we are little more than two years to the end of a millennium, and there was no regard for it…"

"You perhaps search for regard from people who do not exist…"

"Bah, always so negative," Charlemagne rebuked. "You just don't have the ambition, Manon. Imagine a treasure truly brilliant and proud; an object that has been lost for not centuries, but a one or more thousand years."

"There are so many treasures that have been lost," Manon acknowledged. "If you were to put a team together again, I'm sure you could find one truly monumental object with enough hard work."

"Bah, team… that costs money that the company can no longer afford, and that's another aspect to the problem. What a disregard there is to the arts and sciences… Think of an artefact. Any artefact, and tell me to go find it."

"Me? Oh, well… the Ark of the Covenant? The Holy Grail?"

"No," Charlemagne scolded. "I mean something real. Something grand. Something that can make people say, wow – Charlemagne found that."

Manon laughed and shook her head. "I don't know anything like that, *Charles*. Even the most beautiful finds in the last century or so of archeological research there has not been a celebration of the historians, nor should there be. The act of the historian is a selfless act because we seek to elevate the artefact, not the historian. Why do you seek these things? To make yourself be remembered for something you had found?"

"Because I want to be like Christopher Columbus, Manon," Charlemagne answered, "or James Cook, or Hernán Cortes – known for the discovery."

"Ah, well then why don't you travel to Mars. Hm?"

Charlemagne ignored her and replied, "Instead, I listen and hear criticism from others that I've done wrong – that already the press have made complaint that this diamond should return to India as a stolen good as a result of colonialism."

Manon didn't reply.

"The public are a finnicky bunch, but I will show them," Charlemagne asserted. "I will find something that is authentically European and which no person can tell me that I've done moral wrong in locating such object."

"Oh?"

"Yes," Charlemagne expressed, "I may know something too. I came across it when I was in the German archives. What a pleasure it's been, Manon, and I've heard the former Soviet archives to be a treasure trove too – alas, I don't read Russian to be able to understand those, but I am able to read German to comprehend their documents. For nearly fifty years, secrets have been held in the Eastern Bloc, and I intend to uncover them. You must take a look for yourself, my dear. I will show you just what I mean…"

Act 1, Scene 4

Charlemagne exited out from a dark sedan along the same road that he had travelled to arrive at the museum. The Fernsehturm was not too far and loomed over them at the plaza they were at, *Alexanderplatz*. He was dressed in a simple grey suit with a blue striped tie. He walked across the plaza and came around to a café around the corner where Manon was sat, sipping some coffee. Charlemagne entered the patio and sat down in front of Manon. Manon was dressed in work clothes, a long blazer coat and short skirt that went to her knees. The outfit has a plaid white-black pattern to it. She also wore her beret.

"You are late," Manon noted. "We agreed on half eight o'clock."

"I'm sorry, I forgot that meant half an hour before eight o'clock when talking to the concierge desk," Charlemagne casually noted. "Not half-past eight as it is in English."

"You are forgetting your German."

"I have not," Charlemagne responded, "anyways, enough. Let's get going then."

Charlemagne and Manon stood up from the café and proceeded along the plaza at the foot of the TV tower. They came around to a street perpendicular to the main street, jaywalked across, and then came around to the other side where there was an archway entrance into the train station. They proceeded forward to purchase tickets, which Charlemagne took the liberty to do so for Manon as well. Afterwards, they walked upstairs to wait for their train. After a few minutes past when the train was supposed to arrive, it arrived and passengers proceeded to board. Charlemagne and Manon stood up from their seats, boarded the train, and then sat together in the train car.

"I could never live in Germany," Manon remarked, "the people here are so cold, especially in Berlin."

"France is a lovely country," Charlemagne noted, "but the Germans are lovely people. To think that a thousand years ago, it was all one under a Frankish king."

"What is this artefact you believe you can find?" Manon questioned.

"I'm not sure how familiar you are with the subject, so stop me if all this information is familiar to you, but what I hope to seek is a crown that was lost from the French regalia."

"My knowledge of that subject is limited," Manon admitted, "it is a very niche subject to study, so enlighten me."

"During the French Revolution, a lot of the French crowns kept in Saint Denis Basilica were looted by revolutionaries, one of which has been in existence for almost a thousand years in that time – this crown was the Frankish crown, of the Frankish king."

"The Crown of Charlemagne?"

"So it was said and believed to have been, although knowledge of the subject since its disappearance has suggested that it was not the exact crown of Charlemagne for the Frankish Kingdom, but his grandson's crown. I have various points to suggest otherwise, but so far, no strong evidence to support that claim. My interest though is in a document I had uncovered in Koblenz among the numerous documents imported from East Germany that suggest a possibility that this crown may not have had the fate it had. I'll admit, even my knowledge is a tad weak on the subject, because it was my impression that the crown was in Vienna, but of course, that is not the exact crown either. I'm still doing some research on the subject, but what you need to know for the purposes of our visit to Potsdam is that this Frankish Crown is what I'm searching for.

"According to the information that I do know, the exact Frankish Crown, which was a part of the French regalia until 1793, was stolen from where it was kept in the basilica. A catalog of items that I studied last night details (alongside the conclusions of an inept historian), that the Crown is missing because it cannot be accounted for like other items. Many items were transported to the Louvre, while others across the country, but those items that have not been accounted for were presumed lost, and the Crown because it was made of pure metal, melted down, as was common in those times. This conclusion was a leap of logic rather than supported with empirical evidence; faulty work on the historian's part, but taken as fact because no other explanation was made or became as popular. A few fringe theories exist, but like this one, lack evidence.

"This crown had been used for hundreds and hundreds of years, from king to king, and there were two of them, for the king and queen. Either the king or queen variant survived an uprising in the sixteenth century, and a separate crown used for the queen since then until the French Revolution. Imagine – this missing crown could have been on the head of the great king of my namesake, if not his grandson, and was certainly on the head of every French king from Phillip II, Louis IX, Charles V, Louis XIV and lastly Louis XVI."

"And so what makes you believe that this artefact is of such significance?"

"How can it not be? You tell me as a French woman and a historian, how to have the missing Crown Jewel of the original French regalia returned to your rightful country, if not to Germany, the original crown of the former Holy Roman Empire. At a time like our own where European unity and integration is on the rise, foreseeing a future United European state in which either Germany or France will be the dominant power, if not both, how can it not be a big deal? Europe has not known such solidarity and unity since the days of the Holy Roman Empire, and before that, the Roman Empire itself. The European state will be at the forefront of the future world next millennium in a trend that has always seen a unity on the continent. Imagine –

this crown could be symbolic of that destiny that Europe has awaiting it, I know it."

"If you were to find that crown, I guarantee you, the French government will seek to seize it from you immediately."

"I should wish the French government would seek the crown, and I would be willing to give it to them so long as it is well known that I, Charlemagne, recovered it. As I left the museum yesterday, I was informed that the Tuscany Diamond would not even remain on display this season, or the next one, as they verify my research due to questions that arose on its legitimacy. I offered to present my research spearheaded by your father, and they were not interested. We should have never have offered it to that museum – they wouldn't even give mention to me in their tours that I had recovered it and donated it to them. *Bastards…* Sure enough, I will have to do more than recover a single gem to be recognized."

"You don't have to do anything of the sort to be recognized," Manon assured him. "You are known to me, my father, and to all our friends in the historian community."

"Yes, and I am shunned at home though, from the Oxford, McGill, Harvard, even the University of Harlech. Alas, history to do with Britain and North America were never in my taste anyways. The Old World is where I belong, and not on that pungent isle. Here, continental Europe is where I am at home, *avec mes frères* and *mit meine Brüder*. Participation in the European Union was most unpopular in Britain, and should that country ever leave, I should hope to renounce my citizenship and either apply for my French passport as my residence has been in Paris, or Austrian citizenship through my mother. The Cabernet name is a French name anyways, and our place should be here and not abroad."

"If you say so, *Monsieur Cabernet*," Manon replied, giving a gentle smile. The pair then grew silent for a moment as the train proceeded forth from Berlin. Charlemagne looked out the window as they passed through the city and went southwest.

Charlemagne looked at Manon for a split moment, sighed, and then asked, "I've hardly had a chance to have an ordinary discussion with you, Manon. How have you been? It's been a year? Two years since we last saw each other?"

Manon turned her gaze from out the window to Charlemagne. She answered, "A year and a half when we all parted ways. I've been well. Both my father and I have been working at the University of Paris. At the time we learned about your accident, we were working on a project together. He, as you know, studies European History, and I as you know made that subject my specialty too. We've both been looking at the things to do with the former French nobility, before the revolution. He's returned to Aachen to continue our work, while I am here with you – he doesn't mind if I part for a while to join you."

"At any rate, your project seems similar to my own," Charlemagne remarked. "The subject of the Frankish Crown should seem like a grander project compared to whatever it is that you're doing with the petty nobles and such."

Manon didn't reply as she turned a sort of scowl at him.

"I will make all those who doubted me see my genius when I present to them the Frankish Crown, and then perhaps then I should be renowned."

"If you say so, Charlemagne," Manon quietly responded, looking back out the window.

The train continued to travel southwest, leaving Berlin and travelling through a forested area known as Grunewald (Green Forest). At either side, the sight of barren trees could be seen and the grey skies above. The windows held a minor frost at the corners, and the sight of warm-colored leaves on the ground could be seen throughout the forest. After an hour, the train began to arrive back to a settlement, Potsdam, where they passed through this town which was much smaller and quieter than

Berlin. Charlemagne looked out the window as he saw the wide girth of the local river, the Havel. The train continued past this river and stopped at a train station on the other side, *Charlottenhof*, from where Charlemagne and Manon exited.

Once on the streets of Potsdam, Charlemagne hailed a cab and they proceeded to be taken to a specific address, Berliner Straße 98–101. The taxi proceeded to take them east through the town. The streets of Potsdam were clean and the structures simple. Unlike Berlin, these reached a maximum of two stories and many facades of the apartments were not covered in graffiti. The taxi passed the Filmmuseum Potsdam, a single story reddish-tan building with red rooftops and statues of horses and horseman above the front entrance. At the street corner, the car drove north and past a domed church.

"What a lovely place to live," Manon thought aloud. "Not like others I've visited this past year."

"There is something different to settlements in East Germany to those in West Germany. You almost find yourself stuck in the past in the East."

The taxi stopped in a half residential and half commercial area of the town. Charlemagne paid the driver and then exited with Manon. They then crossed the street and came around to a wide two-story building with a brown roof and beige walls. The windows were white and at the center above the main entrance was a clocktower.

"Welcome to the former Deutsches Zentralarchiv, closed in 1992, and still in the process of transferring thousands and thousands of documents to the Bundesarchiv out west. The Bundesarchiv have taken control of this office in the meantime, slowly consolidating files onto trucks so they can transform this government building to some sort of civic centre, I believe. I was here not too long ago."

Charlemagne approached the steps up the turquoise entrance doors. The pair entered into the main foyer where they were greeted by a woman who asked them to present identification, and then state their reason for visit. Manon provided academic credentials, while Charlemagne presented a signed letter from Dr. Dumas that allowed him through. Once past the main foyer, they were led around a corridor, and then deeper into the depths of the three-partition structure, each with an individual courtyard in the center of the building. They entered into a long room where there were aisles and aisles of filing cabinets, stacked documents, and all sorts of other items in a disorganized mess. Charlemagne approached some of the papers and looked around.

"Seems like they're making little progress, which is good, because I don't want to have to travel to their other office out west," Charlemagne remarked. "Well, best place to start is this one. If we split up, we can cover enough ground until we find something."

Manon nodded, removed her blazer, and then placed it on a chair as she proceeded to take her share of the archives. Between Charlemagne and Manon, they each took their time going through piles upon piles, some of which were easy to dismiss for being irrelevant to the purposes of what they hoped to search. However, every once and a while, a document that could somewhat lead into what Charlemagne had earlier found would intrigue either of them, only for it to be nothing of the sort. They worked through the day, and when that wasn't enough, were required to leave to return the next day and then the next. Manon nodded as she read a document and then alerted Charlemagne from the other side of the room they were now in.

"*Charles!* Come!" Manon shouted, rushing towards him. "Look at this this…"

Charlemagne read the document and then looked to Manon with a bit of doubt.

"It's not very clear…" Charlemagne expressed.

"Look here though," Manon remarked, showing him another page.

Charlemagne read the document and then raised an eyebrow. "Is there more?" He proceeded to join her at her side where they searched through papers "Here!"

Manon rushed to his side as they read together, and Charlemagne said, "*By the orders of Reichsführer Heinrich Himmler... a research effort to identify the fate of the Crown of Charlemagne. By my request, an archeological team is to travel to Salzburg...* take note of this address."

"Yes," Manon replied, writing it down.

"There has to be more details somewhere."

Charlemagne and Manon continued to search through the papers, stopping every once and a while with a potential lead.

"I've found it," Manon declared, raising a paper up. "Look here: it is a report to Himmler."

Charlemagne read the report and then began to read aloud as he said, "*At the request of the Reichsführer... an extensive probe has been completed of the genealogy of Scharführer Jürgen Amboise, whose ancestors were rumored to have fled France during the revolutionary period, and acquired and brought the crown with them from France. The ancestor in question was identified as Hilaire Amboise, direct paternal ancestor... No anomalies were detected and the Scharführer was cleared to return to duties...*" He paused for a moment and then looked at Manon. "Do you think – that the Crown could have been retrieved by Himmler himself?"

"Surely not, otherwise we would have known about it by the end of the war," Manon responded, "no less recovered or shown up in propaganda."

"Himmler was a secretive man," Charlemagne remarked. "We need more information..."

Manon took in a deep breath and nodded. She proceeded to resume searching while Charlemagne read the letter over again.

"I can already feel the theories surface around my mind as to what could have happened to the crown, but I am certain as much that it was not melted down."

"How can we be sure that this crown was the crown, the Frankish Crown? The Crown of Charlemagne?"

"We'll have to cross-reference the address with registered landowners in that part of Austria," Charlemagne remarked. "If we don't find anything, then the least we'll have to do is travel to Austria to search further."

"We?" Manon questioned.

"Yes, we," Charlemagne affirmed. "You wouldn't have me travel to Vienna all alone, now would you? I'm still in recovery, and I have enjoyed your company thus far…"

Manon didn't reply. They poured through the rest of the documents in the room they were now in. After another day passed, they left the government building with notes from the files they researched.

"What's the likelihood that the German government went ahead and followed up on this supposed crown?" Charlemagne questioned.

"I would say a good chance because these were rumors about one of their own. Amboise is a familiar name to me, but Hilaire Amboise does not ring a bell. I will have to call my father tonight and get his input," Manon remarked. "If true, then it's likely Himmler would have had the crown seized, but I feel certain that was not the case because we would not have a mystery before us and the Crown would be in the Louvre already."

"There's also the possibility that we've got a red herring," Charlemagne acknowledged. "Perhaps the rumors were false about Amboise being in possession of the crown, or maybe he had it and it went missing. A project was proposed, so that must suggest that the Amboise family was not in possession of the crown, but it was possible for it to be somehow recovered. Perhaps, the intent was to exhume the grave of the ancestor, or follow-up by other means. I think that opens some possibilities and closes some others. We ought to travel to Vienna next though, and I ought to do some more research about these crowns."

Act 2, Prologue

Charlemagne sat on his own atop a small bed in an austere bedroom, his young cheeks wet, light blonde hair combed to the side. He wore a black suit with a black tie, a white collared shirt and small black leather shoes. Charlemagne, seven-years old at the time, fought back the tears that fell from the corner of his eyes, bringing a fist to each respective eyelid. The bedroom had little more than a dresser, a door that led out to the hallway, and the steel-framed bed with the spring-loaded mattress, covered in a quilt and bed sheet, and pillow atop. A suitcase at the end of the bed could also be found. The wallpaper in the room was patterned dark blue and light blue. A window parallel to the single bed looked below. A drizzle of rain covered the window with water, making it difficult to look out to the vineyards beyond. Ahead of Charlemagne, the doorway looked out to a dark hallway from where lights could be seen turned on over the railing to the left to the ground floor where the distant chatter of adults could be heard. Charlemagne sat alone on his bed, continuing to cry.

Suddenly, Charlemagne heard the creak of floorboards at the staircase, causing him to raise his head up and look ahead. He saw a man arrive from the hallway and come towards the door. The man stood at the doorway and looked towards Charlemagne. He was a young man, twenty-four years old at this time, with medium blonde hair and fair skin. He had a chiseled jaw and average body type. He wore a black suit similar to Charlemagne's. He also had blue eyes. The man placed a hand at the door frame and stopped directly below, at an arm's length from Charlemagne.

"Charles," the man spoke in a Western Canadian accent, "your mother wanted me to come up and let you know that we'll be leaving soon." He looked over to the suitcase at the foot of the bed. "Be sure you have all your stuff packed and are ready for us to go. We can't be late to get to the airport. Mum… your grandmother, will be staying with Dr. and Mrs. Dumas as we discussed. I think it would be a good idea to come down and be sure to say goodbye to her."

Charlemagne did not look back at the man and instead looked at his feet. The man sighed and gently knocked on the wall. He then turned around without another word and left. As the man walked back to the staircase, Charlemagne looked towards him from behind and saw him leave. He then stayed put for another moment and fell over. The rain grew harder as Charlemagne continued to cry in solace.

After a few minutes alone, Charlemagne's tears stopped to flow, although his face was still wet. His eyes were red. He slowly pushed himself off the bed and sat up again. He looked over to a clock on the end table and saw that it was nearly six o'clock in the evening. He stood up and went over to the window to get a greater sight of the familiar place he was at, the Dumas Residence in the Val-de-Loire. He could see several cars parked below and the sun to the west as it was about to set. Charlemagne wiped his cheeks and then turned around to slowly walk towards the exit from the bedroom. He walked down the dark hall and came to the top of the stairs, placing a hand on the railing and then looking down. A warmth of light flowed through from the living room to the right where the chatter could be heard; this chatter of which was dismal and somber.

From the top of the stairs, Charlemagne slowly climbed down, stopping at the very bottom where he turned towards the archway that led into a sitting room. He could see an older woman sat beside a younger woman. The older woman had short dark blonde hair and fair skin. She wore a black dress and her makeup was ruined across her cheeks. She held a handkerchief in her hand and the woman next to her had her arm across her shoulders as she consoled her. This woman had medium brown hair and fair skin. Her hair was curled and short. She also wore a dark dress.

"You need to understand," a deep voice spoke in an Orleanist accent, "your father would have never have wanted to be buried in that cemetery. He had a great respect for the men that he fought with, yes, but he never saw himself worthy to be buried with those men."

"If I may interrupt," a man spoke in a North American accent, "with all due respect, Dr. Dumas, but we had a tremendous amount of difficulty to releasing Mr. Cabernet's remains from Belgium as it was – he was set to be buried there, at a war memorial too. The petition we made to the French government was the least we were able to do to have him buried in a place that seemed more dignified."

"Dignified?" Dr. Dumas questioned. "You tell me to have buried Derby Cabernet alongside the men he fought alongside is dignified? A war that he grew to resent for the part he played, believing himself and the men who sacrificed their lives to have been… playthings for government leaders, is a dignified location to have buried him? You have no shame, Mr. Miller."

"The options were presented to Mr. Cabernet – Everest Cabernet."

"These are not options," Dr. Dumas argued. "You are callous men, all of you at Cabernet Corporation, to not even give a damn about the man who employs you. You ought to fire all of them, Everest, for this be treason against your father. Like the inspection report from Mr. Cabernet's accident, they've taken shortcuts rather than care to give attention to find answers to this mystery."

"What answers do you seek, doctor?" Mr. Miller questioned, slightly louder and more annoyed. "Mr. Cabernet was in a motor vehicle accident – accidents happen."

"Get out of my house!" Dr. Dumas demanded. "I've had enough of you – out!"

"Jean – please, no more," a woman responded with a Parisian accent.

"Mr. Cabernet," Mr. Miller pleaded. "Could you please ask Dr. Dumas to be reasonable – we've tried our best..."

A pause came through followed by a clearing of one's throat.

"No," Everest responded with a timid voice, "I believe you." He took in a deep breath and continued to say, "My father believed you and rest of the council fit to lead, so if he could trust you with the affairs of the company, I think I can trust you too."

Dr. Dumas began to curse in French. He then said, "What about the opinion of Mr. Turner? He and I spoke – we are of the same opinion."

"Mr. Turner is no longer with Cabernet Corporation, I'm afraid," Mr. Miller answered. "He resigned yesterday, effective immediately."

"What does any of it matter?" an elegant, but quiet voice spoke in a West London accent. Charlemagne looked and saw that it was the older woman who was being consoled. "My Derby is now dead... his spirit, in a better place than ours no doubt – where his corpse now lies, I do not believe it to matter. The men in suits have done their best, Jean... let us just be at peace too."

"Madame Cabernet... and what about the inspection report..."

Mrs. Cabernet took in a deep breath and replied, "We have all been devastated by the loss of Derby, and I very much liked to have known answers. You tell me, Jean, that my Derby was busy at work on an important project when he was travelling to Germany. He returned to England shortly before he left from his visit to South America, and just like that he was off to get to Dover. At no point did I believe that my Derby was under any threat – so what are these suspicions you have about my love?"

Dr. Dumas did not respond.

"In my husband's excitement, tragedy poured forth from an accident, no more and no less," Mrs. Cabernet remarked. "Such is the way of this world, for one's foot to simply slip and tumble over the edge by chance alone – that's what my Derby believed, and so it has come to happen to him, but... but my Derby and I believed in there to be something greater to console us in this dismal world, and in that I find my consolation. He is received into the arms of God, where his anger against the modern world can be quelled, and he can be at peace. I truly believe that while we weep, my Derby is joyous, and it makes me..." she stuttered as she brought a hand to her eyes, "so much more in pain to know that he is removed from our company, and we are left in this foul place called Earth a little more alone while he is in triumphant celebration in the Kingdom of God." Mrs. Cabernet then continued to cry into her hands and handkerchief. "We must persevere until we too should meet Death."

"How beautifully said..." a woman spoke in an Austrian accent from inside the room.

Charlemagne spun around the staircase railings and passed the sitting room, going into a rear corridor where he walked down and came to the end. He opened a door and found himself in the barn behind the house. He closed the door behind him and kicked a bucket over. He then continued to cry as he sat down on a bench. Charlemagne spun his head around as he heard a door open.

"What are you doing here?" Manon questioned him.

Manon wore a black dress. Her medium-brown hair was cut short at this time. She was also six-years old at this time.

"Go away," Charlemagne remarked, turning around and placing his elbows on his knees to support his head by his hands.

"Why don't you want to talk to me?" Manon questioned. "I haven't done anything."

"Because I don't want to talk to anyone!" Charlemagne aggressively replied.

"It's okay to be upset," Manon acknowledged. "I would be too if my papa died."

"Your papa isn't dead," Charlemagne muttered.

"I'm sorry," Manon said. "I'm sorry if I did something to hurt you."

Charlemagne scoffed and replied, "You haven't – look, just go away, will you? I just want to be alone. What do you even understand, you don't understand anything. You're just a silly little baby, now leave."

Manon didn't leave. She looked at Charlemagne intently. He continued to hold his back towards her as she stood behind him, about an arm's length if not a little further. A tear fell from Manon's eye and she took a step back. She turned around and proceeded to leave, opening the door back indoors, but not without turning around to look at Charlemagne.

"I hope you're able to smile again, soon, Charlemagne," Manon simply remarked. She then left. At the sound of the door closing, Charlemagne turned his head to the side and with a scowl on his face, stood up and kicked over the bench he was sitting on. He then knocked over a mop nearby and kicked the same bucket. He then came down to his knees, facing towards the open exit of the barn and towards the outdoors. He proceeded to weep again, slamming a fist into the dirt.

The door into the house opened again, and Charlemagne jerked his head over to see who it was. He saw Dr. Dumas enter the barn next, looking over to Charlemagne with concern, he rushed over to him and proceeded to assist him onto his feet.

"What is the matter, little one?" Dr. Dumas questioned. "Why are you on your knees?"

Charlemagne continued to cry. Dr. Dumas picked him up into his arms, hugged him, and Charlemagne then hid himself in Dr. Dumas' torso.

"I miss him so much, *monsieur*..." Charlemagne remarked. "I miss my papa..."

"Do not fret, Charlemagne," Dr. Dumas consoled in a quiet voice. "Do not fret, my boy."

"What was my papa doing when he died? Where did he go?"

"Your grandpapa was working on something very important," Dr. Dumas assured him. "He was a very busy man, the busiest he had been in years, and he was doing so because it was an important research project. He left me some of his work to complete though, and maybe someday… I can share it with you, if it is right. Do you still want to be an explorer, like your *grand-père?*"

Charlemagne released his head from Dr. Dumas' chest and looked up to him. His eyes were sunken, both them and his cheeks wet, but he nodded his head.

"In that case, the best you can do to honor the life of your *grand-père* is to ensure that you see it through, yes? Your *grand-père* has always told me how much of an important grandson you were to him, and how intelligent and bright you are, so do not fret, my little Charlemagne. You must study hard, and keep close to your passions, never mind the opinions of anyone else, but be your own man and never forget your *grand-père*, for he has not forgotten about you. Someday, you too will be a great man like he was, I am certain of it. Am I correct?"

Charlemagne looked at him plainly. Dr. Dumas still waited for a response.

"Tell me it will be so, little Charlemagne? You will be a great man, yes?"

Charlemagne nodded to him. Dr. Dumas gave a warm smile.

"I am sure of it," Dr. Dumas encouraged, placing Charlemagne back on the ground, "for you were the treasured child of *Monsieur Cabernet*, and he loved you will all his heart and it will make him very proud to know what a marvel to the world you will have become."

"Charles," Everest called out.

Both Dr. Dumas and Charlemagne looked over to Everest at the doorway into the house.

"Charles, it's time to go," Everest stated.

Dr. Dumas put a hand behind Charlemagne's head and led him towards his father. They stopped just before. He came down onto his knee and brought his hands to Charlemagne's cheeks.

"Remember what we discussed, little Charlemagne. Do not forget, your grandfather is watching over you now."

Charlemagne nodded to him. They embraced and Dr. Dumas hugged him closely. They then parted, and Dr. Dumas waved towards him as he walked down the corridor to leave Dumas' residence, never to return for many years.

Act 2, Scene 1

"With all due respect to the French, there is perhaps no more beautiful city than Vienna in all of Europe," Charlemagne expressed. He took in a deep breath as he continued to walk.

Charlemagne and Manon walked along the side of the *Donaukanal* in Vienna as they left the hotel. He wore a brown suit with a wool coat over top, his breath visible in the chill air, whereas Manon wore a similar overcoat with a skirt, boots, and leggings below.

"May this precious city stay eternally beautiful," Charlemagne remarked, looking across the street. The apartment complexes in Vienna were tall, clean, and unique in all their construction. The complex that Charlemagne looked at had six stories, was constructed of plain white bricks, and had a dormer rooftop adding another floor. The entrance of the building stuck out onto the street and was slightly taller, with balustrades around the rooftop window. A building next to this apartment had balconies attached to them, and rather than a rooftop simply had balustrades along the perimeter of the top level. On the street level, a tram car passed the middle of the street, while traffic was one-lane on the right side, and a wide path for pedestrians on the left side with a green strip between another path and the canal. "Having come to Vienna as an adolescent (my second visit, as I had visited as a child), I could understand what compelled my maternal grandparents to name my mother as such, *Wien*, as she was called from her birth."

"Ah, that's right, Vienna and *Vienne* are exonyms for your mother's name, but she was born in Austria…"

"Yes, admittedly, Wien although beautiful and meaningful in Austria and Germany, is not shared the same emote to the west," Charlemagne responded. "When my mother came to Harlech as a youth, she was called 'Ween' at first, resulting in the taunts of her classmates. She corrected as much as she could to clarify her name was 'Vien,' as the German 'W' is like a 'V' in English. However, tired of such a convoluted explanation, she resigned to just say her name was Vienna, which sounded a lot more effeminate and straightforward. Likewise, when my grandfather helped her immigrate, she changed her legal name to Vienna having been known by all by that name. She resigned to understand that although not the name of her birth, it was the name by recognition of others, and also too she preferred the name. My mother never felt patriotic towards the Austrian state, no less because of the treacherous nature of her family to have abandoned her in her time of need when she was pregnant with me. Even to this date, that family enjoys to not recognize that my mother even existed, to the disheartened heart of my mother no doubt. They had seemingly abandoned her in Canada to study, with no intention that she should return. My mother, so gracious towards them, has always recognized her life to have been better in the New World than to return. Nonetheless, she holds in her heart her brothers and sisters."

"Have you yourself thought about reaching out to this family? To your cousins?"

"I wouldn't want anything to do with a lot like that," Charlemagne remarked. "Certainly, I know about that family, the Neubacher family, but never could I relinquish the wrath that I have for what they did to my mother."

"How tragic..." Manon replied. "I am sorry for you, Charlemagne, to have no family like that. The Dumas family are many, cousins on both my mother and father's sides. Jacques and I have always known my cousins since we were young."

"Who needs family like that," Charlemagne balked. "I can barely loathe my own siblings and tolerate them as they are than to endure much more in half-a-dozen, or a dozen likewise persons. In a family as a large as yours, I would suffer."

Manon did not reply. The pair continued to walk down along the side of the canal. They soon crossed the street and began to walk down a narrow one-way street where there were vehicles parked on the left and many shops to the left more. The buildings maintained the same integrity as those on the main street, and they were very clean too. These buildings were tanned and they ranged from four stories to six stories tall. At the next intersection, the pair crossed the street and then continued along a bend going the same direction as the canal. There were very few people on the streets at this time. The pair came around to another intersection where they turned right again, going down another narrow street, this one of which was made of stone bricks rather than asphalt. They passed many stores, cafes, and bars. They then reached a roundabout and continued straight along the crosswalks to continue forth. The pair continued to walk down until they reached downtown Vienna and the roads disappeared and were replaced with smooth stone brick paths between buildings of which only pedestrians were allowed to walk, and there were many pedestrians.

In this area, Charlemagne observed there to be many high-end shops on the ground floors. They reached a plaza where further ahead he could see the dome roof and entrance of a church. He looked to his right and saw a small store which had statues of bare-chested women that protruded from the beige brick walls like mermaids, hands raised and holding up brackets underneath bay windows from the second floor. There were six of these figures in total, and a pleasant aroma that came out from the store of chocolate and coffee, as this was a café and a sweets store that sold candies and also pastries. The pair walked past this store, but as Charlemagne saw the church ahead, he diverted left and continued down the wider promenade. Manon simply followed suit as he guided her through the city. The pair passed a small fountain that had a marble statue of a bearded man in a robe, holding a cane in his right hand and with a raised index finger at his left hand, left arm outstretched, and head looking down towards a toddler at his side who looked up to him.

Charlemagne quickly passed his gaze from this statue where there were some local youth sat below to a grander one ahead of him. This statue was an amalgamation of all sorts of human figures with gold-colored ornate around. The statue was raised up on steps and surrounded by a balustrade. The statue had three sides with golden crests at each corner. Above one corner, facing Charlemagne and Manon, there was a statue of an angel holding a sheet of parchment paper. On the paper was written in gold letters, '*Deo Patri Creatori.*' Likewise, on each corner more there were two more angels with parchment sheets and gold written letters. Above these angels were an amalgamation of clouds with various angelic figures around, leading up to the top where there were cherubim and all sorts of angelic beings wrapped together to the visible sight of a Christian cross poking out from the very top. The very top of the statue was gold-colored and included a star-like object, similar to a monstrance with rays that shined outwards like petals of a sunflower. Charlemagne observed this statue and then continued down an alleyway in front where he walked away from the promenade.

"What a marvelous statue," Manon remarked. "I am not religious, but it is still beautiful nonetheless, these little things that are remnant of the past."

"I can somewhat recall my grandfather once told me that the past were more humble times to that extent, whatever that means. I also recall something to that extent of the misery of the earth and realization of human fallibility, compared to the glory of the Heavens. You should remember what my grandfather was like, he was a religious man, made sure we went to church every Sunday and more. He was a great believer in a God-centric universe over a humanist approach. He was very old-fashioned; a part of him I least appreciated – just a change of the times we grew up in, I suppose. Of course, I'm not religious either- to me, it's all dribble."

Charlemagne and Manon eventually came out to a round plaza from where there were stands in the center that sold Christmas-themed goods. There were also horse drawn carriages parked around, and very many Christmas lights hung around. This plaza faced a grand structure, arched in being, with black-framed windows. The main entrance had a tall archway in the center, and then smaller rectangular archways that led into a large tunnel through to the other side. These archways each had on either side on pedestals, human-sized marble figures of males trampling and battling demonic figures. The figure on the left-most side held a club and was about to smack two serpent-like heads. The figure next to him held a club and was choking Medusa at his side while trampling a large fish. On the other side, a large, muscular figure trampled another man and an eagle. On the last end, there was a muscular figure that had a one of three heads of a three-headed dog in a headlock with the other hand grasping the beast's tail. The archway in itself had a black gate that was wide open, and above that gate was an ornate black steel-like arch with initials in gold, 'F' and 'J'. Above the archway were two human figures carved into the building, a crown, and words above, some of which read, '*Francus Josephus.*' A sign on the side read, 'Sisi Museum.' Charlemagne and Manon came out through the other side where there was a courtyard with a statue in the midst of Emperor Francis Josephus himself.

Further ahead, Charlemagne and Manon walked through one of their tunnels through the museum which led them to a much larger plaza and much larger arched building. This façade had even more detail than the front of the museum they walked through to arrive. There were also numerous vehicles parked in front. Charlemagne and Manon walked to the front of the entrance, where a sign above read, 'Hofburg' and had various other titles that included 'Nationalbibliotek' and 'Wien Museum,' also called 'Haus der Geschichte Österreich.'

"Here we are," Charlemagne simply noted.

The Hofburg was a large structure with a small entrance above a few steps. The façade of the structure consisted of white brick. The lower level consisted of arched windows with white curtains on the other side, blocking the view indoors. Both left and right there were nine windows with eleven statues between each side on pedestals of clothed persons. Above this level and windows there were double pillars along balustrades that were part of a balcony. Behind the balcony, there were rectangular windows and then square windows above. The entire rooftop of the Hofburg had balustrades along the perimeter and angelic figures at each corner.

"What are we doing here, *Charles*?" Manon questioned as they entered through. "Have you brought me here to take me to a museum?"

"Not just any museum, my dear," Charlemagne remarked. "The Hofburg is the residence of a crown that I need to see for my own eyes and take note of – yet another crown known as the Crown of Charlemagne, the crown of the Holy Roman Empire. I was discussing the situation with your father, and he recommended we make a pitstop here to take notes, and also that I complete my research on the subject beforehand too."

Charlemagne and Manon paid admission into the museum, and then proceeded through the museum halls where there were various objects, decayed marble statue pieces, artwork, and all sorts of collected items laid about the halls of the building.

"The Hofburg was the former principal imperial palace of the Habsburg dynasty since the 13th century, also being the seat of the Holy Roman Empire since the 15th century to its dissolution. Nowadays, it is part government building and other part museum, but nonetheless, in the Swiss Wing, the imperial regalia of the Roman Empire is kept, including the Crown of Charlemagne, or *Reichskrone*."

Charlemagne and Manon came around to a warmly-lit room with red walls. They entered through and stopped to face display cases that included all sorts of items. He took a journal out from his coat and began to list off the items.

"According to documented sources, a majority of these items have been dated and confirmed to have probably belonged to Charlemagne," Charlemagne stated. "In inventory, the Imperial Bible, the Sabre of Charlemagne, and the Holy Lance."

Charlemagne and Manon stopped to look at a spearhead. The object was placed in a large display case with two other objects and was no more than a few inches in length, or just under a foot. At the center of the spear was a gold-colored wrapping. This spearhead was next to a large crucifix with many gems encrusted on its surface and gold-colored. At the mantle below, the emblem of the Austrian empire was imprinted. Next to that crucifix was a smaller crucifix with a sliver of wood.

"According to legend, this item was the very same spearhead on the spear of the centurion that pierced Christ at the Crucifixion – the Lance of Longinus. The shaft was lost a millennium ago – that sliver of wood next to it, on that crucifix, is believed to be a piece of wood from the crucifix Christ was killed on... if you believe in any of that. There's been very good reason to believe that both the lance and that piece of wood are not such, much like that crown of thorns in the Notre Dame cathedral in Paris. It's all just nonsense and myth... and speaking of which, that comes to this..."

Charlemagne and Manon stopped in front of another display case, this one of which held a very regal crown with many gems encrusted on it like the crucifix from the other display case. This crown consisted of eight sides, each arched with the front more arched than the others and with more jewels and a small crucifix above with five more jewels. On the side arches were small depictions surrounded with smaller jewels. The center of the crown was red and velvet, very plush. The crown was next to a sword on the left, and a gold-colored orb on the right. This orb had a crucifix above with more gems encrusted. Some other items on display were clothing items, albs, shoes, gloves, stoles, and robes. As they finished looking around at the regalia, and Charlemagne made notes, they stopped at a portrait of a bearded-man with long greyish-white hair dressed in a dark gold-colored chasuble and cope. He held in his right hand the same sword on display, and in his left hand the orb with the cross. Atop of his head was the *Reichskrone*. He also wore gloves; all these clothing items of which were on display somewhere in the room. On the left of the man's head was the Austrian royal emblem (a black eagle on yellow crest), and on the right of the man's head was the French royal emblem (three white fleur-de-lis on blue). Beneath these crests were the words, 'Karolus' and 'magnus.'

"There you are, *Charles*," Manon noted. "So what is the story behind this crown?"

"The story is that Charlemagne never wore any of these items. Even the items dated from his time period are questionable at the best, and that crown... although shown in this painting to be on his head, was not worn by even his ancestors. The crown was made at least a hundred and fifty years later for Otto the First, and then every successor to the throne when it was removed from the French state. This saber, and this sword, they were not Charlemagne's. Like that sword in the Louvre, crafted for Phillip III, all these items were an attempt to justify the legitimacy of the Holy Roman Empire to its founder. For the past thousand years before the dissolution of the Holy Roman Empire, while the Austrians crowned their king with the *Reichskrone*, the French king was crowned with the actual crown that belonged to Charlemagne."

Charlemagne moved away from the painting and looked back at all these items.

"These are nothing more than propaganda items, which is all the more reason why the German government seized them. I'm not looking for neither myth nor legend, my dear. I want the very true crown that rested upon Charlemagne and Charlemagne's sons' heads. I came to take note to get a visual idea of what the *Reichskrone* looks like with my own eyes. There may be a chance of similarities between that and the Frankish crown. I was made aware of one other contested crown in Italy, but after a little bit more research, determined that although it belonged to Charlemagne, it rests in a church in Lombardy and was one of Charlemagne's crown, but not the one used to declare him Holy Roman Emperor. This crown in question was used to crown him King of the Lombards, a separate title. However, at this time, that crown is the only crown that one can truly be said to have belonged to Charlemagne."

Charlemagne paused for a moment as he looked at the regalia once more, walking from one side of the room to the other to leave. They came into the corridor where they stopped in front of a portrait of a man with short brown hair and blue eyes. He had a parted moustache and wore an ornamental red-white robe with golden branches with golden leaves strewn across. He was positioned in a room, looking outwards with a window that had the Viennese cityscape behind him. A plaque below the portrait read, '*Servus Dei, Carolus I*' in Latin.

"All these items sicken me," Charlemagne confessed. "They seek to make a false claim to something that they did not hold – of the father of Europe and center of power for a German Europe. My grandfather would turn in his grave – he hated Germans, you know."

"And yet his beloved grandson was half German."

"Bah, like my mother, I disown that side of the family – I am Charlemagne *de la* Cabernet, and we are a French family name. I believe it is time that we go to Salzburg to investigate further why a French crown is in Austrian hands."

Act 2, Scene 2

"I'm looking at this map, Manon, and I can't seem to find Lauterbach Street anywhere," Charlemagne remarked, staring down a map placed on a table in his hotel room. "I've looked at this map once over already last night, even picking up a magnifying glass to ensure I got every street, but in all of Salzburg there doesn't seem to be any street of that sort."

"Have you checked the local directories?"

"Yes, I did – stupidly, wasn't my first call, but I did give them a phone call and seemingly there isn't a Lauterbach Street," Charlemagne stated. "My guess, the street was probably obliterated during the war."

"Or also changed after the war to a different name," Manon suggested. "During the war, it was common for defending armies to remove street signs to confuse enemies who relied on archived maps to navigate through. Likely, after the war, the street was lost and/or renamed."

"At any rate, we're never going to locate the principle residence of this Amboise family. We're going to have to rely on Plan B." Charlemagne placed his journal down and pointed to three addresses. "Based on our record search in Vienna, these are the three only persons in all of Salzburg and local area with the surname Amboise. Assuming that the family continues to live in this area, it could be possible that one of these three are our man."

"A lot to assume, since there does not seem to be anyone by the name of Jürgen Amboise in all of Austria. We have a Phineas Amboise, Benjamin Amboise, and Alecia Amboise."

"I have their addresses here, here, and here," Charlemagne remarked, pointing them out of the map. "Let's have a look then. I'm sure at least one of these should be a descendant."

Manon tilted her head to the side as she shrugged and said, "It is possible. I talked to my father and he said that there is a good chance we may be on to something – Amboise… I wasn't sure about the name, but he assured me that it was a name of former nobility. I had my doubts because I knew a Frédéric D'Amboise once upon a time – it is not usually common to come across a person of noble background."

"Well, then let's hope at least one of these are noble by blood."

"Again, it is possible. The Amboise family indeed left France among the émigré who escaped the revolution, and like many others, came to Austria."

"I'm willing to search the entire damn country then to find anyone who may have been related to Jurgen or Hillaire."

"Uh… Hillaire Amboise as a descendant, I am less certain of. There was nobody by that name in the records my father had searched."

"Still, even if a legend, there has got to be some truth to the matter. Let's have some hope here, Manon, I don't want our search to come to an abrupt end."

After Charlemagne finished, he folded the map, placed it in a messenger bag, and then left the hotel room with Manon. They came down to the street level and exited out onto the streets of Salzburg.

Similar to Potsdam, Salzburg was a smaller town than the capital city. With those changes came smaller apartment blocks, smaller streets, and even smaller cars. Charlemagne and Manon exited from their hotel and proceeded down along a street sidewalk to reach a bridge that crossed over to the south part of the city. At the end of the bridge, they crossed the sidewalk and travelled further east below some four-story apartment blocks with plain tan facades. The buildings in Salzburg were less fantastical and the architecture more simple than the ones in Vienna. As they walked down the street, from the other side of the river was a hill covered in trees with orange-red leaves. Atop of that hill was a building with yellowish-tan walls and brown rooftops. Further ahead of that hill, towards the northeast, were further hills and greenery on the horizon. Charlemagne and Manon walked a short distance along the road before they went inwards in search for the first address.

"I have a feeling like this first one on our list won't be it," Charlemagne noted. "We're in the midst of the city and I don't imagine someone just has the crown in their cupboard."

"It is still beneficial to talk and see if this person is in the least a descendant of Jürgen."

Charlemagne and Manon came around to a plaza in front of a church, and from behind the church on another hill, they could see a castle-like structure positioned. They travelled further east some more and found themselves near some fields. At the first address, they found themselves in front an apartment block. As Charlemagne looked at the plain white apartment block, similar to others spaced out on the other side of a field, he shook his head.

"I'll think we'll come back to this one – let's try the next one."

"It is on the other side of town," Manon remarked. "How will be go all the way to there?"

"Let's take a taxicab," Charlemagne remarked. "I'll wave one down."

Charlemagne and Manon were in a quiet part of the town, and so they returned close to the heart of Salzburg where they had an easy time searching for a taxicab which proceeded to drive them back through. They travelled north and passed along many apartments as they travelled along a major road, reaching an interchange where they looked out and could see farmland at the side.

"I've got a better hunch about this one – we can come back to visit Alecia Amboise some other time," Charlemagne remarked. "We shouldn't be searching for the crown in the apartment. I want a family home, an estate."

Manon rolled her eyes as she looked out her window.

The taxicab took them around and then east again as they went along the *Westautobahn* and passed some more farmland. Around this farmland, there were various offshoot roads that tied in with houses grouped together. Additionally, there were offshoot roads that tied together with small suburban communities. The taxi exited out at one of these offshoots, traveling down a lone lane. Ahead of them in the background were the Alps and hills, with a few apartment buildings in the foreground. At either side of the lane were tall shrubs and barren trees. They proceeded to pass some houses, turning around the corner and going past many houses before stopping at one in particular.

"Bollocks," Charlemagne expressed, looking at his map and then over to the two-story home they were at. "I didn't anticipate this end – very well, let's have a looksie."

Charlemagne asked the cab driver to wait for them, paid him in advanced, and then came out with Manon to step towards the home. The house was small with white walls, brown-framed windows, and a small patio at front. At the side was a lane with a decline that went into an attached garage. Charlemagne looked at Manon, and then the pair stepped forward to knock.

After a moment of waiting, Charlemagne turned to Manon and said, "Shame, nobody home. I suppose the last address ought to do."

"Wait," Manon remarked, listening from the other side. She could hear the crying of a child on the other end. The door then opened, and a woman holding a male child could be seen, comforting him as he cried out.

"*Ja?*" the woman asked, looking at them. "*An Ausschreibungen bin ich nicht interessiert.*"

"*Ich bin kein Verkäufer. Wir suchen Benjamin Amboise,*" Charlemagne replied.

"*Benjamin?*" the woman questions. "*Ah... Ben!*"

The woman stepped out of the way, and after a while, a slightly overweight male stepped forward from upstairs and looked over to the pair. He wore a Metallica t-shirt and had sunken eyes. He also very fair, almost sickly fair skin.

"*Was ist es?*" the man questioned.

"*Verkäufer suchen Sie,*" the woman remarked before leaving.

"*Verkäufer suchen mich?*" Benjamin responded.

"*Keine Verkäufer, sondern Historiker,*" Charlemagne clarified. "*Ich bin Charlemagne Cabernet, und das ist Doktor Manon Dumas, von der Universität Paris.*"

Manon looked at Charlemagne with suspicious eyes as he said that. She then looked back over to the male with a friendlier face.

"*Sind Sie der Nachkomme von Jürgen Amboise?*" Manon questioned.

"*Jurgen Amboise?*" Benjamin remarked, scratching his unshaven cheek. "*Ich bin kein Nachkomme, aber der Name ist bekannt.*"

"Really?" Charlemagne questioned. "Wie so?"

"*Ich glaube, ich hatte einen Onkel mit diesem Namen,*" Benjamin answered.

"*Lebt er noch?*" Manon asked.

"*Nein, er ist gleich am Ende gestorben, oder eigentlich erst danach.*"

"Any family from his side?" Charlemagne asked Manon. Manon then repeated the question in German.

"*Vielleicht... ich weiß es nicht,*" Ben answered.

"Do you know - *Kennen Sie einen Phineas oder Alecia Amboise?*" Charlemagne asked.

"*Hm... Vielleicht. Warum liegt Ihnen dieser Teil der Familie am Herzen?*"

"*Wie gesagt, wir sind Historiker,*" he plainly stated. "*Bitte hilf uns.*"

"*Was ist drin für mich?*"

"Was?" Charlemagne questioned, confused.

"Ich sollte eine Entschädigung bekommen."

Charlemagne sighed and took out his wallet. He then provided the man with a few Austrian Schillings.

"Ja, Phineas ist mein Cousin. Ich weiß allerdings nicht, wo er wohnt... vielleicht, wenn Sie in einem Telefonbuch nachfragen."

"No need, my good sir," Charlemagne replied in English. He looked over to Manon. "Let's go."

"Danke, mein Herr," Manon responded, bowing her head to the man. The man closed the door and the pair then walked over to taxi.

"I think we're on the right track," Charlemagne expressed, stopping at the taxi to open the door. "Let's hurry before it gets dark..."

As Charlemagne finished his sentence, he looked up to notice that it was beginning to snow. He frowned and then looked back over to Manon who looked at him and entered into the taxicab. He then entered through and closed the door behind him. He provided the address to Phineas' home on the other side of town, and then they proceeded to drive back to Salzburg as it snowed.

"Charles, I wish you wouldn't lie when we talked to people," Manon remarked as they drove across town.

"Lie? What lie did I tell?" Charlemagne questioned. "I do not lie – to anyone."

"You told that man that we both worked for the university," Manon expressed, "while I admire your desire to be a part of an institution, only one of us is out on official business while you are a mere hobbyist."

"A hobbyist? Very cheeky of you, my dear," Charlemagne expressed, visibly withholding his anger. He cleared his throat and then said, "I believe it's fair to say that I've made a greater contribution to historical society, then you have. Remind me, which of us located the Tuscany Diamond recently? What about one of the Russian Royal Eggs? The Scimitar of the Morning Sun?"

"As if so much depended on you finding useless *knickknacks* from the past," Manon remarked. "You have a list of useless goods to your name, but I have publications contributing to a greater discourse. At least now you seem to be interested in something of modest worth to the academic world."

Charlemagne scowled and then looked out the side of his car. The car proceeded to drive west, passing through Salzburg and going into the back country. After a drive along the autobahn, the cab exited out and drove along a lane, coming around to an estate on the riverfront.

"Hm, if I was a French noble in exile, then I believe something like these homes would be to my taste," Charlemagne noted. "Thank you for your service. No need to wait this time."

Charlemagne paid the taxi driver, and then afterwards the pair exited and saw the driver off. They then turned around to face the Amboise Estate. The house was large, bordered by a tall hedge with a gate in the center. The house had plain yellow walls and white-framed windows. The manor was at least two stories tall, not including the attic viewable by the dormer windows. The estate driveway had a fountain in the center, and the rest of the property encompassed a very neat and well-maintained open garden. Charlemagne paid heed from the outside of the property as he looked in.

"Well, let's see if anyone is home," Charmagne remarked, opening the gate. "Come on."

Manon looked at him and then followed. The gate was easily opened, allowing them to walk through. They then closed the gate behind them and continued down the gravel driveway to the fountain. A few vehicles were parked on the side of the driveway front lot, all of which were Dolores-Ganß sports cars and sedans. Manon looked around the property while Charlemagne rushed to the front door and knocked.

"Even in the face of revolution, the rich survive and are well off," Manon remarked. "Even despite the defeat in war, the rich survive and are well off."

"My mother's parents are a testament to that fact..."

Charlemagne tapped his foot as he waited for someone to answer the door, but nobody came. He hit the door again with hard knocks, awaiting an answer, and then seeing a doorbell button on the right to press. He did so several times.

"It seems as though nobody is home," Manon noted. "Bad luck... it is Sunday after all."

"Sunday, Schmunday," Charlemagne responded. "I know I can find answers in this home – look at the architecture. Did you see the road sign from where we approached? These homes were built in the last hundred years, and the road had the name of a politician in power sixty years ago who was killed by the National Socialists. I bet if we were to dig a little deeper, we would learn that this road was named as such after the war. We're in the right place – this home belonged to Jürgen Amboise."

"*Charles*, even if that were so, do you expect that this man or Amboise would have just had the crown lying around? The family surely would have returned it, or shown it off, or done something to have caused public attention of the matter if they had it, but they haven't. They must not have it."

"Oh, you of little faith," Charlemagne balked, knocking harder. "For all we know, it's lying in their attic. Come on, let's check around the back of the house."

"*Charles*, no – that is trespassing."

"As far as I understand, it's only trespassing when they tell you to leave and you don't, or if what we are about to do is done at night. Now come on..."

Charlemagne and Manon proceeded to go around the back of the house, arriving at a patio that looked outwards to a river lake at the base of a mountain. They came around up a set of stairs above the patio where Charlemagne looked through. He then attempted to open the door, but was not successful. He proceeded down the side of the house from this level and began to check the windows. Manon simply looked back at him until Charlemagne was able to lift a window open.

"Ahah, you see? Come, nobody is home, and I smell treasure…"

"*Charles*," Manon scolded, "no – that is going too far. What are you like?"

"I'm only going to have a little peak inside," Charlemagne remarked. "What harm am I doing to anyone? I'm not going to take anything."

"I will have no part in what you are doing…"

"Very well, then let the history books say that *Docteur Manon Dumas* was too coward to enter through the house, whereas Charlemagne bravely entered through, knowing that the Frankish Crown lied inside where it was greedily kept hidden from public view."

Manon shook her head at him as he then went into the manor. She crossed her arms and stayed put, looking around the wide-open area, sheepishly looking about left and right, left and right, as she awkwardly stood next to the open window. Manon looked towards the river lake where she saw a small boat about to pass. She then looked up to the skies as she saw a V of birds fly over. She looked across the lawn around as the snow had covered the region in a small layer of white powder. Manon shook her head again, turned, and entered through.

The window led into a kitchen. Manon looked around and saw that it was a renovated kitchen with modern appliances. She proceeded down to a corridor and came around, looking for Charlemagne. She quietly walked about, passing a doorway and looking inside to a parlor. She stepped forward and felt a hand come over her mouth. She screamed into this man's hand, squirming as she was caught in an embrace from behind. She kicked behind with her high-heel boots and hit the man, releasing his grip.

"Oof," Charlemagne remarked, grabbing his upper shin and lightly laughing, "look who's had a change of heart."

"*Imbecile,*" Manon quietly cursed at him, hitting him on the shoulder too with a closed fist, "what is wrong with you? Huh?"

"Hush now," Charlemagne reckoned, "and come hither."

Charlemagne took Manon around to the back of the house, past the patio where he unlocked the door, and then over to the other side of the house where there was another parlor, a study, and a recreation room. The items in the house were modern, especially the artwork.

"No heirlooms, no family portraits, and no collectibles anywhere to be found," Charlemagne noted. "What a boring family."

"What are you thinking?"

"I'm thinking that we need to go upstairs to the attic," Charlemagne reckoned. "Up we go." The pair proceeded to travel up to the second floor, searching the bedrooms, many of which were empty and plain. Charlemagne found a staircase that went upstairs, and travelled through, reaching a door that was locked. He pressed himself against the door, and began to bash it forcefully with his side. He managed to open the attic door and then proceeded to look about. "Jackpot, so they say."

The attic contained numerous items in storage, including old furniture, chests and crates, and other stored goods.

"Let's see what we can find," Charlemagne said, going through the crates and chests. He looked around quickly, attempting to find anything he could open to examine its contents. Manon pulled off a bedsheet from a portrait and looked at an eighteenth to nineteenth century figure. He wore a powered wig and wore regal clothes. Atop of his head was a curious-looking crown-shaped object. As Manon examined the portrait,

Charlemagne noticed from afar and came around to look. "Is- is that it?" he said, squinting.

"What do you mean is that it? Do you not know what this crown looks like? I thought you did your research?" Manon questioned.

"I did, and there was a picture of it from the Saint-Denis catalog, but that... I suppose that is close to what it was meant to look like, gems and all, although a little plain. Perhaps this artist just got it all wrong. What does this mean though?"

The pair paused for a moment as they thought.

"It means that the Nazi government had a good hunch," Manon concluded, "but any evidence that the crown was here, or is here, has yet to be seen. In the least we can say that this... Hillaire Amboise, may have had the crown, but whether this portrait is an anachronism, that is to say, imaginary, is for debate."

"Indeed," Charlemagne remarked, "let's keep looking around then, shall we?"

The pair worked tirelessly as they searched through the objects inside the attic. Eventually, Manon approached Charlemagne with fear in her eyes.

"*Charles*, let's leave – the crown cannot be here, and I am worried that the owner of the house should arrive and we'd have to escape."

"Nonsense, look at what I've found here... they're letters," Charlemagne remarked. "Very old letters, the writing of which I'm having a tad bit of difficulty to read, but sure enough it in French. These must have been written by Hillaire. In this letter, he's speaking about his departure from France due to instability and persecution by the revolutionaries. He's left for the Holy Roman Empire."

Manon nodded as she listened. She then perked up as she looked over to one of the windows that looked out below. She saw a car drive in to the estate.

"No mention of any crown in this letter…" Charlemagne stated.

"*Charles…*"

"Not now my dear."

"*Charles…!*" Manon hushed. "*Amboise* – he's here!"

"Oh no…"

"We need to leave!"

"Uh…" Charlemagne hesitated, looking at the many documents below. "You go then… make a run for it. I've got to risk it – there's so much more to clear through."

"What? Are you mad?"

"I'll stay up here until sundown, sneak out through the back when all is quiet," Charlemagne insisted. "Just go…"

Manon rolled her eyes again. She went over to where he was and took a handful of papers. "Who are these letters addressed to anyhow?"

Charlemagne paused and then replied, "They're not letters, but bits and pieces of a journal entry. "I'm going through entries from just around the time they've fled from Paris…"

"I am at arrival in Vienna," Manon relied. "I am scanning each page for any mention of a crown, or any other key words."

Manon quickly went through page to page.

"I am not finding anything…"

"There has to be something…"

Manon continued to scan page to page. "Ahah!" she said. "Here – a few months in Vienna. *Due to the circumstances, where I am like an outcast in Austrian society, I must sell what little I have to make ends meeting, including my beloved crown. Today I met a Hungarian gentleman, a nobleman and an officer in the Austrian Army. I did not catch his name, but he's in charge of a citadel on the border of some badlands. I am not sure where that is, but I will find him when I have regained my wealth. I did not tell him where this crown is from, so hopefully I will be able* to buy it off him again. *This crown is mine – it is my right to rule when I make my return…"*

"That's it?" Charlemagne questioned. "Is there anything else?"

Manon scanned a few pages. She shook her head. "I do not see anything…"

"There must be more information – we have to take some of these pages with us."

"*Charles*, enough, that is theft. You cannot steal these documents; they do not belong to you. Come – we need to leave."

Charlemagne held the papers in his hands, and with a moment of hesitation, let go of them and allowed them to fall back into the chest they came from. The pair then proceeded to leave the estate, sneaking downstairs, and then going out the main entrance rather than around the patio. Charlemagne looked back behind him regrettably as Manon led him forward back towards the gate, and then onto the streets from which they roamed as they returned to Salzburg.

Act 2, Scene 3

Charlemagne was driven around in a grey 1995 Dolores-Ganß van along a narrow cliffside road. On the left of the road was a highway barrier that protected from a steep fall as well as barren trees on the bank of a wide river. On the left was a smooth hill with the occasional barren tree or two, a few properties in rough shape, broken windows, and such. The properties varied in size, from small cottages on the side of the road to long paths that led to larger estates. The skies above were cloudy and there was a minor bit of snow on the sides of the road and on the grass and trees, but otherwise surfaces were clear. Manon rode in the rear passenger seat as she comfortably read a fiction book with both hands, her purse next to her. Charlemagne rode in the front passenger seat, scribbling in a journal with an open map next to him labelled Pest County in the corner. The van was driven by a Hungarian male with fair and warm olive-colored skin. He was an older male, around his forties, and he had medium-light brown hair that was cut short. He also had a stocky figure and he wore a fisherman's vest and cargo pants. He smelt of garlic. This man drove at a modest pace, close to fifty miles per hour.

Charlemagne wrote in his journal, *On our way to an abandoned citadel on the Polish-Hungarian border. Spent the last few days in Vienna checking records again, searching for any potential Hungarian officers that served in the Imperial Austrian Army at the end of the eighteenth century – lots of records from the Napoleonic Wars. Jean-Baptiste gave us a tip that the Imperial Army, also called the Imperial-Royal, was divided among ethnicities and so we would likely find a Hungarian officer in charge of a Hungarian regiment in Hungary – we narrowed a few candidates who lived and served around 1790, and I have a good hunch about this one bloke stationed up here. This citadel was an important castle on the Polish-Lithuanian border, and according to the little information there is about this rock, it became very important during the partitions from 1772-1795, and then Napoleon Wars until 1813 when the citadel was sacked.*

Manon, as usual, seems to disagree with me. Although this citadel seems to be the only one on a Hungarian border in which there could have been a Hungarian general in charge, she believes that because Galicia was incorporated in 1772, it could not have been considered a 'border' citadel anymore but an important command post. I'm more empowered by her words to disprove her foolish hypothesis. Although I appreciate her company, I don't intend to continue this journey much longer with her – she's beginning to irritate me with her concerns for my safety - the disrespect. Even the simplest remark that I wanted to be driven to the citadel rather than rent a vehicle and drive there was met with the question of 'why' from her, as if it is her business. She's a guest on this trip, and I wanted to have time to reflect and research while on the road than to be focused on driving – besides, I don't drive, I prefer to be driven...

The journal entry ended there with a long linear pen mark from the last word as the van hit a bump in the road.

"Oh, damn…" Charlemagne muttered, looking at the page. He closed his journal and placed it into his messenger bag at his feet. He then pulled out a notebook and began to review his notes. He then looked over as the van began to drive along a curve on the river. He looked closer and could see that the river they drove next to merged with another, wider river. The view was mostly obstructed by trees on the cliffside.

After a few more minutes, Charlemagne observed an archway further ahead that consisted of small red bricks with a smaller archway on the left for pedestrians. A pair of cyclists rode their bikes underneath the arch before the van passed through. Charlemagne then observed that the archway connected with some battlement walls on the cliffside. These walls extended approximately twenty meters before coming to an end. On the left, Charlemagne then observed some taller stone walls in front of a cliff besides a tall hill. These walls cut short right at the wall, but continued along the cliffside. The top side of the walls were battered and appeared as though the full extent of the wall had broken off. The rest of the wall travelled uphill. An abandoned structure could be seen near the road in front of the wall, and in front of that abandoned structure was a modern building, a small home. Meanwhile, on the left, although the brick wall ended, the trees no longer obscured the view and there was no steeper cliff between the road and river. Instead, the river could be seen nearly immediately next to the road, and it had calm, greyish-grey waters. A short distance later, more buildings could be seen on the left side while a promenade atop of a wall could be seen on the right side. The space where the buildings were positioned was small due to the steep hill and additional sections of wall that could be found around. However, after a few more minutes, the space widened out and there were more properties, as well as more trees, scattered around. As Charlemagne observed with his eyes, he suddenly noticed his driver turn signal right and merge off the road.

"Hold on, László, what are you doing?" Charlemagne questioned.

"Fuel low," László simply responded. "I buy petrol."

"Petrol?" Charlemagne questioned. "Must you do so now? We're a few ways away from the citadel. You could have gone after dropping us off?"

László ignored him and drove into the gas station. He then stepped out and proceeded to walk towards the mechanic shop while he left Charlemagne and Manon alone. A young worker stepped out and went over to fill the car.

"Well, isn't this great," Charlemagne remarked, looking into the rear-view mirror at Manon. "To think I trusted the hotel to find me someone good and professional to drive us to the citadel."

"Mhm," Manon replied, disinterested.

Charlemagne sat back as he waited. He listened to the pump fill the van, and then when the worker was done, he looked and saw the worker come up to his window and tap the glass.

"What the," Charlemagne remarked. He rolled down the window. "*Ja? Kann ich Ihnen helfen?*"

The young boy politely spoke in Hungarian to Charlemagne, pointing to the machine and then raising his hand as though he wanted something. Charlemagne looked down at his hand and shook his head.

"Sorry, but I'm not the one that's paying for the petrol," Charlemagne stated, where 'petrol' was one of the words the adolescent male had said. He then proceeded to roll up his window.

The male hit the glass more aggressively and began to argue with him.

"I'm not going to pay you; you've got to go ask the man inside!" Charlemagne responded. "Go away!"

The male did not go away. He began to argue with Charlemagne further even though he had closed his window. Finally, an older male stepped out. This man had a thick moustache over his lip, and he had colder fair skin than his son. He wore a greasy collared shirt and his chest hairs poked out from the top. He also wore a vest and trousers.

"Eh! Foreigner – you have to pay him!" the man shouted.

Charlemagne began to roll down his window and replied, "I'm not paying anyone! Where's László! László is to pay!"

The older man began to shout towards Charlemagne in Hungarian, while the adolescent male continued to belittle him.

"Oh, this is madness," Charlemagne remarked, taking out his wallet, "at this point I'd pay them to shut up."

As soon as the adolescent male saw Charlemagne take out his wallet, he quieted down. Charlemagne paid him a few

Hungarian Forints. The adolescent male took the cash currency into his hands and then left.

"I suppose trust a foreign communist country to have some common decency," Charlemagne remarked. "I never imagined Hungarians to be so rude."

"I am sure it is something terrible to live through a communist regime," Manon replied.

László came out and re-entered the van. He started the car and then began to drive out.

"The boy that put petrol into the car made me pay, just so you know," Charlemagne noted. "I'm not sure what you went into the store for."

"He what?" László questioned.

"He filled the car, and asked me to pay for the amount he had filled," Charlemagne explained. "I would have thought you would have paid once you had come out."

"We pay before we fill the car," László remarked, shaking his head. "You did not need to pay no more."

Charlemagne grit his teeth as he held his arms cross. "Unbelievable, that fiendish lad. Turn around then."

"What?" Manon questioned.

"I want to show this kid who he thought he was stealing from."

"And do what?" Manon asked.

"Do not trouble yourself," László remarked, "as when I was inside, I made friends with the owner. He tells me a bit about your citadel. It is a tourist attraction in these parts, lots of foreigners come to see, but there is more that the public does not see."

"Oh?"

"Yes, the citadel was destroyed and abandoned two-hundred years ago, never demolished," László stated.

"I knew that…"

"What you don't know, is that lots of youth come to explore the tunnels below the surface."

"I knew that it was essentially an abandoned pile of rubble too," Charlemagne remarked. "The man we are looking for was stationed here before he fell in battle against the French. I understand that the citadel was just about destroyed and any personal effects may still be inside – I should have guessed though that delinquents would have gotten in by now, which worries me that if there is any item of note, it may now be gone."

László continued to drive the van further into town where they entered a wider stretch of the settlement at its main street intersection. They went east and began to travel through a canyon between some hills, passing homes along this canyon until they were going away from the town. After a few minutes, they reached an off-shoot road and began to travel upwards along the side of a large hill that began to take them up. As the van drove up the hill, they came around to a stretch with an observation point that looked out towards the river and other side where there was another separate settlement that was much larger than the small town they were in. The hill road continued upwards. László continued to drive around the many bends until he finally reached a gravel parking lot where there were a few cars.

At the center of the parking lot there was a path that curved around the rest of the hill up. The citadel was placed firmly atop of the hill on its base with base walls that covered all around in full, mostly undamaged apart from a few small holes. The top of the hill and walls were tall enough to be seen from outward, but at some parts, particularly the rear that faced away from the river, there was a dense smatter of greenery, shrubs and bushes, and then tall barren trees for this time of the year. László joined Manon and Charlemagne as they travelled up and around the hill to reach the top.

The citadel was plain along the top level as none of the walls from the upper structure remained and instead there were only very low remnants of those walls that created an outline of former rooms. The exterior battlements were mostly intact, apart for a few collapsed parts. A few sections that were outright destroyed had been replaced with concrete that noticeably differed from the beige bricks from the original design. As the pair walked through the citadel, it began to rain. Charlemagne also noticed at least two staircases that would have gone downstairs but were caved in with a heap of rubble. As a part of the tourist attraction, cannons were placed along the exterior battlements and at the central plaza there was a tall flagpole with the Hungarian tri-color red-white-green flag. Overall, the citadel was large, but had very little to see. The view outwards towards the river was larger and wider than the view from the observation point further below.

"Well, I've seen enough – I also don't think it's possible to move those rocks, at least not without Konstantin in our party," Charlemagne remarked, "but no less with all these tourists. Let's see about this extraordinary path then."

László proceeded to take them out from the citadel and back along the path. He kept a close eye at the trail, especially around the bushes as he found a very hidden small trail that diverged from the main path. He then proceeded to follow, and Charlemagne and Manon followed suit behind. They entered into the forest behind the citadel and began to come around to piece of destroyed wall that was wide enough to be a pathway. Charlemagne and Manon followed through this pathway, which looked out towards the valley behind and even towards the rear end of the river. This view provided a greater breadth of site towards the trees in the immediate area which still had an array of autumn colors, reddish-orange to gold, especially along adjacent hills. Charlemagne paused for a moment to admire the sight before he continued ahead of László. László proceeded back into the forest where he walked a short distance, came around and then reached a clearing at the side of the citadel walls where there were two collapsed portions inward that provided access into the citadel.

Charlemagne took a flashlight out from his messenger bag, which prompted Manon to do the same. He then stopped as he noticed László stay put.

"Will you be joining us?" Charlemagne questioned.

"No," László denied, "go ahead. I will be right here."

"Very well," Charlemagne responded, leading the way in as he turned on his flashlight. He walked into the tunnel and immediately found evidence of recent life in the vicinity: liquor bottles and plastic wrappers littered about. He walked forward and saw that the two entrances were united together by a small arched passageway. The ground at their feet consisted of dirt and rubble. On the left of the leftmost entrance they entered through, there was a small nook, and then another wider nook. This entrance was a dead-end, so they walked into the rightmost entrance where they found a human-like figure crafted out from bricks collected from the floor. The brick figure was given stick branch arms, and a hat made of tin, like a snowman. "Humorous," Charlemagne expressed, coming around to another side tunnel, this one of which was filled with bricks, but provided descent into the citadel.

Charlemagne walked carefully as he climbed down into the breach. The tunnel curved around and then continued straight. Additional, smaller brick-men were constructed along the path, blocking the way through, but Charlemagne simply walked through them, knocking them over. Manon observed that these brick-men had faces drawn on them. At the end of the tunnel, where they reached an intersection, a Halloween skeleton head was hung from the ceiling, which Charlemagne ignored. From the intersection, to the left, the tunnel continued straight, while on the right it went upwards. Charlemagne climbed up the stairs, reaching around to the top where the rubble blocked any further way through, although Charlemagne did see a small gap in the rubble. He shined his light and then began to climb, whereas Manon stayed back and shined her light towards him. He looked through and only found more rubble on the other side, as well as a mound of dirt that blocked any way through. He exited backwards and then climbed down the rubble to return to Manon. He walked back downstairs and continued forward. The pathway was cleaner along this tunnel corridor and reached a round staircase. Charlemagne walked up the stairs with caution.

"Do you know why staircases were built this way in castles? It was not merely to save space in design, but also because they proved advantageous in castle defense, especially when fighting with a sword."

"Where did you read that bit of trivia?" Manon questioned. "I'm sure that is not the definitive reason why they were built that way. Did you ask all architects across Europe?"

"Very drole," Charlemagne replied. "I'm not saying it was *the* reason, but it was certainly a reason why they proved so popular in defensive structures."

"Perhaps refrain from making generalized statements then," Manon suggested.

Charlemagne gave off a quiet growl at her comment. They reached the upper level and he observed it impossible to continue any further up due to the rubble. He travelled along further another corridor tunnel to reach more debris.

"Hm…" Charlemagne noted, "then that's it then. That's as far as the public miscreants could venture, in which case I think we may have good odds still."

"Oh yeah, and do you plan to move all that rubble yourself?"

"Not exactly, but I do reckon that one of us could climb through the gap above," Charlemagne remarked, shining his light. "Come on, I'll give you a boost. It'll be just like our time in Crete."

"Hmph, I hope not," Manon replied, placing a hand on Charlemagne's shoulder. She then placed her boot and he lifted her up. She climbed through the gap and then began to pull herself through, coming around to the other side. "I'm through!"

"Excellent," Charlemagne replied, "and what do you see?"

"Another tunnel, and also some rooms!" Manon noted as she shined her flashlight. "*Mon Dieu*, they really did not clean at all around here... I hope I don't find any... bodies."

"Nonsense, I don't believe you would..." Charlemagne assured, "or at least I hope not."

Manon shined her light around a small room to her side. She found a lot of rubble, but also some items from that era, cannons and munitions, and small cracks in the wall: embrasures. She also found burnt out lamps. She carried forth and began to go around an unknown side of the citadel. In another room, she found some chairs, a table, some crates and barrels, and also a rack of rifles. She continued forth and reached a tunnel that came upstairs. Manon shined her light around the corner and found this tunnel to be more appropriately furnished with rugs and banners. She even found a room with some books, and a bed.

"I do not know what this man expects to find – this is not our general..." Manon muttered, checking books. She found a large room with a large dining table, crossed through, and then found a larger room with embrasures from where light poured in. This room appeared a lot more furnished by the bed covers and rug. She walked over to a crate, opened it, and found documents inside. She sat down at a chair and began to go through them, but she could not read the writing because it was in Hungarian. "Ugh, if Charlemagne wants to believe his stupid crown is here, he can come and find it..."

Manon left the room and went back downstairs to where she came from.

"*Charles*!" Manon shouted. "I found something..."

"What did you find?"

"Come and see for yourself," Manon noted. "I do not understand any of it – it is written in Hungarian and was found in an officer's chamber."

Charlemagne looked to the side. He smashed a fist against the wall and then looked up. "Alright then, my dear, I'm coming up."

"Uh, wait," Manon responded, but Charlemagne did not wait. She looked about and realized that the gap she had come down from was a simple drop with no manner by which she could climb up without pulling herself up with her own strength. "*Charles* – I believe I may be trapped down."

"Trapped? Why do you say that?" Charlemagne questioned as he squeezed through. "Hello!" he remarked as he popped out from the other side, looking down. "Oh, that's quite the drop – hold on…"

"*Charles*, you are going to get us both stuck in here!"

"Nonsense, I…" Charlemagne pulled himself around, falling down as his entire body forcibly fell through.

"Ah, you *imbecile!*"

"Oh, probably shouldn't have done that with my ribs…"

Charlemagne lay on his side for a moment. Manon reached down towards him. "Are you alright?" she asked with care in her voice.

"Yes, yes," Charlemagne replied.

"Ah, good," Manon responded, standing up without care. "Get up then, and see what you've done."

Charlemagne stood up and looked up to the hole above. "Yes, I see now, but I can just push you up."

"And you?"

"I can… oh bugger," Charlemagne stated. "Right, well never mind that – show me these documents."

Manon sighed and led him around to the top-most level in the casements. She showed him the documents. She even found some books and other items worth to be read.

"Hm… I can't understand any of this – I'm not familiar with Hungarian."

"Oh really?"

"Nonetheless, these are a lot of important documents that deserve to be read through, but the light here is too unbearable. We'll need to transport these items out."

"Oh, and how do you propose you do that?"

"Hm…" Charlemagne expressed, "I suppose I could blow a hole in the wall…"

Manon looked at him as if he was serious.

"Yes, those cannons ought to do," Charlemagne encouraged, walking out the room.

"*Charles!*" Manon shouted.

"Let's see if I remember how to do this – when I was in boarding school in London, we had a demonstration once, very intriguing. I suppose the chemistry should be straightforward, but let's see if we have all the agreements.

"*Mon Dieu*, I am with a mad man…" Manon said. She stayed close to Charlemagne as he proceeded to find a cannon.

"The best place to point this will be the way we came – we don't want to upset anyone by blowing a hole through the exterior wall. Even then, that part of the wall will likely be thickest."

Charlemagne proceeded to attempt to move the cannon, and after a moment of hesitation, Manon assisted. They pointed the cannon towards the way they came. Charlemagne then grabbed a tool from one of the rooms.

"Pour out some water from your bag into this bucket and wet that stick with a sponge at the end. I'm going to make sure there's no debris inside the cannon."

Charlemagne placed the pointed stick with a curved piece of iron at the end into the cannon to ensure that it was clear while Manon poured some water out from her bottle into a bucket. She then wet the sponge-stick and gave it to Charlemagne. He cleaned the inside of the cannon and then dried it with another sponge.

"Just like cleaning an everyday rifle," Charlemagne noted with a laugh. "Alright, now let's load it up."

Charlemagne picked up a grapeshot cannon ball and placed it inside the cannon. He then used one of the tools to ensure it was properly seated, and then came around to adjust the aim of the cannon. Manon stepped back with unease. He went into one of the armory rooms and found a small chord with a metal hook-like object. He then placed it into a small hole at the end of the cannon and looked over to Manon.

"You may want to cover your ears," Charlemagne expressed. "I should do so too... I believe I have some earplugs in my bag..."

Charlemagne placed the earplugs in his ear while Manon covered her head tightly.

"Tallyho!" Charlemagne shouted, pulling the friction plug. The cannon shot forward, recoiling backwards and slamming into the entrance way and causing the debris to fly outwards. Charlemagne had quickly hidden himself back into the armory while Manon hid around the corner in the stairwell. The gunshot had caused a cloud of smoke to fly forward. Charlemagne laughed maniacally as he waved a hand around, picking up his flashlight from a table and looking ahead – the cannon had cleared the entrance just about entirely. Manon poked her head out and looked over to see Charlemagne laughing.

"What is so funny?" Manon questioned, annoyed. "*Mon Dieu*, that was so loud! What is wrong with you?!"

Charlemagne grinned at her and said, "Even with the darn ear plugs," he yelled before removing them. "Even with the darn ear plugs," he quietly repeated, "my ears are still ringing."

Manon did not reply. She looked crossed at him.

"Right then, let's load those books and get out of here."

"And what about these cannons, and all these munitions," Manon remarked. "You will just leave them here for an equally foolish teenager to find?"

"Oh, relax," Charlemagne responded. "We'll inform László, get him to call the police, and they can deal with it. I just want what I consider to be valuable – if we're lucky, we may be able to get all these valuables back to Budapest before sundown."

Act 2, Scene 4

László pulled his van up to the main entrance of the grand hotel in which Charlemagne and Manon were due to stay in. He came out from the driver's seat and opened the doors, and Charlemagne stepped forth with a crate full of documents. Manon lugged her share while László shouted out towards one of the bellboys, who quickly fetched a luggage cart and brought it over. Charlemagne placed his crate on the luggage cart, and then Manon placed her share. He then returned to the van for another haul, alongside Manon, placing additional items they had recovered from the citadel. László pulled the luggage cart out of the way and brought it up towards the door where a bellboy took over.

"To Room 4021," Charlemagne remarked, stopping in front of László. "You have been very helpful, my friend. Here, for your trouble." He paid the man with the rest of the Hungarian cash currency in his wallet. László clamped the bills into his hand received them forward.

"And if the police call you regarding the citadel, you do not know me, and I do not know you," Charlemagne pointed out to him. "Right?"

"Yes, of course."

László promptly left in his van, allowing Charlemagne to turn around and look at Manon. Manon held her arms crossed as she looked at him.

The hotel the pair stayed at was in the midst of Budapest, an Equinox Hotel, with a causeway from where László exited out from and onto the street of the capital city. Across from the hotel was a very small park, or green strip in the midst of a road that wrapped around together. This park had several trees in autumn colors, and towards the centre there were some patches of flowers remnant from the summertime. Further directly ahead from the main entrance of the hotel was an archway onto a major bridge, over the Danube River, known as the *Széchenyi Lánchíd* bridge. Even further ahead there was a domed and very wide structure. The structure was white and appeared to be elevated above the rest of the buildings across the Danube in the foreground. The building had white walls, consisted of at least three stories plus dormer windows at a top floor. There were also pillars in the middle of each partition; left, right, and centre. In the centre, just before the dome, was a short cylindrical tower. This building was warmly lit in the background of twilight. Likewise, all the other structures across the Danube and around the hotel, and the hotel itself were lit, as we were the lamp posts on the street. The structure in question was the *Budavári Palota*, or Buda Castle. The hotel lastly looked towards a green hill to the left, or south where there was a statue pointed southeast; on this hill was *Citadella*, the Budapest Citadel.

Charlemagne entered into the hotel, coming into its grand lobby. The room was multi-stories tall with a chandelier in the centre, directly above the round check-in desk. A fountain ahead of the check-in desk was before a grand staircase that went up a concierge desk. Around the concierge desk were four main pillars that connected with the second floor viewing balcony, as well as the third floor and fourth floor. The ceiling beams then arched together. At each pillar were potted ferns. Besides the fountain were chairs and sofas. To the left from the main entrance, across from the fountain, were the elevators. Charlemagne entered into an elevator with Manon and they proceeded up.

"What will you do now?" Manon questioned. "Who do you know that speaks Hungarian to help translate all these documents?"

"Well, Miklos comes to mind," Charlemagne admitted, "but I believe since the expedition crew parted, he's taken up contractual work in the Middle East out in Dubai and Qatar (my fault). What about you?"

"Nobody who comes to mind, but my father may know."

"Give the old man a ring then, my dear," Charlemagne said, "and I'll see what can be done on my end. I would rather find someone I trust, and I wouldn't dare approach a local university especially if I do not trust them. I believe it will be best to just find a translator of sort to transcribe these documents for us."

The elevator reached the second floor and Manon exited out. She turned to him before she fully went on her way. "We can discuss further in the morning, *Charles*. I'm going to... have something to eat and then have a rest. You should too."

"No time to rest or eat, I'm afraid," Charlemagne noted, pressing a button to go to the fourth floor. "I've got work to do."

The elevator doors closed and he travelled down to the second floor. He got out and took his keys out from his messenger bag. He then proceeded to his room, Room 4021, and opened it. He then stepped forward into the regal bedroom suite, looking around the living space. The windows looked directly outward along the same line as the main entrance, catching a better view of the Buda Castle and Citadelle. To the left was a kitchenette, and on the right was a round dining table and double-set doors into the master bedroom. All the artefacts and crates were piled on the dining table. The king-sized bed faced a pair of windows that likewise looked west across the Danube. On the left was a door that led into the bathroom, and directly across was a locked door that connected with another suite. Charlemagne closed the doors behind him as he removed his coat and took off his suit jacket. He was dressed in a grey vest and trousers, and had an elegant pinstripe collared shirt on underneath. He put on a robe and then returned to the dining room to look at the artefacts. He began to look through the artefacts one by one, placing them aside as he sighed. After a moment of boredom, he walked over to the kitchen and took out a wine glass and poured himself a drink from a complementary bottle on the counter. Charlemagne returned to the dining table and continued to skim through the documents until finally, he sat down and began to read some – this particular set of documents were in German. The room was quiet, very quiet, and all that could be heard was the ambience from the streets below as not a single neighbor made even a bit of noise. Charlemagne studiously examined the documents before him until he took another sip of wine, looked about the empty room, and then sighed. He looked down to his knee, not even realizing that he had been tapping his heel into the floor. He then stood up, walked around, and with another sigh, decided to leave. Before he left, he entered into the bedroom to fetch a piece of clothing and removed his robe. Charlemagne closed the door behind him and walked down the hall, coming around to the viewing gallery and looking below.

From the viewing gallery, Charlemagne walked downstairs on foot and reached the main lobby to see a sign that pointed him towards the thermal baths. He entered through and found himself in the locker room where he got changed from his suit, kept his key close to him, and then walked into the bath itself. The bath was immense, consisting of the entire south face of the main floor and being the approximate size of an average indoor swimming pool. The haze of mist rose upwards from the light blue waters. Composite pillars lined around the edge of the bath, supporting a viewing gallery from above from where ferns and palm trees in pots added to the atmosphere. A series of tall arched windows, translucent, provided a bit of light, while a skylight and lamps did the rest. The walls consisted of dark grey stone lower half panels and white marble upper walls with facial statues carved in grey. Charlemagne walked in his swimsuit towards an edge of the bath, entered down the steps, and then sat down so that the water was up to his clavicle.

A few people could be seen around the bath at this time, mostly older couples. A man nearby Charlemagne sat against the base of a pillar and held his head back. Charlemagne attempted to do the same as he rested his head back, but he was unable to close his eyes as he instead looked upwards. As Charlemagne attempted to rest, his eyes wandered at the sight of movement around him, especially when some left and arrived. Eventually, a young woman arrived, and she appeared to be at least ten years younger than him. She wore a bikini swimsuit and stepped forth. She had fair skin and very dark hair. She was average height and her outward body was without a single imperfection, skin smooth and body slim. Charlemagne sat with unease as she entered into the pool near him.

After an uncomfortable moment in the baths, Charlemagne exited out, had a quick shower, changed back into his suit, and then wandered towards the other side of the hotel where there was a restaurant and bar. He entered and made his way to the bar where he sat down, hunched over, he requested a gin and tonic, and stayed put for more time than he endured in the baths. He made light conversation with those around him, but due to lack of the common use of the English language, Charlemagne stayed quiet. He then looked to his left as he saw a young woman, a few years younger than him, perhaps in her late twenties, arrive in a red dress. She had tanned skin and light brown hair. She was not alone, accompanied with a female with fair skin and blonde hair. Charlemagne looked towards her and then concentrated back at his drink.

"*Jó estét,*" a feminine voice spoke besides him.

Charlemagne turned and saw the woman with light brown hair looking at him with a smile. He smiled back and replied, "*Bitte?*"

"*Ah, Deustcher…*" the woman said. "*Guten Abend.*"

"*Guten Abend,*" Charlemagne repeated. "How about English?"

The woman shook her head and then asked, "*Sind Sie geschäftlich hier?*"

"Ja," Charlemagne confirmed, *"ein wenig. Ich bin Geschäftsmann, betreibe aber auch historische Recherchen."*
"Oh?"

Charlemagne proceeded to have a conversation with the lady, bought her a drink, and then discussed in detail his historical research. She was intrigued at what he had to say and found favor. She followed her intrigue personal questions to do with his business, leading to him saying, *"Mein Name ist Charlemagne de la Cabernet. Und du?"*

"Réka," she answered.

"Réka… Kann ich dich um einen Gefallen bitten?"
"Oh?"

Charlemagne took Réka to his bedroom where he showed her all the artefacts that he had recovered with Manon. He poured her a glass of wine while she sat down, leading to Charlemagne to come around as she began to read some of the contents in German, and for him to take note. Charlemagne would ask her to skim through some of contents, and at times he would ask her to repeat the content or to skip some pages. He took notes while she drank a few sips of wine, laughing as they did so. At the pace that they went, Charlemagne took many notes, but as they continued to do so, he looked anxiously at his notebook to the point that he placed his hands on one of the books she was reading to get her to set it down.

"Sehr gut," Charlemagne remarked, placing his hands over hers. *"Ich denke das ist genug…"*

Réka looked back at Charlemagne with attentive eyes. She leaned forward and placed her lips atop of his lips, only for the pair to be bothered by a knock at the door. He slowly moved himself away from her and looked towards the door.

"Es tut mir Leid," Charlemagne apologized, looking towards the door in hope that it would pass. Another knock came to the door, prompting Charlemagne to stand up. *"Just a moment…"* He opened the door and saw Manon on the other side.

"Ah, *Charles*," Manon expressed, "good you are awake. I just got off the phone with my father, and…" she looked to the side where she saw Réka stand up. "Who is that?" she asked as though offended. "What is going on here?"

"Manon, sorry…" Charlemagne embarrassingly remarked, stepping aside as he looked over to Réka. She began to pack up her belongings and pull her purse over her shoulder. "*Bitte geh nicht.*"

Réka stepped forward and looked at Charlemagne as she was a meter from Manon. She apologized and said, "*Nein, es tut mir leid, es ist spät. Danke für den Wein, Charlemagne.*" She then left past Manon.

Charlemagne watched her walk off, tipping his head out the hallway and then making a slight sound of discomfort at the pit of his heart. He then turned to look at Manon who held her arms crossed. He looked at her distastefully. He sighed and asked, "Sorry, what is it that you had to say?"

Manon looked back at him, placed a hand on her hip and then in a firm tone stated, "I talked to my father, he knows a man who can help us translates these texts, but we will need to meet him in Germany."

"Oh yeah? Well, don't' bother," Charlemagne remarked, entering into his suite and coming around to sit down at the coach. "Réka, the girl who had just left, had helped me with a bit of it…"

"And where did you meet this girl, or where did you find her?"

"I didn't find her anywhere – she was in the bar where we met."

"And what does she do for a living?"

"I… never asked," Charlemagne remarked. "Look, that's not the point – she read a bit of it, and I don't believe that this officer is our mark. His log did not make sense to what we suspected. It also suggests that he was not in Austria at all around the time that Hillaire Amboise sold the crown. We can certainly have someone take a closer look at the rest of the documents, but it's been more or less debunked."

"You *imbecile*, Charlemagne," Manon shot back. "You never listen, do you? I told you that this could not have been the same."

"You didn't exactly have an alternative suggestion," Charlemagne snapped back. "I had the only lead, and when you've got no others leads that's the one you've got to take to rule out. As a historian, you should know that – we're not story-crafting here. We're looking at the evidence in front of us and trying to solve a mystery. You're like all the other hypocrites in the academic field, falsifying a narrative that is convenient to your whims."

"Oh, like all the other historians then? Like my father then too?"

"Of course, not – you know I respect your father greatly."

"But not his daughter."

"I don't want to argue with you," Charlemagne stated. "The point is, this man isn't our man – I'm at a loss. We're back to ground zero."

Manon paused for a moment and then said, "What if we are not? What if there was one than more person who we did not look at?"

"Who?"

Manon took in a deep breath and then stated, "I did not want to bring him up when I saw his name in Vienna, and I wasn't sure if he was entirely Hungarian, but I did a bit more research, and it seems as though he is. His name is Ignác Újlaki – a *Graf* or Count, and a senior officer too."

"When did you find out about this?"

"Earlier today," Manon stated, "that's when I found out he was really Hungarian. My father did some more research on him too. The problem with him is that although his regiment was garrisoned on a border, it was in Serbia."

"Serbia, eh?" Charlemagne remarked, stroking his chin.

"Yes, the very same Serbia in the former Yugoslav countries that is a deadly warzone, and you are not going to go into that country, do you hear me?"

"Excuse me?" Charlemagne questioned. "What do you suppose gives you that authority over me?" he asked, standing up. "I'll go very well anywhere I would like to please – I'll see any sight, travel to any country, and by Jove, I'll dig up any treasure I damn well feel is within my right to do so? Do you know why? It's because I'm Charlemagne and I can do so – there is no authority in this world that hold me back, no less the likes of you, pretending to be my mother. Not even my own mother could stop me."

"You're a lunatic," Manon responded. "You believe that you are… are all that, *Charles*, but you aren't. You're mortal just like the rest of us, and when it occurs to you and when you are able to stare death in the face, perhaps you will pay closer attention and cease to live in this fantasy world that you seem to live in."

Charlemagne scoffed and laughed at the same time, "You're unbelievable – so boring, and so naïve. I've seen more to this world than you've let up, *ma petite cherie*."

"Who are you calling *petite cherie* like I'm some other woman? Like that girl, Rita. I am not someone to be taken advantage of like that, Charlemagne. My father is waiting for you in Nuremberg. Take these books, and go see him if you want them translated…"

"No, thank you," Charlemagne replied. "I'm going to Serbia – I'm going to find out more about this Ignác character and see where he took the crown. Do you know what else? There's nothing you or anyone else can do to stop me."

Manon looked back at Charlemagne with crossed arms, uncrossed them, and said, "Go to Serbia then. I'm done trying to stop you. I will take these artefacts to my father for you, but I will not pursue you to your own death… nor will I enable the actions of a man who takes blatant disregard for his own life, or the care of his family and friends."

"Very well, do what you must," Charlemagne remarked. "Goodnight, Manon."

With those final words, Charlemagne left and went into the master bedroom. He closed the doors behind him and then came around to bed to sit down. He gave off a sigh. Manon went over to the artefacts on the table and began to look at Charlemagne's notes for a moment. Meanwhile, Charlemagne leaned over for a moment, took in a deep breath, and then sat up with a straight back. He then went into the bathroom.

"Who does she think she is?" Charlemagne questioned as he washed his hands. He then looked himself in the mirror, straightened his back further and his fingers above his chest as he said, "I'm Charlemagne – no ill befalls me, nor plight is too great for me." He smiled at himself and then exited the bathroom. He went around to his luggage on the other side of the bed, picked it up, and then placed it down. "I'm Charlemagne," he repeated. "I'm not scared of anything…"

Before the next word could come out from his mouth, Charlemagne felt a gag come to his mouth and then a bag over his head. He immediately began to squirm around as he felt someone began to bind him. His voice was muffled by the bag and he could barely project his vocal chords. In his struggle, he began to kick around, knocking over a lamp and hitting the wall with his foot.

Manon looked over to the master bedroom as she heard a bit of the struggle. She shook her head at him and said, "Effusive idiot…"

Charlemagne continued to struggle. He pushed both legs against a person, causing them to throw someone against the wall. He could hear some mutters from said persons. They spoke a foreign language unfamiliar to him.

"What is he doing in there?" Manon asked as she looked over to the door. "*Charles*, what are you doing?" she asked, louder.

The kidnappers stopped for a moment, prompting Charlemagne to wiggle himself on the bed. He was then grabbed by the ankles and dragged out from the master bedroom and into the adjacent suite.

Manon opened the door and saw that it was empty, although the room was a mess. She looked around and her face went pale. She opened the bathroom door, which was ajar and he was not to be found.

"*Quoi?*" Manon muttered, kneeling down to look under the bed. She then came around to the door to the other suite, but it was locked shut. She shook her head and was as white as a ghost. "Where did he go?"

Suddenly, a knock was heard at the door. Manon quickly went over to the door, looked out the spyhole, but could not see. She stepped back and attempted to peak through the cracks of the door, but could not see either. She then looked at the lock to notice that it was open. She gently placed a hand over the lock, but did not lock it.

"Who is it?" Manon questioned. "*Wer ist es?*"

"*Zimmerservice!*" a voice called out in clear German.

Manon fell at ease slightly, but said, "*Nein danke.*" She then locked the door.

"*Wir suchen Herrn Cabernet,*" the voice on the other side said.

"*Er ist gerade nicht hier.*"

"*Wissen Sie, wann er zurückkommt?*"

"*Oh nein. Er hat es nicht gesagt.*"

"*Ma'am, ich bestehe darauf, dass Sie die Tür öffnen.*"

"*Ich glaube nicht, dass ich das tun werde...*"

"*Ich bestehe darauf...*" a voice spoke from behind.

Manon turned around to see a black clad figure wearing a dark suit and balaclava immediately come at her with a gag. She screeched out and swiped at the man's face, hitting his eye with her nails. She then hit at him and tried to run, but he grabbed her. She swung a fist at him like a hammer. He withheld as he continued to hold on to her. After a brief struggle, the other kidnapper arrived from the other side and cornered her. She stepped back and bumped into a dining room chair. Manon turned to both of them as they slowly approached her, letting out a loud scream which prompted both of them to move in and grab her. She struggled against her captors, but after an attempt to fight back, the gag was around her mouth and the duffel bag around her head. She was placed in ties and carried into the adjacent room where she continued to attempt to move around. Her efforts were fruitless though as her captors began to prick a needle into her thigh, resulting in slow but gradual decreased movement, and then a slip into unconsciousness.

Act 3, Prologue

Charlemagne looked at himself in the mirror. He had medium length light blonde hair at this time that was swept over his forehead. His hair was smooth and silky. His skin was blemish free and his eyes were steel blue. He was tall, nearly six feet and slim. His skin was fair, cold and like snow almost. He wore a plaid collared shirt with the sleeves rolled up, tucked in to his slacks. He also wore tall, pointed leather ranch boots. The top button of his collared shirt was undone. Charlemagne at this time was an adolescent, nearly a young adult. He looked away from his mirror and stepped towards the door near the closet mirror in his bedroom. His bedroom was a fair-sized room with a bed directly behind him. To the right of the bed was a French window that went to a small patio, while on the left was a window that looked down to the outdoor stables, or chicken coop at this time. On the right of the closet was a door that went into the bathroom, whereas to the left was an exit out to the corridor hallway. He passed several closed doors to reach the end of the corridor, a triangular room with an open door on the right. As he was about to exit through, a young girl entered before him and looked at him with a smile. Charlemagne looked at this younger girl; she was eight years younger than him, and she wore denim overalls and a feminine short white blouse-type shirt, and her hair was light blonde, skin fair, and eyes blue.

"Where are you going?" the young girl asked with a smile and local Western Canadian accent. "I thought you weren't going out."

"Alas, but I told you I was going out," Charlemagne responded, looking down upon her with a smile. "I'm going to the Annual Nattau County Derby Festival to meet with a friend."

"We were just there silly…" the young girl remarked, tilting her head slightly.

"You and the others were there," Charlemagne corrected, "but I missed the final show, and besides, it's six o'clock and the festival has only just begun whereas I'm due to return to school next week."

"No..." the young girl said, putting a hand on her hip, "I told you, you're not going back to school. Your options were to either stay here, or take me with you to England."

Charlemagne laughed at her. He waved to her and then took a sidestep to go around.

"I'll be back later today. If I don't see you then I'll see you tomorrow, Allodia," Charlemagne remarked. "Goodnight."

"No, where are you going?" Allodia responded, grabbing her brother by the arm. "You're not going anywhere, Charlie. It's Saturday night and we have church in the morning."

"Correction: you have Sunday service in the morning," Charlemagne remarked. "You forget that I do not go to church with you and the others."

"Yes, you do," Allodia remarked, struggling as she grabbed hold of her brother's leg. "You're a part of the family, so you should stay here with the family and do what the family does."

Charlemagne laughed at her suggestion and pulled her up to the top of the stairs where he did not dare proceed further.

"Very drole, Allodia, now let go of my leg before we both fall," Charlemagne remarked. "You don't want to wake up... *Monsieur Manceau*... do you?"

"No..." Allodia replied, shaking her head, but refusing to let go.

"Oh, I'll count to three... one, two... three," Charlemagne remarked as his sister ducked her head. "*Bonne soiree mademoiselle!*" he said, imitating a cartoonish, but deep French accent as he spoke. "*C'est moi! Monsieur Manceau! Me voila!*" He proceeded to attempt to tickle his sister to let go of his leg, which worked with ease. He then picked her up and brought her into his arms. Allodia playfully squirmed, laughed and cried out with joy. *"Qu'ai-je attrapé ici? J'ai une belle petite mademoiselle ici!"*

"No! Go away Monsieur Manceau!"

Charlemagne carried his sister to her bedroom, pulled over the bed covers with one hand and then placed Allodia inside. She continued to struggle and squirm, still laughing as he restrained her with his body.

"J'ai une coquine qui mérite des chatouilles!" he yelled, beginning to tickle her.

"I'll save you Allodia!" a young voice cried out from outside the bedroom as he charged.

Charlemagne turned his head to see a younger male, at least two years younger than Allodia, dressed in a baseball helmet, and wearing props from a Halloween costume of a sword and shield. He charged towards Charlemagne and began to swipe at him with the plastic sword, causing Charlemagne to laugh as he attempted to playfully swat at the younger male.

"Qui est-ce ? Est-ce Monsieur Salmar?" Charlemagne questioned. *"Pas Monsieur Salmar! Mon ennemi juré!"*

"I've got you now Monsieur Manceau!" Salmar cried out.

"Oh vraiment? Je peux vous faire tomber tous les deux!" Charlemagne remarked, taking hold of Salmar from around his torso with one hand. He swung the covers over Allodia quickly and then took control of Salmar with the other hand too. He picked him up and placed him around his shoulders. *"Que vas-tu faire maintenant, héros?"*

"Let me go evil demon!" Salmar playfully responded, swinging his sword at him.

"Jamais!" Charlemagne responded, taking him to the bathroom and placing him inside. He then stopped him from being able to run out after him as he closed the door, and quickly took the chair from Allodia's desk to jam it. *"Ahaha! Je gagne encore! Jusqu'à la prochaine fois mademoiselle!"*

"Nooo!" Allodia responded, jumping up from her bed and going to free Salmar.

Charlemagne quickly left the room and took the opportunity to come downstairs. He reached the bottom of the staircase and spun around, stopping though as he met with his mother and father.

"What's all the racket upstairs?" Everest questioned, unimpressed. "I can hear Allodia screaming from the garage."

"Here I come!" Salmar shouted, running down the stairs with his sword in hand only to stop as he noticed his parents. Allodia likewise ran behind his brother and stopped as she saw her parents.

"Salmar, I told you no running in the house!" Everest barked.

"Sorry!" Salmar shouted. "Let's go," he whispered to Allodia.

"No shouting either please," Everest remarked, facing Charlemagne. "God dammit, Charles, don't encourage them like that, please."

"Just a bit of fun is all, father," Charlemagne responded, slightly lowering his smile. "They are children after all, aren't they? Are they not allowed to have some fun?"

"Yes, but not to run about like zoo animals," Everest responded, rubbing his temple. He then noticed Charlemagne's clothes and asked, "Where are you going?"

"Just out for a bit, won't be too long."

"You're going to the festival aren't you? Charles – we went as a family this morning. No way am I going to let you go now on your own. That's not fair."

"Fair to whom?"

"To all of us," Everest complained. He then sighed and said, "Look, just be back by your curfew time, that's all I care… I'll be in my study…"

"Could I at least take the old car out for a spin? I've been dying to have a reason to."

"No way," Everest replied, turning around. "First of all, she isn't even yours, and second of all, she's in need of repair. Stay away from her-"

Charlemagne didn't respond. Everest left Charlemagne and Vienna as he walked off and disappeared into the library across the hall.

"What's his problem?" Charlemagne questioned.

"Today has not been kind to him," Vienna clarified, putting a hand on his shoulder. "He's lost quite a bit of money, and I have not been very happy with him."

"Have you been fighting?"

"Goodness, no. You know that your father and me... we don't fight. We just have disagreements, but we come around. No, your father and I are like..."

"Inseparable, I know."

"Yes, anyways, go and enjoy the festival, Charles. Who knows... maybe there will be a girl there you may like... no?"

"Come now, mother," Charlemagne remarked. "How awfully tragic that'd be. I'm due to return to school next week."

"Ah, but a mother can dream for her son, no? Just stay away from any Germans – hm, then again, that's what your grandfather said to your father. Stay away from any French ones – how's that?"

"*Sehr lustig, Mutter.*"

"*Gut,*" Vienna replied, kissing her son on the cheek. "I'm going to check on your siblings. Enjoy the night, Charlemagne."

"*Danke.*"

Charlemagne walked into the sitting room, came down the hall, and entered around to the kitchen. He took the elevator in the pantry closet and went downstairs to the garage where he walked over to a black 1973 Dolores-Ganß convertible. The car hood was polished, waxed, and shined. He came around to a lockbox and opened it to find the car keys, but they couldn't be found.

"Hm…" Charlemagne remarked. He walked over to a workbench and opened the drawers to attempt to find them. He then opened a few cupboards, turning over anywhere it could be hidden to find them inside a tin can. "Gotcha."

Charlemagne walked over to the sports car and ignited the engine. He then drove out from the stall and came around to the garage door. He pressed a button on the remote inside the car and the doors began to open up. He then drove forward, up the side aisle and around to the front gates where he hit another button on the same remote to cause them to open. Charlemagne drove out and proceeded along the road to reach a bridge, and then went over and drove south.

The Dolores-Ganß went quickly along the country roads, driving past numerous farmlands on the left and right, the occasional strip of trees between them and the road. A twilight fell upon the land of Allabrese as the sun set and was replaced with the clear darkness and thousands and thousands of stars above. After a few minutes, Charlemagne approached a large field on his left in which there were many tents, carnival rides, and even a Ferris wheel. The entire parking lot of the Allabrese Equestrian Centre was full, and overflow parking was made on a dirt lot besides the fair where there was plenty of space. Charlemagne pulled into the parking lot and came around to the familiar sight of a pickup truck parked in the corner of the lot, low-beam lights turned on and pointed forward. As Charlemagne came around and parked his car nearby, he saw a male figure stand up from behind the truck and jump down. The Dolores-Ganß went silent as Charlemagne turned the engine off, and then he came out and went towards the pickup truck, a silver 1969 Armstrong K/R.

"There you are, Charles," a young male said, coming around to him. "What took you so long? I thought we agreed on eight o'clock."

"My apologies, Cole, though I ran into some trouble with my parents."

Charlemagne looked over to Cole. He was a young male, same age as Charlemagne, with dark hair and fair skin. He wore dark trousers and a t-shirt tucked in.

"You were about to run into trouble with me if you were anymore late," Cole said. "Let's go already."

"Always on the move and with such haste," Charlemagne muttered, walking over to join him. He walked side by side with Cole.

"You've always moved slow, Charles," Cole complained. "Always the one scout behind the rest."

"Well, you know what they say about wolves – well, perhaps not a fact you'd be familiar with, but in nature, wolves lead from behind," Charlemagne stated. "The wolf is even the herald of the Cabernet family, you know."

"No, I don't know such a useless fact as that," Cole said. "Even if it were true, scouts aren't wolves, they're scouts and they lead from the front."

"It's more than just identity," Charlemagne expressed. "It's about keeping watch of those ahead of you... ensuring that nobody passes you."

"I really don't care for another useless Cabernet fact," Cole remarked. "Let's get inside the fairgrounds already."

Charlemagne and Cole approached the front of the fair. The entire lot was surrounded by chain-link fence situated around to deter anybody from wandering inside. They each bought their tickets, received a stamp on the back of their chosen hand, and then wandered inside. The extent of the fairgrounds was enormous, and the amount of people was packed. Charlemagne and Cole proceeded to navigate around the people as they went to the rides.

"There has to be more people here than in the entire town, nay the entire county," Charlemagne noted. "When did the festival because such a spectacle for outsiders?"

"Always been, don't you remember? The whole point of the derby is to draw people to this weeklong event."

"There must be people here from more than just around Alberta," Charlemagne insisted. "I've never seen this many people in the country before."

"Maybe, but my mom did say that the downtown hotel is full, we're renting out our guest room to a couple out of town for the extra cash," Cole stated. "A bunch of other people are doing the same. Aside from the Stampede, this has got to be the single-most largest event in all of central Canada."

Charlemagne and Cole proceeded to some of the attractions, especially the state-of-the-art portable amusement park rides. These varied from pendulum rides, to high-velocity spinsters, to swing sets and carousels. There was also a portable haunted house, bumper cars, hall of mirrors, and miniature roller coaster. The queues for each ride were lengthy, prompting them to stay back and wait every while. Charlemagne looked towards a rocket ship ride, similar to a spinster but with rocket ship carriages branched to a center piece that spun around. He looked at the machine with awe.

"Imagine the ingenuity to develop such a ride, and to make it portable on wheels as well," Charlemagne expressed. "To be able to send this machine anywhere in the world essentially, and for it to function with ease."

"All I care is that it's right here and I'm about to ride it right now," Cole responded.

"How must they travel, especially the Ferris wheel?"

"You should have seen them pull in at the train station," a young girl said from besides.

Charlemagne looked over and his gaze set upon the young lass. She had pitch black hair and fair skin, like marble almost, although especially as smooth. She wore dark clothes, a black top and skirt.

"You- you've seen them pull in on the train," Charlemagne remarked. "What was that like?"

"You could never guess which ride was on which car," the young girl stated, looking towards the ride with focus. She then looked at Charlemagne. "They were all compact…"

"Fascinating…" Charlemagne said, looking back to the ride as they moved forward in the queue. "If I could just study how they do it, my minds' eye could open to an array of realistic possibilities to invent."

"Oh, you're an inventor? What have you invented?"

"Well, nothing of notable use," Charlemagne replied, "but not to brag or anything, but I am top of my class in physics and chemistry, and I want first-place in our inventor's competition."

"Oh, and what did you invent in that contest?"

"I re-invented the wheel, or at least a mean by which to stop the wheel without significant loss of kinetic energy, especially at high velocities. My research was highly favored by automobile corporations, but I passed those opportunities to do more research and pass it on to Cabernet Corporation."

"Interesting…" the young girl remarked.

"My name is Charlemagne, by the way," he introduced. "Charlemagne Cabernet, of Cabernet Corporation fame."

"Oh, you're from that family that lives across the river," the young girl said. "I've heard about your family. It's nice to finally meet someone from that household. My name is Sabrina Dawson."

"And I'm Cole, Cole Phillips."

"Oh," Sabrina remarked, looking towards him as well, "nice to meet you too, I guess."

"Yes, thank you, Cole," Charlemagne remarked, glaring at him.

"Are you from out of town?" Cole questioned. "You're certainly a new face to me."

"No, I'm from and live here," Sabrina stated.

"How old are you? I've never seen you around before," Cole noted.

"I'm sixteen," Sabrina answered, "and I don't go to school at the high school. I'm home schooled by a private tutor."

"Oh yeah? I heard a lot of the Italian families do that over in that side of town."

"I'm not Italian," Sabrina replied. "I live in St. Allan's Plains."

"I certainly could have suspected that someone of your intelligence is not a subject of the public school system," Charlemagne remarked. "You sound to me like someone who's been encouraged to think for oneself."

"Thank you... I guess," Sabrina responded. "I don't think I'm that different from others my age, although I don't know a lot of people my age. How old are you two?"

"Sixteen," Charlemagne answered, "seventeen in July."

"I'm seventeen," Phillips boasted.

"I just turned sixteen not too long ago," Sabrina remarked. "It's nice to meet people around my age who are nice."

"Thanks," Phillips immediately replied.

Charlemagne looked at him with disbelief and then looked at Sabrina. He said, "What do your parents do, Sabrina?"

"My father is an entrepreneur," Sabrina answered. "He owns a lot of real estate and properties around town. You may have heard of him too, Gordon Dawson?"

"Wait, Gordon Dawson? From the Dawson family?" Cole questioned. "Uh... Charles?" Cole pulled Charlemagne away from Sabrina. He then whispered, "You probably don't know this, but that Dawson family... they're crazy! No wonder I've never seen her before – there's stories about that family."

"Such as?"

"Just stories," Cole insisted, "like being able to talk to the dead, or practicing witchcraft and sorcery. They're weird."

"And who told you these things?"

Cole shrugged and remarked, "I've just heard them is all."

"You've heard them, but you don't know who started these rumors, whether it was rivals in the real estate business, or such. You put too much faith in rumors, and besides, there's nothing wrong with being eccentric. I quite enjoy someone who thinks a little differently."

"Look man, if you want to talk to the witch lady, then by all means, but I'm out." He then left.

Charlemagne returned to Sabrina as they were about to board the ride. He smiled to her and said, "Sorry about that – would you like to ride together?"

"I would like that..." Sabrina remarked, nodding and her cheeks turning red.

Act 3, Scene 1

Charlemagne sat with his back against some sort of surface. Both his hands and his feet were bound, and he sat with his knees raised up to his legs, at a slight bend. His hands were atop of his knees. His face was covered with some sort of potato sack, and his mouth tightly wound with a cloth around his head. The air where he was seated was cold and he could only hear on occasion a foghorn, the occasional chatter from afar in an unclear foreign language, or the sound of a bell ringing. The surface at his bottom and feet was smooth, and he occasionally felt an abrupt halt or startup of movement. An unknown amount of time from the moment that Charlemagne awoke from his anesthesia to the present had passed, although he sat in place for several hours until he heard a door open and the footsteps of a few people come towards him. He heard them speak loud and clear in his ear, speaking some sort of Middle Eastern language amongst themselves. The men stepped forward towards Charlemagne, picked him up by the arm pit and elbow joint, and then guided him up and forward. Charlemagne did not resist as he was guided forward and around a corner. He was brought around to a set of stairs where the echoes of a sort of cellar were replaced with the loud cries of gulls and sound of still water. He was led forward and then left, onto a metal ramp and then down. He placed his feet on a wooden floorboard and then brought forward again, and then left into a room with a hard smooth surface. Charlemagne was sat down onto a chair, hands untied and then brought around behind him so they were then tied.

Suddenly, the sack was raised from his head and he found himself in a warehouse-like room. The room had an open ceiling, wooden ceiling beams across, and a four-pane glass window on his left where light poured in from outside. On the other side of the window, although barred, he could see a brick wall with graffiti and rubbish laying around. Before him, there was a bucket on its side and a hose stretched out and going behind him. Near where he was, there was a drain and small puddle of water around that collected at an adjacent dent in the smooth concrete floor. To his left was a metal door, and on the left and right of that door were four-pane windows that looked inside to the rest of the building. His captors stood behind him, and as Charlemagne looked around the room, he could see one of them to his left, dressed in a grey suit with a dark lavender turtleneck shirt and sunglasses on. He appeared to be Middle Eastern with a bald head and thick beard. Another captor came around from Charlemagne's right, a crowbar in right hand, smacking it in his left as though to intimidate. He wore a black suit with a collared shirt. He was Middle Eastern too and had a thick black beard and short black hair. The men spoke openly in their foreign language to each other, as though to decide what to do. Charlemagne breathed rapidly as he looked at the crowbar and the other man as he paced around the room.

The door then opened and Charlemagne was met with a familiar man, Le Havre. He looked at him and his eyes scowled. Le Havre spoke to his comrades in Arabic and then stepped forward towards Charlemagne.

"So, we meet again, Mr. Cabernet," Le Havre spoke.

Charlemagne made a faint murmur sound as his mouth was still gagged.

"What's that? I can't hear you," Le Havre remarked. "You may want to speak up, my friend, especially when we start to ask you a few questions. As you may assume, our client was not happy that we could not retrieve the diamond from you. You made me unhappy too, because a slippery fish like you, I can handle, but humiliation in front of my client and my men? That is unacceptable. I lost a lot of money, but not faith in our client when he overheard you had interest in a new artefact of considerable value. We had a hard time tracking you down, and now that we have you right where we want you, far enough from

Western civilization, I have some questions for you. Are you ready to comply?"

Charlemagne simply looked back at Le Havre with a fearful look in his eyes. Le Havre snapped his fingers and spoke in Arabic to have one of the henchmen remove the gag from Charlemagne's mouth. As soon as the gag was removed, Charlemagne spoke, "You really are a worthless bastard! I'm going to ensure that the likes of you are far removed from Europe, you o-"

The henchman punched Charlemagne across the face, causing him to nearly fall over with the chair he sat upon.

"Now that is not very nice, Mr. Cabernet," Le Havre remarked. "You have two options: either you comply with my questions, or I move on to ask your lady friend what she has to say about your little adventure here."

"Manon?" Charlemagne questioned in a quiet voice. His face grew angry as he looked at Le Havre. "You wouldn't dare harm a hair on her head. I will make you pay, all of you…"

"I would choose my words wisely, Mr. Cabernet," Le Havre suggested. "Your fate right now is being offered back into your hands. Comply or we will take that freewill back into ours to decide whether you can return to civilization or never be heard from again."

"Empty threats. I know your client, and he wouldn't dare pay you to kill me."

"No, he hasn't, but at this moment, with all the humiliation you've put us through, I will happily do it for free."

Charlemagne looked at Le Havre plainly and said, "Empty threats." He gave a nervous laugh, "Honestly, you expect me to believe that you would kill another person? All that effort for what – an artefact?"

Le Havre laughed in return, "Yes," he said, "it is a silly thing for a Westerner like you to believe, isn't it? Do not worry, Mr. Cabernet, I will not kill you… but I cannot say the same for my friends. We certainly wouldn't have dared to hurt you in Germany, but you are not in Germany right now."

"Where am I?" Charlemagne asked.

"In a place worse than hell," the person who was circling him replied in broken English.

Charlemagne looked at him, down to the crowbar, and then over to Le Havre. "So what do you want to know?" he asked.

"My client wants to know what you are looking for," Le Havre stated. "A simple question."

"Yes," Charlemagne responded in a nervous tone, "well, to give a simple answer, I'm looking for the French Crown Jewels – the original crown jewels, which were stolen from France during the French Revolution."

Charlemagne proceeded to comply with their demand that he provide information. He proceeded to summarize his journey to Vienna, Salzburg, back to Vienna, and then Budapest.

"Based on our current research, the Crown Jewels could be in Vojvodina somewhere – that is, northern Serbia, the extent of Austrian rule in the region at the time – however… however, that is just a theory we had with no justifiable evidence so far as we had yet to investigate the possibility."

"Very good, Mr. Cabernet," Le Havre stated. He had sat down on a chair similar to the one that Charlemagne was strapped to, except backwards. "You may have just saved your own life… be sure that he suffers, though not too much," he said, standing up. "I will now verify this information with the girl."

"What?" Charlemagne questioned. "It's the truth, by Jove, I swear it - oof!"

The crowbar was swung into his side, below the ribs. Le Havre left the room.

"Please, don't…" Charlemagne begged, "Aaagh!"

The crowbar was swung into his abdomen. The henchman proceeded to roam around the room afterwards as tears came down Charlemagne's eyes. The henchmen spoke in Arabic, prompting the one with the crowbar to stop by the chair Le Havre sat on and take a break. The other came around, cracking his knuckles. He swung a punch across Charlemagne's face. Charlemagne rocked sideways in his chair by the force of the punch. Another fist came towards him from the other direction.

"Please…" Charlemagne begged again, "please, don't…"

The henchman gave a sinister laugh as he threw in another punch, this time hitting the temple. He was knocked out.

Charlemagne woke up, eyes barely able to stay open, and blood dripping from his mouth. His chin rested on his right shoulder and he murmured in pain. He slowly began to turn his head to look around the room. The henchmen had left and it was still daylight outside, although dim, no doubt due to cloudy weather. He slowly began to regain consciousness, although his head stayed tilted to his front and sides as though severely groggy. His stomach rumbled and his skin was fair. He spat out some blood onto the floor and looked around again. He then lowered his head and fell asleep. Charlemagne woke up again, eyes able to stay open a bit longer and blood no longer pouring out from any orifice.

"Wake up, Mr. Cabernet," Le Havre remarked, standing before him.

"I'm awake…" Charlemagne muttered.

"Good…" Le Havre stated. "You've provided the information that we need, but I regret to inform you that we have no intention in releasing you."

"W-what?"

"You've been a nuisance for quite some time now, and rather than be humiliated again, I believe we will simply sell you and your friend to some Algerian friends of mine. They are on their way to take you to Albania from where you will be taken to North Africa. Our rivalry has been a pleasure, Mr. Cabernet, but I'm afraid that from here we are due to part. All else I can say is that it has been an honor, but alas, it seems that I've bested you. *Au revoir, mon ami.*"

"No…" Charlemagne quietly replied.

"What's that?"

"No, you haven't, and I have no rival – not you, not your friends here, and not Ali… Nobody is worthy to best, Charlemagne… or call himself my rival."

"If you say so, Mr. Cabernet," Le Havre simply stated. "Fairwell."

Le Havre left the room again, this time with his henchmen, and he was left on his own. His stomach grumbled again, and he stayed put with his head down for a few minutes, then an hour or two. Finally, he raised his head up and began to look around again. His head suddenly jerked up as he heard a scream from nearby.

"Manon," Charlemagne said, livening up. He looked around the room with more enthusiasm and then felt the ties behind his back. Charlemagne growled and began to tilt side to side in his chair until he fell over. He cringed as he fell on his side, but the drop caused his ties to slightly loosen. He squatted in place and then pushed himself up from the chair, causing the chair to slide off from being attached to him and his ties. When he was free from the grip of the chair, Charlemagne began to stand up and look around for something to use to cut the ties. Another screech came from nearby. "Manon, I'm coming…" he quietly said.

Charlemagne picked up the crowbar placed nearby and used it to smash the window. He then gripped a shard of glass and began to use it to cut his ties. As soon as he felt the ties loosen, he dropped the sharp piece of glass and began to manually free himself from that bondage. He then picked up the crowbar and walked over to the exit, peeking through the window before he continued forward. He could hear cries coming from a room not too far from his. He opened the door and maintaining a squatted position, he began to venture out into the warehouse floor. He walked down the aisle towards a room at the other end where he could see light pour through. The warehouse was dark and there were no others that could be seen. Charlemagne came around to the window into the room and peeked in as he saw a fierceful Manon, gritting her teeth as two henchmen stood before her. The blouse she had been wearing was slightly undone, revealing the top of her bra underneath. Charlemagne held the crowbar in his hand as he watched.

"*Venez ici, salauds!*" Manon shouted. "*Je t'arracherai les doigts avec mes dents si tu essaies à nouveau de me toucher comme ça!*"

The henchmen disagreed in Arabic as they attempted to discuss her behavior. They began to approach her, one from behind, each with a cloth similar to the ones used to gag them. At that moment, Charlemagne slowly turned the knob and entered inside the room. Manon quickly looked over and Charlemagne entered swinging, hitting a henchman across the head and causing him to fall over knocked out. The other henchmen turned and pulled a knife, but Manon leaned forward and bit his hand, causing him to swipe towards her, though she dodged. Charlemagne swung the crowbar again and hit him across the head.

"How's that for hospitality..." Charlemagne remarked, dropping the crowbar. He looked over to Manon, "Oh, Manon," he said, "what's happened to you?"

"What do you mean what's happened to me? Do you not see that I've decided to follow you into this lovely spa, Charlemagne. What a question to ask me – shut up and get me out of here, *Vite maintenant!*"

Charlemagne picked up the knife and came around to untie Manon. She did not hesitate to stand up, adjust her clothes, and then go over to pick up the crowbar. She spat on one of the captors and then turned to Charlemagne.

"Let's go, before more of them arrive," Manon suggested.

"Good idea," Charlemagne replied, holding the knife.

Manon looked at the knife and then to him. "What are holding that for? Take a gun from one of these men – you won't defend us with that…"

"Oh," Charlemagne agreed, "right." He put the knife away, keeping it on his person, and then went to one of the henchmen to search them for a handgun. He picked up a Beretta and a spare cartridge, and then turned to Manon who was looking out the door. "I haven't felt one of these in my hands in a long time. I forgot how heavy it is…"

"Silence," Manon hushed, looking out the window. "*Il y a une personne là-bas… Je vois une ombre.*"

"*Le Havre?*" Charlemagne questioned. "Their leader, perhaps? There aren't usually more than three of them in one place… I've dealt with these people before in Germany, they…"

Manon looked at Charlemagne. "Ah, so these are your Turkish friends then," she quietly said. "How nice of me to join in your suicidal adventures well and done. As soon as we are out of here, no more, Charlemagne."

"We can talk about it later," Charlemagne said with a humph. "Let's focus on getting out of here alive. Are you alright?"

"I'm fine," Manon insisted, "let's go."

Manon opened the door and proceeded through. She came around to the end of a shelf in the warehouse space and stayed put. Charlemagne followed and stuck behind. As they waited to move, Charlemagne weighed the Beretta in his hands. He looked at the gun and then shook his head. He moved forward with Manon, going from shelf end to shelf end in the warehouse until they reached the large open doors that looked out towards a dock. The dock was empty, the ship they had seemingly come on was not moored in port and the ramp visibly removed. Manon looked around and saw a stairwell up towards a catwalk above, but it was across an open space before the dock where there were two henchmen looking around suspiciously. They talked quietly in Arabic as they looked about, guns drawn. Both Manon and Charlemagne looked above at the catwalk, seeing that it bridged over the open space and came around to an exit on the left. They moved out of the way and began to look around for an alternative exit, but none could be found except one which was locked. Manon turned around to face Charlemagne.

"What do we do? There's no way out," Manon expressed.

"There's always a way out, either through the docks or above," Charlemagne insisted. "Come now."

Charlemagne led her down the aisle, opposite from where they had been, with the stairwell directly at the end. They stopped at the furthest shelf end before the open space and looked over to where the henchmen had been. They were gone.

"What..." Charlemagne questioned, eyes looking around, "they're..." He then spotted a pool of a dark liquid on the floor. He slowly stepped out and saw behind a workshop bench where the corpses of the two henchmen lay. A gunshot pierced both of their heads, and they laid on the ground, open eyes towards the ceiling and handguns not too far from their right hands. "How? What?"

"*Charles*, I do not think that we are alone..."

"Neither do I," Charlemagne agreed. "Let's leave, shall we?"

Charlemagne stepped across the room, stepping out onto the boardwalk. The boardwalk stretched a few more yards at the end, coming out towards a wide body of water that stretched from this coastline to the other. The width of the body of water was similar to the Danube. Lights shined from the other end, from buildings that side of the river, like stars in the skies, whereas the side they were on was dimmer and less bright. At one end of the dock was the end of the dock, going out onto the river, whereas at the opposite-end was a chain-link fence, which looked out towards a street. Across from the street were some rundown homes. Charlemagne stepped towards the chain-link fence and looked up.

"No way out this way," Charlemagne expressed. "We best try the stairs."

Charlemagne pivoted his foot to return towards the warehouse, but as he did so he could hear something speak in Arabic from within the warehouse. He paused and came around to the corner. He could see someone on the catwalks, looking down towards the dead bodies.

"On second thought, perhaps this exit will do," Charlemagne noted, stepping back. "Come on, I'll give you a leg up here."

Charlemagne boosted Manon up and she climbed over the fence. She then stayed in between the median and offered her hand to Charlemagne. He took ahold of her hand, but she could not lift him.

"*Sacre Dieu*," Manon cried out as she attempted to lift him. "You're too heavy/ I can't lift you."

"In that case, hold on and I'll try and lift myself up," Charlemagne said, attempting to climb up the fence by his feet. He released Manon's hand and fell back down to the ground as he heard gunshots from the warehouse. He immediately crouched and kept his head down, freezing for a moment while Manon raised her hands to the side of her head. Charlemagne looked towards the warehouse and then up to Manon. The pair saw the beams of some headlights approach, prompting Manon to panic. "Get out of here!" Charlemagne remarked. "I'll find another way out." He then ran back into the warehouse while Manon called out his name.

"*Charles! Charles!*"

Charlemagne looked above but could not see the figure that was walking around the upstairs catwalks. He quickly dashed across and began to climb the stairs to the top of the catwalk. He then saw some offices at the end, as well as an open door at the opposite corner. He took the handgun out from his pocket and began to approach with caution. Charlemagne looked ahead of him and kept the gun pointed up.

"Alright, Charles, just like we learned in boot camp."

Charlemagne stepped carefully towards the door, placing a hand forward and causing it to open wide. The doors opened with a creak. He entered into a rectangular room with barred windows that looked down to the same alleyway below. He stepped forward towards another door into the next room. He pushed the door as it was ajar, looking down to discover another male who was shot and killed. This male wore a teal suit and had reddish-tan skin and dark hair. He was face forward on the ground, directly in front of an open safe with the door left ajar. Charlemagne stepped forward towards yet another door that was also left ajar.

The door creaked open, and with the handgun pointed forward, he looked into the room to see that there was seemingly nobody present. He then turned to right and found a promising door. However, before Charlemagne could rush to the door, he felt a cold sensation come upon his head, as though a piece of round metal was placed upon it.

"*Nye dvigat'sya,*" a voice quietly remarked.

Act 3, Scene 2

Charlemagne stood with a slight hunch, shoulders tense, as the gun to his head remained in place. He did not dare to move. He could still feel the coldness of the end of the barrel touching upon his hair; colder than the air around as apparent by his visible breaths, breaths of which were sharp, in tune with the rate of his heart. He held his hands apart from his body, wrists extended and palms out, and slowly raising them to be equal with his head. He then slightly turned his head to the right to see what was behind him.

"*Nye dvigat'sya*," the voice remarked again in a stricter tone before he could see. The voice spoke in a soft, but masculine and slightly nasally voice.

Charlemagne looked straight forward again. His hands trembled. He quietly replied, "I don't know what you're saying. I don't speak whatever language you are speaking in, but I mean no harm."

"English?" the voice questioned. The accent of the voice shifted from a Slavic one to a thick southern Ulster accent. "What's a *sassenach* doing about here?"

"Irish?" Charlemagne remarked. He felt the cold touch of the barrel of the gun fall from his head and the tension in the room shift. He slowly turned around to see the man staring at him.

The man wore dark, pitch-black clothes. He had fair skin and was unshaven. He had a slight cleft in his chin and a tall nose. He also had greyish-green eyes and medium reddish-brown hair apparent by his thin eyebrows. His cheek bones were visible, and his eyes were tired and sunken. He wore black a beanie cap. He wore a long-sleeved turtle-neck black wool British commando sweater that covered his neck. He also wore black cargo pants with ample pockets, and around his belt he wore a tactical utility belt with pouches for ammunition and a holster. His sweater was tucked into his pants, and his pant legs were tucked into his black army boots. He was nearly the same height as Charlemagne, though shorter by one or two inches. He held a Makarov pistol in one hand, still pointing it at Charlemagne, but aiming from the waist.

Charlemagne noticed that the handgun was still pointed at him, looked at it, and then looked at the face of the Irishman whose eyes like the gun were still pointed straight at him without loss of focus. Charlemagne said, "Easy now. I don't want any trouble. I was kidnapped from my hotel room in Budapest by these men here."

"Budapest?" the Irishman replied. "You're a long way from Hungary then."

"I wouldn't have the faintest clue where I am now…"

"You're in Belgrade, lad. The former capital of the Yugoslav Republic."

"Serbia? I'm in Serbia?" Charlemagne responded with surprise. "I suppose we were supposed to be taken to Albania, so makes that as much sense then."

"You were being taken to Albania by these men?"

"Yes, these men… they belong to Musa Le Havre, a French-Algerian crime boss who's been a pain in my side for better part of a year," Charlemagne stated. "He told myself and my compatriot who I was travelling with that they intended to sell us to some friends of his out in Algeria. Imagine that – to sell another human being as if this were the days of the slave trade."

"The days of the slave trade never ended," the Irishman remarked. "What you and your friend nearly found yourselves in was just that – consignment into slavery. We can talk more about it in a second – you said you had a friend?"

"Yes, a female friend," Charlemagne stated.

"Where's she now?" the Irishman asked, taking a sidestep and looking out the window down towards the warehouse floor. "She taken away?"

"No," Charlemagne responded, "she managed to escape out onto the streets. I was frightened by the gunfire and thought I was done for just now…" he said, looking at the gun still pointed at him. "You… you aren't going to hurt me, will you?"

"Well, my English friend, that depends on what else you can tell me about yourself," the Irishman responded. "You say you were travelling and these men captured you?"

"Yes," Charlemagne agreed. He proceeded to explain the kidnapping in detail before he said. "These men were hired by the son of an oil baron, Ali Al-Suli, who I imagine takes great dislike in me because of my friendship with his father, Harun Al-Suli. He sees me as a rival of sort (not that we are), and although devoid of any archeological or historical experience, resorts to hire these goons to come after me to steal my self-earned glory in my quests."

"Right, and what brought you out to Budapest? You say you're an archeologist?"

"Not professionally so," Charlemagne corrected, "just an amateur historian. I've been in the region searching for the French Crown Jewels, lost during the French Revolution, likely to have travelled east."

"Oh really? That's interesting… and what's your name there, friend'o?"

"Charlemagne – Charlemagne *de la Cabernet*."

"That's quite the name for an Englishman isn't it? Sounds a tad bit French if you ask me."

"If you – could you please point your firearm away from me," Charlemagne requested, looking at it again. "Please don't hurt me."

The Irishman laughed and replied, "Relax there, bud, I'm not going to hurt you." He put his Makarov pistol back into the holster and then said, "Well, I'll tell you what, *Charles-man*, you've found yourself in nice company here. The name's Cael, Cael Monaghan, and I'm with British Intelligence."

"British Intelligence?" Charlemagne questioned, lowering his hands. "How'd an Irishman come to the service of Her Majesty's intelligence agency?" Charlemagne asked. "Your accent doesn't sound like it's from Northern Ireland."

"Aye, it's not," Cael affirmed, "I'm from the north of Ireland proper, but I've been of use to the Queen's services, I assure you."

"And with a license to kill, I suppose at that..."

"Ah, well, it's not a part of the job description, but I tell you, they fall over just the same as the Reds did. Come now, why don't we go find your lass friend then."

Charlemagne nodded and proceeded to walk with Cael out through the exit to the top landing of a metal staircase. They then proceeded down together.

"How long have you been doing all this?" Charlemagne asked.

"I was an informant from when I was a wee'lad in the seventies, then shortly after I turned eighteen I was recruited in the eighties. I tell you what, I've been doing this for fifteen years now."

"You're young then," Charlemagne remarked, "younger than me."

"How old are yuh?"

"Thirty-six."

"Ah, not too much older than me," Cael remarked with a laugh.

"No, not by much," Charlemagne remarked, looking down the alleyway, "but you may be just the person who can help my friend and I out of Serbia. Although I would very much like to be in the Balkans right now for my research, I need to return to Budapest to fetch my items from my hotel, assuming they're still there and not been burglarized."

"Where were you and your friend staying?"

"At the Equinox in downtown Budapest, dead-set besides the Danube River."

"Right," Cael replied, "well, I could very much help you in getting out of Serbia, Charles-man, but if you're interested in staying to look for them Crown Jewels, it may be harder for you get back in."

"And this is advice from a member of Her Majesty's Intelligence Agency?"

"Ah, well, what can I say, I'm out here looking for criminals and insurgents and all that, but you don't seem to be anything like that – who am I to deny you a bit of tourism?"

"How kind."

"Yes, she's seen better days, but Belgrade is something to see for sure, especially after the war, but if you go any further south, be weary for certain – the Moslims out in those parts are worse than wears towards strangers."

"I'd like to stay in the part I'm in now, but I don't have any money or anything. I've left all my credit cards and wallet in my hotel safe. Is there any place for us to be taken to? An embassy or consulate?"

"I could take you to the embassy, but it was vacated since the war and they still haven't returned. You'd have to travel up north to Croatia if you'd want out," Cael said as they came towards the end of the alleyway, "but like I said, coming back in could cost you."

"I just care to get my friend out of dodge, then I'm right back in," Charlemagne remarked. "I don't plan to go anywhere near Kosovo where the action is – I want to stay in this area, I need to do some local research."

"Very well," Cael remarked, squinting as he saw headlights approach. He took his firearm out and came down onto his knee. "Do me a favor there, Charles-man, and go find your friend down the street. I've got a job here to do and will be with you in a second."

Charlemagne stepped forward to see the red pickup truck that had just parked further ahead. The doors opened and men with firearms exited out. He looked towards them and then down to Cael who attached a suppressor to the barrel of his Makarov.

"I'll get you and your friend to a safehouse in town, but bear with me just now. Act casual, and go."

Charlemagne nodded. He then slipped down the alleyway as he passed the front of the warehouse. He put his hands into his pockets and proceeded down. He came around to the opposite alleyway where he turned and found Manon huddled behind some bins.

"*Charles!*" Manon remarked, embracing him. "Oh, I thought something terrible had happened to you..."

"You're alright," Charlemagne replied, looking down at her as she held her arms around his neck. He placed his hands at her waist and slowly pushed her away. "We need to stay down – more of them have just arrived. I ran into an intelligence officer with MI6, British Intelligence, upstairs. He's the one that had killed those gang members. He's going to get us out of here."

"*Merci.*"

Charlemagne pushed Manon away and then came around to the building corner as he awaited Cael's conflict with the gangsters. He watched the gangsters approach the building – three in total. Cael then appeared from around the corner, with his suppressed Makarov pistol drawn, and shot one of the three in the back of the head. The two others immediately sprang into action as they turned around, one of them opening fire with their submachine gun while Cael rolled into cover behind a vehicle parked at the curb. The gangsters shouted out in Turkish. Charlemagne watched the gangsters as they had their backs to Charlemagne, and he felt in his pocket as he still held on to the Beretta pistol. The gangsters immediately encircled the parked vehicle that Cael took cover behind, but as they approached the behind, they were astonished that he was gone. Charlemagne then saw him climb out from the end, take a clean shot at one of the gangsters and then turn to finish the other one off.

When Cael had finished, he looked around the narrow street and then went down towards where Charlemagne was. He detached his suppressor, re-loaded his pistol, and then holstered it.

"That was brilliant," Charlemagne remarked.

"T'was nothing," Cael insisted. "Let's be going. They've startled the neighbors with that noise and local guard will be here any second now."

"Why don't we take their vehicle?" Charlemagne suggested, pointing towards it.

"Because these lads riddled it with holes," Cael remarked, looking towards Manon. "Hang on, this your friend here?"

"Hm?" Charlemagne questioned, turning to Manon. "Oh, yes, it is."

Cael stepped forward and placed himself in front of Manon. He offered his hand. "Cael Monaghan, British Intelligence, pleased to meet you."

"Manon Dumas," she replied. "*Charles*, tells me that you will get us out of here?"

"I can bring you out to a safehouse, but won't be able to get you out tonight," Cael replied. "I've got a job to do still, so best be quick, shall we?"

"Yes, let's go," Charlemagne agreed, eyeing Cael with Manon.

Cael proceeded to lead the way down the street and into an alleyway on the adjacent part of the street. They then came into a short alleyway followed by an intersection to a perpendicular alley. From the other side, Cael knelt down while the others huddled behind him. In the distance, the sound of police sirens could be heard.

"Due to recent insurgent attacks, Belgrade is in lockdown, won't find anyone out here who isn't up to no good, and there are checkpoints throughout. We'll need to lay low if we're to get you to my place."

Cael then led them across the street and into another, slightly cleaner alleyway. The architecture shifted from rundown apartments and warehouses to stone architecture and pathways. The alleyway from here led out to a small lot with cars parked in front of a tall building. A few lamps around and attached to the buildings provided minimal light, but it was otherwise very cold and quiet. Cael brought them around to the side of a black sedan as one could hear whistling from afar. After a moment, Cael stood up and went down behind the vehicles towards the intersecting street. He stayed close to the side of the buildings and made his way towards an arcade, but then turned left at the intersection and came around to a parallel street to the parking lot. He then continued forward, across the street, but stopped behind a parked van as he saw a male in army gear standing around the street corner ahead. He signaled the pair to keep hold as he pulled his firearm out, attached the suppressor, and then walked down behind several vehicles. Charlemagne watched from afar as Cael snuck down the sides of these vehicles, and then waited for the soldier to turn his sights away before he crossed the street and continued down, hugging the walls of the buildings as he quickly snuck down towards the sidewalk and checked his corner. He was a few feet away from the soldier. Charlemagne watched with anticipation; the police sirens had stopped, but he could hear a helicopter rotor from afar. As the rotors became increasingly loud, Cael stepped forward and put the soldier into a chokehold to knock him out. Cael then signaled Charlemagne and Manon to come over, so they rushed down the street and joined him at the street corner. The helicopter made a pass from nearby, but not directly above them. Cael then led them around the corner along a stoney road that went uphill.

The group stopped again as they were just about at the top of the hill where there was a three-way intersection, not including a set of stairs directly ahead that led up to a park. Charlemagne could hear footsteps, prompting him and Manon to hide in a nook while Cael crossed to the other side of the street and came up to the corner. From where Charlemagne was, he could see ahead as a soldier patrolled forward. He took notice of the soldier, dressed in urban grey camouflage with green vests and camouflaged caps on. They held AK-47 rifles in their hands. The soldier came to the intersection, paused, and then turned around. Cael made his move forward before he approached the next corner, wrapping his arms around him and then knocking him out. Afterwards, Charlemagne and Manon approached while Cael dragged the body to hide it behind a furniture truck. He then went towards the street corner and looked ahead.

"Bad luck," Cael remarked, "a blockade up ahead and too many of them to fight through. We'll need to go through the park here. Stay low."

Charlemagne followed Cael as he led them forward and then around up a set of stairs. The park in the midst of the city was elevated with chiseled stone walls around them, topped with black steel fences. Cael brough them around to the middle of the park where there was a fountain and hedges. They stayed low and Charlemagne noticed a pair of soldiers at opposite exit.

"I'm going to need your help here, Charles-man," Cael whispered. "I need you to distract one of these guards here to separate them. It'll be the only way we're getting through. You got it?"

"Uh… sure," Charlemagne replied.

"Good."

Cael moved out from the side and proceeded to come around the trees and shrubs. Charlemagne stayed put.

"What are you going to do?" Manon whispered.

"Hush," Charlemagne replied. "I know what I'm going to do."

Charlemagne looked towards the guards and towards a tree nearby where a raven was perched upon a branch. He looked at the raven and then stepped back. Manon moved out of the way and stayed where she was, back to the hedge, and Charlemagne picked up a rock. He looked towards where Cael had went and saw that he was gone, but then as he came back around to the corner of the hedge and looked towards the guards, he saw him not too far from them at the side in some shrubs. Charlemagne looked at the raven and threw the rock at it, causing it to let out a loud shout and then fly off.

The guards immediately turned towards the raven as it flew off and the rock landed not too far and hit the fence. The guards talked to each other in Serbian and one of them proceeded forward, while the other continued to look in Charlemagne's direction. Cael moved in on the one guard while Charlemagne and Manon withdrew. They came around the hedge where Cael had tipped the body of the soldier over the stairs and then made his way to the last. This soldier had a lot more fight in him than the other one, causing Cael to wrestle with him. Charlemagne rushed in to intervene as the soldier came onto his back. Cael punched him across the face. Charlemagne landed atop of the feet and was immediately kicked off. Cael punched him across the face again, and that was enough. Cael then stood up and walked over to help Charlemagne back onto his feet, but he refused his help and instead stood up on his own.

The group continued out of the park and came onto a wide street with a ramp on the right. They kept right and proceeded down and around the corner. They came out towards a sort of elevated plaza with cars parked on the side. They were brought down some stairs to the lower level streets, made their way across, and then hid in the nooks, going from nook to nook as the sound of the helicopter could be heard closer again. The perpendicular street at the next intersection was slightly diagonal with an arcade directly across that cut through the buildings to another street. This street was wider. They travelled left and then right at a large arch above the road. A separate smaller arch came over the sidewalk, and these arches led into a plaza from where the helicopter hovered above. At the opposite side of the plaza was another soldier. The group hid behind a van. A searchlight lit up the middle of the plaza and the helicopter began to slowly look around as it rotated above. The group stayed close to the sides of the buildings as they went counter-clockwise around the plaza.

Cael led them right and then around a bend in the road where there was another soldier at the end, patrolling down. Cael moved in while the others stayed behind, and again he took him out before they could proceed forward. They came around another bend, and then carried forward. The helicopter began to move again. Cael took them down an alleyway and away from the wider streets. The alleyway curved around, passed a garden, and then came out to a bent smaller street. The street then went downhill to where there were two soldiers at either side of the street corner, standing around. Cael stopped them a few yards back.

"Same here," Cael remarked, "I'm going to need you to set a distraction. See about tripping one of them car alarms."

"Right."

Cael crossed the street to approach the nearest solider at the street corner, while Manon stayed back and Charlemagne went forward to one of the cars parked just about at the street corner. He took out the Beretta and used it to smash a window in, setting off the car alarm. He then fled backwards to hide behind the car behind it. The soldier furthest looked over and stepped forward while the other stayed put. Cael stepped forward to the closer one, proceeded to knock him out, while the other turned to him and then raised his firearm up as he saw Cael's actions.

"*Nye dvigat 'sya!*" the soldier shouted.

Charlemagne took out the Beretta again and then immediately moved in towards the soldier as he stepped towards the street. He took the handgun and knocked the soldier behind the head with it, causing them to lose ground and tip over. Cael through his comrade to the ground, and then swung over the hood of the car in front of him to rush in and tackle the soldier to the ground. He then used his own assault rifle to knock him out with the stock of the gun. Charlemagne took notice of whether anyone else had noticed, and then they continued forward, going around the right street corner and uphill. They went left into another alleyway, which led out to another street that bent rightwards and then carried on straight. The helicopter was now far from them. They went into another alleyway, which went left and right, and then came out to another street where they stopped as an armored car passed by with soldiers above. Charlemagne took a step forward with Cael as they went further along the street, coming around and then entering into another alleyway. He quickly rushed them into a nook before he took cover behind a parked vehicle in the alleyway as the sound of rolling tires could be heard on approach. Another armored vehicle passed before they could carry on, stepping forward along the alleyway and then turning left to a dead-end where from above the sound of bells could be heard loudly. Cael entered into a nook at the side of the building they were at, knocked three times and saw a slot open with eyes poking out. Without a word, the door then opened and they entered through into the dark room. A man dressed in dark clothes like Cael, but like robes from top down wandered away. Charlemagne took a step inside and the door closed behind him.

Charlemagne looked around and saw that they were in some sort of storage room with barrels and crates. There was also a wardrobe with robes inside in different colors, very ornamental and colorful. On a table were some silver-colored and gold-colored plates and chalices.

"Where are we?" Charlemagne asked.

"In a safe place," Cael answered. "I can't stay, as I said I have work to do, but go out from here, right, and then left at the end of the hall to find a way down to the cellar. If you're hungry, the local cleric is still awake to cook you up a meal."

"Cleric?" Charlemagne questioned.

Cael then left. Charlemagne looked around the room again and looked towards Manon. Manon said, "Where are we, *Charles?*"

"Belgrade, my dear," Charlemagne remarked. "You said you didn't want to follow me, and yet here we are…"

"What a fool I've been to follow you into danger," Manon sneered. "I should have known better…"

The pair exited out of the storage room and came into a small foyer with a red carpet in the middle. The room had two large arched doors left and right, where they had come out of rectangular double doors and also faced another. The room was dim and lit by a chandelier above. They turned right as Cael had instructed, went forward, and pushed through the doors to come into a small church. Charlemagne froze as he entered inside and looked around the dim room.

The church consisted of pews left and right with archways on the far left and right up to the sanctuary. A low wooden fence stood in front of the sanctuary with a gate before the altar. The sanctuary consisted of an altar with a tabernacle above and tall candles left and right, four in total. Around the sanctuary were arched steps that came up to a statue of the Virgin Mary that loomed above with arms spread out. The statue merged with a mural painted into the domed ceiling of Jesus Christ sat above a throne, which in itself was behind a suspended crucifix with a large life-like and human-sized figure of Jesus Christ gruesomely nailed in.

Charlemagne looked at the entire scene with a bit of fright and then directly towards the tabernacle at the end of the aisle.

Manon looked at him with confusion. She then slapped Charlemagne in the chest with the back of her hand as she said, "What's the matter with you? Hm? You look as if you've seen a ghost."

"Sorry," Charlemagne replied, catching himself. "I just… I wasn't sure if we were alone or not is all… Cael said that the cellar is to the left.

Charlemagne came around the side aisles of the church where he found a side room with a trap door in the floorboards. He raised the trap doors and saw a ladder in the hatch. He then climbed down the short distance to come into the lower crypt.

"Well, isn't this lovely…" Charlemagne expressed, picking up a lantern on a table and lighting it with some matches, "sleeping with the dead in this place."

Charlemagne observed the crypt to be small and roughly the same size as the transept and nave of the church. There were a few empty tombs that had nameplates on them. He placed the lantern down and proceeded to light a few candles with Manon. A makeshift hideaway existed in the crypt with cots laid out. In the corner of the room was a cot with blankets thrown over and some personal effects. Charlemagne continued to light a few candles to give some more light. He then found an electric lantern and used that to help him around. Charlemagne observed a monument slightly near where the altar would be above with an enclosed tomb. Above the tomb were statues of saintly figures and angels looking down. At the side of the monument were more statues of people looking towards the tomb. He looked at the monument and saw a plaque below that written in Latin, '*Gloria in Excelsis Deo.*' Charlemagne observed and then took a step back, placing his heel onto a grate in the floor. The entire crypt was surrounded by a grate system.

"So do we wait here for Kyle to return?"

"Yes," Charlemagne responded, "until he returns, and then he'll take us back to Hungary, so I believe, and we can both be on our merry way. I'm to return to Belgrade on my own, better equipped, and venture forth to find this Ignác Újlaki and see what I can learn about him."

"After all we've just been through, you'll voluntarily come back into this country to carry on this futile search?" Manon questioned. "What is wrong with you, *Charles?* Why do you do this?"

"I have a responsibility to carry out in my historical research to not let a potential important secret be left uncovered."

"What responsibility? You have no responsibility to nobody, that's who you are, *Charles.*"

"Oh, here we go…"

"You are a solitary man, *Charles,*" Manon complained. "You have said so yourself, so what is this commitment to find the Frankish Crown? You do not seek to fulfill any sort of commitment, or responsibility, but a pursuit for fame to be known as something you are not or ever will be."

"You just watch it now," Charlemagne warned.

"Or what? What will the brave *Charlemagne de la Cabernet* do to me?" Manon encouraged. "You are a fool, *Charles,* because you do not understand it. Oh, how noble it is to be named *Charlemagne* like the great king," she teased, "and be of the Cabernet family… your grandfather never took to brandish such notoriety, no – he understood his place in this world, and so has your father, but seemingly you have not. You believe yourself to hold a grand place in this world, when not even your own hometown could bear you as a burden, so what makes you think the world can too?

"I said be quiet," Charlemagne threatened.

"Believe me, *Charles,* you are a fool to believe that the world even wishes for what you believe you have to offer – the Frankish Crown… a few more people will blink at you if you were to find this stupid crown that I imagine you dream to place upon your own head."

"Oh, this is madness…"

"Yes, madness… madness to have followed you to Vienna, then to Hungary, and now here?"

"I told you I was going to get you out…"

"And yet here we still are, in the basement of some church," Manon remarked. "And what do you expect me to do when we get back to Hungary? To let you leave and endanger yourself further? To allow those bad men to take you captive and be the last one to have seen Charlemagne de la Cabernet? Oh, you'll be famous then, for certain, when the world learns that a rich man like you has gotten himself kidnapped, and then the world will promptly forget about you as it does…"

"I've had enough of this…" Charlemagne remarked, walking over to Cael's belongings and searching them. "I'm not going to stick around and listen to this dribble. Call me a fool all you want, Manon, but you're the one that's the so-called followed a fool. Admit it – you've followed me not for that reason. I know why it is you've followed me – it isn't some pursuit of your own for my wellbeing."

"Oh really?" Manon questioned.

"Honestly, Manon, I see it plain as day – you're had it in me for me."

"What?" Manon responded with a nervous laugh.

"You're nostalgic for the adventure of the old days, and just like Ali, want a piece of what I accomplish, to be a part of the pathway of a true historian, an adventurer and explorer, to seek the unknown rather than sit behind textbooks and books all days, teaching in mildew classrooms to the less than interesting students of yours. You seek me – you idolize me."

"You're a fool then, Charlemagne," Manon simply replied, shaking her head. "You truly do not know what I do for you, or have done."

"Oh, deny it, but I know it's true," Charlemagne responded, taking out a set of keys. "Ahah, see what I've found here: some car keys, and some currency."

"What are you doing? Put that away," Manon stated.

"No way," Charlemagne expressed, "stay here if you'd like, tell Cael I've stolen from him (though I will pay him back), but I'm not going back to Budapest. I'll find some place safe away from Belgrade and phone for help myself, but I won't be staying here. I have adventure to seek…"

"Oh, and where will you go exactly?" Manon responded. "You do not know what county Ignác Újlaki was from, or where his castle is."

"Do you?"

"Yes, and I will not tell you," Manon replied.

"Very well, then I'll just have to do so myself," Charlemagne replied, putting on a poncho he found. "Fairwell, my *cherie*, enjoy yourself in this dungeon."

Charlemagne then turned to leave, climbing up the ladder and leaving. Manon stayed put, crossed her arms and looked about the damp room she was in. She tapped her heel into the ground anxiously, and without another moment of hesitation, left to follow Charlemagne.

"*Merde… je déteste cet imbécile…*"

Act 3, Scene 3

A few days later, Charlemagne drove the vehicle he had found parked besides the church and the keys of which he found in Cael's personal belongings. The vehicle was a red 1983 UAZ-3151, an off-road light utility vehicle. At some point in the past few days, Charlemagne changed out of his suit and now wore cargo pants, boots, a long-sleeved sweater and a vest. He also wore a bucket hat. Manon likewise changed out of her clothes and now wore cargo pants, boots, and a denim jacket. She also tied her hair up and wore a cap. Manon studied a map of the local region while Charlemagne drove. He drove the vehicle along a forested road.

"I told you that we ought to have asked for directions, we're lost now," Charlemagne scolded. "We're in the middle of Serbia with no idea of where we even could be going, and without a lick of sense to what any of these signs and such mean."

"Uck, *Charles*, I told you kilometers before to turn right, and you did not, and now I have not an idea of where we could be."

"How was I supposed to turn right when we had already passed the turn?"

"Turn around," Manon argued. "Is it that hard?"

"We've been going around and around, as if this jeep has unlimited fuel when we've used up half a tank already," Charlemagne remarked. "At the next sign of civilization, I'm going to ask for help to get a sense of where we are."

"Well then," Manon commended, folding the map, "it's in your hands. What do I care if we cannot find this castle? Let us get lost in the forest as well – sure, if we find a village, the chances that anyone may speak English, German, or even French are in our favor."

"Can you please at least attempt to get a sense of where we are by the signs," Charlemagne requested. "We cannot be too far from where you lost track of us."

"I lost track of us? I lost track of us!?! Charlemagne, you are at the wheel! How can I know where we are when you are driving like a madman?!"

"This petty discussion isn't getting us closer to our destination – look there's a sign up ahead. See if you can find where we are…"

Manon looked ahead and read the sign. The sign had Cyrillic letters, and she proceeded to attempt to decipher their location, while Charlemagne continued to drive.

"Almost a hundred years since the end of Austrian occupation, and not a bit of this place makes any sense to me. How can I expect or hope that this supposed castle continues to stand, or hasn't been turned into a museum?"

"It stands," Manon insisted. "My father assured me. What little he was able to find out has said that the count's castle is abandoned, in the middle of this forest, and of no objective use since the World War, no less because of ghost stories surrounding it."

"Hmph, as if a little children's tale should deter us," Charlemagne remarked.

"No, our concern is arriving there and not being left behind in this forest," Manon reminded him. "Even with that sign, I still cannot find where we are. Next time, you can navigate, and I can drive… even then, you would still find a way to blame me, I'm sure…"

Charlemagne didn't respond. They drove through the remainder of the forest and came out to some hillside farms. They then slowly approached a village. A few cars were parked on the side of the rundown buildings in this small village. All the buildings in the village looked the same: white walls with terracotta rooftops. They consisted from single story to double story in size, and the lots were surrounded by chain-link fences. There were telephone and electrical wires on poles everywhere, connecting from building to building, and these buildings of which were condensed and clumped together with hills on either side and naked trees. Charlemagne pulled over and grabbed the map from Manon's hands.

"Give me that," Charlemagne barked, "I'll find someone who can help us."

"Ah, good luck."

Charlemagne looked around the village and began to wave towards some people as he cried out in English, "Hello? *Hallo! Does anybody speak English? Spricht jemand Deutsch?*" His shouting caused a few onlookers to steer their gaze towards him, but none to approach him. He caught the attention of a few men who exited out from a pub to look at what all the commotion was, but then re-entered inside. After a few minutes' effort, Charlemagne sat back into the jeep and passed the map to Manon.

"How was that?" Manon questioned.

"Shut up," Charlemagne replied, turning the car keys and driving out. He came to the intersection, turned right and came into another part of the town where he did the same, except without the map. He shouted out in German, "*Hallo? Spricht jemand Deutsch? Englisch? Wir wissen nicht, wo wir sind!* We need help to find out where we are!" He looked about but none caught his attention. He lowered himself back into the cabin of the car and faced Manon. "This is hopeless. We may as well go back the way we came and return to Vršac. We need a guide for this – there must be someone who in the least speaks German there."

"You look for English?" a man asked from nearby.

Charlemagne looked out of the car and towards an elderly man. He had a long beard and a hunch to his stature. He wore peasant clothes, a sweater and coat, and he had lengthy grey hair that came out from the sides of his cap. Manon exited the vehicle and joined them.

"Yes, you seem to speak it," Charlemagne expressed, taking the map and going over to him. "We were travelling from Vršac looking for Vukašin Castle."

"Vukašin Castle?" the old man questioned. "No, you don't want to travel there."

"Why not?" Charlemagne asked.

"Because, nobody goes there, and it abandoned. The bridge destroyed. Go home."

"I understand there are superstitions around the castle, but I'm not travelling for those. I'm traveling because this castle was built in the late eighteenth century to defend against the Ottomans, and it belonged to a count of that castle."

"No, not for defense no more, just bad luck."

"Look, could you at least tell me where I am right now? We're lost."

"No, turn around, and go home."

"Will you at least tell me why? What's so damnable about this castle that I should not get to see it? I'm only interested to learn more about Count Ignác Újlaki."

"I do not know that name – only Vukašin... and his son..."

"You seem persistent to keep me away from the castle, so enlighten me – why is the castle called as such and not after Count Újlaki? What is so sinister about this castle that we ought to stay away?"

"Because of *Chovavuk*," the man warned.

"Chovavuk?" Charlemagne questioned. "What's that?"

"Half-man, half-wolf," the older man clarified, "the son of Vukašin. His son by blood, or his son by law, we do not know. We just know that he took care of it like his own, and kept the world away from it."

"Right... how old is this tale? Sounds like a medieval legend..."

"One-hundred years ago, or so," the old man stated, "which is why it is all the more reason to be careful. The castle is...

is…" the man struggled for the word, "foreign. It is not Serbia. It is foreign land in the middle of Serbia. It is of that man, Vukašin. He lived with that *zver*… while we lived here. Listen… one time a hundred years ago, *Chovavuk* once came here… to this village, and it killed one… two… three boys. The people tell Vukašin to go away, so Vukašin does not listen, but he stay with it in the castle. The people tell him to keep it in the castle, but it keep escaping and escaping, and the young boys… they go missing. So the legend says, the monster knew – the monster knew what it is, but it still killed. It killed with resent, for humanity and for its own existence. The monster knew that we the people hated it, would want it dead and to kill it, and he hated the people. It knew it was a monster and all rejected him except Vukašin. Was it half-man, or full wolf? It did not care – it killed many until the people had enough. With guns, a few men and a political chief went to the castle to investigate. When the doors opened, they were met with the terrifying stare of what they thought, like you, to be myth. The creature was tall, seven feet tall, and large – at least three-hundred pounds. He had sharp teeth, red eyes, and greyish-black fur on all his body. He wore clothes like you or me, a black cloak. A man shot it with his rifle, wounding it, but they did not kill it. It ran and the caretaker, Vukašin, came out and defended the castle until they left. The monster was wounded, and Vukašin took care of it, and when he was ready for his revenge, that wolf came to one of the villages searching to devour more of our youth. He preyed on one such boy, watching him from the trees, and when he was home, he came out to grab him, but as he was to break down the door, he heard a sound. The boy played on the piano a soft tune…" the old man began to hum the song. "The beast ran away, and the boy, *Tadija*, was unharmed. For nights afterwards, the beast would come to listen to *Tadija* play music. He would hear him sing, both at home and at the church. The beast listened to his words, these were the Psalms and hymns and spiritual songs, and they pulled him back, caused him to fear for his own existence, to know what sort of creature he was, and what he had done to others, and for the first time, the creature cried – he cried because it had come to love *Tadija* and his music to hate what he desired to do – still desired to do, to the boy if it was not for his songs, to devour him; to the boy if it was not for this transformation within him. According to the village priest, the creature made its approach upon him and asked for him to baptize him. Listening to *Tadija's* music converted his heart, and for the rest of his years, he is said to have lived in that same castle until he passed away."

"So… what's the danger then?" Charlemagne questioned. "Assuming any of this story to be true, what's the threat towards us? The wolf-man is dead, and the castle is abandoned – do you suppose we'll come up against his vengeful spirit?" he asked with a laugh.

"That is the story, so much as you wish to believe. It is bits and pieces, the last half of which with *Tadija* the church adopted for its own. Today, it is known as the church of *St. Tadija*, for this very story… and it is as so as you believe… Tadija was our village priest until he died some decades ago. He told the story to us. He preached it to me when I was a little boy. To me, the *Chovavuk* continues to live at that castle and is not dead. He continues to hunt young boys and men in the fields at night, going missing here and other villages, because he is alive, and you must stay away."

"Hmph," Charlemagne responded, "let me tell you what, my dear friend. My name is *Charlemagne de la Cabernet*."

Manon rolled her eyes.

"The Cabernet family herald is that of the wolf, because our ancestors were noble wolves who fought for what he had. So the saying goes, we fought our foes in the morning and in the evening we shared in our rewards together."

Manon looked at Charlemagne with confusion.

"An urban legend such as that of a wolf-man is not going to frighten us," Charlemagne remarked, "so where is this church of *St. Tadija* then?"

"Right here, in this village," the old man confirmed, pointing down the street to the white domed Byzantine-style Church. "You are there."

"And just as such, it seems we are at our destination," Charlemagne remarked to Manon. "Let's get going."

"Wait," the old man cautioned, "you must be careful… who know what evil spirits remain at that castle…"

"Thank you, my good sir," Charlemagne commended, "we'll be sure to let you know if we find any remnants of large wolves and be sure to bring you back a fang for good measure!"

Charlemagne got back into the car, threw the map aside, and then started the jeep engine. Manon sat down and crossed her arms. He then drove off.

"Must you be so cruel? He was only trying to help you…" Manon scolded.

"Oh, please, he's just a sullen old fool who believes in his mumbo jumbo superstition. I don't have time for that folly. I have a crown to find, and if this castle is as abandoned as such and we're on the right track with our *graf*-count, then I could hazard that if true, our wolf friend may have kept our prize safe and sound for us."

Manon did not make another comment. She sat back as Charlemagne proceeded to drive. He pulled over once he was out of the village to re-examine the map. He then proceeded to continue to drive along the road, re-entering the forest for a few miles until he reached a junction that deviated from the main road. He then continued to drive along a dirt road that took him deeper into the forest, and uphill, similar to the one that travelled upwards to the citadel in Hungary. Eventually, Charlemagne and Manon arrived at an iron gate and they examined it from within the car to see that it had a chain wrapped around edges of the two gates to hold them together. Likewise, on each gate door there were signs written in Cyrillic in capital letters. Each gate was attached to a brick column, which likewise connected to additional sections of gate that went into the forest. On each column were effigies of wolf-like human creatures that hung from string wrapped around the top ornaments.

"Hold on, there's an assortment of tools in a crate back here," Charlemagne remarked, turning his neck to open a weapons crate in the backseats of the car. He rummaged through the few items and pulled out a bolt cutter. He then carefully brought the bolt cutter into both of his hands, opened the car door, and went towards gate. He snapped one of the chains and then began to pull the chains out and drop them into the dirt. He then pushed each individual gate open.

After Charlemagne had finished cutting the chain and opening the gate, he returned to the jeep as it began to lightly pour down. He sat down, turned on the windshield wipers, and then proceeded to drive forward. The rain turned to a mild drizzle, and the road continued uphill until it came to a fence between two columns. The chain-link fence had a sign on it with an exclamation mark at the end. Charlemagne took the car into park and then looked ahead to see if he could see anything, but the clouds and tall trees made it difficult to do so. This time, Charlemagne grabbed his poncho stored behind, put it on, and then stepped out to take a look. The bridge was completely destroyed and collapsed, revealing a gulley several feet deep. He looked both ways and then forward across the bridge to see the road continue to bend right slightly. He then examined the sides of the gulley again before he returned to the car.

"So?" Manon questioned.

"It's collapsed, but this is an all-terrain vehicle, and I see an alternative path," Charlemagne remarked, shifting gears. He then turned left and began to drive along the cliffside of the gulley. Manon held on as they began to drive through shrubs.

She looked through her window which looked directly over the cliff. Charlemagne focused on the path ahead of him while Manon held tightly.

"Oh, *Charles*, be careful," Manon begged. "Do not fall…"

"Relax, I know what I'm doing…"

Charlemagne turned right and then with a sudden drop, the car fell forward slightly, but continued to drive along. They drove down a slope and came to the bottom of the gulley, from where Charlemagne backed up and then changed directions to go right. Right before the collapsed rubble, Charlemagne drove up the cliffside and came back onto the road. He then carried forth the rest of the direction to arrive at the castle outer walls that surrounded an open field at the front of the castle entrance. These walls were mostly destroyed and ruined, with even the arch entrance being completely collapsed and rubble cleared away for them to drive through. Past these walls, the road led up to the main entrance and castle seated.

Vukašin Castle sat upon the top of the hill in the midst of this forest surrounded by inner walls. The walls surrounded most of the hill with select sections partially collapsed but none like the exterior walls. At the end of the road was the enclosed portcullis and adjacent square towers that prevent any further travel further ahead over another bridge over another gulley, or moat, around the castle. On approach, Charlemagne and Manon could both see the elevated walls of the castle building from within with the pointed terracotta rooftops. The castle design was less than a traditional medieval castle, but of a mansion-like estate surrounded by battlements.

Charlemagne drove right up to the portcullis, put the car into park, and then turned off the engine. The car went silent and then all that was left between them was the sound of rainfall as it got worse.

"You may want to put on a poncho in case you get wet," Charlemagne remarked, fetching one from the back of the car and tossing it to her. He then fetched a small backpack for himself, and then exited the car. He examined his surroundings and went towards the tower on the right, but there was no way in.

Manon exited out with a spotlight flashlight in hand. She shined the light forward for Charlemagne who turned to her.

"It's a castle, *Charles*," Manon expressed, "how do you expect to infiltrate?"

"Oh, I'll find a way," Charlemagne expressed, climbing down into the moat. "You forget that I am…"

"*Charles!*" Manon shouted as Charlemagne almost slid down. He managed to grab hold of a root in the cliff as she yelled. "*S'il vous plaît, faites attention!*"

Charlemagne looked down and then let go to gently slide down to the bottom of the gulley. He then accepted the spotlight from Manon, who gently made her way down to join him. They walked under the bridge where they looked around for a way up. They proceeded to walk along the moat until they found a section of collapsed wall for them to climb up, bringing them level along the side of the exterior wall to walk around. Eventually, they came around to the entrance as the raised section dropped down to the ground and went around to the bridge. Charlemagne looked around the other side of the portcullis to see if there was a means to raise it. He entered into one of the guard towers and found a crank. He proceeded to pull the crank, raising the portcullis for them to exit in and out of. He then turned around to Manon. Charlemagne looked at her and then carried on forward.

"That should make it easier, I think," Charlemagne expressed. He then walked towards the front doors.

The bridge came around to the front of the castle at a slight bend, reaching a set of tall rectangular front doors. He raised his hand to the door handle.

"Charles," Manon interrupted, "what if there were some sort of beast inside?"

"Oh, don't you start," Charlemagne dismissed, "the only evils in this world walk among us already. There's nothing sinister in here than there already isn't out here."

Charlemagne then brought his hands to the door and pulled at the handles. With a bit of force, the doors began to pull out and open.

Act 3, Scene 4

Charlemagne turned on his own flashlight as his eyes pierced into the darkness within the castle foyer. The foyer was small, rectangular with the elongated walls on the left and right. On the left and right were narrow columns too, and likewise at the end of the hall there were another set of double doors with narrow tall windows beside them covered by curtains. A stairwell curved on the left and led upstairs. On the right was a smaller double doorway, while on the left further ahead there was a single door going in that direction. The room was tall and dark, but a bit of light from outside seeped through a curved window above. He looked around the room, eyeing a tapestry on the wall on the right and suits of armor left and right beside the main entrance. Charlemagne turned to Manon as she entered in behind him.

"I don't see any signs of life in here," Charlemagne assured her. "Count Újlaki must have lived here through the early nineteenth century, and the story of the wolf-person and his master was set to be late nineteenth century. I would hazard that the idiots of the nearby villages have preserved this castle as it was for us, and whoever inhabited this place before it was abandoned kept it in stasis. We will have to explore a little to find where Count Újlaki's personal belongings could have been left behind – the primary places to search will be bedrooms, studies, and libraries, if the latter exist here. Otherwise, an attic or basement storage area could also be ideal."

"I'm right here with you, *Charles*," Manon expressed. "We can search together – I am not going my own way in here."

"Suit yourself," Charlemagne responded, "just keep up."

The main entrance doors closed behind them, and the pair proceeded to walk down to the end of the hallway. Charlemagne peaked through the curtains to look out to a plain small courtyard in the midst of the castle building where through the stone pavement bunches of tall grass had overgrown and scattered throughout.

"It doesn't look that large of an estate," Charlemagne expressed as he looked at the building structure. The structure was rectangular, U-shaped on the right-side, at least four stories tall, with battlements and smaller two-story houses conjoined on the left side. He removed some matches from his backpack and lit a candle in the foyer to provide some light. "It'll be easier for us to return and know where we've been if we light a path for ourselves." He then waved the matchstick and placed it besides the candle. "Come along now, Manon, we've got a castle to explore."

Charlemagne pushed through the doors on the right and entered into a grand hall with doors on the right into adjacent rooms. The floor consisted of polished wood, although the floor had a long red rug that extended from end to end too. The walls on the right were decorated with large murals around the arched doors into separate rooms. These murals depicted noble figures, some of them on horses, in lavish scenes of gardens and balconies. A mural was painted on the wall at the end of the corridor, next to a carved wooden door. This figure was a noble figure too in a blue coattail suit and powered wig. The eyes of the figures looked down upon anyone in the room. On the left were tall windows covered with arched curtains. Between each window were candle stalks that could be lit. In front of each mural were chairs lined together, over two dozen chairs in this corridor alone, pointed outwards. On one half of the room there was a wooden grand piano placed in a corner, while at the other was a small round table with more wood chairs at each end. The ceiling above consisted of beams and wooden panels, and from these beams were chandeliers with candles.

Charlemagne went to the first archway on his left, and found a similar room that extended outwards like a small ballroom. Overhang reinforced windows provided light from the wider wall, and mirrors surrounded each of the walls in this room rather than murals, which instead were painted above in garden-like scene with depictions of Greek cherubim. Charlemagne came to the end of the corridor where there was a set of arched doors on the left at the end of the row of arched windows. He pushed through those doors and came into a larger foyer than the one before. This foyer had staircase on both sides that led up to a balcony around the second floor that viewed down. On the left was a large arched door that led out to the courtyard. Besides each door were more suits of armor in place. Beside the entrance door were arched windows covered with curtains. Charlemagne went to the centre of this foyer and looked around with his flashlight.

"I don't see any wolf-creatures," Charlemagne taunted Manon. "No – no evil creatures in sight around here. Where do you reckon he was buried? Out in the yard?"

Manon quietly growled and did not respond. She sheepishly looked around while Charlemagne went further along to the east wing. He entered into another corridor, which went down a short distance and then came around a corner to a sitting room with a fireplace. On the opposite end from the fireplace was another arched door that led out to a veranda outside the wall. Charlemagne followed an archway into another corridor on the right with a staircase on the left and a short passage further right. This led to a small foyer that connected with the other large foyer from before to the right. On the left was another set of arched doors, though no windows beside them. Manon quietly looked around as Charlemagne pushed the doors open, revealing a chapel inside.

The chapel had a transenna screen with a wooden door that divided it in two parts. Rectangular, wide chests were placed before the transenna. On the immediate left was a herald crest that depicted a wolf on two feet, carrying a patriarchal cross, while on the right was a large icon that depicted a young male in a black outer cassock with smooth fair skin, blue eyes, and reddish hair. A halo surrounded his head and he looked gently forward with a hand raised with pointed fingers to the words, 'Тадија.' The chapel was decorated with colors of gold, and the walls in half panels, one-half a smooth beige stone and the upper half decorated with icons, many icons, of saintly figures whose eyes followed through the entire room. The chapel had a small transept on the left and right, about four pews before the sanctuary, and a small altar. Atop of the altar was a tabernacle, itself secluded behind a screen gate that kept this golden cabinet-like box secluded further in a dark nook. Above the tabernacle were twelve icons, in a three by four grid of the apostles, met with three medium-sized icons on the left and right, John the Baptist and Saint Paul on the bottom, Saint Michael and Saint Gabriel in the middle, and Saint Joseph and Saint Mary at the top. Above the three-by-four grid was a large icon that depicted the crucified Jesus Christ.

Charlemagne's eyes fell towards the tabernacle directly across from him as he held the doors open. He stared at it for a whole minute as Manon looked at him.

"*Charles*, what's the matter with you?" Manon questioned.

Charlemagne flinched and looked back at her. "Sorry, I was lost in a thought – churches like these remind me of my youth… back when I used to attend church service, in East Anglia with my grandfather and in Allabrese with my parents until they allowed me to stop… and I never turned back since then. Why would I? None of it matters…"

Charlemagne closed the doors and then returned to the foyer. They continued into the large foyer where they began to go under the staircase into the south wing where there was a lavish hall with tall arched windows and an elongated dining table. At the end of the hall was a fireplace, and opposite the windows were additional murals painted. Above each archway in, one from the small foyer and another from the large foyer, were paintings placed above that depicted noble figures too. Charlemagne and Manon briefly looked about, seeing doors that went out onto the battlements that surrounded the dining room like a covered veranda. A side door in the west wing demonstrated the kitchen with a few primitive kitchen hardware, another fireplace, and a smaller dining table with overhang windows. Charlemagne closed the door behind them and journeyed back to the large foyer to climb up to the second floor.

The east wing of the second floor consisted only of a foyer corridor with suits of armor, these with medieval and early modern weapons, including halberds, swords of different types and sizes, maces, and other primitive weaponry. The room had many arched windows that were covered with curtains. Directly above the dining room was another ballroom like room, but with primitive and regal sofas and chairs with arched windows that looked out towards the hill. Rather than murals, this room consisted of wooden panel walls with the occasional portrait of a noble figure sporting a powered or dark-colored wig. In the west wing, the corridor was approximately the same size, but had more doors on the west end that entered into smaller and austere rooms with chairs, sometimes a small table, and cabinets or wardrobes, but no beds. The walls of these rooms consisted of smooth beige stone and the floors were covered with thin rugs overtop wooden floorboards. At the end of the west wing, directly above the main entrance foyer was another foyer corridor, with more portraits and arched windows on either end with restricted light, covered in curtains. On the left was a passageway that led down to the main floor, centre there was an arched door that led out to the battlement walls, and on the right was a passageway that led up to the third floor.

The west wing of the third floor consisted of similar sized rooms and corridor, but these contained primitive twin to queen-sized beds. They also had at least a wardrobe, chest, and a small stove in the corner with arched windows. At the end of the corridor was a primitive washroom. Directly above the large foyer and ballroom in the south wing, the pair found a two-story library with tall bookshelves and windows that looked southwards further. Charlemagne looked with awe at the contents of the library.

"Imagine the worth of all these books two-hundred years ago," Charlemagne expressed. "Now this is wealth…"

"Yes, immensely so, but is it new or old?" Manon questioned.

"Who cares, if there are books here, there may be something related to the Count."

Manon rolled her eyes. She began to examine the books before she joined Charlemagne to light some candles. They then sat their stuff atop of a large square table in the center of the room.

"I will examine some of the books," Manon remarked. "I am now convinced there is no harm here – go and look through the rest of the floors. I do not want to be here forever."

Charlemagne did not argue with her and came out to the east wing. On the third floor, the wing consisted of a short corridor with access to a stairwell that went up and down. Directly adjacent to the library and this wing was a storeroom with maps littered about in pigeon store holes. Beside this map room, there were also two bedrooms, which contained a lot more decoration and furniture than the other bedrooms but did not reveal any personal effects left behind that were distinct from other items. Notably in this corridor were portraits that bore the last name Újlaki on plaques. There were three in total, on the right of each door in this corridor, and the names on each plaque were written in Latin alphabet letters. These people were Farkas Újlaki (1658-1735), Etele Újlaki (1715-1775), and Ignác Újlaki (1763-1820). Ignác had fair skin and dark eyes. He also had dark hair with singes of white in his sideburns. He wore a military officer suit in his portrait fit with a hat. There was a fourth portrait, next to the exit, of another male, Géza Újlaki (1795-1873). After

Charlemagne finished examining these portraits, he came around to the stairwell corridor, climbed up, but could not get through the door at the top. He attempted to push through, but it would not budge. Charlemagne did not waste his energy to push through and instead went downstairs and returned to the library.

Manon ignored him, and he carried through to the west wing again, and up the stairs to the top level of that wing. The bedrooms were similar to the ones downstairs in this room, and exiting out in to the south wing, there was a veranda besides the rooftop with some windows looking into the library below. Charlemagne crossed the outdoors as it continued to rain, reaching a door at the end that led into the fourth floor of the east wing. He opened the door and came into a regal corridor, similar to the ones on the main floor, but without the murals and instead lavish portraits of figures with labels upon them. The men in these portraits were Csaba Újlaki (1826-1876), Dušan Újlaki (1854-1911), and finally someone named Vukašin Újlaki (1876-). There was no death year for Vukašin Újlaki. The portrait of Vukašin had also been torn off from the frame with a claw marks through. Charlemagne looked with unease as he saw this sight and stepped back. He looked towards the windows, pulling the curtains open, but it had grown darker since their arrival as the sun began to set. Charlemagne hugged the corner of the corridor and then turned to the door besides the portrait of Vukašin. A flash of lightning filtered through the room, followed by rumbles of thunder. Charlemagne ignored the weather and instead approached the doorknob and turned it open.

Charlemagne stepped into the bedroom and found it to be a lavish room with regal ornamental garments atop of the bed and plush pillows. The room had windows ahead and to the left as it was at the corner of the wing. In the corner of the room by these windows was a desk. He opened the drawers of the desk, revealing pencils inside, and also a few sheets of faint paper. He looked with unease at what appeared to be like claw marks around the base of the desk. He then turned around and took a closer look at the bedroom, seeing claw marks on the walls too. At the opposite corner of the room was a table next to a wardrobe, and atop of this table was an early twentieth century phonograph. Charlemagne stepped out of the room, quietly closed the door, and then stepped forward to the adjacent bedroom.

The adjacent bedroom was the master bedroom, larger than the previous one, but with more furniture including a chest, duvet sofa, and larger wardrobe. There was also a bolt-action rifle at the side of the bed, between the bed and an end table. Charlemagne checked the drawers to find some bullets inside. He then closed it and went over to a desk, but likewise with the desk in the adjacent bedroom, it was empty. He left the master bedroom and approached the final room at the end of the corridor, adjacent to the library rooftop. He entered into this room and saw that it was a study, with a chandelier in the center above a square thin rug, and a lavish desk on the far side. The windows in this room were rectangular. Charlemagne held the door open as he examined the contents of the room. He found more bookshelves on the left, a globe on the immediate left, and suits of armor behind the desk on the left and right. The desk also had a cushioned chair. Between the bookcases was a fireplace. Across from the fireplace were thin tables in front of the windows. At the far-left end was a mirror. Charlemagne made his way towards the bookcases as he searched for clues or other useful items. He slowly swept through the bookcases, shelf by shelf, seeing only encyclopedias and almanacs stored. He finally came to the end of the row and positioned himself in front of the mirror. He looked at his own reflection, at which point a flash of lightning entered the room and he looked at the left corner, reflecting the opposite corner of the room, as he saw the sight of a wolf-like face. Charlemagne gasped and immediately turned around, pulling the Beretta kept in his pocket and aiming it towards a tall painting that depicted a wolf, just a wolf, seated and eyes looking forward.

"Bloody hell…" Charlemagne remarked, looking towards the portrait. "What a fright…"

Charlemagne examined the unfinished painting and then looked beside it at where there were paint brushes and dried up acrylic paints. He stepped towards the door to exit, but stopped to notice a cloak hung behind the door. He placed his hands over the cloak and felt it was thin, black, and also large in size covered in fur as if an animal had brushed up against it one too many times whilst shedding, or it had caught shedded fur in the wind. Charlemagne examined the cloak, opened the door, and then left the room.

"I've concluded," Charlemagne said as he rejoined Manon, "that there is no wolf-man, while at the same time, I further assert that the wolf-man, *Chovavuk* as the old man called him, was not named as such."

Charlemagne explained to her the portraits detailing a genealogy of the Újlaki family by six generations.

"Whoever the last son in this family was, I believe he would have been the so-called wolf-man," Charlemagne expressed. "His name Vukašin Újlaki, where Vukašin is a first name, not a surname, and so this castle was named after the last son when it should really be known as the Újlaki Castle."

"What makes you certain that Vukašin Újlaki is the wolf-man?"

"His birth date," Charlemagne remarked. "The old man told us that the wolf-beast lived in the late nineteenth century and was raised by a caretaker. I believe that caretaker was Dušan Újlaki who died in the early twentieth century while Vukašin was born in the late nineteenth and his date of death… who knows when, but was likely sometime after his caretaker had died too. I don't know what the lifespan is for a potential half-man, half-wolf beast, but I'm in the least intrigued to do some follow-up later on when I can bother to do so and am not sca-scrambling to know what became of his grandfather…"

"Hm…" Manon responded, reading some journals, "well, luckily for us, Ignác Újlaki wrote in German in his journals, not Hungarian or Serbian, and so I can read much of what he's written here. In 1816, he writes that the castle was ransacked by bandits who stole from some of the most priceless items he held on display throughout the castle. He also expresses grief with the local authorities in the land, complaining about the lawlessness, and laments to live in Serbia surrounded by… Slavs. He then writes that he's going to seek to recover his items himself by hiring a Hajduks… Whatever that is…"

"Hm… we'll need to follow-up on that end then. What else?"

"Well, there's a list of missing items that he's eager to see returned to him, various jewelry items, a couple of mantle pieces, and then this one item, a bejeweled crown."

"Right?" Charlemagne remarked with intrigue. "Go on…"

"In the next entry, he says he's found a man named Zarko Jović who he paid to search for the bandits. Afterwards, there are a couple of gaps before an update is provided… A couple months later, Zarko arrives at the castle and informs Ignác that the bandits were themselves robbed by *Zigeuners*. What is that?"

Charlemagne chuckled and replied, "Gypsies – *tsiganes* in French."

"Ah," Manon affirmed, "well, the journal states that Ignác sent them back out to find the gypsies, doubling the reward." She then continued to flip through. "Let me see if I can find an update from there…"

Charlemagne nodded. The room then fell silent, which prompted Charlemagne to come to the window and see that it had grown even darker. However, as he looked out towards the rain, he noticed a group of men below on the plaza. These men had assault rifles in hand, were stocky figures, and appeared to be looking around as they split up into two groups of three.

Charlemagne looked at them closely and saw they appeared to be of fair skin.

"Oh dear," Charlemagne expressed, "er, Manon? We appear to have some company below…"

"What? What do you mean company?"

"I mean, it seems like either the Serbian Army, or British commandos have found us, and it's time to go…"

"I'm not done yet," Manon expressed, continuing to look down.

"It's time to go, my dear," Charlemagne remarked, pulling her arm. "You can take whatever you want with you, but we are leaving…"

Charlemagne took Manon's hand while she stuffed the journal into her backpack. The pair came into the east wing and Charlemagne took her down the staircase to the ground floor where they came out and moved towards the large foyer. The bandits entered in and began to look around, weapons drawn and looking about.

"*Charles*, who are these people?" Manon quietly questioned.

Charlemagne didn't immediately respond, but listened to them as they chattered in a Slavic language.

"Definitely not British," Charlemagne answered. "Come along now, we'll need to find another way out…"

Charlemagne took Manon back to the east wing, and they exited out through the veranda and came onto a patio besides the battlements that looked northeast. From the exit, there was a set of stairs that went down into the sublevel on the right, while directly ahead were collapsed stairs up along the battlements around the north end of the castle. The other group of bandits stayed put in the midst of the field as they looked around, keeping post at that exit point at the main entrance foyer. Charlemagne took Manon and they went downstairs into the sublevel.

"We'll have to keep low and go around," Charlemagne expressed. "I've had a second thought – they don't look like they're from the Serbian Army. Their uniforms are all different… I think these may just be hooligans looking to rob us of a treasure we didn't find, possibly sent in by Le Havre, maybe Al-Suli, I don't know, but they look worse than the Turks, that's for sure."

Charlemagne led Manon through the basement level cellar, and then around to a corridor beneath the south wing where they passed kitchens, store rooms, but as they were about to turn into the west wing, Charlemagne heard a whisper. He turned his head and faced one of these mercenaries straight on, resulting in them raising their firearm up and shooting bullets straight at him.

"*Merde!*" Manon shouted out.

"Hush," Charlemagne silenced. "Run!"

The mercenary shouted in his Slavic language as he found them. Both Charlemagne and Manon ran back the way they came, coming around to a tunnel besides the stairway out, especially as mercenaries entered through from outside and opened fire at them.

Charlemagne and Manon came out to a dead-end with a ladder that went up. "Climb! Climb! Climb!" he encouraged before doing the same. Manon then ran forth along the battlements of the north section of the castle while Charlemagne pulled out his gun and took a random blind shot down the hatch at the bandits. "Away with yee!" He fired another indiscriminate shot, and then the gun jammed. "Oh damn…" Charlemagne quickly ran off to join Manon as she went along the battlements, to a house at the end. As they entered the house, the initial group of bandits exited out from the large foyer and opened fire at them. The windows in the house shattered as gunfire sprayed in, causing both of them to duck down. "Crawl! Crawl!"

"*Tais-Toi!*" Manon shouted. "*Je sais ce que je fais!*"

Charlemagne followed Manon as she crawled to a staircase and then climbed down. They came to the ground floor and then turned around to find the exit through to the main foyer. The gunfire ripped through the courtyard door and windows. Charlemagne followed Manon out to the bridge and hurried straight towards the jeep parked behind the portcullis gate.

As the pair were about to enter into the car, Charlemagne took notice that the bandits had parked their GAZ-72 jeeps, colored army green, behind, blocking Charlemagne in.

"Oh, that's not very nice," Charlemagne expressed, fumbling around his pockets for the keys. "Where'd I put those keys…?"

"*Imbecile!* Here!" Manon remarked, pointing at them in the ignition.

"Ah, right," Charlemagne said, turning the engine on. He then hit the clutch and drove backwards, hitting the parked vehicle behind him with full force. The car slid back after some brief resistance. He then pivoted and exited in reverse just as the bandits exited out through the main entrance. "How about that?"

Charlemagne drove off from them, exiting out through the outer walls and along the road. He began to laugh as he looked to Manon who appeared terrified as she held on for life.

"Relax," Charlemagne remarked, "we made it."

"The bridge! Bridge!" Manon shouted, causing Charlemagne to brake immediately. He stopped right before the drop downwards to the rubble.

"*Faites attention! Imbecile!*" Manon yelled.

"*Je sais ce que je fais!*" Charlemagne responded to her in French.

"Ah, sure!" Manon mocked in English.

Charlemagne reversed backwards and then down the cliffside the way he came to pass the gulley, but as he came around to the upward slope, he noticed the mercenaries soon arrive and exit from their vehicles.

'Heads down!" Charlemagne encouraged Manon. Manon ducked. He attempted to drive up the side of the cliff, but could only reach a certain distance before the tires became stuck in the mud. After releasing his foot from the accelerator, the jeep began to slide back. "Uh oh…"

Bullets began to hit the side of the car, causing Charlemagne to duck down and cover himself too. The car continued to slide backwards, prompting Charlemagne to change gears, and reverse without looking. The car moved quickly backwards, hitting the back of the gulley. He then turned the wheel and drove forth and away from the bridge along the gulley as if it were a canyon.

After a moment of driving along, Manon raised her head while Charlemagne looked ahead with determination and fright. She released the tension from her position and looked ahead too. She was silent. Charlemagne was silent. He looked into the rear-view mirror as if expecting their pursuers. Eventually, the gulley merged with a clearing, and Charlemagne drove onwards as he passed the map to Manon.

"Tell me… tell me where I could pull off from here…"

Manon took the map and began to locate them. She then instructed him around and they came out onto a road in the midst of the forest from where they drove. They drove without end to the nearest town, and stayed put for a moment as they took a moment to breath. Charlemagne made no remarks. Manon read the journal and turned to Charlemagne.

"Zarko Jovic tracked the gypsies near a monastery – I have the name here: *Skete of Paraceletos*."

"Lovely," Charlemagne remarked. "And?"

"Oh… they were all dead," Manon expressed, "every last one of them – Ignác Újlaki is unsure what Zarko meant in those exact words, but according to Zarko Jović, they were all killed and their bodies looted. Ignác expresses doubts that it could have occurred, especially when Zarko provided no possibilities as to what could have happened. He believes that Zarko killed them all and looted their bodies, stealing the crown from him, but nonetheless, that's the end of it... Zarko and his men buried the bodies in a mass grave near the monastery grounds... and I suppose that's the end of it for us too..."

"We need to find that grave..."

"*Charles...*"

"No, I'm going to Romania to find that pit – it must still be there, and I want to learn more about this Zarko character while we're in Serbia too."

"*Charles*, that must be impossible... this Zarko, he is like a... mercenary, you can't expect him to have a journal like Újlaki or Amboise, and even if he did, where would you find it?"

"He must have been buried somewhere, have relatives..."

"You do not know Serbian..."

"I'll find someone who does..."

"And what about these men behind us?"

"Bah, just more bandits, like the ones that stole from Ignác no doubt, looking to steal from us too. Just a one-off encounter, that's all..."

"Impossible, who would dare go up to that castle expect us? They followed us, *Charles*."

"No, not possible," Charlemagne remarked. "Le Havre followed us, and he's been on my tail for a while, but that was because of Al-Suli. That Irish bloke took care of the lot of them, and I doubt that Le Havre would bother to come after us anymore. These were just some Serbs looking to get rich, hearing about us travelling around, but we'll lose them."

Manon shook her head in disbelief.

"Come along now, I still have a bit of money left," Charlemagne remarked. "We'll fill the car up and make our exit from this country in the meantime. Romania should be much safer, and I should be able to make contact with Mr. Adlington from Bucharest. We can have our things delivered to us, and we'll make a fresh start, right from where we left off – no more of this dangerous country, that's for sure."

"I don't believe you," Manon remarked, tilting her head to the side. She looked out towards the darkness beyond. "You are going to get us killed."

"Me? You and I killed?" Charlemagne questioned. "No, that's impossible – no, you're riding with Charlemagne, my dear. Did anyone ever get themselves even a bit injured in all those years we adventured together abroad?"

"Yes, you did, many times," Manon pointed out, "that's why we had to hire a doctor to join us, because Monsieur Adlington demanded it so."

"Ah, but did anyone else get injured?"

"No…"

"You see, nobody gets injured when adventuring with Charlemagne. Now how about a smile, my dear. Cheer up, I'll drive us to someplace nice, we'll have a meal, a rest, and we'll be back at it tomorrow morning. The adventure is not over yet; that crown is somewhere eastbound, and we are coming for it. If the pair of us can't find it, then no one can."

Charlemagne turned the car engine and drove back onto the road. Manon looked with unease as she continued to look out the car window.

"Why do I feel like you will be the death of me, *Charles*?"

"You're easily worried," Charlemagne answered. "Take in a deep breath… it'll all be alright."

"I am going mad… like you…" Manon expressed. "No more, *Charles*…"

"You wanted to join me on this adventure. You're here by choice, and if you want me to let you go once we're in Romania, then by all means, it's your choice. I'm happy to carry on by myself."

"I do not know how much more I can take of this…" Manon remarked. "I fear for you, *Charles*, I really do…"

"Nonsense, nothing to be scared of," Charlemagne remarked with a nervous laugh. "We've just been having some rough patches here and there, but we'll be fine from now on. I promise you."

Manon did not say anything more. She remained quiet for the rest of the car ride, and the rest of the night.

Act 4, Prologue

"Charles, I need to tell you something," Sabrina said, taking Charlemagne's hands. The pair sat beside each other in his Dolores-Ganß. The vehicle was parked at a drive-in theater at night. "Please don't take this the wrong way, but I'm worried about you…"

"Me? Why's that?" Charlemagne questioned. "What's wrong?"

"My dad was not impressed the other day, with the way you talked to him, and to be honest, I was not impressed either," Sabrina stated. "And then there was that other day at the diner, in front of those boys – that was not nice, Charles – that wasn't you."

"Those boys had disrespected you," Charlemagne stated. "What kind of a man would I be if I allowed them to say what they had without any consequences to it?"

"Alright, strangers are one thing, but my dad?"

"I didn't touch him. All I said was for him to mind his own business, because to be quite honest, Sabrina, he has you in his grasp like a tyrant that he is," Charlemagne expressed. "Is that how you like to feel at home? How long until he controls your thoughts too? Provided he hasn't already gotten to that point by the way he's brainwashed you and your brother, but pretty soon he'll be demanding to know what you think the more you come to think for yourself. What then?"

"Charles, it's my family, not yours. He's my dad, I grew up with him, and I can very well take care of myself when it comes to him and his parenting style than to have or need you to fend for me. Do you understand?" Sabrina asked. "The same goes for my brother. We don't need you to… to not be yourself in a way, because…"

"Not be myself?"

"Yes," Sabrina affirmed, "when you're mean or rude, it's not you. The you I know is the sweet you, the kind you, but throwing punches to other boys, and getting into a verbal dispute with my father, that's unlike you and I don't like that."

Charlemagne didn't respond.

"And to be quite honest, I feel like what you did in town the other day has somehow something to do with it – as if what you did was to try and impress me."

"How so?"

"You caused a county-wide blackout," Sabrina said, "the night of a meteor shower the same day in which I told you my father wouldn't let me go out with you."

Charlemagne gave a nervous laugh and replied, "Pure coincidence, that one. I didn't want to go out without you, so I stayed home and was tinkering a bit... How was I supposed to know that the power-grid was so fragile that my work would cause it to fail? At any rate, how is that any different than when I turned the tap water green? You loved that and thought it was hilarious."

"Because the water conveniently being my favorite color is nothing compared to the loss of power across the entire city, no less the hospital."

"Bah, hospitals have run without power for decades," Charlemagne remarked, "and besides, the power outage did not last very long."

"So you did do it then... on purpose..."

Charlemagne didn't answer and instead said, "You were able to look up at the night sky and see the shooting stars, weren't you? What more do you need to know than that?"

"I need to know because up to a month ago, the things you would do for me were too cute and meaningful, and played into your ingenuity, but now they seem impulsive and... increasingly reckless that I'm scared of what you would try to do for me, or how far you would go to do something for me in a way that would get you hurt."

"Don't worry, my dear," Charlemagne expressed, placing a hand over her hands on his hand. "Your fear for my safety as though you were to blame, but what I do is not because of you, it is because of how I am. I am Charlemagne, and I know no less to expect that all will be fine before I act."

"You told me the police were considering criminal charges for the power failure, and getting into a fight at the diner, that nearly got your arrested too. If my father didn't mistrust the police, he surely would have called them to kick you out of our house – by the way, he says you're not welcomed back anytime soon."

"Not to worry," Charlemagne brushed off. "It's all fine, it doesn't matter anyhow, dear, because you are very much welcomed at the manor."

"Except not by him."

"He doesn't need to know you're really there."

"I'm not lying to my father, Charles. You need to apologize to him, make it up to him somehow, because he's about an inch away from not letting me see you again. If he wasn't away right now, and my mom allowed me out now, we wouldn't be able to be together right now."

"And you will let him do that? To dictate your life?"

"Enough, Charles," Sabrina warned, "look, I just want to be assured that you won't do anything to hurt yourself and that this pattern of reckless and escalating behavior isn't because of our relationship, or anything like that."

Charlemagne smiled and released his hands. "I promise you, Sabrina, it is not. Now let's enjoy the film, shall we?"

Charlemagne and Sabrina both sat back in the convertible as the movie on the big screen ahead began. Just as the movie proceeded, a red convertible drove into the lot and parked next to them. Charlemagne looked over to see a male with dark hair and tanned skin sit with a female who likewise had tanned skin, but medium blonde hair. They were both young, around Charlemagne's age, but as they sat together, Charlemagne could hear them speaking to each other in Italian. They were having some sort of argument.

"Ugh, the nerve of this lot," Charlemagne muttered to Sabrina.

"Forget about them, Charles," Sabrina replied. "Just let them be…"

The Italian couple continued to argue together as the movie began, causing Charlemagne to bite his tongue. The male was more aggressive in his tone and hand gestures while the female passively complained and attempted to look forward towards the movie screen. Charlemagne looked over to them as the movie screen provide more light to see.

"Hang on, I recognize this pair," Charlemagne remarked, "that's Enrico Pinelli. That dodgy bastard was at the diner with Angelo. He ran off like a coward before the mounties arrived."

Charlemagne observed Enrico Pinelli from nearby. He had medium tanned skin and lengthy brownish-black hair. He also had dark and thick eyebrows. He wore a collared shirt and denim jeans with a sweater overtop. His girlfriend wore a brown jacket and denim pants with a pink scarf.

"Leave him be," Sabrina insisted. "Please, let's just enjoy the movie."

Both couples grew silent, and as the movie went on, Charlemagne extended his arm over behind Sabrina's neck. The film, a romantic comedy, drew laughs from the audience, but even as they and Sabrina laughed, Charlemagne continually eyed his foe over nearby.

After a few more minutes, Charlemagne began to hear them chirping to each other again. He heard their quiet murmuring, and although noticeable, he kept quiet and only occasionally paid attention until it grew louder. Enrico began to argue with his girlfriend, although he did so in a hushed tone, and she would respond with breathy and quiet rebukes to his statements. After another moment, Charlemagne overheard Enrico speak in a normal volume voice to his girlfriend as he continued to disagree with her. Enrico began to argue loudly, causing Charlemagne to tense a fist in his lap.

Finally, Charlemagne spoke and said, "Oy, can you two shut up! Some of us are trying to watch the film!"

"Charles," Sabrina scolded.

"Eh, what did you say to me," Enrico remarked in a perfect local accent, nodding his chin towards Charlemagne and giving him a lone stare. "You have something to say, *mangiacake?*"

"What did you just call me?" Charlemagne questioned.

"Charles, stop," Sabrina pleaded.

"Listen to your woman and sit down, Cabernet," Enrico remarked. "You're embarrassing yourself."

"I'm embarrassing myself? You're the one talking aloud during a movie – have some common decency, you… pasta-eating toad."

Enrico laughed at him. Charlemagne growled. Enrico continued to talk to his girlfriend in Italian as he ignored Charlemagne.

"Charles, I swear," Sabrina whispered to him, "just let it go. You don't have to prove yourself to anyone."

"It's not about proving myself to anyone," Charlemagne muttered. "It's about… ugh, you wouldn't understand, my dear."

Enrico continued to argue with his girlfriend, although he had quieted down, Charlemagne continued to listen. After a few minutes passed, Enrico returned to his normal volume as they continued to speak as though in opposition.

Charlemagne growled and picked up the drink he had in the cupholder. He slung it over and it landed atop of the hood of Enrico's car as he shouted, "Shut up!"

"What the hell?!" Enrico remarked. "You've done it now, *frocio*!"

Enrico jumped out of his car. Charlemagne got out of his seat and stepped out. He raised his fists up, but Enrico stepped forward without hesitation. Both males were about the same height. Enrico grabbed Charlemagne by the collar of his shirt. Before a fist could land at either person, a whistle blew and a loud voice in a P.A. system remarked, "No roughhousing in the drive-thru. Both drivers, please return to your vehicles or you will be asked to leave."

Enrico looked at Charlemagne with hatred. He slowly let go before he just flat out pushed Charlemagne back. He composed himself immediately and kept his eyes on Enrico.

"After this movie is over, you're dead…" Enrico threatened.

"I doubt it," Charlemagne remarked, "you'll be out of here with your tail between your legs. I know you – Enrico, you're all talk, no bite."

"Stop it, both of you," Sabrina intervened as she sat up. "What's wrong with you? What's with all this violence? I swear, if either of you lay so much as a fist on each other, I'm telling the police."

"Don't be ridiculous, Sabrina," Charlemagne replied.

Enrico laughed, "You have no control over your woman. You're weak, Cabernet."

"I'll show you – fine, she doesn't want us to fight, but I bet that I can out-run you in that bucket of bolts you call a car…"

"Oh, is that a challenge?"

"If I need to spell it out for your dull mind, then yes," Charlemagne replied.

"Alright then, Charlemagne, you're on – outside, now."

"What are you doing?" Sabrina questioned. "I told you – no."

"I'm sorry, my dear, but you said no to violence, but this isn't violence."

"If you race him, I'm leaving," Sabrina warned.

Charlemagne turned behind him. Enrico told his girlfriend to exit the vehicle, which she promptly did. He then turned back to Sabrina.

"For your own safety, I would advise you do so then," Charlemagne remarked.

Sabrina's jaw dropped at that word. She did not hesitate to open the door and step out. Charlemagne then started his car and drove around. He followed Enrico out of the drive thru and came out to the street ahead where he followed him around to a quieter part of town. The drive thru lot was on the outskirts of town, on the other side of the river, in the midst of the forest at the base of the mountain hills.

"First one from here to the other side of town at Calabrese Plains wins. The finish line is at the city limits. Rules are to stay on the freeway."

"Easy peasy," Charlemagne remarked. "You're on."

"At the end of three: three... two... one... GO!"

Charlemagne sped forward in the Dolores-Ganß while Enrico drove his 1976 Fiat 124 Spider. The cars sped off, reaching the intersection ahead with the freeway where they both turned right at the red light and without looking for oncoming traffic. Luckily, the streets were quiet and clear, and so they both made sharp and wide turns onto the freeway and then continued forth. The cars sped along the right lane of the freeway and began to try to keep up with each other. Charlemagne's car ticked up in speed, forty-miles to sixty-miles per hour. After a few seconds, they passed a single car that was travelling northbound on the freeway. The freeway ran along the river with the rail line besides. They drove along, reaching another intersection with a flashing green light, and carrying on through until they reached the interchange before the bridge. Charlemagne and Enrico both made sharp left turns and then sped forth to cross the Nattau River bridge. Charlemagne sped forward, catching air as he ran over the train crossing in the road.

Enrico sped along and the cars approached the intersection directly ahead after the river crossing. The light was red, but neither car cared to stop and they instead simply continued forward. They sped along through St. Allan's Plains, passing the farms on either side, and approaching the uphill section of the road that went up to Allabrese Plateau. At the top of the steep hill, both cars soared and then continued straight. A car driving the opposite direction honked at them, catching the driver by surprise, they continued to roar past the suburbs and approach the downtown core. The cars passed the RCMP detachment on the right, and then the office buildings further ahead. They passed downtown and continued along the eastern suburbs as they soon met farmland again in Champion Plains. The freeway had a slight curve to its design as it stretched across this large open space of farmland and fields. They passed three intersections, all of which had green lights, and they continued to drive forward as the end of the county jurisdiction was not too far away. Enrico sped forward ahead of Charlemagne as the Carella River bridge was not too far away.

Each car passed a sign that read, 'Leaving Nattau County,' at which point Charlemagne looked at the rear-view mirror to notice sirens followed with the wail of those sirens.

"Drat," Charlemagne remarked, "I can't be left in the dirt like this…"

Charlemagne sped forward and drove right up next to Enrico. The cars passed over the wooden bridge, passing the low and calm waters of the Carella that slithered along the flat plains. The cars continued forward for the last stretch neck to neck. Charlemagne pressed down on the accelerator with the RCMP cruiser behind, but as he was about to pass Enrico, Enrico pulled back and tapped Charlemagne's car on the corner, causing it to swerve out of control. Charlemagne took his foot off the accelerator and began to immediately attempt to regain control of his vehicle while Enrico sped off and won the race.

"No, no, no, no..." Charlemagne muttered as he gently applied the brakes, causing the vehicle to vibrate. "Oh damn, the brake rotors..."

The convertible slowed down, but flew off the road and into a field. It drove a few yards forward as Charlemagne hit the brakes forcibly, causing the car to come to a complete halt. Before Charlemagne could even flinch, the airbags activated and he was knocked out.

• • •

Charlemagne awoke a few hours later, a bandage wrapped around his head and seated on a stretcher in the midst of a clinic space. His arm was in a cast and in a sling, and he was lying back with a moan. He muttered, "What happened...?"

"What happened?" Vienna repeated, standing up as she sat beside him. "What happened? Have you lost your mind?" she questioned. "*Was ist los mit dir?! Ich werde dich töten, wenn wir nach Hause komme!*"

"*Mutter... wo bin ich?*" Charlemagne questioned.

"*Du bist im Krankenhaus. Ich werde den Arzt finden...*" Vienna replied. She then left.

Charlemagne continued to sit back. He looked up at the bright light above him, and then looked over as the curtain opened. Sabrina stood at the other side of the curtain and looked back at him with an unimpressed glance.

"Oh, Charles," Sabrina expressed, "you're alright."

"Yes... of course," Charlemagne replied, sitting up. "I suppose I had a bit of an accident?"

"A bit of an accident?" Sabrina questioned. "I saw your car – it's totally ruined."

"I could have won if that fiend had not knocked himself into me..."

Sabrina shook her head and replied, "I'm sorry, Charles, but I can't do this... all of this... this adventure is too much for me, and I'm not up to it. I'm sorry, but I... I'm breaking up with you... Goodbye."

Sabrina did not wait to say another word or receive a response. She left. Charlemagne looked back at where she stood, nodded, and then tilted his head back and stared into the lights above with a plain look upon his face.

Act 4, Scene 1

"Unbelievable," Charlemagne acknowledged. "You'll never guess what's just happened." He stood at the side of the UAZ jeep as it was parked on the curb of a street. Manon stood at the hood of the vehicle, examining a map of the local city spread out along the hood. At the bottom corner of the map it was written, *'București.'* They were parked on a quiet street in the midst of the city, surrounded by tall apartment complexes that were at least six stories tall with curved grey rooftops. "I swear I had my wallet with me from when got in the car, to when we parked and I got out. There's no logical explanation to what has just happened now. I went to the nearest teller machine, and in that moment I'm certain that someone's snatched me wallet from me trousers."

"What?" Manon questioned. "What are you saying, *Charles?*"

"What? What does it sound like I'm saying, Manon, I've just had my wallet stolen with the last bit of cash we had, and I haven't got the slightest idea of how we're supposed to contact Mr. Adlington now, or retrieve our belongings from Budapest, assuming they haven't been tossed or pawned off by now. I'm livid…"

"How could you have lost your wallet, *Charles*? Are you sure you did not leave it at the hotel?"

"I precisely remember having it in my hand as we left the hotel," Charlemagne argued. "There's no way it could have gotten lost, and my mind tells me that it was swiped of me." He came around to the driver's seat, opened the door, and began to rummage through.

"*Ah, mon Dieu,*" Manon swore. "What are we going to do?"

"I don't know, and I don't have any local currency or coins to use a payphone," Charlemagne said. "I don't have any sense of the Romanian language, even as a Romance language and being fluent in three of them. All I have is a bit of the currency left from Serbia, though I doubt anyone be willing to trade for it for Romanian currency."

"We cannot be stuck here, *Charles*."

"We don't' even have enough petrol in the car to be able to move any further than we are, so yes, you may as well believe that we are stuck here. Best bet, I think, is if we try to find the British embassy that way we could find some help... wherever that is..."

Charlemagne looked around the street as though it were supposed to be nearby. He then turned around and looked over to Manon.

"Does that map you bought at the inn point to anywhere?"

"No, not really..." Manon responded, looking slightly up though avoiding eye contact. "Since when do maps show place names, *Charles*?"

"Alright, alright," Charlemagne dismissed. "Let me think..."

"Why don't we just start to beg on the street, *Charles*, otherwise we will starve and die from this cold..."

"No," Charlemagne immediately denied, "we are not going to start to ask for strangers for money as though we were vagrants of some sort. I will not stoop to such level of poverty. I would rather die than face that humiliation."

"Humiliation? *Charles*, we are in the middle of a foreign city, who will humiliate you?"

Charlemagne didn't respond. He instead said, "I'll walk around, go from café to café until someone takes my money. I shouldn't need much to make an international call, assuming that even be possible. Take note of where we've parked, provided nobody jacks the car while we're away."

"Yes, I've done it," Manon replied. "Let's go..."

Charlemagne and Manon walked down the residential street they were at and came around to a street corner. The street corner took them around to a curved road that led to a roundabout. From the roundabout, they went further down the street to reach an avenue. The avenue was flanked by trees on either side, decorating the straight road, though the trees were far from decorated as every leaf had fallen from its branches and they were barren. The traffic along the avenue was tame, and after a moment wait, they crossed the street to the other side to try a café there. Charlemagne and Manon walked out a minute later after the Serbian currency was refused, and so they continued south.

The pair walked along the avenue, passing lavish stone apartment blocks that were barricaded behind stone and iron fences. These buildings were not very tall, and some were in need of maintenance over a crack in the wall or collapsing loose tile. Eventually, they reached a large intersection, round but not a roundabout, with many buildings around it and traffic driving through the centre in a peculiar manner. Some traffic drove around the centre as though it were a roundabout, while other traffic just went straight through. Charlemagne and Manon walked along the pavement and crosswalks to continue along a large street with four lanes in each direction. The buildings on this side, the south side of the intersection, were double the height like skyscrapers made of stone. These apartment and commercial buildings flanked either side of the busy street, though after half a mile on the right-hand side there was a wide pathway with parking on the right-most side. The pair observed the extent of commercial advertisements on large posters and billboards along this street. Additionally, some of the buildings varied from vintage like the apartment blocks from earlier, to modern in a brutalist construction with wide tinted windows and blinds. The heights of the apartments and commercial buildings varied from six to ten stories tall. The pair walked along the street until they reached a promenade to the right that passed along numerous cafes.

"There's got to be one in the dozen here," Charlemagne remarked.

Before the pair set forth along the lane, they stopped at both restaurants on the left and right, both of whom rejected Charlemagne's currency. They then walked further along the promenade to the rest of the cafes. The buildings along this lane were single story to double story in height, and at the end of the row of cafes they reached a regal white building. This building had columns grooved into its façade with brown cross windows and motifs of eagles in the corners. They walked further along where they reached a driveway that led to the main entrance of the building where up some steps were some thick white columns supporting a triangle pediment. In front of the structure was a rectangular and neatly kept garden, surrounded by low balustrades. In the midst of the garden was a statue of a nude woman. The front of this building, the *Ateneul Roman*, was surrounded by a plaza, which in itself was surrounded by three-story tall apartment complexes in a similar baroque architecture with columns, white to crème facades, and arched and sometimes flat rooftops. They continued down a perpendicular street where they passed another structure, this one longer and larger than the one before with an iron fence around the property. The façade of the building was crème with arched windows on the first and second floor, and then square windows on the third and fourth. It had no rooftop, balustrades in front of the even-numbered windows as well as the roof. There were also columns etched into the façade along the second and third floors. At the main entrance, a humble entry way compared to such a grand structure and had the Romanian flag at either side of it. The front garden around the main entrance, on the other side of a driveway around, was nearly trimmed. The pair set forth further along where they saw a round plaza across from the museum with a triangular statue almost like a thick needle. Around the top of the needle was a mesh of iron in the shape of a ball.

The street the pair followed along consisted of one lane in each direction, but it passed some beautiful sights and the architecture continued to consist of the Neo-Romance and Renaissance architecture in this section of the city. Additionally, on the right-side, Charlemagne found more cafés to attempt to exchange his money to. He was thrown out of each of them, forced to continue to walk until he reached another beautiful sight. This building consisted of two turrets on the left and right with square domed ceilings. The front partition had stairs that went up to the main doors, two columns on either side etched into the façade, and then an arched pediment. Underneath the arched shelter that the pediment created was a motif of two angels resting with a clock between them. Below this motif were rectangular windows, and then the main entrance doors. On either side, between the main partition and turret, there were three windows on the first and second floor, and overhang windows below around a basement level. Behind the pediment was a tall domed glass-centre. The front gardens were thin but better kept than other buildings with evergreen trees and shrubs. There was also a low green iron fence around the property. This building was called *Casa de Economii și Consemnațiuni* and was a bank. The street followed along a short distance to reach a bridge over a canal.

"*Charles*, we are walking too far from the car," Manon cautioned. "How do you know how to return?"

"Trust your map, just not your navigating skills, my dear," Charlemagne remarked. "I would rather die trying to trade this currency than to return to that bucket of bolts."

"You say that..." Manon muttered.

The pair continued along the next set of buildings across the river. These buildings were dissimilar to the rest of the ones they had seen. From the intersection across the river, there were numerous twenty story tall apartment buildings in a sort of art deco architectural style. They then walked inward to one of the streets that branched from the main road and found themselves between smaller buildings, but in rougher shape with graffiti tags on the walls and barred windows. They wandered around a street that surrounded by apartments until they finally found an exit to the main road. Here, they found themselves at another avenue, but this one divided by more trees and either side flanked by a consistent line of the same apartment block for half a mile. Charlemagne looked down the avenue with a bit of fright. He then began to walk forward. The pair continued down this avenue but did not see any cafés ahead.

"How awful," Charlemagne acknowledged. "I was never one to get involved in politics, ever, though I never sympathized with the Communist World, but I've heard stories of sights like these – apartment complexes like these, lined up, all the same, one and all. It's to become lost in… to question which is yours and what is your own. It's a frightening thing to say the least, no less than to actually live in that totalitarian system and way of life. Who could truly want it?"

"*Charles*, look," Manon said, prompting him to turn around.

At the opposite way from where they were walking towards was a large semicircle plaza surrounded by the road. They walked to the intersection and Charlemagne observed how even the apartment blocks curved with the road though keeping continuous with the rest of the apartments. Behind the semi-circle plaza where there were vehicles parked was a grand palace, like a casino in appearance, though it sat upon a tuft of green lawn in four layers of lawns bordered by low hedges and surrounded by trees in the background. This building was immense from side to side roughly three-hundred yards in length. The building was stacked like a cake. The first layer being the largest and four or five stories tall, the second layer placed upon that, two-thirds the size, and another five stories tall, and then the final layer being a third of that second layer right in the middle and center of the building at three stories tall.

At the plain centre of the roof was a pole that waved the Romanian flag.

"How fitting... imagine having to look at that from your low-income apartment," Charlemagne rebuked. "No wonder the Romanians had their way with their leaders nearly ten years ago..."

Charlemagne and Manon wandered down the street on the left and hey came to another unorthodox roundabout intersection where they were able to find some more restaurants and cafés to attempt to trade the currency with. Eventually, Charlemagne met with a man in a café which had a payphone inside it.

"You give me: coins for the payphone," Charlemagne spoke, attempting to annunciate his words. "I give you this..."

The man spoke to an older man behind in Romanian, and then they completed the trade and Charlemagne was given some coins for the payphone.

"Thank you, very much," Charlemagne acknowledged, putting his hands together and bowing. "Finally..."

Manon walked with him to the payphone. He inserted the coins into the payphone and then picked up the phone.

"Let's see if I remember how to do this..." Charlemagne muttered. "Should be just like this..." He dialed a '1' and then proceeded with a ten-digit phone number. He waited as the number dialed. He looked at his watch as he waited. No answer came through. "What the devil? Where's that man?"

"*Charles*, what a time difference we must have," Manon scolded. "Here, let me phone my *père*." She took the phone from his hand, and with the last coins in their hands, they inserted them through and waited. "*Allo, papa. C'est moi, Manon...*"

"Perfect, thanks," Charlemagne remarked, taking the phone from her hand. "Hello, Dr. Dumas?"

"*Allo, Charles*?" Dr. Dumas remarked. "What's happened? Where are you and Manon?"

"Funny story, professor, don't worry about us. We're in the Romanian capital, lovely place really. We've been safe and sound out here, still searching for those Crown Jewels, but we've run into a bit of a pickle… you see, I seem to have lost my wallet – fancy that, less than a second on the streets of Bucharest and already had myself pickpocketed…"

"Oh, that's too bad…"

"Yes, well you see, I'm going to need a favor – I'm going to need you to loan me some money… I can't seem to reach any of my people in Canada because it is late, you see, so I- we were hoping you could loan us… say oh… a couple hundred Francs?"

"What about Manon? What happened to her wallet?"

"Manon's wallet? Oh, yes, that too… not with us at the moment. She seems to have, uh…" he said, looking at Manon. "Left it behind in our hotel in Budapest and doesn't seem like we'll be going back to get out things from the hotel. We were staying at the Equinox Hotel and just like that… we're now in Bucharest, so if you could send a money order in for us at any post office in Bucharest, that'd be grand, old chap."

Dr. Dumas sighed and replied, "*Bien*, I'll go to the post office then… What progress have you made so far, *Charles*?"

"Tremendous progress, another step forward towards finding that crown, certainly. We're on our way to a grave site near a Paraclete monastery in Romania to inch us towards that next clue. I'm certain it's out east somewhere here, and we'll find it, I assure you."

"*Bien*, I trust you, *Charles*," Dr. Dumas remarked, "but please be careful, especially with my little girl. I'll send your money, but please give the phone back to Manon."

"Very well, thank you, Dr. Dumas," Charlemagne replied, passing the phone. "He wants to talk to you."

Manon uncrossed her arms and received the phone into her hand. She proceeded to talk to her father in French while Charlemagne went and sat down. After a brief conversation,

Manon placed the phone down and then walked over to where Charlemagne was sat. She held her arms crossed again.

"Finished?" Charlemagne asked.

"*Oui*," Manon replied.

"Excellent, I believe I saw a post office nearby," Charlemagne remarked. "I've heard of money being able to be sent instantaneously thanks to the wonder of the World Wide Web. Let's hope this forsaken land has reached that level of technology and isn't still using carrier pigeons."

Charlemagne and Manon travelled from the café to a nearby post office. They waited for a moment, and thankfully, they used a computer. The clerk slowly typed the name Charlemagne had spelled out on a piece of paper.

"*Hier ist es*," the clerk spoke in broken German.

"*Gut*," Charlemagne replied.

"*Ausweis, bitte*," the clerk asked.

"*Wat?*"

"*Ausweis*," the clerk remarked. "*Identifikation?*" He then spoke to a colleague in Romanian while Charlemagne tensed his fist atop of the counter.

"*Ich habe meinen Ausweis nicht dabei*," Charlemagne answered, placing a hand at his heart. "*Aber ich bin bekannt. Kennst du mich? Ich bin Charlemagne de la Cabernet...*"

The clerk looked at him dumbfoundedly and shook his head.

"*Tut mir leid... ich weiß nicht, wer du bist. Ausweis, bitte...*"

"*Ausweis!*" Charlemagne yelled, slamming his fist onto the counter. "*I don't have any bloody identification with me! How can you be so dense to not know who I am? Why I... oh, what's the use...*"

The clerk shouted out to his colleague who came over. He began to bark at Charlemagne in Romanian.

"Oh, shut your mouth, you brute," Charlemagne remarked, irate. "I've had it with this place... I'll go to another post office. Bloody youth, can't even recognize this face."

Manon stayed quiet and followed him outside. They walked around before they came to a café where they sat down at a table. Charlemagne thought for a moment.

"*Charles...*" Manon remarked, "why don't we go back to Budapest and get our things?"

"Nope, no can do," Charlemagne immediately denied.

"Why not?"

"Not enough petrol in the car for a start..." Charlemagne remarked. "I also don't want to go to Budapest. Look, I'll phone Mr. Adlington and have him send someone to Budapest to fetch our personal effects, but I won't go there... no way."

"Why?" Manon insisted.

Charlemagne shook his head and said, "We've got to keep moving forward. We can't look back or go back. We can't waste time. We need to... we need to just focus right now on getting to that graveyard or mass grave, or have you."

Manon looked at Charlemagne with concern. She observed his knee bouncing up and down as he tapped his foot into the ground. He also looked around his surroundings as though suspiciously.

"*Charles*, what about some help then?"

"Don't need it? Why would we need help?"

"A tour guide?"

"With what money? I can't even seem to be able to bloody get the money your father sent to us..." Charlemagne cursed. "I'm just trying to... trying to think of a way to get that money. I'll have to keep going to post offices until someone recognizes me... maybe I should shave..."

"Yes, please do," Manon remarked. "I do not like the beard..."

"What?" Charlemagne replied, touching his beard. "What do you mean? I though the beard was well-received, at least that's what I've been told... I've received more affirmation than to be clean-shaven."

Manon sighed and looked aside. She then turned the other way as she noticed a glance. She squinted at the person ahead, prompting Charlemagne to look as well. This woman waved at them and came forward. She held a smile on her face. Charlemagne's eyes focused on her.

"Do I know this woman? Why is she so familiar?" Charlemagne asked aloud.

"Hello," the woman greeted. The woman had fair skin and dark black hair. She wore a winter wool coat and leggings underneath a skirt with high heel boots. She also wore a fur cap and designer purse. "What a pleasant surprise…"

"I remember you," Charlemagne said, standing up, "you were at the museum in Berlin. Fancy that – much pleasure to see you again, my dear." He shook her hand with both his hands. "I don't seem to remember your name though, what was it… Helena?"

"I don't seem to remember telling you my name," the woman responded. "The name is Irina – Irina Pachayevskovna…"

"Ah, Polish?" Charlemagne questioned.

"No," Irina flat out denied. "What brings you to Bucharest, Mr. Cabernet?"

"Oh, well, just in town for a bit of an expedition…" Charlemagne remarked. "I'm on another adventure, out here in Eastern Europe, looking for something more enticing and valuable than the Florentine Diamond was. Me and my partner – research partner, that is. Ms. Pachayevskovna, this comrade of mine is Dr. Manon Dumas, expert in European history, her father himself an expert in European history too."

"Pleasure to meet you," Irina remarked.

"What brings you to Bucharest then, miss?" Charlemagne asked.

"I'm in town for some shopping," Irina replied. "My boyfriend and I live out of town…"

"Ah, really? Your boyfriend, huh? Is he the man you were with at the museum?"

"Yes."

"How fascinating…"

"What are you searching for at the moment, Mr. Cabernet?" Irina asked. "My husband, you see, he's a bit of a… collector of rare items."

"Oh, is that so?"

"Yes, he was jealous that he was unable to pocket that diamond for himself," Irina replied. "He likes to collect whatever he can, and he can afford it too, mind you."

"Can he now?"

"Yes," Irina remarked, "and not that a wealthy man like you needs that sort of financial assistance, but as a wealthy collector and man of connections, he may be able to assist you while you are this side of Europe."

"Really?" Charlemagne asked.

"Yes."

"Is that so?" Manon remarked, looking over to Charlemagne. "*Charles* – why not?"

"No," Charlemagne denied, "no thank you."

"What?" Manon questioned. "Do not listen to him," she said to Irina. "*Charles*, how can you say such a thing?" She looked back at Irina and apologized, "Do not listen to him. We have not had the best of luck it seems… We are… *fauché*… out of money…"

"Nope, no we're not," Charlemagne remarked. "Do not listen to her – the great Charlemagne is not a poor man. We're well off and don't need any sort of charity from anyone."

"Hm…" Irina responded, "very well. I respect if you do not want to work with my boyfriend, but a word of advice to you both… Be careful as you travel through Romania and the rest of Eastern Europe. The people in this part of Europe are… not as friendly as those in the West. The people here would not hesitate to hurt you, steal from you, or both to even kill you for what you own. Please, tread carefully…"

194

Irina took some currency notes from her purse and placed them on the table, nearer to Manon.

"Be careful, and if you change your mind... here..." Irina remarked, writing on a piece of paper. She then slipped it towards Manon.

"*Merci beaucoup*," Manon acknowledged, bowing her head. "*Merci beaucoup*."

Charlemagne crossed his arms and Irina left. He watched her off and then looked distastefully at Manon.

"What is wrong with you, huh?" Manon questioned. "Are you such a stubborn fool to not accept a bit of help?" She stood up. "*Incroyable...*"

Act 4, Scene 2

"Just so we're on the same page," Charlemagne said, "just because I've had a change of heart in the matter of whether we visit them at their home does not mean that I would seriously consider their assistance."

"Is that so?" Manon questioned, unimpressed.

The pair sat in the UAZ jeep as Charlemagne drove along a road that stretched across hill after hill, separated by either farmland, grassy pasture, or dense forests.

"I seem to remember that the noise from your stomach made you realize that our situation is dire, *Charles*. We are in the middle of nowhere, no money, no identification, and with who knows who behind us trying to capture us, kill us, or sell us to slave masters."

"Yes, well, that's an unfortunate situation to be in, but adventures these days come at a price, especially when you're this world renowned."

Manon rolled her eyes.

"I've heard it be said that the next millennium will be age of connection, especially with the innovation of the Internet. I've spent my fair share in the computer sciences, lending my expertise to a laboratory in the United Kingdom, and we all knew that what we were doing was revolutionary – the technological revolution. Pretty soon, every man, women, and child too, will be able to have a computer at their disposal, and it will be that item of which they come to rely on. The computer has become the single-handedly most important invention since the wheel; the computer is representative of the very notion of technological advancement. The computer has made it possible for one to communicate with a person from say Japan to another in Europe in mere seconds. The progress that is made each year only becomes greater and greater… just you wait…"

"I am waiting... waiting to see what point you are trying to make."

"My point is, my little dear, is that when I began to roam the world a decade or two ago in search of historical secrets, who had yet been blessed to know my name? I had just yet had my time. When my father resigned from Cabernet Industries, he divided his shares which were around sixty percent, into three-thirds to each of my siblings. His idea, no doubt, was to have us cooperate like some sort of triumvirate and make the decisions to spite the corrupt leadership at the time. You haven't met my siblings, but those two were not the ones that should be making such decisions. My younger brother had only just turned eighteen that year, and so I advised him and my sister on what needed to be done, and they knowing of my genius entrusted in me to do what needed to be done. However, I knew that I could not rely on their trust forever, so I maneuvered myself to consolidate power and in that short period, I became known to the world. I was on magazines and newspapers in every country from Harlech to New York, to London and Berlin, all the way back around to Beijing and Tokyo. The people asked themselves, who is this Charlemagne de la Cabernet? I though did not have the stomach for business decisions in the long run, so I placed the people I could trust in seat of power, who to my advantage themselves did not seek the fame and attention I could relish in, but I did not want to be known to the world as a business magnate. Cabernet Expeditions was to be what I wanted to be known for, but the stupid media did not want to cover Cabernet Ex, so I fought for the spotlight and with time, I've gathered it – the Florentine Diamond will no doubt be the most media coverage I've managed in a long time, and it came at a cost. Although media outlets have not had much interest to recognize my brilliance, those in the black market and other nether regions have taken notice to me. What can I say? I'm a wanted man, by and large, just by the undesirable and crooked. Not now though

– now I will find that crown and I will return to the West as a spectacle – what great things Charlemagne has done for us, they will say. Yes… they will say…"

Manon looked back at Charlemagne and then out the window. The UAZ continued to drive along the Romanian countryside and they drove past the hills and came into a forest. By evening, as the sun set, they eventually reached a settlement, a small town, from where they began to pass some houses. Manon looked at a map she bought and began to navigate them through.

"I do not know what to expect from this home," Manon said, "but it could not be here, could it, *Charles*?"

They continued to pass small homes as they drove along a stone brick street. The car came around on a bend and then forward. The houses in this village were single-story and constructed of red brick with red tiled roofs. They followed the brick street and passed a commercial building constructed purely out of red bricks. Across from them at an intersection was another building of entire brick. In the background there was a plain concrete cylindrical tower with a metal ladder on the side. Charlemagne turned left and came along a paved road that passed an enclosed park on the left with tall grass and trees, and shrubs and trees on the right with gravel lanes that stretched out. They continued past some plain white buildings with pointed red tile roofs.

"What's that…" Charlemagne remarked. "Looks like another bloody church…"

Charlemagne observed a tall, peaked tower in the background ahead, stretching upwards from a brownish-grey brick building with turrets and tall reddish rooftops. As they went further along the road, they both took notice that that this structure was a castle sat atop of a tall hill in the midst of the town. The castle was well-lit with spotlights around the perimeter to shine incandescent light upwards along the tall outer walls of the castle. Along some of the turrets along a lengthy partition of the castle there were some banners in red and blue, displaying a black bird symbol upon them. Atop of the pointed rooftop of the turrets were flags that bore the Romanian colors. Charlemagne observed that as they drove around, the castle loomed over them while Manon continued to study the map.

"Oh great, another castle," Charlemagne muttered.

"What do you mean? We are in Europe – the only building there is more of in Europe than castles are churches and monasteries."

"Why do I get the feeling that this castle is our destination."

"What lane are we at? It may be…"

The car drove around and proceeded to go uphill. They continued upwards up until they reached a stone arch at the end of the lane. The arch had an iron gate with another arch made of black iron within. The gate led into a courtyard on the other side that was surrounded by a ten-foot stone wall. In front of the stone arch was a small kiosk. Along the stone wall there were floodlights that illuminated the perimeter. The car drove into the short driveway to reach the kiosk where a man in a suit sat inside on a chair.

The man opened the window and looked at Charlemagne. He looked at the bullet-ridden car and then back to Charlemagne as he asked a question in Romanian.

"Sorry, don't speak, uh… er, Romanian," Charlemagne said. "*Englisch oder Deutsch?*"

"Reason for visit?" the grunt spoke in a heavy Romanian accent.

"We were invited," Charlemagne answered, "by Ms. Irina Pech…youskayovna."

"*Pachayevskovna?*"

"*Da-* I mean, yes."

"Name? Identification?"

"No identification, unfortunately, but the name is Charlemagne de la Cabernet…" He looked over to Manon. "And

Dr. Manon Madeleine Dumas, also without identification. We spoke with Ms… with Irina a few days ago. Go ahead, call her."

The man looked at him and then picked up a phone in the booth. He spun a rotary phone and then waited. He spoke in Romanian and had a brief conversation. Charlemagne overheard his name spoken, prompting him to look at Manon and raise his eyebrows with confidence. After a quick minute, the man put down the phone and turned to them.

"Just one minute," the man remarked. "We are verifying with Lady Pachayevskovna."

"No problem, take care your time…" Charlemagne replied, tapping his fingers on the steering wheel. The man stood tall in the booth as he waited while Charlemagne awkwardly looked at Manon. The phone rang after a few minutes and the man picked up. The man answered in brief positive responses, "*Da…Da…Da…*" He then hung up.

"Lady Pachayevskovna could not be reached, but Sir Rubashkin has welcomed you to come inside," the man remarked, pressing a switch and causing the gate doors to automatically open, though slowly. "Welcome to Castle Samandar… please park inside and walk to the bridge."

"Much thanks," Charlemagne responded, rolling up the window. He drove in and came around to the courtyard. The courtyard was triangular shaped and the base that looked towards the castle had a lower wall with turrets in each corner. At the center of the base were a few steps up to a ten-foot-wide bridge up to the main entrance. "Well, here we are…"

Manon looked over to the castle as she continued to sit in the car. "I could not imagine paying the electricity bill of such a place." She then opened the door.

Charlemagne and Manon walked from the car to the steps up to the bridge. They walked across and it was a fair length bridge, about fifty feet up to a tall arched wooden doorway. As they walked, Charlemagne looked over the bridge and down to the drop by about another fifty feet to the bottom of a gulch that ran straight through. The castle stood tall from the other side of the courtyard, the base of the structure being fifty feet. The castle was surrounded with tall trees.

The pair approached the main entrance of the castle where the arched door loomed over them. Charlemagne sheepishly approached forward and knocked. He then stood back and looked up at the door, but then a small rectangular door within the door opened on the right and another man in a suit looked towards them.

"Oh, hello, we…"

"Come," the man simply spoke, stepping aside and ushering them in.

"Oh, thank you," Charlemagne responded, allowing Manon in first.

They entered inside and came into a square foyer with a tall vault ceiling connected with columns. The walls around the castle were thick grey stone bricks with a rough texture. The floor on the other hand were wide smooth tiles. Along the columns were dual-head lamps that provided electrical lighting into the foyer, and above them were the same red-blue banner across the length of the corridor to the right. This corridor consisted of dual vault ceilings and columns, approaching a shorter wooden archway door at the end, and with two archways with scarlet red curtains on either side. Along the floor on both sides of the corridor were wide velvet rugs. There were also plenty of furniture; narrow tables, chairs, benches, and duvets, addressed along the wall. The windows on the right-side of the corridor also had red curtains.

"Well, at least it seems a lot more livelier here," Charlemagne acknowledged.

The man closed the door behind them and then led them forward. They came to the end of the corridor where he opened the doors and entered into long and tall hall with more vault ceilings. The room was dim, on the right-side the curtains along the narrow, pointed windows were shut, and before them were tables with the occasional vase or token, and in between these were tall suits of dark-colored armor with swords and other weapons. The knights were positioned with their legs a foot apart, hands together at the front, clutching the base of their long weapon and the tip of the weapon firmly on the ground. On the other side, there was a similar sight, though instead of windows there were mounted heads of apex predators: a rhino, a saltwater crocodile, and a grizzly bear. In the middle of the room was a long and wide rug up to a fireplace at the end where there was a coffee table, a couch on the right and an armchair on the left. The fireplace was lit and its fires glowed light and radiated warmth. At either side of the fireplace were two more suits of armor, and above these were two more mounts, though empty. Above the fireplace mantle was a tall portrait of a man seated in a chair with a Rottweiler at this side. The man wore a suit and had his right ankle placed atop of his left knee, hands together, as though he were rubbing them together, if not folded over. The man had a fairish to tan complexion with a hooked nose and dark eyes. He also had short dark hair and almost slanted eyes. The man who led them inside offered them a seat at the couch and then left. Manon sat down, while Charlemagne looked around and rubbed his chin as he went around the fireplace before turning around at the sound of a door opening behind the armchair. Charlemagne saw the silhouette of a figure enter through the doors. The man closed the door behind him and then stepped forward towards the fireplace as Manon stood.

Charlemagne identified the man not just as the one in the fireplace mantle picture, though with a slight widow's peak, but also as the same person who was with Irina in Berlin. He wore a dark suit even now with a black collared shirt and tie, and he approached Charlemagne with a light smile.

"Mr. Cabernet," the man spoke with a nasally East Slavic accent, "such a pleasure for you to come to my home."

"Mr. Rubashkin," Charlemagne responded. "Please, call me Charlemagne. With me is my colleague, Dr. Manon Dumas."

"If you are just Charlemagne, then I am just Avdiyi. Irina mentioned to me that you were in Romania, and I had hoped you would come to visit, to collaborate with me. Isn't that right?"

"So the thought was," Charlemagne simply replied, looking about. "Irina told me you were a collector of various goods. Where do you keep your collection?"

"Throughout my home, some in storage," Rubashkin responded. "In this room, all these animals you see here, I have shot and killed with my own hands."

"You mean with your own rifle," Charlemagne corrected. "You must be quite the marksman nonetheless."

"As a citizen of the former Soviet Union, of course," Rubashkin replied. "I was trained well, not just in military training, but in recreation. I've hunted since I was a young boy... What about you?"

"Apparently I've been out to hunt ducks before with my grandfather before he passed away, up north in Scotland, though I'm told it was rather uneventful nor can I remember it," Charlemagne simply stated. "What about these then? What do you intend to put here?"

"Here," the man pointed to the left, "the head of a lion, taken from the savannahs of Africa. There," the man pointed to the right, "the head of a grey wolf, taken from the tundra of North America."

"How exciting," Charlemagne replied, "what else do you have?"

"Come and see," Rubashkin insisted, taking them away from the lounge. He led them through to a corridor on the other side. The corridor had paintings on the left opposite windows, and before the windows tables with more vases. "You'll find in my home paintings the likes of which you have never seen before, and although beautiful, these are not just any works of art. These are the works of famous painters: Guido Reni, Peter Paul Ruben, Eugène Delacroix, Caspar David Friedrich, Francois Xavier Fabre, Ivan Aivazovsky… to name a few."

"I'm not much of an arts historian…" Charlemagne expressed, "though I know about half of those names."

"You are not, but I am," Manon expressed. "In university, I adored to learn and admire the great works of art…"

"Ah, a lady of good tastes then, it seems," Rubashkin remarked. They passed a few scenic paintings attributed to Aivazovsky and Albert Bierstadt, and Frederic Leighton. A specific painting on display near the end of the room showed a scene from antiquity, a young, ruddy adolescent with wavy reddish-brown hair in a tunic robe playing the harp while cross-legged before a throne with an older male seated in majesty with a scowl across his face.

At the end of the hallway, they entered a round room where in display cases there were numerous suits of armor of different varieties and different cultures, from East Asia to Africa, and back to Europe. In a display case between the suits of armor and also against the walls were many different weapons on display, swords of all sorts of varieties and cultures too.

"These were taken from Japan, dating to medieval times," Rubashkin explained. "Here you have the traditional suit of armor for a samurai, while here you have the traditional suit of armor of the European knight and next to it, a British commando shock trooper from the Great War trenches."

Charlemagne looked at the contrasting samurai suits of armor, one in red, and the other in yellowish black. He then looked at the European suit of armor, which was black and engraved at certain parts such as the gauntlet and chest. He then looked next to it to the armored uniform of a British soldier, fit with an elephant trunk gas mask, flat helmet, and trench coat.

Charlemagne also looked at the armor in the centre of the room, which consisted and was made of bones; a helmet of bones and mane out of feathers. The material was primitive, though the costume was beautiful crafted.

"Ah, these were taken from Central to South Africa, and the ones behind from America. Come around here, you can see the traditional armor of an Aztec warrior, this one recovered from Central Mexico and the other from the Caribbean Islands along the coast of north South America."

Charlemagne looked at the last suit of armor, also consisting of bones though its helmet was spiked with horns protruding outwards in different directions, and two central horns that protruded outwards like a ram. The rest of the protective pieces of the outfit consisted of bones, while the fabric was reddish-black and like a robe.

"From this particular island, the chief warrior was also the chief priest," Rubashkin explained. "The weapon of the soothsayer on the battlefield was also the weapon at the altar."

"Very peculiar…"

Rubashkin then took them to another corridor where they passed some more artwork, this time from classical antiquity scenes, while between them were display cases that contained decorative egg-shaped objects inside.

"These were recovered after the collapse of the Soviet Union," Rubashkin remarked. "They were believed to be from Russian nobility, confiscated and kept by the communist government."

"And how did you come to them?"

"Please, Charlemagne, I have my secrets," Rubashkin remarked. "For me, it is not difficult to ask and receive in Russia. I have friends all around. Surely you must understand, as a businessman yourself, to have connections across all North America."

"Hm, I suppose," Charlemagne simply replied. "You are in business?"

"Yes," Rubashkin affirmed, "my company is among the largest producers of natural gas and oil in all of Eurasia. We just recently acquired Petrolgrad Neft as well. You must have heard of my company, Strannik Neft."

"I believe I have," Charlemagne remarked. "My apologies, but a lot of these new companies that have entered into the international market in the past five years, I'm still learning. I've been away from the business in a certain sense to focus on my historical ambitions. I would not be surprised if my company deals with your company."

"Indeed, we do," Rubashkin replied, "but I fully understand. Sometimes too, as a collector, I can be detached from the business, though I do try to pay attention. Come, I will show you the heart of my museum."

Charlemagne and Manon entered into a grand hall, two stories tall with a staircase at the end that went up to the second-floor veranda corridor that stretched down left and right. This room had numerous bookshelves against the walls, some of which were encased with wooden glass cabinet doors to store texts on the other side, or sometimes other effigies, small statues, or other items. Between some of these bookshelves were larger rectangular display cases, or small square ones with items on display atop of plush cushions, or one raised velvet stands inside. Charlemagne and Manon entered separate corridors as they looked and then joined Rubashkin before the staircase.

"I'll say, if this is all what you have on display, then I don't want to know what you have in storage," Charlemagne remarked. "There seems to be quite a lot. Very impressive..."

"So, how could I be of assistance to you, Mr. Cabernet?" Rubashkin asked. "Take a seat."

The group walked towards some seats in the center of the library.

"What are you looking for at this time?" Rubashkin questioned.

Charlemagne looked at Manon, and then over to the collector. "I'm in Eastern Europe searching for something quite precious, the French Crown Jewels, more specifically, the Crown of Emperor Charlemagne, thought to have disappeared at the start of the French Revolution."

"And what progress have you made?"

"A fair bit to come around to Romania, but seems like the item was lost around this part of the world around the early nineteenth century, most likely the 1830s when it was taken off some gypsies. At this time, we're a bit lost at that dead end."

"Hm, very unfortunate then," Rubashkin remarked. "Let me say though, there are many treasures in this part of the world. The Soviet Union greatly ignored the historical studies, choosing to focus on what they could do to enhance their ideology than to participate in the progress of historical research."

"Yes..." Charlemagne affirmed.

"I did my best five years ago to collect what I could in encyclopedias, anthologies, and other texts to store them in this library," Rubashkin remarked. "Before like the Great Library of Alexandria, that wealth of knowledge could sink into an abyss, I took hold of it and here it lies."

"Is that so? Interesting, except neither of us would speak any of the local languages from the Balkans or Mother Russia to know what they say. In that sense too, we are a bit of a loss."

"So, you need help then."

"We're seeking some assistance, yes," Charlemagne confessed. "I would not say we need the help, but it would make the task ahead of us easier than to roam on and on. I just have one concern though – my interest in locating this crown is to have it on display for others to admire, and for the entire world to know what was once lost in the dark is now for sight in the light."

"Yes."

"If I were to consider working with you, I would need some sort of assurance that it would be so and not locked up here. I'm intrigued to the say the least, and you have connections, so maybe we could work out some sort of deal."

Rubashkin laughed and replied, "No, I believe I have more to sell to you than you sell to me, so I will have to insist that you let me have the crown if we were to partner, but to let the crown be on display... I would not be opposed as long as it were mine and all people know it was mine. If it is the admiration of the crown of everyday people, then it can be done."

"Hm... your crown, eh?" Charlemagne said.

"Yes, you can have the crown go anywhere you'd like to be on display in whatever museum, but as long as when that ends, and the public lose interest, it can rest with me here, and that wherever lent to they know it is mine, then that should be no problem. Now, I have much to offer you, lots of resources to aid in that search for the crown, but with your mind and my resources, we should find this crown in no time."

"I am thinking that if the crown was here, then it could have gone anywhere from south to north to even east over the Black Sea," Manon remarked. "We would need access to shipping logs, rare items, anything that could be checked to see what went in and out of the country."

"Yes, Dr. Dumas is the expert here," Charlemagne expressed. "Why don't you tell him what we need, and I'll be right back. Do you have a washroom I could use?"

"Yes," Rubashkin responded, snapping his fingers to the attention of a guard wandering around. He spoke in Romanian to him, and the guard guided him out.

Charlemagne was led out of the library and into another corridor where there was a room on the side. He entered into the room, flicked a light switch, and then saw the room light up and reveal its marble floor and spacious space. In the corner of the room, on a small pedestal, was a marble statue of a nude young male with a hand to his chin and looking aside. The statue was at least seven feet tall and next to a large tub in the corner which separated from the other side of the room by a glass screen. Charlemagne walked over to a counter next to the screen with a mirror and he looked over to the exit and ran the sink. He then began to walk around the room, coming around to a cabinet near the marble statue. The small display case had numerous rocks and fossils inside. He attempted to open the display case, but it would not budge open. He then walked away from the display case, passed the nude statue that loomed over him, and then towards the countertop. He saw a large ammonite fossil on display in the corner of the countertop, but it was as large as his head. Charlemagne quickly washed his hands and then dried them with a towel.

"All done," Charlemagne expressed, exiting the room. "Where to?"

The guard brought him down the corridor and back into the library.

"Thank you," Charlemagne said to the guard. "I'm just going to walk around, stretch my legs…"

The guard did not reply and so Charlemagne walked around the library while Manon and Rubashkin continued to talk. He came around to the stairs and looked over to them.

"Don't mind me, just admiring your collection."

"Please, feel free," Rubashkin responded, continuing to discuss with Manon.

Charlemagne went upstairs, began to look at the items on display there, and saw numerous artefacts, ancient Egyptian and Greek statuettes of anthropomorphic figures, and then some gemstones and jewels. Finally, some jewelry. Charlemagne looked around suspiciously and then opened a cabinet to pick up a ring on display. He weighed it in his hands and then looked beside it at a large spherical polished stone. He picked that up and held it in the palm of his hand, and then placed it in his pocket. Charlemagne went downstairs to rejoin the others and he stood next to Manon.

"Could I interest you in a drink? Perhaps a fine wine from the cellar," Rubashkin offered. "I have many bottles."

"No, I think that Manon and I ought to retire for the night," Charlemagne expressed. "We only just arrived at your village, and we ought to check-in our hotel. I am quite tired as well. We would be very interested to meet with you tomorrow morning to continue our discussion as there is much to discuss."

"Yes, of course," Rubashkin remarked, standing up. "Allow me though to offer you a room here though, free of charge."

"Appreciate the offer, but we've made reservations at the local inn and already paid our deposit, so wouldn't want that to go to waste. I'm also a loud sleeper, deviated septum, I'm afraid, so we wouldn't want to disturb you in your home."

"Very well."

Charlemagne and Manon were guided to the main foyer of the castle where they stopped to bid farewell.

"I look forward to continuing our discussion, Mr. Cabernet," Rubashkin remarked. "Thank you for visiting."

"Thank you for having us," Charlemagne replied, shaking his hand. "We'll be here at, say, nine in the morning."

"Good."

"*Merci beaucoup, Monsieur Rubashkin,*" Manon expressed, shaking his hand.

"Right, shall we?" Charlemagne asked Manon.

A guard went to open the door, but as he did, Charlemagne overheard the sound of steps approaching. A guard entered the adjacent corridor and walked towards them. He shouted out in Romanian, prompting the guard at the door to not open it.

"Uh oh," Charlemagne muttered, looking by his periphery, "best be off…" he muttered.

The guard spoke loudly in Romanian, causing Rubashkin to look confused.

"What's going on?" Manon questioned.

"I wouldn't know," Charlemagne said, "come, my dear." He took her hand and attempted to push through the door on his own, but a guard caught him and detained him. "Get off me!"

"What are you doing?" Manon asked, turning to Rubashkin. "Get him to stop!"

The other guard ignored them and began to pat Charlemagne down. He then pulled the orb from Charlemagne's pocket and showed everyone.

"How did that get in there…" Charlemagne muttered.

"*Charles*!" Manon scolded.

"I don't believe this…" Rubashkin remarked. "You've come to steal from me, haven't you?" He then spoke to Romanian to his men as more guards appeared from nearby.

The pair of guards each took one of Charlemagne's arms, while the others approached Manon. Rubashkin had them arrest Manon too.

"What did I do?" Manon questioned, fighting them off. "Get your hands off me!"

"Call the police, and take them away until they arrive. I'm insulted, and here I thought we would collaborate…"

Charlemagne and Manon were taken downstairs to a cellar where they were thrown into a cell which had a toilet and a bench. Once thrown in, Manon immediately hit Charlemagne in the shoulder.

"Knock it off," Charlemagne responded.

"You idiot," Manon said, "you did not intend to work with them at all, did you? You had me talk to him, discuss what we needed, and you just wanted to rob them like a common criminal."

"I do believe I told you that I had no intention to work with them," Charlemagne remarked. "Besides, it was not my intention. I just had the idea in the heat of the moment. I could have sold that rock and we could have enough money to get to Moldavia where we needed to get to... Did you think that I needed help? Me? Help? I never..."

"Ah, and who will help you now to get out of here?" Manon rebuked, sitting down at the bench. "I am at the end of my nerves with you, Charlemagne."

"So they'll take us to the police, we'll be asked questions, but come now, nothing will come out of it. We still have a few Romanian leus. I'm sure it would be enough to get by, though we did need that to find a place to stay tonight..."

"I should better hope they would throw you away," Manon expressed, putting her hands into her face. "Where you need to be, locked in a jail cell, or an insane asylum."

"Now don't be dramatic..."

Manon fell silent. Charlemagne stood around, looking about the cellar they were in.

"Let's see if there's a way out of here," Charlemagne expressed. He looked about, left and right, and there was not much to see. He shook the gate of the jail cell, examined the lock, but after a moment as he glanced to Manon, resigned and went to slide down and sit in the corner. He looked over to Manon. She held her hands at the side of her head, slightly covering the side of her eyes as though massaging her temples, though her fingers did not move. "If we have a moment to speak, I'll ensure that the police understand that you were not involved and unfairly incarcerated here with me. You can take the jeep, the rest of the money, and drive back to Budapest if you so wish, return to the hotel, and leave. I'll manage on my own..."

"You'll let them throw you in jail?"

"I'll get a hold of the Canadian embassy, British embassy, anyone that would hear my plea, and I'll have my people respond. I'm sure my arrest may cause some scandal in the papers, but it should be fine. I should… re-examine my position here, see what funds I can salvage, and return with some proper assistance, perhaps get in contact with Konstantin in the least… That gravesite won't go anywhere, nor that monastery…"

Manon removed her hands from the side of her face.

"I don't know why you continue to bother with me, Manon," Charlemagne expressed. "You clearly aren't enjoying yourself, and I know what you're really on about… You're just here to put your father at ease after that scare you had at the Berlin hospital."

"Do not even presume," Manon shot back. "You do not know what I do, *Charles*, or why I do it."

"Why then? Why do you bother with me?"

"You imbecile, *Charles*, we've known each other for many years, since we were both babies, even if we did not see each other since your grandfather's death, my father and I still held your family to ours like we were one. If I have been with you, it is no more than because I care about you and fear for you, for your existence, because clearly that is something that you have not feared. You do not fear death – you do not care if your actions result in your death – it is like you do not care about yourself or others, just this obsession of yours to be recognized by others. Even as a child, you were always obsessed. As our leader, you were obsessed. Alone, you've grown more obsessed, and I do not know why, but I have my suspicions…"

"Oh, and those are?"

"Either you are suicidal, or you have become so obsessed because you are unsatisfied, like you say. Even if it was the former, there would need to be a why."

"Suicidal? You think I'm suicidal?"

"Your actions certainly say so."

"Oh, be quiet, Manon," Charlemagne said. "Spare me your psychoanalysis, and don't bother to stick around if it's out of concern. I've allowed you to stay because I thought your knowledge to be useful, and it has, but a babysitter? I do not need."

Manon shook her head. "You are a fool, Charlemagne. You've always been a fool, but older, you've become a greater fool."

"You've lost your zeal," Charlemagne shot back. "I remember as children, you loved it when I would take you around the farm in Val de Loire, or the shores in East Anglia, or the surrounding parts of the manor in Alberta. You've stayed this far because that zeal is not yet all lost, I'm sure of it. Either way, go – I don't need you to slow me down."

"Slow you down… I've done less than slow you done. If it were not for me, who knows where you would be right now… *Mon Dieu*, who would know."

The pair silenced as they saw a light switch turn on in the adjacent room. They then listened to steps come around and the door open into the cellar room. Charlemagne recognized a woman in a bluish-lavender dress step forward.

"Irina!" Charlemagne remarked. "Listen, you've got to get us out of here…"

Irina took a key and unlocked the jail cell. Charlemagne pushed the cell open and walked out. Manon stood up and joined him behind.

"Rubashkin told me what happened," Irina said. "Your financial situation seems to be most dire, but you've shaken my husband, and also peaked his interest in what you search for."

"Well, not like he knows where to look next."

Manon cleared her throat and replied, "If you had not wandered off to steal, you would know that I did tell him where we were going next."

"You what?" Charlemagne questioned. "Oh, and you call me the fool."

Manon growled at him and raised a hand to hit him. "I am not the one that stole from another man!" she argued.

"Enough," Irina said, separating them, "here, take this..." She gave them a few more high-value bank notes. "I will let you go through a passageway out. I will call to have your vehicle taken to the nearest inn. When you are there, take your car and drive away from this place and never return. Am I clear?"

Charlemagne did not respond and instead simply nodded. "Thank you," he finally said.

Irina proceeded to lead them out of the cellar and down a stairwell to a passageway. The passageway led out through a false door in the exterior walls, coming out to a street. They walked along the street until they were in the suburbs of the adjacent town where Charlemagne took to count the notes.

"Should be close to a few hundred dollars here," Charlemagne expressed. They stopped a street corner. "Here would be a good time to part. I'll go to the inn, and you take your money and go back to Bucharest, board a train, and get the hell out of here." He handed half the money to her. He then offered a hand. "It's been nice to see you again, Manon. Stay in touch."

Manon looked at his hand with a plain expression looked back at him.

"You are truly the world's greatest imbecile, *Charles*," Manon expressed. "Do you think that I've sacrificed so much to be here now for nought?"

"Sounds like a bit of a sunk cost..."

"Do you think that your grandfather sacrificed all that he could for you, or your mother and your father, if not for nought?"

"I see what you're getting at, but..."

"If I leave now, I would be only leaving you to the other wolves that await to ravish you, like a lamb."

"I'm no lamb."

"No, a goat," Manon corrected herself, "and a stupid one at that who only intends to get eaten."

"I'm not going to have this argument with you again."

"Put your money away, *Charles*. We are not done yet – I'll follow you to the monastery, but I will not follow you any more than that. I do not think that this crown can even be found at this pace. The sources and evidence are shrinking at around feet; we are at our end. I want to at least see you safely return to Germany in one piece."

"Suit yourself, but for one that complains so much, it is a bit of a bother to keep hearing and then seeing you stay."

"When have I not ever complained, *Charles*, or be known to complain."

"*Touché.*"

Act 4, Scene 3

"The Monastery of the Paraclete is not too far," Manon said, reading the map in front of her. "Keep following this road, and it should be a few miles."

"Roger that," Charlemagne replied, scratching his beard. "Let's hope that the monastery has not expanded its claim on territory in the past two-hundred years. If what those mercenary bandits reported is correct, then the gravesite should be in the forest to the southeast."

The UAZ jeep drove along a poorly maintained paved road in the countryside of the region of Moldavia in northeast Romania. The sight around them consisted of very low hills, pastures, and varieties of farmland and farmsteads. On their left for example were grassy plains that stretched for miles, separated from the road by a low wire fence. To their right were an assortment of shrubs, the occasional tree or two together, and then a rundown house. They would occasionally come across larger homesteads, some with iron gates or barbed wire chain-link fences, and at other times there would be the continuation of a telephone pole on their right. There was minimal traffic, though what traffic they did come across was either passing them in either direction. Not too far ahead, the sight of a settlement could be seen, as well as an overpass for a train that cut perpendicular with the road and continued onwards. Like many other settlements the pair drove through, the UAZ drove ahead and passed along, continuing onwards to the next landmark.

"At the next town, you want to drive through and continue north until you enter into a forest. From that forest, comes the entry road to the monastery."

"Understood."

The pair continued to drive along the freeway as they passed another larger settlement. The entrance into this settlement was parked with a stone pedestal that held a stone Orthodox crucifix. They passed some buildings under construction on the left, and a tall hedge on the right. Further ahead, they came to pass a large industrial building on the left and a few rundown warehouses on the right. They then entered into the town outright where they passed numerous homes, all of which had some sort of fence or wall around them. On the sides of the road were thin trees with no leaves that decorated the narrow way forward until they came into a commercial sector with taller buildings, ground level shops, and then a large, crowded graveyard on the right. The pair continued forward while Charlemagne looked to his side.

"Oh my, what happened here?" Charlemagne questioned. "Looks like a massacre passed through. How is there so little space?"

"You've not seen a cemetery in Europe before, have you?"

"Of course I have, but this one?"

The cemetery continued forward a fair distance. A white church could be seen at the corner of the property. A male in a black cleric Orthodox cassock could be seen in front of the church, talking to another man. They both looked towards Charlemagne as they slowly drove past.

"I've just had a thought – what do you reckon happened to that British intelligence officer? Do you think that he's looking for us? I suppose I did steal this vehicle and a sizeable amount of money from one of Her Majesty's agents."

"If the Romanians won't arrest you, then surely the British will."

"Bah, I don't think so," Charlemagne remarked. "Besides, what makes that officer believe that he really met Charlemagne de la Cabernet? I'm sure he's got bigger fish to fry out there."

"Fish to fry?"

"It's an idiom. It means he's got more important tasks to do catching, or killing, Albanians."

"I thought the NATO-aligned countries were supporting Albania and the Kosovo independence movement," Manon remarked. "Pardon my ignorance, but I do not keep up with geopolitics."

"Neither do I, but that is a good point. At the same time, who can know what the British government is up to these days. My grandfather, as you probably know, was always skeptical of the government. I wouldn't say he was ever a political man, either. He was apolitical, I believe. He was a man who simply wanted to be left alone, to live alone, and live a life outside of government interference. I suppose you could call him a libertarian of some sort, though also a believer of public order and safety."

"I do not remember much about your grandfather, *Charles*," Manon said, "but what I do remember was that he was always kind with me. He was patient with me. He loved me. My father said that he would often joke about wishing I was his granddaughter; we were his grandchildren, especially since he treated my father like his youngest son. He said that my father was the only man in all universities who was willing to put up with your grandfather and his projects, because others despised your grandfather and did not want to work with him. My father saw differently; he saw a man of immense instinct and intuition, and it was true what they said- to trust in Derby Cabernet was to gamble, and gamble he did, and it paid out immensely for him. Now my father is one of the most respected historians in all of Europe because he chose to follow Derby Cabernet, and Derby never wanted any sort of recognition or glory for his work, but to simply let the work be done in contribution to the humanities. He let my father have all credit with his peers because he knew it would be good for his career, and it was."

Charlemagne did not respond.

"Your grandfather, *Charles*... I am told he had no fears, and he was a very moral man who hated the evils of the world.

Perhaps though he had one fear, according to my father, and that was to live a life that did not do all that it could to fight the evils of the world; that his existence should be short-lived and in vain, especially as it applies to those he left behind close to him."

"I could never make sense of it," Charlemagne quietly replied. "My grandfather was not an old man. He was shy a few months to his forty-ninth birthday that August. I last saw him leave the summer home in East Anglia to go to the continent, and the next day... the news of his accident while driving through Belgium. It felt, even as a child, wrong. Even now I can't explain it – we live our lives knowing the people in them, and it never crosses our mind that they should just be removed from among the living, no less after you had just seen them not too long ago. The reality of their deaths hits you like a grave violation of the natural order, like the claw of death snatching them and pulling them away into oblivion, never to be seen again. When I returned to Allabrese shortly after my grandfather's funeral, I took to reading the Bible to comfort me, because he would commonly read it to me at night. He wanted to get through the entire thing in a year, imagine that- of course, we never made it and stopped short at the Book of Nehemiah, I believe. Still though, a distinct memory I had was that in the Book of Genesis, shortly after the Fall of Man. My father explicitly emphasized that through the Serpent, Sin and Death entered into the world. As I read through Genesis on my own in that immediate time, I thought about those two and I recognized the terror of Death, that our existence should be able to end in such a short notice, suddenly, and seemingly there is nothing in our power that we could do to stop it. My grandmother... the neglect of her family and her unwillingness to join us in Allabrese, caused her to slip into a state of deterioration. To this date, those pillocks, the Mountbattens, have not been entirely transparent with us, but during my visits there nearly ten years ago, I began to uncover bits and pieces that it was a cognitive decline to a loss of willpower to live. In letters we received when I was young, all they had said to us was that she had become ill and it was a gradual news of her decline of health before eventually it was a news that she had slipped away at night, suddenly stopped breathing, and passed away peacefully. Her death was not sudden for us, though it was the other hand of Death that had gotten to her and pulled her out of this world, and now, who knows where those two be. Who knows what happens to us at the end of our lives, whether that be an eternal hellfire as the superstitious choose to believe, or a great reward for the virtuous, or simply nothing – to cease to exist. It is no wonder that for years, not just in European cultures, but in other cultures too, Death has taken on a personification of a terrifying being. In the end, it is not what Death does to you, but where he takes you that is unpleasant, that unknown that should happen to our existence."

"Do you fear death, *Charles*?"

"No," Charlemagne replied, smiling as he looked at her. His smile then lowered. "At least not for myself though at times I do for others. I spent a lot of my youth in existential crisis, questioning how a God, if he existed, could be so unmerciful and unjust when it comes to that being, Death. I questioned how God could not simply crush Death and free us from that burden, despite what have you about this Original Sin upon mankind. Eventually, I stopped being fearful. I realized that as long as I feared Death, Death had power over me, so I stopped fearing. I surrendered to accept that if Death wanted me, then here I was, and that I was free. Death did not seem so powerful at that moment, and I've lived as such state since. I am not afraid of Death no more."

"What a perverse way to live, *Charles*," Manon commented. "Either you are lying, or you have not truly stared Death in the face to be able to say those words. Everybody fears Death."

"No, that's not true either," Charlemagne interjected, restraining his anger. "People, too, sometimes think they fear Death when they don't. To some, like me when I was twelve, the possibility of being pulled spontaneously or gradually from this world is a terrifying feeling, but for all persons, it is the fear of the unknown after Death takes you – it is the fear of our existence, to not understand our existence, so much so that civilization has built upon a mythos of the afterlife or reincarnation to bring comfort to such questions, but those are just what they are, beliefs, not proofs. Even the most devout believers still fear for their existence, to wrestle with the question of why – why are we on this Earth? None of us truly have that answer – we may think we do, but none have it truly certainly. Even for me, I stopped caring about that answer long ago, and it's a more comfortable way to live."

Manon did not respond. The pair drove out from the larger town and continued along the countryside. The day had been partly cloudy, but as they arrived at the third town just before the forest, it grew cloudier. The town was not very large and they drove in and out, and continued along the farmland as they saw the forest up ahead as the road curved.

"I certainly hope it doesn't rain," Charlemagne expressed, looking upwards. "If we're going to have to do some excavating, then it will be no fun in the rain. If we're going to have to do some camping out in this forest, likewise."

The UAZ jeep drove into the forest and began to proceed along the freeway for another mile until they reached a convergence in the road going right. They then proceeded to follow the dirt road into the depths of the forest, travelling uphill and then downhill, passing a solemn lake, and then continuing at a curve along until they finally reached the gates at the end of the road where the monastery sat. The UAZ jeep drove off road right before the gate to park on the side of the road.

"Here we are," Charlemagne remarked, pulling his poncho from behind. He passed the other to Manon. "Safe is safe, as my mother used to say, as well as that there is no such thing as bad weather, just bad gear."

Charlemagne exited out from the vehicle and then opened the door behind him to remove some of the equipment, including a small backpack with a shovel. He then turned to face the monastery gates, seeing the building on the other side. The monastery had a tall circular belltower and pointed dark grey rooftop. The walls of the building were white. The front gate had a depiction of the Holy Spirit painted along the archway. Charlemagne looked at the sight with disgust and then turned towards Manon. Manon put on the poncho and then followed Charlemagne as they ventured into the forest together for a short hike along a path. The path took them downhill where at the base of the monastery they found a small cemetery. They stopped for a moment to look at the map, and then they continued off-trail into the forest. They wandered the forest for a brief moment until less than a mile away from the cemetery that found a large clearing in the midst of the forest that consisted of dirt and small patches of grass and protruding roots. Charlemagne exited out the forest first and looked around before he gave a thumbs up to Manon.

"This would most likely be it," Charlemagne expressed. "It's a bit more space than I anticipated, but I'll poke around a bit and if we find any remains, then we'll set up tents. This could take a while…"

Charlemagne proceeded to stick his shovel into the dirt and began to dig up brief patches. After close to an hour of digging around, Charlemagne hit his shovel into a hard object. He squatted down to raise some dirt out and found himself gripped with a narrow object. He swatted at some of the dirt and saw that it was white and hard.

"Bingo," Charlemagne said, "we've got some remains here. Seems like a forearm bone, or leg bone of a small child."

"How awful," Manon quietly remarked.

"Relax," Charlemagne replied, overhearing, "she's been dead for quite some time."

Charlemagne continued to dig, removing what appeared to be an arm. He then proceeded to clear some dirt to find the rest of the remains. As he did so, he found another arm.

"I would say this is another person, unless this initial person had two right arms," Charlemagne pointed out, climbing out of the hole he made. "We should set up tents – this'll take at least another day to complete."

"*Bien*," Manon replied, going to set up the tent.

Charlemagne dug and dug, clearing out more dirt and putting himself in a 3x3x3 hole. He had excavated at least half of the remains, finding a set of copper earrings which he showed Manon. She proceeded to examine them near a fire she had set up. Charlemagne dug and dug into the evening, stopping to drink some water Manon fetched from a nearby stream and boiled, and then continuing after a dinner of some military rations they had bought.

After a few more hours, Charlemagne had made a decent effort to excavate a few remains. He came around sit down near the fire where Manon was reading a book.

"I don't think I'll finish tonight," Charlemagne remarked, "but the night is pretty, could be colder."

"What are you hoping to look for, *Charles*?" Manon questioned. "To find the Crown buried with these people? Let the dead have their rest…"

"Oh, I believe they're resting plenty – they're just bones, Manon. Just dense calcium, nothing else."

"They were once a part of a human being," Manon argued.

"So is the dust in an apartment if you consider the shedding of dead skin cells on a daily basis," Charlemagne sneered. "There is no humanity left of these remains."

"They are human bones, *Charles*. One day, you and I will be just like them."

"Hopefully not together..." Charlemagne muttered.

"Pardon?"

"Nothing," Charlemagne replied, standing up, "I've found the energy to dig a bit more."

"Ah, good, then I am going to sleep."

Charlemagne proceeded to a dig for a bit. He removed some dirt around another body he had found in the pit and began to clear it off. He thrusted the shovel into the dirt and then heard a loud clang.

"Hm?"

Charlemagne threw the shovel in again and began to clear some clumps of dirt to reveal a shiny metal object. He reached in to grab the item, seeing that it was sharp and long. He then began to clear some more dirt as the sharp object protruded outwards. As he continued to clear the dirt, he noticed that the metal object was curved with a pointed tip. The approximate length of the sword was three feet. Once Charlemagne had unearthed enough dirt, he removed the object and pulled it out. Charlemagne threw the sword over the edge and then climbed out, picking up the spotlight nearby to provide a clearer bit of light.

"Look what I've found!" Charlemagne shouted. "It's a sword!"

Manon looked over as she prepared her sleeping bag near the fire and under the tent.

"It's a very peculiar sword. Too bad I don't know my weapons that well," Charlemagne expressed. He picked up the sword and brought it over to Manon. "Do you think the Romani people here had used it, or did it perhaps belong to the bandits?"

"Where did you find this?"

"Where do you mean I found it? I found it right over there in the mass grave."

"No, what part?"

"Oh, over there," Charlemagne pointed, "in the corner. I've been excavated towards that end where I found a body, a large one too. Been working on the feet and legs when I found this…"

"Keep looking, maybe you can find something else," Manon remarked. "I will log this item…"

Manon gently took the sword with a towel and placed it near the fire. Charlemagne meanwhile returned to the pit to dig away some of the dirt towards the hip where he found a belt buckle. He picked it out and brought it around. The buckle had grooves around it and was ornate. It had some words vertically along it too.

"Looks Cyrillic," Charlemagne remarked. "Perhaps it was a fallen soldier of the Serbian troops."

"No, Zarko made no mention of losing any men, or even having to fight anyone."

"I thought we were operating under the assumption that he and his men had killed these people. If we failed here, we were going to return to Serbia to learn more about him and see if he took the crown."

"We'll need to verify, but I'll log this item too. Keep digging and see what else you can find…"

"Aye," Charlemagne replied, returning to the pit. He took his shovel and continued to dig around the corpse of the fallen warrior. As he dug, Charlemagne suddenly heard a branch break in the distance. He stopped digging and looked out to the darkness. He squinted as though he could see something, and then kept the shovel in place and backed up to fetch the spotlight. He picked it up and then shined it out into the forest. "H-hello?" No response came. He turned off the spotlight and then moved back to the camp where Manon wrote in their logbook. "I just heard something in the forest – we may not be alone."

"What do you mean? It is a forest, no? Could it not be a wild animal?"

"It was a fairly heavy crunch," Charlemagne quietly noted. He walked to the backpack and picked out the Beretta and checked its ammunition. He then put it into his pocket. "I'm going to walk around..."

"You will leave me here?"

"You're free to come with me," Charlemagne pointed out.

"I am busy doing your work."

"Well, hurry it along then, because we may have to go."

"Where?"

"To the car," Charlemagne said, feeling the keys in his pocket. "Be prepared to run..."

"*Charles*, you are scaring me."

"Good, get that adrenaline going, Manon. You are going to need it..." Charlemagne stated. He then cleared his throat and spoke loudly, "I think there's a wolf or a bear out there. I should try to scare it..."

Manon looked out towards the forest and then picked up the buckle and placed it into her pocket. She then picked up a spotlight to shine it outwards. She froze on the spot.

"*Charles*..." Manon remarked.

Charlemagne squinted and could see the cap of a person poking out from ahead. He then looked over to Manon and quietly said, "Follow my lead..." In a louder voice he said, "I don't see anything. I guess I was just seeing things... Come now, let's put out the fire and get some sleep."

Both Charlemagne and Manon put out their spotlights, one after the other, and Charlemagne then picked up the sword and with another hand, poured out the fire. He dropped the pan and then picked up his backpack. Manon stayed close to him, putting her bag around her shoulders. He could see her breath before him. With his other hand, he took her hand.

"*Allons-y*," Charlemagne quietly spoke in French.

"*Oui.*"

Charlemagne and Manon proceeded to carefully walk away from the campgrounds, into the forest and away from where Manon had seen a capped man. He used the sword to guide him away from trees, and once he was fair distance, they began to pick up their speed. Charlemagne then heard a loud shout in a Slavic language from behind, prompting him and Manon to increase their speed while Manon turned on the spotlight.

"Bloody hell, I knew we were being watched… Who are these lot?"

"How should I know?!"

Charlemagne and Manon ran through the forest together, hands continued to be held. They soon arrived at the gravesite and then found the trail where they continued along. At the sight of the end of the trail, Charlemagne sprinted, encouraging Manon to keep up, and they reached the UAZ where it was parked with two Soviet-era GAZ jeeps in front of them. The pair panted as they made their exit and came to the car, but before they could rest, Charlemagne saw two mercenaries at the hoods of their vehicles, sharing a cigarette. They parted hands and Manon went around to her side of the car, while Charlemagne immediately took the Beretta out from his pocket and fired at them. The shot hit a beam of the car light and caused the others to withdraw and take cover. Charlemagne took cover at the hood of his car, joining Manon.

"Here," Charlemagne said, handing the keys. "I'll fend them off."

Manon took the key and went back around to her side of the car to unlock it and then climb in. She climbed into the back of the jeep and kept prone. Charlemagne continued to fire shots until he was out of rounds and threw the Beretta towards them. He then got into the car and climbed into the driver's seat.

"Where's the key?" Charlemagne questioned.

"In the ignition!"

"Thanks."

The UAZ roared to life and seeing the mercenaries encroach on them, he shifted gears and then immediately pulled backwards, hitting them both with the car.

"Sorry, lads."

Charlemagne shifted gears again, drove around and then sped past each of the cars as he went along. Some gunfire came out from the forest just as they were on their way out.

"Who are they?"

"They look like the same lads as those from the castle in Serbia!" Charlemagne shouted. "Luckily, this road has no bridges, so we should be safe…"

As Charlemagne finished his sentence, he found another pair of GAZ vehicles parked up ahead with mercenaries pointing their weapons towards them. He immediately drove out of the way and into the forest, causing the jeep to bounce up and down as they ran over shrubs and evaded trees.

"What happened?"

"We seem to be in trouble…"

The UAZ leaped upwards as they ran over a mound and then flew towards a road. The car hit the base of a tree, but Charlemagne was able to back up and pull backwards as he stopped for a moment.

"Drat, which way to the exit? Both ends look the same…"

Charlemagne looked back and forth. He looked back again and squinted as he could see some vehicles on approach. He immediately hit the accelerator and drove forward along the road as he continued downhill. The headlights of the GAZ jeeps continued to descend upon them, followed with a volley of gunfire that caused Charlemagne to duck his head while Manon stayed put prone. The rear glass of the jeep shattered and Manon covered her head. She stayed in place on the cushions and swore aloud as the cars continued to accost them.

"Oh no…" Charlemagne muttered.

"What now?" Manon cried out.

Charlemagne observed a pair of GAZ jeeps at the intersection with the freeway, blocking the exit out. Rather than steer out of the way, Charlemagne accelerated more. He eyed a two-foot gap between each car as they were parked slanted, and he also saw the mercenaries ahead with their weapons pointed, taking cover around the side of the hood of the car. He drove forward and ducked his head down as he kept the steering wheel straight.

"Hold on!"

Manon looked over as she saw Charlemagne ducked down, prompting her to do the same. The UAZ jeep went full force towards the GAZ jeeps, resulting in them to open fire. Charlemagne peaked over as the UAZ made its collision course towards the mercenaries. Suddenly, a tire blew out, causing the car to lose control. Charlemagne raised his head and instead hit the brakes. The car steered off road. Manon looked up right when the car hit impact as he braked.

"*Merde!*" Manon shouted. "What is your problem?!" Manon sat up and looked over to Charlemagne. The vehicle did not have airbags and Charlemagne was thrusted over the steering wheel and knocked out. "*Charles!*" Manon yelled, climbing over to shake his shoulder. "Ah, *Charles, réveilles-toi…*"

The vehicles that pursued them stopped nearby. The others at the checkpoint further ahead marched upwards. Manon looked out towards the road as she should see them position around. She then looked down to the sword. Suddenly, the door at the passenger side opened and she was yanked out. Yet again, a bag was placed over her head, but this time, with the strength of a few more men, she was bound with ease and carried to one of the vehicles. She stayed put, squirming around, but the back of the vehicle was small to move around much. The vehicle she was in stayed put for several minutes until she felt the jeep move. The vehicles that pursued them proceeded out from the road, turning right and continuing along the freeway as Manon continued to panic in place.

Act 4, Scene 4

Charlemagne slowly regained consciousness, opening his eyes and then looking around. His wrists and ankles were tied together, and his mouth was gagged with a thick piece of rope. He breathed quickly as he looked around his surroundings. He was in the rear of a GAZ jeep that was moving along in the dark of the night on a thin road. Inside the jeep were four mercenaries that wore similar uniforms to those that he and Manon had seen at Vukašin castle. The odor in the jeep smelt strongly of cigarette smoke. The barrels of the Avtomat Kalashnikov (AK-47) rifles poked outwards as they sat between the two mercenaries in the rear seat. Charlemagne observed the mercenaries speak in a Slavic language amongst each other as they bantered. He looked at each of the men and observed that they had fair, cold skin. All the males had dark hair, from medium to dark brown, and they were rugged and stocky males too. Charlemagne slowly began to control his breaths and then slipped down as he looked around his surroundings in the trunk of the jeep.

The rope around his wrists was wound tightly, and likewise those around his ankles. There was nothing around him in the rear of the jeep to observe. He brought his hands to his face and began to tug at the tightly wound rope around his mouth. He also began to chew at the other side with his teeth until the rope slipped down to his neck.

"Oh great..." Charlemagne muttered. He began to quietly move to his side and look at the door of the rear of the jeep as he searched for a safety release of some kind, but he could not find one. The jeep then suddenly hit a bump in the road, pushing Charlemagne's body towards the side of the trunk and hitting it straight on. "Ow!"

The mercenaries quickly quieted down as they heard Charlemagne speak. A mercenary looked over to Charlemagne, but in the quick moment he put the gag back into his mouth and closed his eyes. A mercenary reported what he saw to his comrades and the jeep continued to drive. Charlemagne groaned in pain and came onto his back. He looked up towards the light above him with difficulty, partially maintaining his eyes open before he rolled onto his other side to stare at the back of the rear passenger seats. He then fell asleep.

At an unknown amount of time later, the rear trunk door opened and Charlemagne was pulled out and thrown onto the floor. With that pull, the gag fell off from Charlemagne's face and came to his neck.

"Ah, you bastards…" Charlemagne muttered.

A mercenary spoke and two of them came around to pick Charlemagne up onto his feet, while another came around from behind to tighten the gag around his mouth. As the mouthpiece was fixed, Charlemagne looked around. He found himself in a large overgrown lot with shattered concrete and trees poking outwards. In the nearby area there were five story concrete apartment blocks with barred windows. The skies above him were grey and it was foggy to be able to see any more than he could, as well as still dim with the sun nowhere to be seen. A mercenary spoke and Charlemagne was turned around, seeing behind him at the long road ahead with tanks, numerous T-84 tanks, parked along the side of the street in unison, all cannons pointed upwards towards a hill with a plain field behind them. A jeep was parked ahead, this one with an open top unlike the others that were sheltered. A mercenary spoke and Charlemagne was guided to a rear seat where he was sat down in the middle, while other mercenaries came around to sit around him.

Charlemagne observed as he was brought from one side of the lot, down the road to the other side where there were arched concrete structures with thick doors. There were three of them, each accessible via a separate road that spread out from the main tarmac. Two of them were open. One of them had a Mil Mi-24 helicopter, otherwise known as a Hind E, while the other one was cleared out and had people inside. To the one with others inside, Charlemagne was brought to and the jeep stopped in front of. He was pulled out from the jeep and brought forward inside where there was a table with some maps, chairs, and a few other tables around the sides with equipment. At the very back there were numerous assault rifles hung up along a rack, more than a few dozen in total. Beside this rack were crates upon each other. On the far sides of the hangar were some cots, and there were numerous mercenaries like the ones that apprehended Charlemagne stood around. Charlemagne observed a male at the head of the table, looking down at a map and then looking upwards.

This male had white hair and a chin curtain beard in the same color. He had fair skin, cold and almost sickly pale, and he had very fine blue eyes like a Husky. He was average height, about the same height as Charlemagne, and unlike his compatriots who wore military vests and cargo pants, he wore a simple uniform; an olive-green military fatigue with two large breast pockets and collars. He also had epaulettes at his shoulders that bore three stars. The suit jacket was button up and underneath he also wore a similar color collared shirt. Around the waist he wore a military belt. The suit jacket was long and came down over his lap with pockets at the side. The pants had no pockets and the cuffs were tucked into black boots. The man had thin white hair in a Caesar cut. He picked up a military cap in the same color and placed it over his head. He then crossed his arms as Charlemagne was brought forward to them.

Charlemagne was kicked onto his knees, and the man came around from the table to look down upon him. He then snapped his fingers at his men, spoke in the same Slavic language, and the men came forward and removed the gag from his mouth. He then had him raised onto his feet so they were eye level.

"H-hello," Charlemagne greeted. "Who are you?"

The man slapped Charlemagne across the face.

"That's for talking out of turn," the man spoke in English. He then observed Charlemagne while he slowly retracted his face back to looking towards him. "So, you are Charlemagne... Hmph..." The man began to pace around him as he observed him. "Do you know who I am?"

Charlemagne didn't immediately reply. He looked over to the man and then asked, "Sorry, is it my turn now?"

"Yes," the man responded, "speak."

"No, sir, I don't seem to know who you are. We've just met..."

"I am Krum Berezovsky, former major-general of the Bulgarian Army," Krum spoke. "Now, commander of these loyal men, and dealer of arms to the third world. I've heard much about you, Charlemagne."

"Not surprising," Charlemagne replied, "I..."

Krum raised a hand to hit Charlemagne, causing him to duck and flinch. He held himself back as he was about to hit Charlemagne, laughing at his reaction. He spoke in a Slavic language to his men while Charlemagne slowly stood up straight again.

"I do not think that the legend could be true..." Krum stated. "For this man to have killed all of La Havre's men?"

"W-what?" Charlemagne questioned. "Pardon, but what did you say? I've killed Le Havre's men?"

Krum ignored him and spoke to his men with a cheerful face.

"Yes, we heard from Le Havre what happened to his men, but I see you now and think that it is impossible. You – little man, you... are no killer. Still, that is not my interest... Le Havre tells me that you seek treasure. He has passed on this information to me, and I have sent my men to find you because I want this treasure."

Charlemagne remained silent.

"What is it that you are looking for in these parts?"

Charlemagne looked at him as he paused and then spoke himself, "I don't know what you're talking about. Le Havre is a nasty man. If you and him are colleagues, I would suppose you are the Albanians we were meant to meet?"

"Albanians?!" the man questioned, insulted.

"Bosnians?"

Krum immediately backhanded slapped Charlemagne, causing him to fall over.

"We are no such foul creatures," Krum remarked, spitting at Charlemagne's side. "We are Bulgarians."

"I'm sorry…"

Krum kicked Charlemagne's ankles while two soldiers came over to help him onto his feet. He spoke harshly to them in Bulgarian and they did not help him up.

"Now, what is it that you are looking for?" Krum asked, picking up a tin case on the desk and opening it. "Tell me – Le Havre said it was most valuable."

"Why do you want it? What does a mercenary chief need a crown for?" Charlemagne questioned. "You want to wear it?"

"A crown?" Krum questioned, bringing a cigar to his lips and lighting it. He blew some smoke and then held the cigar in his right hand. "Hm… What does this crown look like?"

"I don't know," Charlemagne complained. "I have a vague idea of what it could look like, but I don't even know if it still exists. I'm doing research at this time…"

"Who did this crown belong to?"

"To the French kings," Charlemagne answered.

"Ah, like Napoleon?"

"No, not him," Charlemagne said, "the kings before him, before the revolution. From Louis XVI to Charlemagne, a crown that has lasted close to a thousand years."

"Ah, Charlemagne… Charlemagne the Great… Like you? Yes, I remember him from school. Yes… What is this crown made of?"

"Gold, most likely, and valuable gems encrusted on the side."

"How much would a crown like this cost?"

"What? I don't know. You can't put a price on something like that – it's priceless. It's a one of a kind item. Any… any collector would fight tooth and nail to get it…"

Krum fell silent and spoke to his men in Bulgarian. He then looked down to Charlemagne again.

"So, what have you learned about this crown?"

Charlemagne proceeded to briefly explain that the crown was situated at the Basilica of Saint Denis where it was taken out and thought to have been (presumed) melted down into currency, as was common in that time. However, Charlemagne explained his source to believe that the crown had no such fate and instead a French nobleman took it to Austria where while impoverished was forced to sell it to another nobleman in the Austrian Empire, a Hungarian officer, Count Ignác Újlaki, whose castle in Serbia provided information that he had the crown (unbeknownst of its origin), stolen from him by a group of unknown bandits. He then proceeded to hire some bandits of his own, led by a Serbian named Zarko Jović to search for the bandits, discovering them and learning that they had lost the crown to some Romani wanderers. Jović was able to track down the location of these wanderers to Moldovia where they were discovered to have been brutally murdered.

"I was in Moldavia, eastern Romania, to learn more about the crown," Charlemagne clarified. "Before your men showed up and brutalized us, I was… Oh that's right, where is… where is Manon?"

"Manon?"

"The- the woman I was with… where is she?"

"Nearby," Krum simply replied. "What did you learn in Moldavia? Do you know where the crown is?"

"No, I don't – look, let me tell you something… historical research is not some cut and dry operation. It's an investigative process, like a criminal investigation, where we look at the evidence before us, evaluate it for truth, or bias, or confusion or lies. All that I've told you, it's a partial portrait based on what we've been able to uncover, backed by the evidence we have, but it's also based on our interpretations of that evidence. Altogether, we've acted upon the assumption that this crown that the Austrian nobleman had brought with him from France is even the Frankish Crown, which in itself has the minimal evidence I could tolerate.

"Right now, all I can say is that there are two likelihoods to this crown: either Zarko and his men lied to Újlaki, or the gypsies were indeed massacred and the crown stolen from them. Who could have killed them? I don't know, but that's what I was trying to find out before I was kidnapped and brought to… who knows where…"

"You need not worry for where you are," Krum replied. "Where do you think this crown is now?"

"Based on the two theories, if Zarko and his men lied, then it could be anywhere in the former Yugoslav Republic. If Zarko told the truth, then possibly somewhere in Romania, or out East to even South. We've done as much as we could to track the crown down from the 1790s to the 1830s. From 1830 to 1914, Eastern Europe was a very different place, divided between the Catholic Austrians, Orthodox Russians, and Islamic Ottomans. Even if it were in one of those three places after it was taken off the gypsies, it could be anywhere from here to France again, to Moscow, or south to Jerusalem for all I know. The world changed so quickly from 1914 to 1945."

"Yes, it did…" Krum remarked, thinking for a moment. He brought his cigar to his lips. He then crouched down and blew the smoke into Charlemagne's face. "Let me tell you something, little one, before the Soviet Union fell into dissolution, I was an important man – I was a very important general in the Warsaw Pact. By 1989, I had lost everything I had worked my entire life towards, or so I had thought. I had to act fast, make deals, break laws, but I survived – we survived, from where we were once respected men to become… like the word you used, bandits. I am where I am now because of the decisions I have made, and in doing so, I have made lots of connections. The Soviet Union has many treasures spread throughout, but like my comrades, I never paid of interest." Krum waved his hand for the soldiers to come and bring Charlemagne onto his feet. He then came around to the table where his map was placed. "Look and see…"

Charlemagne observed that the map detailed Eastern Europe up to the parts of Russia around the Black Sea. The countries it depicted included Lithuanian, Poland, East Germany, Czechia and Slovakia, Austria, Hungary, Yugoslavia, Albania, Greece, Bulgaria, Turkey, Georgia, Azerbaijan, and Armenia. It also depicted Belarus and the Ukraine on the map where across this area, including the Russian lands, there were pins marked atop.

"The only ones who have been greatly interested in the harvest of artefacts and cultural items from the Soviet Union in the past fifty years has been the Germans. When the Nazis invaded all of Europe, trains upon trains of cultural items transported these goods back to Germany, and at times, they arrived to be stored until they were returned. At other times, they never returned or left the train. Sometimes, they never left where they were meant to be stored. Take a look here…"

Krum showed Charlemagne a binder which detailed a list of items. All of these items were written in a Cyrillic language. He placed a hand over his shoulder as he expected Charlemagne to read.

"Sorry, I can't read this handwriting," Charlemagne expressed.

Krum pushed Charlemagne away and called a soldier over to pick up the binder and read. He listed the items off, including earrings, necklaces, chalices, broaches, amulets, scepters, royal eggs, paintings, portraits, statues, and more. Along this list, the soldier stated 'foreign crowns,' which peaked Charlemagne's curiosity.

"Where is that list from?"

"From Soviet archives, a list of all heritage items that were stolen from the Soviet Union and not recovered," Krum stated, "completed in 1951. If an item was not returned, it was either stolen to a personal collection, or never survived transport. These plots are approximate locations of those such areas: trains, storage caches, and more."

"Seems like you have quite a good rap on it," Charlemagne remarked. "You surprise me to be a bit an amateur treasure hunter then."

"But it is not my work," Krum shouted, slamming a hand on the table. "It is Soviet work, incomplete… which is why I need you, Charlemagne, to help me."

"You want me to help you locate… what? Lost treasure…?"

"Yes," Krum remarked, "because your crown may be there, and I want that crown if Le Havre wants it. You work for me now…"

Charlemagne stood in place, looked over to the men around him, all of whom held Kalashnikov rifles. He cleared his throat and replied, "Very well…"

"Tomorrow, we roll into Ukraine and begin to search. For now, rest, Mr. Cabernet… whatever you need, you will have it."

"How about these ties off?" Charlemagne requested.

Krum spoke in Bulgarian to his men. They cut the ties from his ankle, but kept the ones around his wrist. He was guided back to the jeep where he was taken away from the hangar and back towards the buildings. They passed a few of the apartments, and then peeled through to come to a square lot with additional hangars, though these made of metal. The vehicle came around to the front of one of these open hangars and Charlemagne was led out and brought towards one of three cages.

"Manon!" Charlemagne remarked, seeing her in the furthest one, lying on a cot. Her hands were cut loose and free.

A mercenary opened the gate of the middle cage, stopped Charlemagne to free his hands, and then pushed him and closed the gate. Charlemagne immediately went over to the cage and began to rustle it as he repeated, "Manon! Manon!"

Manon slowly woke up and turned on her back. She looked over to Charlemagne.

"*Charles…*" Manon quietly said. "Ah, *mon Dieu*, where are we?"

"I don't know," Charlemagne replied, "seems like some sort of military base by the looks of it, possibly in Bulgaria. Those men who've been after us seem to know Le Havre, the Algerian who had kidnapped us, and they learned from him what we were up to and became interested. They now expect me to help them find the Frankish Crown."

"Ah, well, at least that should be it then…"

"What do you mean?"

"We help them, they find the crown, and we get to leave with our lives…"

"Only if you believe them," Charlemagne remarked. "Listen, I'm going to find a way out of here. They intend to send us to Ukraine tomorrow…"

"Us?"

"It better be us, and I'll insist on either them letting you go or coming with us," Charlemagne remarked. "I'm not going to let you get left behind…"

"How kind…" Manon responded, sitting up. "What are you going to do to try and get out of here?"

"I'll wait and see," Charlemagne remarked. "If we could escape Le Havre in Belgrade, then we can escape this man, Krum, somehow."

"And you will keep running..." Manon said. "Why not let him have this crown, *Charles*? Why not resign that it is too dangerous?"

"Did I ever lead you to believe that I was some sort of quitter?" Charlemagne questioned. "As if I did not have a single degree of perseverance."

"Perseverance? *Charles*, this is not perseverance, this is madness – this is persistency..."

"Relax, I'm sure we will be safe. We just need to hold on..."

$$\bullet \bullet \bullet$$

Charlemagne and Manon were kept in these cages for just about the entire day, provided meals on metal trays, while Charlemagne was provided with reading materials that were of no use to him.

"I wish'd they stop assuming I spoke Cyrillic..." Charlemagne remarked, looking at the letters in the book. "I'm not about to start now to read that silly alphabet, though I suppose it would be worth to know the alphabet at least."

Charlemagne and Manon were kept in the hangar where the cold air came through. A stove near the cells was used to burn firewood and also keep the guard they were with warm. A few hours after sunset, the guards changed and this one put his feet up on a table and read through a book. Charlemagne was provided with a lantern that he used to read through a book, while Manon wrapped herself around blankets and lay on her side.

"*Charles*, give it a rest... go to sleep, please... you are driving me crazy..."

Charlemagne looked towards her, closed the book and placed it aside. He looked over to the guard who had his backs to them and then sat down at his bed again. He pulled the blankets over him and then lay on his side, opposite Manon as his cot was parallel hers and the cage wall separating them.

"I'm sorry this adventure has not exactly gone in our favor," Charlemagne remarked, "but I did give you ample opportunities to leave. I suppose you can't complain that I have been unfair... How could I have been if I did not consistently attempt to offer you a chance for redemption before it was too far gone as it has now, of final entrapment?"

"*Charles*, how can I not say the same to you? I've been here with you not for the reasons you believe to be a voice of reason to you – this is farfetched and dangerous, and while it did not begin this way, it will certainly only worsen. I told you to be careful many times... I do not know how many more times I can say it and offer you to step away before it is too much for me, before it is too late for you to turn around."

"Don't worry about me," Charlemagne doubled-down on. "I don't need help from anyone. I'm my own man."

With that final thought, the pair quieted down and went to sleep. Charlemagne shuddered through the night, waking up and opening his eyes as it became too much. He looked ahead of him, out towards the base as the doors were kept open. He then came onto his back and looked towards the guard who had fallen asleep. He rolled his eyes and then looked up above him.

Suddenly, Charlemagne overheard the sound of gunfire in the distance. He then heard the sound of shouts. He lurched forward and looked around, but not even the guard that was with them had noticed and continued to snore. Charlemagne slowly lowered himself and lay back in the cot. He heard the sound of dogs barking and closed his eyes. Suddenly, again, Charlemagne heard a peculiar sound, a quiet voice that spoke his name, "Charles.... Charlie-boy... Charles-man."

Charlemagne opened his eyes, looked outwards to his side and then came onto his back. He looked forward and then jumped upwards as he saw a dark figure looking at him from behind the cage.

"Bloody hell…" Charlemagne remarked, looking over to where the guard was and seeing him collapsed on the ground. In front of Charlemagne's cage was Cael, dressed in the same garb as he was seen to be wearing in Belgrade. "Oy, it's you…"

"Aye, it's me," Cael affirmed, looking at him, "you look worse for wears, lad."

"Listen, Kyle, you've got to get me out of here," Charlemagne begged. "Manon and I have been kidnapped and forced into labor for these mercenaries."

"I'll say," Cael agreed, "I was following a lead on these boys, heard they were supplying arms to both sides of the Kosovo conflict, and low and behold I find you here too. How'd that happen?"

"It's a long story, but these lads are related to the same lads who kidnapped me in Budapest and brought me to Serbia. Now I seem to be here in Bulgaria or somewhere…"

"Not even close, Charles-man. We're in Moldova. Suppose all that explains a lot then, because I was just hunting for that man you told me about – thanks for the tip, friend, by the way."

"So, you'll let me out?" Charlemagne requested.

"Ah, you did steal from me, Charles-man," Cael pointed out. "In fairness though, I did have to take a sidestep and steal back from you."

Cael retrieved an item from his pocket and threw it over to Charlemagne. The item was brown, rectangular and made of leather. Charlemagne picked it up and opened it.

"My wallet," Charlemagne remarked, looking inside to see his driver's license. "How did you? You went to Budapest?"

"Aye, couldn't find your luggage, but did find the safe and all that was inside, so thank you for that…"

Charlemagne observed that the wallet was empty aside from his ID and credit card.

"Call us even, Charles-man?"

"Yes, well even, especially once you get me out of here," Charlemagne requested.

"Oh, relax, I was going to let you out anyways," Cael remarked, fumbling with the keys. He opened the cage and Charlemagne walked out.

"Catch," Cael remarked, tossing the keys to Charlemagne who caught them. "Let your pretty friend here out and we'll be on our way to get you out of here."

Charlemagne went to Manon's cage and opened the gate. "Manon… wake up…" She slowly woke up. She looked over to see Charlemagne ushering her out of the cage and immediately put her shoes on to leave. She looked over to see Cael knelt down keeping an eye out at the exit from the hangar.

"Ah, *mon Dieu*, what a relief…" Manon remarked, "but where are we going? We are in the middle of a bee's nest."

"A hornet's nest, my dear," Charlemagne corrected, "but likewise, where are we going?"

"We are going to have to do a bit of sleuthing around to get on out of here," Cael remarked. "We'll need a car to get out."

"How did you get in?" Charlemagne questioned.

"A one-way in," Cael replied, "should have worked to get me out, but not all of us."

"I saw a few cars parked up ahead," Charlemagne noted, "on the other side of the military base."

"Ah, so I thought it would be," Cael said. "Right, you two ready? We're going to have to lay low…"

"Ready…" Charlemagne affirmed.

Cael stood up and kept his own Kalashnikov rifle in hand pointed down. He led the way to the back door and then exited out. He then walked forward, knelt down to look about, and then continued forward with the others behind him. They made their way down the darkness of the side grass, along the tall grass and bushes, to pass the hangars and reach the apartment buildings.

The middle of the pass through the apartment blocks were well lit, and the perimeter of the facility was well lit too. Cael stood up and came over to a window, ushering them to follow him through. They entered into a devoid room, furniture and all manner of items, wiring, and other items ripped out. They came around to a corridor and Cael proceeded to lead them carefully down, stopping at corners ever so often to inspect them until they reached the end. They eventually reached the end where Cael looked out and could see some watch towers lined up along the perimeter fence with spotlights covering the grass. He looked forward for a moment and then turned to the others. Cael stood up and climbed over the wall and then stopped to point to the tanks and signal them to follow him.

Charlemagne and Manon kept their heads low as they arrived to the tanks. They were guided along to the very end where they approached the concrete barracks. The helicopter could still be seen parked in the middle hangar, while the other two were closed shut. Cael brought them behind the one closest to them, which was the only one in which Charlemagne was uncertain of. Cael brought a hand to his mouth to signal to them, and then they carefully walked over the pavement behind the concrete barrack to reach the other end. They then quickly passed around to the front of the helicopter hangar where they went along to find the jeeps parked in front of the fence behind these structures. Charlemagne and Manon kept their head low as they reached the corner of the final structure.

"Won't we need keys?" Charlemagne asked. "They may be inside."

Cael and Charlemagne came around to the rear of the bunker that Krum had talked to Charlemagne in. He began to work on the lock behind it to unlock it, doing so with ease, and then entering inside. He turned on a flashlight and the pair found themselves in the presence of tall machines with rotors that spun and spun.

"Hello? What do we have here?" Cael questioned. "You may have just given me a gold mine, here, Charlie-boy."

"The keys are on the other end," Charlemagne expressed.

"Right, you get them while I have a look here."

Charlemagne opened the next door and looked inside with caution. He could the table with the map and manifesto placed beside. He could also hear some soldiers snoring as they slept in the cots around. He could not see Krum though. He walked towards the table, picked up the manifesto to close it, and then began to remove the pins in the map. He placed them aside, and then folded the map into four and placed it atop of the manifesto. He then silently exited the room and returned to meet with Cael. Charlemagne closed the door and then passed the room to exit out to join Manon.

"Nope, no keys," Charlemagne expressed to Manon, kneeling to put the items into his backpack.

"What is all this?" Manon questioned.

"A hint in the right direction."

"Where is Kyle?"

"He's having a look at the computer machines inside," Charlemagne expressed. "We still need those keys... I had a bad feeling that they would be in the other bunker. I suppose though we could just hotwire one of the cars..."

"What about Kyle?"

"Forget him," Charlemagne remarked, "he's just going to slow us down. Besides, where would he take us? Back to Budapest?"

"Charlemagne, what are you doing?" Manon scolded. "Stop!"

Charlemagne began to feel the handles of all the jeeps parked along the row. He went by the ones without tops, and then to the canopy ones, and finally to the entirely covered ones like the ones that had hunted him down. He eventually found a jeep that opened, prompting him inside. Manon opened the other door and sat down.

"What are you like, eh?"

"My dear, I grow tiresome with your discourse. Do you not see it yet? You are no different than me, as the old saying goes, who is more foolish? The fool or the fool following the fool?"

Manon did not respond to his words. He looked behind him and opened the trunk. He then pulled out a toolbox and took a screwdriver around to pop the ignition cap. He pulled wires out and began to fiddle with them.

"Ow!" Charlemagne muttered, flicking his hand. "Shocked myself..."

"*Charles*, please," Manon pleaded. "This Kyle has been so nice to us, why leave him here?"

"He got himself here in the first place, he can get himself out. Besides, I led him to a treasure trove of information. He'll likely haul those rolls out and take them to a jeep and drive out – perhaps it'll be enough to get Krum arrested for arms dealing former Soviet equipment. Can you believe this? We're not in Bulgaria as I had thought – we're in Moldova, one of the small former Soviet republics. We are in the former Soviet Union..."

"Where do you intend to take us then?"

"I've got my wallet back, thanks to Mr. Monaghan," Charlemagne remarked. "I'm going to drive into the Ukraine and make contact with Mr. Adlington. He'll send us some money, and we'll be right as rain again, my dear. We're back on track, and as we slip out of here quietly, we won't have those pillocks here follow us for sure."

The car engine began to start and Charlemagne shifted gears and then rolled forward.

"Just like that, Charlemagne is back in the game... Nothing holds me down."

Act 5, Prologue

"Honestly, you can't have me believe this nonsense," Charlemagne expressed. "Special relativity?"

Charlemagne held his arms crossed as he looked across from in front of a chalkboard to where another person sat on a chair about three yards away. Charlemagne appeared a few years older than he was when he raced Enrico Pinelli in Allabrese. He remained slim, though he was his modern height, and he wore a light blue sweater and blue-white plaid collared shirt underneath. He also wore brown trousers.

"Albert Einstein was a fraud, hailed as a genius when he never was, and he's still venerated in modern academia, particularly physics, when his idea on E equals MC squared was never his own."

"Charles, how can you even make such a radical assertion," the man across from him stated. "Everyone knows that Einstein published his paper on the matter in 1905."

The pair argued in a nook of a small apartment. A large chalkboard behind Charlemagne was in front of a pair of cross windows. The chalkboard had various mathematic equations and calculus symbols. Besides the chalkboard was a small workbench with scraps of metal lying around. The nook was slightly elevated in comparison to the rest of the apartment, and the man that Charlemagne argued with sat backwards in a chair across from him. This man had fair skin on the warmer side with unshaven facial hair and dirty blonde hair. He was slim like Charlemagne, but wore black glasses. He also wore a t-shirt and denim jeans. The rest of the apartment was modest, though unkempt. Across from the nook was the living room adjacent to an open kitchen. A corridor besides the kitchen led to a bathroom, and then two bedrooms on either side. The pair continued to argue.

"Have you actually read Einstein's paper, my friend," Charlemagne rebutted. "His 1905 paper makes no such claim to the equation in question. I can tell you, and this may come as a shock, but I've read the published paper of a lesser known scientist who in 1903 did coin that exact equation."

"Oh really?"

"Yes, and his name is Olinto De Pretto, and his publication was made in a scientific journal. Let me also address to you the works of Henri Poincaré, who adapted the works of a Hendrick Lorentz. Do you know where Einstein was at that time of his life, in 1903?"

"No."

"Einstein was in Switzerland, a country which borders both Italy and France, working in a patent office. He had graduated with a diploma in sciences less than two years ago, and based on biographical accounts of his life, read the works of others so it highly likely to believe that the lesser known Italian and French publications made its way into his hands to inspire his own dissertation which he published two years later, which in my opinion, is just enough time for someone to do such an act. What is perhaps more tragic is that Einstein was young, a new face in scientific community at that time, whereas De Pretto and Poincaré had dedicated his entire life to his research. Ironic to that tragedy, just as Einstein's fame set off, De Pretto died, and that fraud went on to travel the world, partake in the Manhattan Project, and so on... all while standing on the shoulders of another. No doubt, the cheap victory must have gnawed at him to want to leave behind something that truly was his own, and because of the false credit he had as a 'genius,' others believed in him. At no fault to the ignorant masses, he is still given false credit, and it angers me for the glory of one to be misplaced in another. For a man to be so arrogant to stand upon not his own success; so hallow inside – I have no respect for the man. Now his special relativity and this emphasis and reliance on the theoretical and supposed belief that we can not truly 'know anything,' is absurd."

"Well, that's a crazy story, Charles," the man said, looking at his watch, "and it's torn right into our time to work on this equation."

"Hm, so it has," Charlemagne agreed, looking at his watch. He tossed the piece of chalk in his hand in front of the chalkboard and then turned to his friend with a smile. "Well, enjoy your evening, Barry, but I suppose I'll duke it out here on my own."

Barry stood up from his chair and looked over to Charlemagne apologetically. He said, "Come on, Charles, another night all alone? Why don't you come out with us and live a little?"

"No, no," Charlemagne denied, "no can do, friend. I promised myself when I came to university that I wouldn't steer off the path of contribution. I told myself that I could..."

"Really make a difference," Barry repeated with him. "You've certainly made an impression on the folks around here, also some enemies, so it seems, but come on, give the ol'noggin a break and come join us. Felicity and I are going to a brand-new café that opened up on campus this semester. It's called Casa Java, or Java Casa, or something like that. All I know is that they sell coffee, and tonight is their poetry night."

"Poetry... hm, no thanks," Charlemagne remarked. "I took my mandatory English arts course in first year, and those tribulations were enough for me for a lifetime. Besides, I hardly consider it appropriate to partake as a third person on your date night."

"Oh, it's not a date night," Barry replied. "We're going with a friend of hers, and one of ours. Come on, it'll be fun."

Charlemagne thought for a moment and then remarked, "Very well. If you insist."

After the pair were ready to leave their apartment, they travelled downstairs to the lobby and came out to West Queen Boulevard on the south side of the campus. Both Charlemagne and Barry wore coats, where Charlemagne wore a blouson coat, and Barry wore a cotton jacket. They walked down along the boulevard to pass numerous commercial buildings along the street. At the intersection with the teaching hospital, they crossed northbound and then continued along Davidson Avenue to walk through the east side of the campus. Just before Marham Mall, the pair crossed the street and continued east again, coming along a promenade next to the School of Business. They soon reached a plaza near the student union building designed in brutalist architecture. From here, they came around to another plaza next to the bus station on Barcote Street. They passed the bus stop station, crossed Barcote Street, and reached a market square where the coffee shop was one of the shops inside a courtyard. After the pair were inside the shop doors, they travelled down a set of stairs into the basement level where they passed through a screen of beads to enter into the dim café lounge.

"Hm, where do you reckon Felicity is?" Charlemagne questioned, looking around. "I must admit, I quite like the quiet atmosphere, though I'm not too impressed with the lighting."

The café had an L-shape with the coffee bar on the shorter end to the left, while the tables along the narrower section ahead. There were U-shaped booth seats all along the longer wall, and a strong ambience of bluegrass jazz music and a bluish glow within. Some table seats could be found on the left with some jazz art on display.

"There she is," Barry said, looking over to a table near the end.

Charlemagne walked behind Barry as they approached the table, and he went ahead to sit down with a girl. She had deep red hair and fair skin. She appeared to be about the same age as them. She was next to a young girl who did not look the same age as them, but younger. She had fair skin and light blonde hair. She also had blue eyes that looked back at Charlemagne with focus. Charlemagne walked up to the table and back at her with minor intrigue.

"Hi Charlie," Felicity greeted, "have you met my friend? She's in engineering too."

"Oh?" Charlemagne questioned. "No, I don't think I've met this friend yet."

"She's a new friend," Felicity clarified. "This is Charlie…"

"Charlemagne," he clarified, "Charlemagne Cabernet. And you?"

"My name is Judith," the young girl greeted with a north Londoner accent, "Judith Cook. It's so nice to meet you."

"Very nice to meet you too, Ms. Cook."

"Your accent, what part of England is that?" Judith asked.

"East Anglia," Charlemagne answered, "I was raised out in those parts since I was a young boy, went to boarding school in London up until I came here when I was eighteen."

"Oh, how fascinating," Judith remarked, "and you're in engineering?"

"Yes, Barry and I are both in our third year."

"Where's Huel?" Charlemagne asked. "I thought he was going to join us when you said one of our friends was coming."

"I don't know," Barry asked, looking over to Felicity suspiciously. "I suppose he had better plans…"

"So what sort of program are in you, Charlemagne?" Judith asked.

"I am in Engineering Physics," Charlemagne answered. "A plethora of all that I love."

"Oh, I'm not sure what that one is all about," Judith said. "Do tell…"

"Engineering Physics is all about innovation and inventions," Charlemagne remarked, "which I am particularly talented in.

I've also recently become interested in computer engineering and the application of those studies to my current field. If I could recommend any program in Applied Sciences, it would be this one for the creative liberties it provides. What sort of program did you hope to pursue?"

"Oh, I'm not entirely sure," Judith said. "I do have a passion for research, but I do not only want to learn what I study, but make applications of it into technological advances. I ultimately decided on Applied Sciences because of what it had to offer in the 'applied' part. I thought I would be restless stuck in just the research components in Sciences."

"Yes, you've made a wise choice there, my dear," Charlemagne said. "What's the good of all this knowledge that we as humans come to grasp if there is no manner in which we can live it out? Do not get me wrong, there is a tremendous importance in researchers, but only as long as what they are doing can have some sort of application, and it is the best of both worlds to do both, and understand both, to unlock the secrets of what it is that awaits us. Look at computers for example, which have been the result of mathematics, not any relativist theory in the sciences..."

"Oh boy, here we go..." Barry quietly remarked.

"Do you anything about Olinto De Pretto?" Charlemagne asked.

Both Charlemagne and Judith carried on having a deep conversation related to physics, application of physics in engineering, and then hobbyist subjects.

"I've taken a history class for all of my electives," Charlemagne said. "Barry here chose literature studies and language classes, but I had no need to learn another language. I'm already fluent in German and French from my childhood, Latin I learned in school, which aided me greatly to learn both Italian and Spanish to tie it off. What else do I have to learn?"

"Oh, I remember taking Latin in school too, it was such a nightmare," Judith expressed. "It's so different from English."

"Ah, but not so different from German in structure, and French in words," Charlemagne remarked. "I found it to be a cakewalk, just a game of memorization, which I saw no challenge in."

"Can you two pipe down?" Barry requested. "The poems are about to start…"

Charlemagne and Judith looked at each other as they sat next to each other, and then over to the stadium as the lights dimmed even more. A woman in all black, sporting a black beret, approached the stage.

"Good evening, everyone," the woman spoke in a soft voice, "and welcome to tonight's poetry night. I wanted to start tonight off with something simple to set the mood… *What does it mean, these changing days? I can hardly ever feel your rays… In me too, a transformation… I do not know if I have the patience. Yet I am not alone in these times, as all my friends, I do not recognize. What does it mean, this life of mine… When I fall face first just to die?*"

There was an intermittent pause. The poet placed the microphone back in the stand, while the audience began to snap their fingers. Charlemagne, who was about to clap his hands, looked around to every one else, and with his friends caught on to the trope.

"Oh, I get it," Judith murmured to Charlemagne. "The poem was about a leaf changing color in autumn before falling from the tree."

"Ah, yes, I see that…" Charlemagne acknowledged. "Very good – you, I mean, to have caught that. I was never any good with poems."

"No worries, I was best in that in my studies," Judith remarked. "I don't know why, but just something clicks in my mind when I hear a poem, like I can see something that others can't. I could never write one of these, or mind you, get up on stage and share one. What about you?"

"Never any good at it in interpretation, never any good at it in creation," Charlemagne said. "I've been taught how to analyze them, break them down by parameter, and this and that, but still couldn't be bothered to stitch one together."

"It's not that difficult, really," Judith remarked. "It doesn't even need to follow any particular rhyme scheme or metric, though those can be fun. A poem can be whatever words you so choose to craft together, in whatever length or prose."

"Quiet," Felicity hushed, "I want to hear the poems."

Another poet stepped up to the stage and gave their poem. A few more approached, followed with a somber one from a male in all black.

"Behind your parents, I knew you before you were even born. From the moment you were birthed, did I see you. In the watches of the night, was I there in the shadows when you were a child, but only as you grew older to an adolescent could you even think of me or know my name. As a young adult, you loathe me, but as the years go by you begin to fear me as I encroach. By then, many come to meet me sooner rather than later, your friends I would come to know first as though for you it would be late. By the time we finally meet, you too can call me friend."

The audience responded with snaps to that poem. Charlemagne gave some brief snaps before he sat back again and turned to Judith. He quietly said, "Well, that one was something..."

"Yes, I'm a bit puzzled at that one..." Judith responded, looking forward with fingers pinching her chin. She then suddenly looked over to Charlemagne with allure in her eyes. "Do you have any favorite poem, Charles? Anything you've come to read in your studies?"

"Not particularly," Charlemagne replied, looking plainly forward. "What about you?"

"Oh, yes," Judith answered, looking forward as well. "When I was in sixth form, I loved Percy Shelley's *Ozymandias* immensely."

Another woman stepped up to the stage and recited her poem as she said, "*From dust to dust, we trek this place, To what do we owe all this strife? Of all of us from here to outer space, For what do we live this life?*" The stanza was interrupted with a tap of some drums. "*Who are we to think and be, And yet to only rise and fall? What is there for us to see, And not believe that we are so small?*" This stanza was likewise interrupted with some taps from the drums. "*Why is that we should scavenge, When life is such a challenge? How can any of us be so great, When we all share in this same fate?*" Another tap of the drums, followed by a pause. "*My existence does not leave me frightened, So long as I should love, and be enlightened.*" A heightened tap of the drums follows suit, and the poet bowed and then left the stage. The room filled with snaps as applause, and Charlemagne sat back and pondered.

"Oh, I liked that one," Judith remarked to Charlemagne. "That one was good…"

"Hm… yes, but what does it mean?"

"Come now," Judith replied, smiling at him, "I don't think it was that hard to grasp. Live, love, and let yourself be enlightened."

Act 5, Scene 1

Charlemagne pulled out a backpack from the rear of the GAZ jeep and brought the straps around his shoulders. The backpack included various brand-new equipment, as well as a sleeping mat. Both he and Manon appeared refreshed and awake, each in sets of brand-new outdoor apparel that included the same ponchos they wore for a while now. Charlemagne closed the trunk door and then turned to Manon.

"Shall we?" Charlemagne asked. He then left the rear of the GAZ as it was parked around some trees near a dirt road. "Lots of kilometers to get through, my dear. We have a full day ahead of us."

"*Charles*, we are getting off track," Manon noted as he started to make his way into the forest for a hike. "How can you be so confident that the crown is among this treasure?"

"There is about a one-hundred-and-fifty-year gap between when the crown went missing, and it could have gone anywhere. We've seemingly reached a dead-end at that graveyard, so it's time to start anew. The least we know based on our current research is that the Frankish Crown could not be in western society. Between its disappearance in Romania to now, it would either have to have wandered through the Ottoman Empire or the Russian Empire, and given that both of those civilizations are both obscure to us, I would hazard it to still be in one of those two. The Germans were hauling valuables back to the West during their invasion of Russia, and this manifesto cites crown jewels that are 'foreign,' as in, neither German nor Russian."

"But we looked through the German archives and there was no mention of anything else to do with the crown since before the war," Manon remarked. "Besides, we did not finish looking at the clues in the cemetery.

"What clues? A wonky sword that we lost in the car wreckage?" Charlemagne questioned. "I'm not backtracking to

Romania to pick up that sword, besides, from the moment I saw it I knew it had a Balkan design to it. The sword clearly belonged to one of Zarko's men, and that bloody liar must have killed those gypsies, and he plundered the crown for himself."

"If so, then what are we doing here in Ukraine?"

"Like I said, a hundred and fifty years have passed. Let's assume that Zarko did plunder the crown and it came back to Serbia or sold in Romania at the time. From that point, it could have gone anywhere. For nearly a hundred years after the Napoleonic Wars, Pax Britannica, like Pax Romana, enhanced trade in Europe. I'm certain that the crown is nowhere in the West, and I would have to include Yugoslavia and Greece in that mixture, which means it is somewhere around the Black Sea region."

Manon did not reply.

"Based on the information that Krum was carrying around, an armored train that set out from Kiev is supposed to be in this forest," Charlemagne said, stopping to look at the map Manon was still looking at. "If you look at the map of the Ukraine that shows the rail network, not much has changed. The train was supposed to come to Lvov, but never did. I've read of something similar happening in Poland with a train full of gold, where in that example it was suspected that the train was hidden away in an off-shoot tunnel and rail line."

"Ah, and why did you not go looking for that train then?"

"What desire do I have in an abundance of gold?" Charlemagne questioned. "You assume as though I do what I do for the wealth of it – you know better than that."

"Yes, for much worse," Manon muttered.

Charlemagne continued to hike forward as they entered into the forest. The surrounding forest had a glum expression to it; almost all leaves of these tall deciduous trees had sunken, and what green did exist came in the form of tall, but thin coniferous pine trees and shorter pine trees with long branches. The ground consisted of dusty dirt and roots protruded outwards from it. There were seldom bushes and shrubs to cover the ground, but what there was plenty of were leaves, all the leaves covered the ground around the trees from which they fell from, though they had lost their color and were faded to a near grey.

"This forest is somewhat similar to the one in Romania," Charlemagne noted, looking about. "Perhaps my favorite experience, one that I cherish from Cabernet Ex in particular, was the opportunity to hike; to just hike and camp in the outdoors. I so adore the opportunity to be in the midst of nature, to inhale the fresh natural air and to just muse as I walk the brisk walk. My mother, perhaps the German in her and I, enjoyed to hike, though my father too though I'm told she pushed it onto him."

"Ah, but the hike is the German pastime," Manon acknowledged. "Certainly, not as popular in Germany as it is in France."

"I do enjoy appreciating the flora whilst on a hike," Charlemagne remarked. "If I had to guess, based on the geography about us, this forest would be typical of Central European mixed forest. I see the notorious Scot pine tree among the cone-bearing plants and oak trees among the leave-falling plants. To think that once upon a time, bison used to roam these forests, like those in the United States, before they were all hunted. Mind you, all sorts of animals used to roam the Europe before they were hunted out of existence. Even lions used to roam these lands, though I can imagine as beautiful as a sight it must have been, how necessary it was to reduce them, though not to extinction."

"My father would always tell me, 'Manon, if you are to be a good historian, not just any historian, but a good one, then you need to immerse yourself in the land long past.' It is too easy to understand the world as we know it, but like you say, not all remains the same in our lives. Perhaps with your knowledge,

Charles, in all sorts of disciplines, you could have an easier time than me, but there is so much to consider in a time since past. My father would also tell me not to be so fast to judge a world past, as we too may be judged in future. In my own studies, I've tried to look at the cultures of different societies to understand their actions and it too changes so quickly. We are so quick to assume a bias about past culture, so too we assume a bias about the physical world."

"That we do," Charlemagne affirmed.

"My father would often criticize the arrogance of other historians and critics, to assume and let their biases corrupt their opinion about a subject matter. What is history to be but the truth of the past, good or bad, and who are we to judge or believe that we are better than a people past? It is a dishonesty to believe that we are better than others, or that what happens in the now is just and pure."

"Yes, that is most true," Charlemagne responded. "I recall that about your father very well. It's those outlooks that have made him so skilled in his field. Your father… taught me much of what I know, and I'd do him no good if I were to not find this damned crown."

"Do not believe that my father would not love you anymore than he has if you do not find this crown, *Charles*," Manon quickly interjected. "Why do I suppose at times you put yourself in danger just for his sake?"

"I do no such thing," Charlemagne rebutted. "I'm out here of my own accord. I'm only saying as we talk about him now, as a student of his, I do him no honor, as well as others who have reared me, if I do not do something great."

Manon did not respond. The pair continued to hike through the day. They continued through a consistent ambience of a forest, to occasional clearings to the odd open pasture with tall grass. Eventually, as the sun began to set, Charlemagne stopped them to decide to locate a campground where they set up for the evening. Charlemagne did not speak much as they enjoyed a camp-side meal and sat around a fire by a creek across from each other.

Manon sat on a log near the fire while Charlemagne sat on the ground. He would occasionally scratch his thickened blonde beard. He would stroke it; he would pick at the side of the moustache and pull at the odd hair. He would also bring his hand around his neck. Manon read a book near the campfire as he did so, writing in his journal about the trek and fondly making notes about the flora, fauna, and his companion in this adventure, Manon. Charlemagne poked at the fire on occasion with a stick and then would resume jotting down a thought. Manon sat awkwardly on the log and would at times look over to him, especially as he scratched beard.

"*Mon Dieu, Charles*, why not do away with that beard?" Manon questioned. "You are doing yourself no favor."

"It's not a problem to me," Charlemagne replied. "Is it a problem for you?"

"No, let yourself suffer for all I care, but stop scratching it, please."

Charlemagne picked up the stick again and began to poke the fire instead. He then let the stick down and placed his hand around the lower end of his beard. He then said, "I wouldn't mind giving it a trim, but only problem is that I couldn't see what I'm doing out here. If it's a bother, I could do something about it…"

"No bother," Manon responded, "just stop scratching…"

Charlemagne resumed to write in his journal. However, after only a few minutes, he lowered his pencil to bring a hand to the beard and scratch the side. Manon looked over to him and he slowly stopped.

"I'll be candid," Charlemagne confessed, "it is a bother for me. I would be quite relieved if you could help me give it a trim."

Manon looked at him, closed her book and set it aside, and then looked at him intently. She replied, "You want for me to help you?"

"Yes... I mean, I couldn't do this myself..."

"What if I told you that I like the beard," Manon expressed. "I've come to enjoy it – it looks good. Like a real man."

"As heroic as it may seem to be, it is quite a bother," Charlemagne begrudgingly remarked. "If it pleases you though..."

"Give me a knife and scissors," Manon asked, "I'll see what I can do."

Manon fetched a sharp knife and a pair of scissors. She then placed a small pale of water next to them and set to work. She knelt in front of Charlemagne and began to trim the longer hairs of the beard, gently doing so until the beard was just about trimmed except around the moustache. She then took a bar of soap and began to apply it around the cheeks, chin, and jaw to rightly shave to the skin. She took her time, bringing the blade down the cheeks, and then the chin, and around the jaw until she left behind smooth skin on all reaches except around the moustache. When she was ready, Manon began to work around the moustache as she trimmed around that area and stopped. She looked at Charlemagne with loving eyes for a brief moment and then turned away as she blushed.

"You look so much like your grandfather, *Charles*," Manon noted. "Sorry, it was not my intent, but with the moustache, you really do look like him."

Charlemagne did not respond and instead brought his hand to his moustache. "I wish I could see..."

"Wait," Manon remarked, looking around her bag to bring out a small mirror. "Here..."

Charlemagne opened the mirror and then looked at his face. Above his upper lip was a chevron moustache consisting of golden blonde hair. He examined himself carefully and then passed the mirror back to Manon. Manon inched forward with the blade to finish shaving his face, to which he raised his hands to stop.

"How about we leave it like that," Charlemagne requested. "I like it…"

Manon nodded and then washed the blade and scissors in the pale. Charlemagne looked at himself in the mirror again and then returned it to Manon when she was done washing the tools.

• • •

The next day, Charlemagne and Manon set forth from the campsite and continued to hike through the forest. After a few hours, a quick midday lunch, they hiked up a hill to reach a cliff that overlooked a distance of many trees. Directly below them, Charlemagne saw a gulch. He followed the cliff, following the gully below until he began to see the gully turn to a gulch where overtop there was the sight of a right trapezoid shaped box car with turrets at the top.

"Bingo," Charlemagne reckoned, looking ahead with a pair of binoculars. "I'd say that's our treasure nest."

Manon looked through the binoculars while Charlemagne prepared some rope for them to climb down a few feet to the ground below. They then trekked along the side of the gulch until they were looking down at the armored car stuck within the earth. The outlines of rail tracks could slightly be seen in a linear fashion through the gulch and along to the gully far ahead. The armor car before them was trapezoid in shape and at least twelve yards in length. At the rear of the car from where they stood was a turret with a medium length cannon pointed forward. Behind this car was a twelve-yard flat bed followed by an ordinary twelve yard rectangular box car and an armored box car. The train then continued lengthwise for several yards down the gulch.

"She's quite a long train, isn't she," Charlemagne acknowledged, looking down to see several armored boxcars. He paused for a moment as he examined the extent of the train with his eyes. He then hopped over the three-foot gap and landed atop of the rectangular box car. His landing caused a loud echo inward. He looked left and right and then pointed towards the way they came as he said, "Seems as though this is the front of the train as the coal car is that way." He then helped Manon cross over.

"Where do you think the cargo is kept?" Manon asked.

"If I had to guess, right below us in the cargo hold, but it is an armored beast, so I wouldn't be surprised if it was elsewhere," Charlemagne answered. He turned the other direction and looked past the twelve yard armor car behind them. Behind them was a twenty-five-yard flat bed, followed by a very long armored car.

After a brief observation, Charlemagne and Manon climbed down a ladder on the side of the armored car to reach the ground. As they walked, Charlemagne flashed his flashlight along the ground as he observed the wheels had sunken into the earth, and likewise the rail line was not visible either. The flat bed was directly atop of the ground, while the armored car ahead of them had its base directly touch the ground too. "I don't believe this rail line was on very sound ground," he noted as he flashed his light around. "If I had to guess, shoddy Soviet craftsmanship or quick improvisation to be the cause of this poorly made rail line. Both also possible."

The pair continued to walk down approximately fifty yards in length, reaching the end of the initial length armored box car. This car had four turrets, two at the front and end. At the end of the armored box car was at least a forty-yard gap. Charlemagne observed with his flashlight as the connector with the armored box car was submerged in the ground, and likewise the last half of the armored car was sloped inwards to the ground more than the initial half. He walked down the forty yard length where there was another fifty-yard box car, more submerged than the other as the initial half sloped downward, and the rest of it could only been seen top half up.

"Well, that's no good. It seems like we've lost a bit of it to the mud…" Charlemagne stated, looking forward. He came around to the rear of the rear-most armored box car where at either end of these trapezoid-shaped cars were sloped doors slightly raised by steps. He attempted to open the doors, but they would not open. "Damn, seems as though the handles are a little too rusty." He stepped back and then looked over towards the length of the train they had already passed. "I wish we had visited Konstantin before we had come here. We could have used his expertise."

"Expertise… in trains?"

"No, in explosives," Charlemagne corrected. He proceeded to walk back the way he came, reaching the opposite set of doors. He attempted to open them, but they would not open either. They walked fifty yards to the other side, and likewise the doors would not open. They came around to the twelve-yard armored car, and it too would not open. They then came around to a rectangular box car exposed to the elements as it had no door, and there were a few crates inside to examine. Charlemagne passed through to the end and found the last twelve-yard armored car. He attempted to open both sides, and then came around to the rectangular box car as that failed.

"Well, seems like we're unable to get in," Charlemagne remarked. "Let's have a look at what's in this car." They examined the contents of the crates, locating a crowbar to open the crates, and finding routine supplies. These were rations, medical supplies, and industrial materials. "What kind of treasure is this supposed to be…" He opened the last crate and began to take out boxes of items labeled with warnings. Charlemagne's eyebrows raised as he read the label in German. "Hm…"

"What is it?" Manon questioned.

"Iron-Three-Oxide," Charlemagne answered. "Quite a lot of it… and aluminum flakes… Altogether, I could make some thermite and melt through those door handles…"

Charlemagne opened one of the small boxes of iron oxide which contained a red powder substance inside. He began to mix it with the aluminum, using some plastic bags from his backpack to create a small package.

"The only problem with thermite is that it needs a lot of heat to ignite," Charlemagne remarked. "The lighter in our kits won't be enough. We'll need to create heat by some other means, and it will need to be a constant source…"

Charlemagne thought for a moment and then walked over towards the armored car behind the coal car. He placed the package of thermite he had made along the handles of the door. He then retrieved an aerosol can from his backpack and a lighter.

"You will want to stand back for this," Charlemagne requested, prompting Manon to stand behind him. He sprayed towards the thermite package and then immediately lit the lighter to turn the aerosol spray into a flamethrower. He continued to spray in the direction of the thermite, eventually causing it to catch fire. At first, the fire was typical as the thermite caught fire, but then flew outwards and Charlemagne immediately retreated away as a violent reaction took place. "Thermite does not explode," he explained. "It causes intense heat to come around it, melting whatever it touches, including metal."

After a moment, the reaction subsided, and a hole was left where the handles were. The area glowed orange-red for a moment. Charlemagne took the crowbar and used it to pry the doors open, revealing the inside of the armored car. This armored car revealed a luxurious inside with polished wooden walls, carpet floor, and a door ahead. Charlemagne opened the door and found a private quarters with a bed, desk, and various documents laying around.

"Hm, not a storage hold as I thought it would be," Charlemagne acknowledged. "Still, there may be some information here we can scavenge."

Manon began to go through the documents. Charlemagne meanwhile took a brief look around before he returned to the other box car to make more thermite. He made another package, placed it on the car behind the box car and then lit it in the same way. The reaction set off and melted through the door, allowing him to enter in. However, rather than treasure, this car stored munitions for the cannons above. He then returned to the box car to make another package of thermite. Charlemagne walked to the fifty-yard train that was not submerged and closest to the box car, placed the package, and with his makeshift flamethrower, lit the substance, but as he finished spraying, noticed that he was out of aerosol spray.

"Well, it better be in here," Charlemagne quietly spoke. He pried the door open with the crowbar and then began to step inside. The fifty-yard box car was divided into four segments, each separated by airtight doors. The initial car was similar to the one before with munition crates, except there was a desk with a radio as well. He opened the door behind it and found a living quarters with three beds on the right side, a washroom stall in the corner. He opened the next set of doors and found another living space, and then followed at the end he found another munitions storage area with the ladders to the cannons above. "Drat..." He walked forward and opened the set of doors to the armored car length at the very rear and then returned to join Manon.

"I've run out of bug spray," Charlemagne acknowledged, placing the can on the desk, "and there is one more car I have yet to search before we call it quits. I've not seen anything to suggest there to be treasure here."

"Ah, but treasure there may be," Manon noted. "These letters are from a Waffen-SS officer, in charge of this train and the delivery of its contents to East Prussia. According to the officer, these items are of most important to the German high command. This letter is dated September 1943."

"What hope is there to crack through," Charlemagne stated, arms crossed. "I'd have an easier time throwing one of those shells at the door than to use the crowbar, I..." He paused for a moment. "Hang on..."

Charlemagne walked down the entire length of the train again and reached the second-last armored car. He opened one of the crates with the shells and then began to examine the turret cannon. Manon joined him as she watched.

"What are you doing?" Manon questioned.

"I've always wanted to do something like this," Charlemagne expressed, climbing the ladder and taking control of the turret cannon. He began to spin it around and point the cannon at the doors he needed to get through. He then loaded the shell into the cannon, but before he fired, he went around to the roof to ensure that the cannon was clear of debris before he came back up the ladder to pull the trigger. "*Feuer!*"

Manon quickly brought her hands to her ears and the cannon fired, ripping through the armored door and causing shrapnel to fly upwards and around the surroundings, including the roof of the box car they were in. Charlemagne laughed as the looked ahead. He then climbed down. Manon quickly looked over to him and growled.

After the smoke settled, Charlemagne walked ahead and entered into the sunken armored car. He found that the initial car was like the others, except there fewer munition crates and also beds in this area. He came to the next door, opened it, and rather than living quarters, he found crates stored inside, and paintings lined about.

"Hm, nobody tell Rubashkin about this place, lest this artwork come into hands," Charlemagne stated. "Look at this though... what a trove."

The pair walked through the narrow aisle to reach the other side, opening the door to find more of the same: artwork, crates, and chests that contained numerous valuable goods no less. The final segment of the train was like the others in that it had more munitions. Charlemagne attempted to open the final doors out, but they would not open. The pair returned to the cargo and Charlemagne took his crowbar to open one of them.

"Let's see what is in crate number one, *fraulein*..."

The crate opened and inside revealed gold ingots stacked upon each other.

"Oh my..."

"*Charles*..." Manon remarked, eyes widening. "What have we found?"

Charlemagne immediately raised a mild scowl. He came around to anther crate, and likewise, more ingots. He opened all the crates in this segment, and they all had that gold shine; more ingots. He entered into the other segment and opened those crates, and there were more ingots. He then opened the chest, and inside he found jewelry. He opened the other chests and there was more jewellery and other trinkets. Charlemagne's scowl deepened as he turned to Manon.

"I don't see a crown here..." Charlemagne noted. "Just more gold... useless gold..."

"*Charles*, there must be more than a million dollars worth of gold here."

"Easily, but what use do I have for gold?" Charlemagne questioned. "I want to find the Frankish Crown, not apparel pieces and money. What use do I have to have the extent of wealth of Mansa Musa?"

"Hmph," Manon responded, crossing her arms. "What a thing to say, eh? There is more money here than I could hope or know to do with in a lifetime, and you dismiss it."

"And I'll leave it here too," Charlemagne said, walking out of the car as he finished examining for other chests. "Do you think I'll haul this much treasure through the woods? Perhaps I'll send someone for it, but right now, I couldn't care for it. Come now…"

"At least Mansa Musa knew what his wealth was worth," Manon noted to him as he left. "Not frivolous adventures, nor to sit upon it nor dismiss it."

Charlemagne stopped for a moment as he heard these words, and then continued to step forward. He came around to the officer quarters where he looked through the papers and sat down. Manon soon joined him. He briefly looked at the papers, and then at his watch. He proceeded to gather all the papers together and put them into his backpack.

"I'll have to look at these later, but this cargo came from somewhere, and I intend to know where because there we'll find this foreign crown I was promised," Charlemagne said. "Let's get a move on before it gets dark."

Act 5, Scene 2

Charlemagne looked out his balcony in the early morning as the looked towards a figure atop of a column in the middle of a small plaza by a city street. The column was tall, and the figure was greenish-grey, dressed in a robe. The top and bottom of the column were gold-colored, and above the figure as it had its armed stretched outwards, was a golden arch. In front of the monument was a flagpole with a blue-yellow flag flying in the wind. Charlemagne drank some coffee as he looked around the city. Around this area of the city were various buildings in the same typical architecture seen throughout Central and Eastern Europe. On the other side from where Charlemagne was there was a white building. At its base, the building consisted of arched windows, but above it there was an area around the perimeter in which one could walk around and followed with two-story tall columns that supported the rooftop, which was the same size as the base and flat. Near this structure was a church-like building, and then across the street there was a large eight-story building consisting of beige stone and with a sign that read 'Bank' in Latin alphabet. Directly in front of the monument was an arched plaza with five-separate roadways branching out at the end. Charlemagne looked above and saw that the skies in Kiev were dark grey, and as he continued to drink his coffee, he looked to his side as a neighboring door opened and a person stepped out.

Manon wore a robe and began to light a cigarette caught between her lips. Charlemagne wore a grey suit with no tie. He raised his mug to her and greeted her, "Good morning." The cigarette lit and she blew the smoke out from her mouth as she brought one arm to her abdomen as though to cross her arms, but with her right arm she flexed and held the cigarette.

"*Bonjour, Charles,*" Manon greeted.

"I was able to make contact with Konstantin Sakharov," Charlemagne said, turning around to place his backside against the railing as he continued to drink coffee. "He's well, happy to receive us, and I noted his address though it seems like he lives not too far from here."

"*Bien.*"

"I also had a read through those documents – that train was never meant to leave station, I think. I think it got lost because it went off-course. It was stationed here, in Kiev, and before that it was in an area referred to in German as '*Yuzivka*,' but which I cannot find. The train was half-loaded with goods when it left station due to advancing Soviets, the rest of the items left behind in a salt mine, the entrance of which was demolished. If we're going to find this mine, then we'll certainly need Konstantin to join us."

"Ah, good, one more pyromaniac to join the party," Manon remarked. "I'll be sure to bring ear covers this time, before I lose my hearing because of either of you. I do not look fondly on our time with Konstantin… the anxiety with all that man carried with him was never easy."

"Ah, don't you worry now, he's an expert. He's an army veteran and the most knowledgeable man in all of the former Soviet Union in things to do with explosives. Besides, he speaks just about all the languages we've hoped we could understand. He's the most perfect asset to our team."

"I do not want to travel with explosives, *Charles*," Manon remarked. "As much as an expert he is, it was never him that was the problem. He was a kind man, but with all the people who have been after us, shooting at our vehicle, I would rather not…"

"Oh relax, will you?" Charlemagne rebuked. "We're in a different land now, the outback of the former Russian Empire; literally, a country whose name means 'borderland,' separated from whence we came. The only danger I suppose from here is the local authorities, or if we were to somehow make any new enemies. I wouldn't anticipate we've been followed – we ditched that jeep and bought a new car. We haven't used any of my credit cards and have only paid for things in cash. We're off the grid, so to speak, and completely untraceable even by today's standards."

"I spoke with my father last evening," Manon said. "I told him that we were in Kiev and on the hunt for this Nazi treasure. He questioned me and asked what happened to our lead in Romania, and I told him that we hit an impasse there. I have not told him about all the trouble you've put us through, but even with the acquisition of this map, and the insinuation from yourself that this could be a shortcut we need, he doubts it to be. He also condemns this cheating, so to speak."

"Cheating? What cheating? I found a map, it leads to some treasure, some of that treasure includes a crown – what more is there?"

"You are so confident in your stupid map, but it was not even yours to begin with."

"I never said it was mine, besides, it's got to be it. There aren't many Crown Jewels in the world that have gone missing, and besides, the ones that have are likely to be in their geographical regions – the Irish Crown Jewels, for example, or the English."

"Yes, he made a joke some time ago," Manon remarked. "He said when you are finished here, perhaps you can find the English crown."

"Very funny..." Charlemagne responded. "The Hawaiian crown is also amiss. You know two-hundred years ago, the Scottish Crown was also considered to be missing. They were hidden during the English Civil War to prevent Oliver Cromwell from destroying them. They were placed in a chest and thrown under some linen in Edinburgh Castle. Shortly after the civil war, the Scots unified with the English to form the United Kingdom, and the crown stayed put in Edinburgh until about a hundred and fifty years later where it was exactly where it was last placed."

"What is your point, *Charles*?"

"My point is that you can leave something for a hundred and fifty years, and it won't have moved. I don't anticipate the Frankish Crown to have done much moving about and that it is most likely exactly where it had come to rest after a moment, and that moment being the Second World War and in these salt mines where they rest."

"If you say so, *Charles*," Manon replied, putting out her cigarette. "I'll be with you in an hour while I get ready."

Manon re-entered her room. Charlemagne re-entered his room and went to brush his teeth. When he was finished, he continued to read through the notes from the German officer and then joined Manon outside their rooms so they could venture forth to the bottom of the hotel. The hotel they stayed in was simple, and the lobby small. A taxi waited for them in front of the hotel, and the pair got inside, and Charlemagne provided the address to the driver.

The taxi driver spoke in Ukrainian to them, to which Charlemagne replied, "Sorry, only English." The driver then went quiet, and they began to drive along.

"Never in all my years did I ever anticipate I would be in Kiev, the city where it all began for this part of the world. There is so much history here, my mind could melt..."

"You're welcome then," Charlemagne responded, taking his journal from his suit pocket and opening it to write. "I was in Moscow a few years ago with Mr. Adlington, as part of a mission to open ties with the Second World after the collapse of the Soviet Union. A beautiful city, for certain, in some parts, but in others there is an aura of dread that follows this land. As if the souls of every innocent man, woman, and child killed in the communist regime haunts the land."

"Ah, perhaps there you met Rubashkin. He did seem to think you knew who he was."

Charlemagne paused for a moment and then looked at Manon. He replied, "You know what, come to think of it, I perhaps did – yes. We met with so many people in those few days, I could not be certain, but his name does strike me as a little bit familiar, Avdiyi Rubashkin." He paused for a moment as he looked out the window. The car drove uphill on a slope, driving along a brick street surrounded by trees. There were small apartments on either side, separated by wide sidewalks and each building with its own front lot, mostly consisting of bushes, a path up to the door, and mowed grass. They then passed along a tighter street in which there were no more front lawns, but longer apartment blocks of buildings with grey stone foundation and sand beige brick facades. He looked out for another moment and then into the rear-view mirror as he noticed the taxi driver looking at him. He then looked back at Manon. "Of course, who can blame me to forget this man's name? We met close to five years ago... I'm not in the business of remembering people's names, especially nobodies from this nobodyland. What I do know is that after we returned, we received word that it was not entirely in our favor to do business with the ex-soviet states. Those people were had met... they called them 'oligarchs' in the press. I was told that they were a group of entrepreneurs and businessmen who had exploited the collapse of the Soviet Union through corruption with the Russian government and opportunistic moments to seize on the nationalized wealth that became privatized in the emerging free market economy. Later on, I've also heard from those blokes that they were the ones primarily responsible for the collapse of the Soviet Union themselves, for the sole intent of reaping the wealth of the nation and such."

Charlemagne looked to his side again as they passed a park. In the front-middle of the park was a short red tower with a black portcullis. The tower was at the front of a wooden structure with numerous layers upwards, three in total. Around the side of the peculiar structure was a statue of a man in a robe seated.

"Ah, that must be the Golden Gate..." Charlemagne noted.

The driver took a right turn further ahead. They drove along a very narrow and dirty street with short apartment blocks consisting of stone. Many of the buildings had barred windows, the upper levels with balconies. The walls were tagged with graffiti, and the streets cracked and littered. The road soon narrowed further so much so that only one vehicle could pass in one direction. Numerous cars were parked on the curb too. They soon passed a white wall on the right with additional white brick apartments on the left. After they passed the wall, the car came to an intersection and turned right again. They then went down a wider street that was cleaner with taller apartment blocks that did not have any graffiti. At the end of the street was a bend on the right, and on the right was a large plaza consisting of grey stone in cross-like patterns of darker grey stone. The plaza was surrounded with bollards, and in the front-middle was a statue. The car drove right and came onto a much wider road that passed in front of the plaza. The statue consisted of a soldier in medieval armor, on a horse looking inward to the plaza while atop of a mossy mound of large stone bricks. Within the plaza was a large basilica, the main tower of which had four levels with a golden domed crown atop, and at the very top of this crown a Christian cross. These levels were like layers, the bottom-most larger than the top with open arches in the middle. There were similar towers around the side, one in the middle a portion of the size of the original tower surrounded with six or seven others that were turquoise and only the very top gold-colored. The basilica was white and overlooked the plaza. They passed along, continuing along the wider street that also consisted of stone bricks.

Charlemagne noticed them pass the Golden Gate again. He paused for a moment and then turned to Manon and said, "I think we're being taken along for a ride. I've heard about this before

– where the chauffer takes you for a spin and you stand in awe at the sights, but they only mean to squeeze you for a penny more in the ride."

Manon nodded. Charlemagne leaned forward and said, "Excuse me, we are being taken to that address we gave you, right?"

The chauffer did not respond. He pointed to the note he gave the driver, and the man spoke in Ukrainian to him, to which Charlemagne responded in German.

"Wir werden zu der Adresse gebracht, die ich Ihnen gegeben habe, richtig?"

The man raised an eyebrow and then nodded. He replied, *"Natürlich."* He turned right and then right again further along before going right once more as they came to a large street. The street took them forward where they eventually reached another plaza with a gold-crowned basilica. A statue in the plaza consisted of four white marble statues on grey pedestals. The tallest of the pedestals displayed a female figure in a white robe looking forward. The other two had smaller pedestals, one of which had two figures. The basilica was similar to the one they had formerly passed, but the main tower had one less layer and its walls were light blue and white. After a drive along, the car reached the intersection with the hotel, turned right, and then went down the same major street they had gone down before. Charlemagne tapped his fingers impatiently, but rather than go right they turned left at another intersection and continued along a boulevard in which he saw many billboards and other advertisements on display, many for products he recognized.

"The amount of commercialization even in Kiev is astounding," Charlemagne remarked. "Earlier when we arrived in Kiev, I had seen many of the fast-food joints typical in North America."

"Ah, of course, thanks to the Americans, those are seen in all of Europe. Certainly there are many of them in Paris. I remember as a child being enthralled at such a sight, but now as an adult, the presence of these venues and their cheap products is an eyesore."

"I'm certain that your reaction is everybody else's reaction."

The taxi drove through Kiev along this freeway where they eventually reached an interchange. The car passed an overpass and then peeled left in a fork in the freeway, turning left again to come along to the lower road perpendicular with the freeway. The car drove down a slope in which on the right there were apartment blocks and on the left hills covered with many green bushes and tall barren trees. There were also more billboards on either side of the freeway. Charlemagne looked ahead as the freeway curved right and through the greyish-brown hills he could see a silver-colored statue. This statue poked through the foreground. The figure had its arms raised in either direction, back towards the freeway and looking out to the sky. In one hand, it held a shield, and in the other a sword pointed skyward. As the car came closer, Charlemagne saw that the statue was atop of a grey pedestal at the top of a hill across from the freeway. The taxi drove to a larger interchange, but carried on forward as they went uphill slightly.

The car passed a waypoint on either side of the road with four columns atop of a flat roof to create a slight shelter. Above the roof there were four poles with banners that had the Ukrainian flag flying in the wind. The car continued along with lamp posts on either side of a three-lane bridge. The bridge was long and crossed over a wide blue river surrounded by trees with a city horizon on the other side.

"Feels a little bit like Harlech..." Charlemagne muttered.

At the end of the bridge was another interchange where this time they pulled out and then continued left. They drove down a plain road with clean structures on the right and a park on the left. They journeyed along until they pulled right and drove through a sort of suburbs with many apartment buildings.

Finally, they arrived at one apartment block, in similar architecture to the many buildings across the river in Kiev.

Charlemagne paid the driver and then they exited out. He walked towards the front gate of the building and found an intercom. He searched for Konstantin's name and then buzzed in.

"*Hallo?*" a voice spoke out from the end.

"Good morning, my old friend," Charlemagne greeted. "We're at the front door, old chap."

"Ah, Karl, yes! Come in."

The door unlocked and Charlemagne and Manon went inside. They walked upstairs to the fourth floor and then down a hall to an apartment at the end where then stopped. Charlemagne knocked on the door and the door quickly opened.

Konstantin looked down upon them from the other side. He was a tall man, three inches more than Charlemagne, stocky, and he had a blackish-white beard and neatly combed medium length peppered hair, shorter on the sides, and blue eyes. He had fair skin at an olive hue, though slightly wrinkled at the forehead and side of his eyes. He wore a brown suit with a blue tie. He appeared to be in his mid-fifties.

"Charlemagne, there you are!" Konstantin greeted, stepping forward and embracing him. "How have you been my old friend?"

"Well, quite well," Charlemagne responded. He then let go and looked at his side to Manon.

"Ah, and you are with Manon as well!" Konstantin remarked. "Hello, my beauty!" He took Manon's hand to greet her and shook it with both of his hands.

"*Bonjour*, Konstantin."

"I did not expect you to bring company," Konstantin remarked. "Are you not here to interview me for that job we talked about?"

"Interview?" Manon questioned.

"No, that won't be necessary," Charlemagne remarked, looking to Manon as she looked at him. "Why don't we go inside?"

"Why would you interview him, *Charles*?"

"For the job, of course," Konstantin answered. "With Cabernet Industries."

"Oh, is that what we call it now?" Manon jestered, looking at Charlemagne.

Charlemagne budged forward into the small apartment, passing the toilet closet and then kitchen on the left, bedrooms on the right, and entering to the main living space with a balcony looking outwards to a park.

"Where's Olga?"

"She went out. I told her I had an interview with you."

"Yes, about that... congratulations, you've got the job," Charlemagne remarked. "My only question is if you are still in contact with those vendors of yours."

"Vendors?"

"Yes, the explosives dealer," Charlemagne said. "If you're to join us, we're going to need explosives – lots of them."

"Ah, yes, but why do I need explosives?" Konstantin asked. "I thought you were taking me with you to Canada. Is it safe to bring explosives there?"

Manon looked at Charlemagne again, and then he turned to Konstantin and remarked. "Yes, that's a part of the bargain, isn't it... but never mind that right now. You're not bringing explosives to Canada, just transporting them around in Ukraine. We have a job to do here. Just like the jobs you used to do for Cabernet Ex, remember?"

"Of course. Of course... eh, explosives, I can provide, but what for exactly? I need to know *for* which kind."

"I'm looking to explore a salt mine out in the *Yuzivka* region," Charlemagne clarified. "I've done a bit of research since arriving in Kiev, and it seems like my interest is an abandoned salt mine from the empire days. I'm going to need your assistance to pinpoint the location – are you still in contact with Igor Ivanov?"

"Igor? Yes, why?"

"I'm going to need his assistance as well," Charlemagne noted. "I would assume that he has plenty of access to the former Soviet archives and more."

"Yes, I can do that… uh, but what explosives do you need from me. There are many *kind*."

"Well, it's a mine, with possible sections that have caved in. I have a bit of thermite for any thick metal that needs to be bypassed, so I would say an assortment of everything possible would be best. Do you have any hiking equipment? We may need to do some camping out in the woods for a few days depending on where this mine is. If not, that's okay. I can buy you some…"

"Hiking… yes…" Konstantin remarked, sitting down, "that may be a bit of a problem…"

"What?"

Konstantin chuckled and said, "A few months ago, Karl, I had a bit of an accident…" He rolled up his pant sleeve and showed them the prosthetic leg that came down from a nub in his lower right foot. "Not very good for walking anymore. I hope it is not a problem… if so, I can still hike…"

"Er…"

"*Charles*," Manon scolded before he could speak.

"Is it safe for you to walk on that for extended periods?"

"No problem at all. I swear… I can do the job, please. Whatever you need, I can do."

"*Charles*," Manon again scolded, looking at him. "What is going on here?"

"Alright, alright," Charlemagne beckoned. "Konstantin, don't worry about the job offer. I promise you, I'll get you and Olga to Canada, and I'll ensure there's a job for you at the brand-new Cabernet Industries research facility in Allabrese. Cabernet

Industries will assist you with immigration, work permit, and we'll go from there, but right now I just need to focus on you being able to help me with my current expedition. I need to tackle some abandoned mines in *Yuzivka*, and for that I'm going to need explosives of all sorts. Just teach me how to use them, and I'll take care of them, but I need you to provide and help me out here."

"Yes, certainly," Konstantin replied, standing up, "without a doubt. I will see what I can gather and do whatever I can to help you in this mission. Thank you so much, Karl, you've always been a good friend."

"Yes, of course…" Charlemagne plainly responded as he shook his hand. "Right… I think I need to have a sit down."

"Please, sit," Konstantin offered him.

Charlemagne sat down besides him, and Konstantin offered a seat for Manon who received it. He then sat down himself, but not before standing up again to offer something to drink. He went to the kitchen to put the kettle on the stove.

"How many years has it been?" Konstantin questioned. "Too many…"

"What are you doing in Ukraine nowadays?"

"Ah, a little bit of this and that," Konstantin answered. "Not much someone like me can do anymore in this place. The work I did with Cabernet Exploration was the most a man like me could ever hope to do, and a job with Cabernet Industries is a wonderful opportunity. You say it is a research facility?"

"Yes, for research and development, formally it will be known as Cabernet Technologies," Charlemagne remarked. "A bit of a spit in the face on my part to my father, who shut down their predecessor. I've been slowly relaunching it these past ten years or so, culminating in a lab in Allabrese. With my current chief executive officer's help, I've slowly been migrating high skill work to Allabrese, in addition to supporting the construction of houses out there for our workers at a subsidized price to attract the best staff to find. A friend of mine, Dr. Bartholemew Lambert, is spearheading the operation with his wife. This project has been the culmination of our ambitions to create a centre of the brightest scientists in the world to innovate and create."

"Scientists?" Konstantin questioned. "I am not a scientist, Karl."

"Yes, of course," Charlemagne replied, "and that's quite alright. You have an immense expertise in explosives, and so the role best suited for you will be an advisor position."

"Advisor...?" Konstantin repeated. "In Russian, we say '*Sovyetnik*,' but I am sure it must have a different meaning in your country."

"An advisor is one who advises on their experience and knowledge to another," Charlemagne clarified. "Nothing to do with trade unions or that sort of thing."

"*Da*, good."

"If you have a moment, I would like to run some documents through with you, to translate," Charlemagne requested. "I've been scouring the map of Ukraine and cannot seem to find this *Yuzivka* region. Do you know where it is? Is it in Russia?"

"*Yuzivka*... no, it is not a place I am familiar with, but let us see..." Konstantin picked up an atlas from a bookshelf nearby and placed it on the table. He flipped through and displayed a map of the Ukrainian Soviet Republic, but there was no place of that name. He flipped a few pages back as it was known as *Malorussiya*. "Here –" he said, pointing to a southeast region. "In the Soviet days it was a region known as *Stalino*, but nowadays it is known as *Donetsk*."

Act 5, Scene 3

A few days after Charlemagne and Manon met with Konstantin, they left on their own to drive to a small town in the countryside of the Donetsk region. Unlike Kiev, the rest of east Ukraine was covered in snowfall, which in the plains of this part of the country created miles upon miles of an untampered clean white blanket upon the country land. They passed numerous villages from Kiev to Donetsk, stopping in the regional capital before they ventured north towards a forested region. They passed along up to a suitable location on the road, parked the car on the side, readied themselves with equipment, and then continued on foot into the coniferous forest. A light blanket of snow covered the forest, and the snow was not too deep either. They ventured along relying on a handheld device titled 'GPS' and 'CaberNET' on the top. The handheld device showed an olive-green screen with a geographic map of the nearby area. Below were buttons, including an arrow pad and an enter button. After a full day, the duo retired for the night and then continued in the morning again as they went deeper into the forest.

Eventually, the pair located a trail. They followed the trail, and it led them to a tunnel through a cliffside that then continued along a winding path. The path then took them to an abandon industrial area within an open space within the canyon. Within the snow, decaying, was a supply truck parked in front of some garage shutters into a concrete building. The building was L-shaped with the right side consisting of overhang windows and a metal balcony.

"How curious," Charlemagne remarked, looking about. "I recognize this truck though. It's a ZIS-5. There was one of them in the dealership. It's a Soviet-era logistics truck."

The roadway continued on the left, venturing upwards and then around at a curve. They eventually reached a dead-end in the road, but not the pathway as a trail curved out from the side and continued upward. On both the left and right there were tall coniferous trees, fallen over trees, and shrubs covered in frost. The trail eventually led to another roadway that curved forward. The sun shined down as it continued to rise from the east. Charlemagne, looking at his GPS device, continued eastward. The road led to a stone bridge, completely unused since the snowfall and with vines overgrown on the pillars. On the other side of the bridge, the road continued along a gully, curving rightward before reaching a large clearing.

Charlemagne examined his GPS and then began to lead himself and Manon rightward into the forest. He stated, "If we follow this road, we'll be going away. We're close, but still have a bit to go."

"Why did we not just drive here...?" Manon remarked, chattering her teeth.

"This road wasn't on the map," Charlemagne replied. "If it had been, we would have."

They entered into a denser part of the forest as they continued along. They eventually reached a pipeline in the midst of the forest. Charlemagne examined it, saw icicles on the sides, and letters on the pipe. He then passed underneath it as it stood above the ground on metal pillars, and continued forward on the trail. They proceeded to travel uphill without any clear sense of passage until they eventually reached a natural path in the forest. They continued along the path until they reached a frozen pond in the midst of them. They walked around the pond and then continued along a vague path ahead of them, coming around to an uphill path that finally led to a cliffside along a mountain. Charlemagne guided them around the side of the mountain until a nook was noticeable, and within this nook the rubble of a cave in. Charlemagne entered into the nook to examine the rubble closely.

"Yes, based on my understanding of what Konstantin was trying to tell me about these explosives he gave me, we should use the larger one here with ammonium nitrate. These are harder to come around since they're modern, and I only have one of them for this purpose."

Charlemagne retrieved a large pack of explosives, prompting Manon to step away from him. He looked over to her.

"You'll need to get a fit further than that to escape this bomb," Charlemagne acknowledged. He stepped towards the debris and placed it within the center of the rubble. He then took a blasting cap and placed it inside. Afterwards, Charlemagne took a roll of wire, hooked it up to the explosives, and began to lead it away from the mine entrance as he walked along the side to exhaust the entire roll. When he was finished, he took a boom box out and tied it with the wire. Manon joined him as he took refuge near the trail. She took out from her backpack a pair of earmuffs, prompting Charlemagne to the same. "Fire in the hole!"

Manon closed her eyes as a rumble could be heard and debris shot out from the mouth of the mine. A large cloud of dust flew outwards in all directions and small bits of debris shot forward as close as to where they knelt down. They waited for a brief moment before they took off their ear protection and then went towards the mine entrance. The explosives cleared most of the debris, allowing them inside. Manon looked around from the mine entrance while Charlemagne turned to her with a smile.

"Now thermite cannot do that, can it?" Charlemagne acknowledged.

Manon looked at him, unimpressed, and then walked inside with him. She took out her spotlight and shined it forward. The mine entrance revealed a lengthy but slim cavernous tunnel. The tunnel walls were at least twenty yards in height, sloped inwards. A metal rail loomed over their heads from the ceiling with unlit lamps. As they walked a few yards in, the cave began to shake as behind them, the entrance collapsed in again. Manon looked in horror while Charlemagne shielded himself, but then let up to look with likewise a bit of concern.

"Oh dear…" Charlemagne remarked.

Manon looked ahead with stupor and then turned to Charlemagne with fury as she began to hit him in the side.

"Oy, stop it," Charlemagne reacted, shielding himself.

"Damn you, Charlemagne!" Manon shouted out. "You've very well just killed us! We're trapped down here with no way to go out now!"

"Now now," Charlemagne replied. "No need to get all upset. I'm sure it's not so bad…" He then looked over to see that the rubble was much the same as it was a few minutes earlier before he used the explosive. "I… I'm sure there must be some other exit out, or otherwise… a way out…"

"Did you think that I wanted to end my life this way? To be trapped in a cave with you?"

"Look, let's just remain calm," Charlemagne insisted. "I've got some explosives with me, not powerful ones, but perhaps it could work."

"Ah, then get us out then."

"I… I can't…" Charlemagne replied. "We've got to explore the mine first… if I blast a way out, it could just tumble back in and then we'll have wasted a day in the half out here."

"*Ugh, je ne peux pas croire cet idiot…*" Manon cursed. "*Nous allons mourir ici.*"

"You know I can understand you," Charlemagne rebutted, "and besides, it's not like we'll have to use anymore explosives from here on out. Now let's get going before we waste precious day time."

Charlemagne turned on his spotlight and then began to travel down the tunnel. The tunnel was at least a hundred yards in length before it led to an open space. Charlemagne examined with his flashlight as he saw crates around, empty crates, and concrete nooks that had more empty crates. He looked on both sides of the open space and then towards Manon who looked at him begrudgingly. Charlemagne turned forward and saw that the tunnel continued, though at half the height.

The pair continued along, coming around a curve in the tunnel system. They soon reached a junction that went two ways, going left to reach a dead-end supported with a concrete pillar in the center. Charlemagne observed a rectangular metal box on one side of the artificial pillar. The box was the approximate same size as a fire extinguisher box, but was closed shut with the mark of a skull on the side. Another nook in the cave wall held a few small empty crates. They backtracked and went the other way, continuing forward in a curved pathway that came out to another large space. Several crates were stacked up on the right. A nook on the left had a few more crates, but also to their interest, artwork and empty frames. Charlemagne observed and then went to the right side. He also saw some mine carts lying around with piles of a fine grey dust. He went around to the rear of the open space where there was a tall reinforced concrete rectangular entryway with doors that were open. Below the entryway was the start of a rail line for carts. This entryway also led into a tall square tunnel that curved to the left. Occasional segments of the mine were supported with concrete pillars in the walls, each with a metal box, and the cave walls curving around before reaching a long straight path. The pair continued along this path to reach the end, which led out to a side path into another pathway that entered into a large room where mine cars were littered around.

A nook at the end of the room had some more paintings, empty frames, and empty crates. There were some natural cavern pillars around the open space, and likewise these had metal boxes. On the left was another shorter tunnel that reached an elevator at the end.

"I don't suppose this elevator has power," Charlemagne acknowledged, "nor would I know where to even begin to look for its power source. There must be some sort of coal or lumber engine somewhere. No matter..." He walked forward to the elevator gate and began to pull it open, revealing the car on the other side.

"What are you going to do? Find the generator?"

"The generator is probably nowhere to be seen anymore," Charlemagne noted. "No, these shafts always come with an emergency ladder on the side, to rescue workers in case of an emergency. This elevator is of no use to me, so I'm going to blow it..."

"You'll waste the little explosives we have to do what?"

"I'll still have explosives to get us out, don't you worry," Charlemagne assured her. "Just stand back."

Charlemagne knelt down and took out some plastic explosives. He set them up around the side of the elevator shaft and then placed blasting caps in them. He attached the wires and then took them a fair distance back with a boom box. Without another word, Charlemagne detonated the explosives, causing a horrible screeching sound of metal to tear through the tunnels followed by the collapse of the elevator outright. Charlemagne peaked around the corner to see that the elevator was surely gone and in its stead was a black void. He then knelt down to look at where the elevator collapsed at the very long bottom of that abyss.

"Hm..." Charlemagne remarked, looking around the side, "there we are."

"You may go down, but I will not go with you," Manon remarked, crossing her arms. "It is too dangerous for me."

"Very well, hold your light," Charlemagne expressed, lighting a flare and throwing it down. "I'm going in."

Charlemagne came around to the ladder, carefully lowered himself, and then took hold of the rungs. He then slowly lowered himself down the shaft. Once he was a fair distance below, the light from Manon's beam could not reach him, forcing him to slow down to feel for the rungs before he could continue. He began to slow down immensely as he felt for the rungs, dropping a few inches every minute or so. He also stopped for a moment outright. The mine was incredibly silent. He could hear the drop of water, or some other liquid from somewhere. He could hear the pulse of his blood from his ears, and his heartbeat. Charlemagne came down another step and then muttered to himself, "Bloody Manon, always a worrywart, can't let me just be…"

After a few more inches down, Charlemagne began to see the glow of the flare he threw allowing him to increase his speed. The mine went down a sum of a hundred yards into the earth. He carefully climbed onto the wreck of the elevator car and then slid down to the base as he looked ahead. He took out of his spotlight again and began to enter into the lower levels of the mine.

Charlemagne found himself in a rectangular open space with a tunnel ahead that sloped upwards. A rail line immediately followed through, while mine carts were littered about. He noticed some concrete steps in the side which led up to a small nook with a table and some filing cabinets. Charlemagne opened the cabinets to see they were empty, and then he rummaged around the desk to see that it was likewise vacated. Atop of the desk were blueprints that showed the layout of the mine. He also noticed markings at certain points. He ventured forth into the mine as it led into a small open space with mine carts on the side and natural pillars, followed by a larger open space with numerous natural pillars, and more metal boxes. There was also an artificial pillar each with a metal box, and a nook in the side with more treasure. Charlemagne examined the treasure around to see paintings, but also chests with jewellery, chalices, and books. There were also some empty crates lying around. He continued down the mine pathway to reach a set of vault doors. The walked over to the valve in the doors, but it would not budge. He examined a locking mechanism that required a key, prompting him to take a bit of thermite out from his bag and place it atop. He then took a blowtorch out from his backpack and ignited the thermite. He stepped away as the thermite set off and melted the lock. He then went to the valve and began to pull the doors open, allowing him to walk through and continue into a narrow corridor with a platform on the right. The narrow corridor led to a smaller tunnel that began to slope downwards at a steep angle. Charlemagne found himself in a large room than the other ones with a large pit from which the rail line crossed over atop of a makeshift wooden bridge. The pit went down a few yards.

The mine continued from the other side to another narrow corridor supported by artificial columns, these with metal boxes too. A nook in the side had all sorts of valuables: jewellery, furniture, artwork, and even gems. Charlemagne passed this treasury to continue along the mine pathway as it curved and continued to slope downwards further. He reached a very large open space supported with artificial columns. On his left was a nook with more of the same, and directly ahead of him another nook, and on his right some vault doors. Charlemagne approached the vault doors, seeing it had a similar lock as the previous doors. He placed his final bag of thermite and then lit it on fire to melt the lock. He then pulled the vault doors open and entered inside. The mine came to an end as he found the last room; the room was massive, at least forty yards in height, twenty yards in width and a hundred yards in depth.

Charlemagne looked around as he stepped inside. The walls and floor of the room consisted of white rock. There were numerous empty crates lying about, but also more artwork, chests, and other items lying about in open crates. He looked through the chests and the crates, but nothing struck his eye. He spent more than twenty minutes looking through the massive room until he found a metal safe. Charlemagne looked at the combination in the safe and then took out his last explosive, a stick of dynamite. He placed it in front of the safe, used his blowtorch to light the fuse, and then stepped back to let it pop off. He then returned to see that it had blown off the safe door and revealed a wooden box inside. Charlemagne looked at the box and then brought it into his hands, and with abated breath, he lifted the lid from the box to reveal a gorgeous golden crown.

The crown inside had four fleur-de-lis gold curved plates connected together over gold headband, fitted with two arched bands that looped over one another in a cross shape in the middle. At the very top of the cross bands was a small gold orb with a cross above. Each fleur-de-lis plate was decorated in gemstones in a similar pattern. At the very top of the top-most petal there were pearls, and three more around this same petal. The crown was cushioned with a burgundy velvet cap inside, which Charlemagne used to hold the cap as he had his hands inside the cap.

"At long last... here she is... just as it was described..." Charlemagne remarked. He brought the crown up and then brought it over his head. "No..." he muttered, "not now... I need to find a way out of here."

Charlemagne placed the crown back into the box, and then he removed some items from his backpack to place the box inside. Once he was finished, he began to look around to see if there was something he could use in this room to blow through the caved in wall, but there was not. He then backtracked through the mine and began to look at the chests and crates closely again. When nothing could be found, he looked intently at the metal boxes he could find at the pillars that supported the ceiling of the cavern. He walked to one of them and released a hatch lock. He then pulled the crate open and found a bundle of cylindrical plastic tubes connected together via a wire with a clock above. His eyes widened and he immediately fetched a wire cutter in his backpack to untie the explosives from the clock. Charlemagne stored the explosives in his backpack, and went about gathering as much as he could. Eventually, he returned to the elevator shaft to begin to climb upwards. Charlemagne placed his spotlight on his belt side to keep providing him somewhat light and then climbed up, but as he climbed up, he did not find Manon.

"Manon! Manon, where are you!" Charlemagne shouted out. He then backtracked along the mine corridors. He collected a few more explosives, but without anymore space in his backpack, he carried the rolls of this unknown explosive in his arms as he went around. Eventually, Charlemagne returned to the main entrance of the cavern where he found Manon examining the cave in. "Manon! Manon, I found it," he acknowledged, placing the explosives atop of a rock in the debris. He lowered his backpack, took out the rest of the explosives, making Manon uneasy, and then showed her the box. "Look – it's just like in the pictures."

Charlemagne showed the crown and held it in his hands as Manon shined a light on it and examined it with less glee and excitement than he held. She held a plain face, pensive, and then looked over to Charlemagne.

"Hm... I suppose..." Manon admitted, looking at it suspiciously. "Let's take a closer look when we are in a safer place. Just because we've found the crown, doesn't mean we don't have to verify it as the one."

"Come now, it is the one..." he insisted.

"Ah, and what will you tell the press? You found it on a whim? On a stolen map from some Bulgarian bandits? We've jumped across history, but now we must verify where it went from that monastery grounds to wind up here, *Charles*. It's what your father and my father would have wanted; to finish the story."

Charlemagne lowered his smile and looked at her with a strict face. He replied, "Very well. Let's do just that then. Come now, let's get out of this mine and back wayside. Hopefully Konstantin can at least have a bit more excitement. Now get back, I'm going to tie wires with these explosives I found down here."

"What is that?"

"I haven't got a clue, but I don't believe the Germans had that many advanced explosives like we do nowadays. If I had to hazard a guess, these rolls are just simple trinitrotoluene, better known as TNT," Charlemagne said, piling close to twelve rolls of explosives atop of the center of the debris. "I believe this much should have the same punch as the ammonium nitrate."

After Charlemagne had piled the explosives, he took a roll of wire from his backpack and began to bring it down the corridor to the very end where he and Manon were set to take cover behind some crates. He then lowered his backpack against the crates, looked down the corridor as he held his spotlight and then came back around to join Manon. He tied the wire to his boombox, and then looked over to her as she applied her hearing protection. He did the same, and then placed his hands on the trigger.

Without a word, Charlemagne pressed down on the lever and the ground shook. A large cloud of dust flew inwards into the open space, causing them to raise their arms to their face to shelter themselves. The cloud persisted, causing Charlemagne to just swat at the air around him. He untied the wire from his boombox, placed it back into his backpack, and then brought his backpack around as he came around to look outwards.

At the end of the tunnel, light poured in from outside, prompting him to remove his ear protection and look to Manon.

"Let's get out of here, my dear," Charlemagne encouraged. "We've got the crown, but we have a bit of work ahead of us before we relish in this victory."

Act 5, Scene 4

A week after Charlemagne and Manon had left the salt mine in the Donetsk region, the pair sat at a table on a patio that overlooked a calm, light blue ocean. Below them, down a slope, was a lengthy, but narrow beachhead with fine white sands. The skies ahead of them were still grey, but it did not take away from the palm trees and the warmer temperatures than they had experienced in eastern parts of the country. Along the horizon, one could see the stretches of the sea on the left, while on the right the harbor of the port city was visible as well as a simple white lighthouse tower with a red top. At the present moment, both Charlemagne and Manon could sit outdoors and not see their own breaths. Before them, atop of a towel on the table, the crown they had recovered sat between them as they stared at it.

"As far as I am concerned, this crown is just like the one I had seen in the Saint-Denis catalogue," Charlemagne remarked, sitting back. "A few modifications can be expected, of course. It has been in the hands of many, I could expect it to have been damaged at some time, but insofar as the modifications are concerned, it is the crown."

"Ah, but is the Ship of Theseus still the ship of Theseus even if all the parts have been removed and replaced?"

"Don't get me with that Theseus paradox, bollocks," Charlemagne denounced. "We're not dealing with absolute replacement of all the parts. Based on my research, the only original part of that crown in which Charlemagne had worn for certain was this part here – the head band. The fleur-de-lis components were added on afterwards, as were the gemstones. Otherwise, this crown is the very same. We are not dealing with replacement, but adaptions to the original."

"Aside from repairs, what reason could there be to add more fleur-de-lis?"

The door onto the patio from inside the house they were at opened, and a man stepped forward with a book in his hand. This man was average height, slim, and with pale skin and sunken and bored eyes. He had dark grey hair, glasses, and grey eyes. He was clean shaven and had a bony complexion. He wore a dark navy-blue suit, collared shirt with a tie, though the suit looked like it was too large for him as the pants were very baggy. He also wore black shoes. He stepped forward with the book and placed it before them as it showed depictions of numerous crowns.

"It seems as though," the man spoke in a thick Russian accent and bored tone, "among the crowns lost to time, this one could be one of many."

"How is that possible, Dr. Ivanov?" Charlemagne questioned. "I assure you; this crown matches the one taken from Saint-Denis."

"I cannot say it doesn't," Ivanov responded, removing his glasses, "but I cannot say it is. This image you refer to, from what year was it?"

"Of the top of my mind, it was supposed to be dated 1706," Charlemagne answered. "I know that is ninety years before it was removed from the collection, but it looked just like this: a golden headband, fleur-de-lis plates coming out from atop (a French symbol, no less), and gems bejeweling the side of it. These arches over the cap, golden ball and cross, I'm not familiar with, but the fleur-de-lis design of these sides of the plates; who else would share in that design?"

"Before we say for certain that this crown is the Crown of Charlemagne, we need to be sure too that it is not a replica and is the original crown," Ivanov asserted. "You told me that you had followed the alleged transport of the Crown from Austria to Serbia, and from Serbia to Romania, but what happened in Romania?"

"In Romania, the crown was in the hands of some Romani nomads," Charlemagne explained. "The Serbian mercenary, Zarko, and his men, tracked them down to a forest near a monastery in Moldavia. According to our sources, Zarko described that he had found many butchered corpses as though a massacre had taken place: men, women, and children of the Romani people were killed and their bodies left to rot. Zarko mentioned to his client that his men took the liberty to bury the dead, but in doing so did not find the crown. As Manon and I have debated, whether Zarko is telling the truth is not verifiable. We went to that crime scene and found the bodies, and although there were lots of dead bodies, we also found the corpse of a possible warrior. This warrior had a sword, a curved sword that seemed foreign and not particularly Western European in design."

"Where is this sword?"

"Unfortunately, due to unforeseen circumstances, we had to leave it behind."

"Ah, but I did draw it in best detail as I could," Manon remarked, lifting up her handbag. She took out her own journal and showed the sketch of the sword. Ivanov picked up his glasses from the side of the table and put them on.

"Hm…" Ivanov thought aloud.

"Come to think about it, we also found a belt buckle with some markings on it," Charlemagne said, "but I believe that too had to be left behind."

"No!" Manon corrected, rummaging through her handbag. "I have it here too… I cleaned it up not too long ago to see the markings better, but I cannot say what it says."

"You what?" Charlemagne asked. "When did you do that? I didn't realize you had taken it with you. I thought we left it behind…"

"Ah, but you were so certain that where we were going here in Ukraine was where we needed to be," Manon responded, placing it on the table. "What was I to say?"

Charlemagne shook his head and then picked up the buckle. He looked at it closely and then said, "The problem with this thing is that these letters are noticeably Cyrillic..."

"Let me see," Ivanov asked. He received it into his hand and then examined it. "Hm... yes. These are Cyrillic alright, but that is not a problem."

"If these are Cyrllic, then what was a Serbian soldier doing dead amongst the gypsies?"

"Supposing that the dead man was not a gypsy who had this sword and belt buckle by chance," Manon added.

"No, not Serbian," Ivanov denied. "Although Cyrillic, these letters are not used in Serbian. There are differences in dialect between South Slavic languages and East Slavic languages."

"Are these East Slavic then?"

"Yes..." Ivanov said.

"So this buckle belonged to a Russian?"

"No... You see these letters here: it is like the backwards 'R' in Latin alphabet."

"Yes..." Charlemagne replied.

"This letter is used in both Ukrainian and Russian, but this letter here, like the 'I' in Latin alphabet, is not used in Russia, but Ukraine."

"So, the soldier was a Ukrainian then?"

"Or a gypsy with a Ukrainian belt buckle," Manon pointed out.

Charlemagne ignored her and looked at the drawing as Ivanov picked it up to show them.

"I believe that based on these two evidence points, it was a Cossack, specifically of the Zaporozhian Host. The Romani are not typically armed with swords like the one you have shown, and even if they were, where would they get it from? This sword is distinctly used among the Cossack warriors, which in combination with the buckle, suggests it was a Cossack that had died."

"So, a Cossack was lying with the slain gypsies then? Could it not have just been one man among a group of gypsies?" Charlemagne suggested.

"These Cossacks did not live in Moldavia, but in southwest Ukraine, north from where we are here in Odessa and not too far. Perhaps I should explain that the Cossacks were not like gypsies or these Serbian bandits. They are closer to what you have in the West with the Prussian Army; a professional army at the service of the Polish-Lithuanian Empire and later Russian Empire. These were an autonomous group of horsemen with their own laws, code of ethics, and systems of government. What I should emphasize to you two is that they did not kill indiscriminately. If they were the ones who had slain the gypsies, it was likely as a reprisal for actions against them. What the Cossacks did do was plunder from their defeated enemies though, so the Crown, if in the hands of these gypsies, would have been taken from them for certain. The problem then is that the crown, as a symbol of a king, a monarch, would not have survived, nor did the Cossacks enjoy treasure to adore but to provide. If I were to guess then, the Crown and other items stolen from the gypsies were sold while travelling back to their land. A popular location for Cossacks to sell their goods is right here in Odessa, at the port where merchants gather.

"Bloody hell..." Charlemagne acknowledged, "so from that port then, it could have gone anywhere connected through the Black Sea, including outward in the Med. Alright, but supposing this crown here is that very same crown, which I still believe, it must have been sold to a merchant who then sold it to a Russian noble or some bloke."

"Maybe..."

"Well, I suppose that's enough of a connection. Right, Manon?" Charlemagne asked. "Do you think your father would be satisfied with that conclusion?"

"I do not think he would."

"Well, I'm not about to go searching around the entire Black Sea or Mediterranean Sea to see where it ended up. Sometimes there are just dead ends to mysteries, but I'd bet my entire self-worth that this crown is the crown I saw in the catalogue taken from Saint-Denis. I firmly do not believe it could belong to any other monarchy. Insofar as to whether it is a fake, we checked it out already and this crown is made of real gold, and these are real pearls and gems. It isn't a fake."

"Just because its material is real does not mean that itself is what it is," Manon pointed out. "The Crown of Napoleon was designed to look like the Crown of Charlemagne, but that only made it a replica."

Charlemagne did not respond. Ivanov instead spoke and said, "You have found a crown here, Charlemagne, but in order to assert to others that it is a Crown that belonged to the Franks then you must assert its legitimacy. You will need to track it from 1940 back to 1830."

"How the hell am I supposed to do that? We've exhausted our leads here, and even with what you're telling me, that's a bit of a stretch to think it was sold. What if it wasn't? What if it was kept in the hands of the Cossacks?"

"No, that is not possible. A crown is not just a… a fashion piece. It is a symbol of authority, and this symbol would not have been appreciated in the Cossack Host."

"Alright, so what if it was sold – what makes you so certain it was to a merchant here in Odessa?"

"Odessa was one of the largest ports nearest their homeland, a gathering point for all sort of merchant activity. What came into the Port of Odessa was always noted with what came out, and those records are available at the Odessa Museum for us to view."

"Really? How convenient for us. Let's go there then," Charlemagne asked, standing up. "Come now, I'll drive."

Without much persuasion, the trio exited from Ivanov's home and found themselves in a gravel road beside a sandy grass field. The UAZ was parked near the entrance into the beachside home, which allowed all three of them to enter in and for Charlemagne to drive out. He drove down the gravel road and then took a left turn as he drove through the field lot and approached a major road on the other side. Once at the major road, Charlemagne waited for the opportune moment to turn left and drive through the quiet suburbs of Odessa. On the right were some stucco-based homes with orange terracotta tile roofs, while on the left the field continued with tall trees. They continued to drive along as they entered a small commercial district with more trees along the sidewalk.

"I have to say, of all the places we've visited so far, Odessa has won my favor as the most beautiful. A shame really that we've come here in late autumn."

"Yes, she is a beautiful city, of the few there are in Ukraine," Ivanov agreed as he sat in the back of the car.

"Ah, then I suppose then *Charles* will not offer you a complimentary migration pass out of your country in exchange for your services," Manon commented.

Charlemagne looked over to her as he continued to drive. "Nevermind her," he replied. "Odessa used to be a Greek settlement, isn't that right? I certainly get that feeling, a bit of both the Russian and the Greek influences."

"Odessa was founded on what used to be a Greek settlement," Ivanov affirmed. "Its name is from that same settlement, *Odessos,* which disappeared more than two thousand years ago, a detail in which my son never has me forget. He studies ancient histories."

"Father like son a bit then," Charlemagne bantered. "I knew a man whose father, son, and grandson all became engineers. Of course, of different varieties, one was a draftsmen, the other a geologist and so on. What is your son up to nowadays, Dr. Ivanov?"

"He is working in Saint Petersburg as a professor at the university in near east studies," Ivanov answered. "He has been busy, in and out of the country a lot. I do not see him much."

"Perhaps I should catch up with him some time for some projects I had in mind," Charlemagne acknowledged. "He's the reason I even met Konstantin, because he was aiding him for some projects out in those parts of the Levant and such. I owe him a favor or two for sure."

The jeep continued to drive down the freeway as they passed a variety of single-story commercial buildings. Some of these buildings appeared rundown, while others brand new and beautiful. Eventually the freeway split up into two roads, one going in each direction, the other far from the other closer to the coast. They passed some mechanic shops and gas stations as they continued to drive the narrower road with three lanes. They also passed some rundown industrial buildings, some condemned buildings, and also some plain lots of land.

"I say, there is so much potential for business in this land," Charlemagne acknowledged. "What is the primary economy? I would assume it is maritime based..."

"Yes, Odessa was founded for the port and is still relied on for the port. During the time of the regime, it was the busiest port in the entire country, despite what others may say about Sevastopol or Vladivostok."

"I could imagine – I see huge potential for shipping and warehouse services still," Charlemagne acknowledged. "It would be such a shame to continue seeing a beautiful city like this suffer... perhaps I'll have a word with my people when I get back to Allabrese, if that ever happens anytime soon."

The jeep drove past more industrial buildings, a lot of fenced-off buildings and then the large rail lines on the left. After a fair stretch of that zone, they entered into a quasi-residential and commercial zone with more single-story buildings on either side. At the end of the freeway, they drove under an overpass and then reached an intersection that went two ways, left or right. Charlemagne was guided to the left and drove along a short distance to reach a fork in the road. He stayed left again and drove past some four-story rundown apartments on his left, and a hill on his right with billboards. At the end of that long road, the jeep drove up to an intersection to come to a halt.

"You'll want to go straight here," Ivanov directed. "Not too far to go…"

"No worries," Charlemagne responded, looking about. He turned to his right and saw a tall pedestrian bridge overpass the road on his right through two elevated parks on either side. On his left the road reached a checkpoint and then curved around to consist of a bridge perpendicular to the way they were going. At the green light, the jeep continued to drive down as they continued below the bridge on its right side. On the left side was a stone wall with the elevated park on the other side. "What's that way? The harbor, I assume?"

"Yes, that's where that goes," Ivanov answered. "On your right is a park, known as Greek Park, of course. You'll want to keep driving until you reach a parking lot on the right."

Charlemagne did so and after a few minutes found the parking lot. He turned right and came into the lot to find a parking space. He observed that the lot was besides a set of low stairs into the park. He locked the car once everyone was out and began to walk to the sidewalk. From the other side of the sidewalk, Charlemagne could see the rail line next to the harbor. Ivanov led them around to the stairs, to which Charlemagne observed them to be a wide set of stairs going up.

"Do you climb these stairs every morning to get to work?" Charlemagne asked as they went up. "Seems a bit exhausting."

"Every morning."

At the top of the stairs, they reached a plaza with a statue in the middle. The statue looked upon them and was of a male figure in a white toga. He held one hand up as though asking for spare change, while the other was down at his side. On either flank of the statue were three-story tall apartment buildings with an inward curve in their façade. These buildings were yellow with black-framed windows, no rooftops. There was a road in between each building, continuing straight forward from the stairs and into the city. Charlemagne briefly turned around to catch a better sight of the harbor from up top. Ivanov took them to the left rather than straight through where they walked along a neat promenade with park benches and lookouts from above. There were three strips of green along the promenade, each bordered with low wrought iron fences. Numerous trees were plotted along these green strips, as well as very low green plants. The trees along this strip were orange and not all yet fallen off, while some on the left were still green, much like other trees in the city though those being different than these very thin trees. At the end of the promenade, they reached another plaza with another statue. This statue was that of a bust of a man with mutton chops and curled hair. He also wore a robe. Along the sides of the monument were fish that spat water out into a basin around the bust. Besides the statue on the left, looking out towards the lookout was a cannon surrounded by a bed of flowers. More noticeable than these monuments was a building directly ahead with a white façade. The building was two stories tall, consisting of two partitions at either side of a wide center partition. The center partition had twelve Greek columns and a very low pediment with a clock and two marble statues, back-to-back of the clock sides as they sat down atop of the pediment, one of a male and the other of a female in toga robes. Above the clock was a pole with a red-white-yellow flag. In small alcoves on each side partition were marble statues, a female on the left and a male on the right.

Charlemagne and Manon followed Ivanov as he took them around the right corner of the building. They walked down a wide path and came around to an intersection with some beautiful apartment buildings around. Ivanov led them away from the intersection though and towards a building on the left. This building had two pathways up to a set of stairs that converged to a veranda that overlooked the lawn in the middle. At either side of the lawn were very tall evergreen pine trees, and the perimeter of the lawn was surrounded with a very low iron wrought fence. In the center of the lawn was a marble statue of a man struggling with a serpent. At both sides of the man were smaller humans, also struggling with the coils of the serpent. The museum was a small single-story structure with four columns supporting a triangular pediment at the entrance. The structure was tall and beside the main partition were two arched windows.

Ivanov brought them into the main lobby of the museum, and down to the basement where there were rows upon rows of filing cabinets. He seemingly navigated the many rows and aisles with ease, finding one in particular in which he pulled documents out, leather-bound manifesto books and began to pile them atop of the filing cabinets as he went from one to another. He pulled out close to a dozen manifestos and had Charlemagne carry them to a desk. Ivanov brought a chair back, turned on a lamp, and then sat down as he began to open each book.

"You tell me that the year Zarko and his men found those bodies was 1828, so let us start there…" Ivanov remarked, opening a manifesto He then began to read; slowly read, one page at a time, prompting both Manon and Charlemagne to sit down, and wait and become bored as each page went by. Soon an hour passed, followed by another, and another. He went through a few books until he stopped and leaned in. He fixed his glasses, and then he pulled back and shook his head. The hour then went by, at which point Charlemagne began to tap his fingers on the nearby desk impatiently. "Ah…" Ivanov remarked, stopping and putting his finger down, "here we are. September 1st, 1828 (though keep in mind that in Russia at this time…"

"Used a different calendar, yes," Charlemagne interrupted, "but what does the entry say?"

Ivanov read and then said, "Received from the ownership of Volodymyr Trebukhin, into the care of Shama Lazarovich, one gold crown with leaves around the side, coated in various gems. Sold for the sum of one-thousand rubles."

"One-thousand rubles – what is that? Is that a lot?"

"Today, no. In 1830, yes. For a Cossack looking to dispose of pillaged items, it is quite a lot. Today, it would be close to a million rubles."

Charlemagne whistled in affirmation and replied, "A fair bit, though with all those gems, I wouldn't have settled for that much, I think."

"How much is that?" Manon asked. "In dollars if not in francs."

"About ten-thousand American dollars, give or take, though of course remember now, neither the Cossacks nor this merchant know what the real worth of the crown is. Still, we weighed the crown, and it is about five kilograms in total, minus the gems, at least two kilograms in gold alone. A kilogram of gold, like one of those ingots we saw, is worth forty-thousand dollars today, so I would say that the Cossack was ripped off for what that Crown was physically worth let alone really worth. At any rate, does that log say who it was sold too?"

"I am looking…" Ivanov replied, flipping to the next page. He flipped through several pages as he thoroughly searched. Suddenly, he stopped and said, "Here – From the ownership of Shama Lazarovich, one gold crown with leaves around the side, to *Osman...ski, Osmanski* diplomat; an Ottoman diplomat, there is no name. It was sold for ten thousand rubles."

"Ten thousand rubles? No name? What the hell?"

"I am not sure, but there is no name," Ivanov remarked, pointing. "See, it says *Osmanski,* which in Russian means Ottoman."

Charlemagne looked over to where Ivanov pointed and sure enough, he vaguely saw what he referred to in Cyrllic.

"So, we travel to Turkey then to get to the bottom of this – sure enough the Ottomans were adept record-keepers. We'll find a diplomat who travelled to Odessa in the year – 1830, and then we'll get to the bottom of how that crown came around to return to Donetsk in that mine."

"*Charles*, travelling to Turkey? Is that not dangerous with those gangsters who were after you? What if they capture us again? It is not safe."

"Hmph, what then?" Charlemagne replied. "We need to visit Turkey to learn more. Do you suggest I sit down with Al-Suli and make peace? He's not a negotiable man, and if he catches wind that I have the crown, it'll be a forever war until he has it in his own hands. We need to keep the existence of the crown a secret amongst us."

"What if we hire some protection? To come with us?"

"Mercenaries? Where am I supposed to do that?" Charlemagne rebuked. "I'm not a man with many connections to that extent. I could ask Konstantin, but doubt he'd know."

"And what about Rubashkin? Why not ask him? He's a connected man. He may know."

"Rubashkin? Rubashkin would rather snag that crown from us than help us... of course, perhaps he doesn't need to know we have the crown... I suppose it could be worth a shot. In exchange, I could offer him all that treasure in the salt mine we'll need to retrieve; I won't dare to give him the gold from the train, that's mine." He paused for a moment and then groaned.

"Alright then, I believe we have his telephone number. We'll give him a call, apologize, and then we'll set off for Turkey with him, to satisfy your father and give a probable excuse to how we found this crown in the first place."

"*Bien.*"

Act 6, Prologue

"Right," Charlemagne proclaimed, "not a word of this leaves this room. We all know our stations. Team One are to put the target in position at the side of the Richard Harlech building. Meanwhile, Team Two and Team Three will make their way to the roof of the building where they will lift the materials needed to construct the Device. From that moment, Team One will ensure that the target is ready. Team Three will begin their dynamic stretches, making sure those muscles don't get pulled, and Team Two will put together the Device and supervise its function. At the sound of a whistle, we will communicate each phase of the plan. At the sound of two whistles, we will speed up. Three whistles, indicates trouble with the Law and evasive maneuvers. A long whistle will signal an emergency and our need to take emergency action. Any questions?"

Charlemagne, aged twenty-years old, looked around a table in a dimly lit room. He wore a black turtleneck sweatshirt and dark jeans. He also wore black boots. Likewise, the eleven other youngsters around the table overlooking a campus map wore dark clothes.

"Good," Charlemagne affirmed. "We strike tonight, on the night of the new moon, with a forecast of clouds – a night perfect for our intentions. Team One will fetch the target from its hideaway, while Team Two and Three will begin to transport the *materiel*. Off we go now."

The twelve split up as they left the table. The table was positioned in the middle of Charlemagne and Barry Lambert's apartment. Barry left with Felicity out the door, leaving Judith alone with Charlemagne as they were about to leave.

"Such a brilliant scheme, but what if… what if we run into unforeseen trouble? We've observed the patrols of the campus security, and sure enough the RCMP detachment only has one or two officers at this time of the day, but still it could be dangerous for us all."

"Nonsense," Charlemagne dismissed, bringing his hand to Judith's chin. "The only way in which this plan could go awry is if someone were to snitch. We've planned this operation for weeks, and its details have been kept secret under sworn oath. There will be no betrayal under my watch, and besides, everything should go along without a hitch because of our extensive planning. Now let's get going – you're due to join the others to fetch the mark from the shop."

"Okay..." Judith replied, leaning over to kiss him on the cheek, "for good luck as they say."

Judith then ran off and Charlemagne closed the apartment door behind him. He locked the door and then went downstairs to the main floor where he met with Barry as he led Team Three. The night was surely very dark, skies covered in dark clouds and not a light above them aside for the streetlamps and buildings around.

"Right, let's move out then, lads," Charlemagne encouraged. "There is mischief to be done."

The team of nine divided into five and four, and each got into one of two vehicles parked on the curb of West Queen Boulevard, one of which was a double cab pickup truck and the other an SUV. Charlemagne sat in the passenger seat of the Asano SUV. Each car pulled out from the curb and set forth westbound. They came around to the intersection at the end of the road at West Marshall Drive, merged right onto the freeway that span around the campus, and set forth to travel northbound at a great speed. The cars were quick to pull at the northeast end of the campus, passing the East Parkade, and then turning left. They passed a quiet section of the campus where there was nobody on the sidewalks. They passed tall barren trees on their left and the Ancient Studies Building and Psychological Centre on their right. At Renfrew Mall, they turned right and continued around the Jessica Chin Psychology building, coming to an alleyway where they then turned right. The alleyway was narrow and not meant for vehicles, but they travelled along anyways, coming to an intersection where they drove slowly through, followed by a series of pathways that led to the School of Law. They drove around the law building and then passed down the middle of the promenade with the School of Law Library to reach the base of a tall eight-story office building adjacent to a large manor. They drove around the rear of the office building and parked their vehicles at the corner, slightly to the rear of the building. The team of nine quickly exited the vehicles and Charlemagne came around to the rear of the SUV to help carry some toolboxes towards the rear shutters of the loading zone. They placed their tools down, while those in the pickup truck helped carry long metal poles and thick steel wire. A student knelt down in front of the metal door besides the shutters and began to fiddle with the lock. He was soon through, opened the door, and students began to filter through while others began to carry material around the eastern side of the building. Charlemagne held the door while he watched two students place a large plank on the side of the building, while the other two began to carry the large equipment and place it atop. When all the equipment was placed, another two students carried smaller poles in with them and Charlemagne then left two students below. He joined them at the elevator where they soon realized the length of the poles were too large to bring into the elevator.

"Take the stairs," Charlemagne remarked. "We'll meet you at the eighth floor."

Charlemagne entered into the elevator with a toolbox in his hand, went up eight stories, and then exited out. He came into the stairwell adjacent the elevators and then climbed up to a ninth story where he found the rest of the team fiddling with the lock. The lock was soon opened, and the team filtered out onto the roof. They placed their equipment down near the rooftop exit. Charlemagne exited out and looked about; the rooftop was simple, a few HVAC machines around the corners, and nothing more. As Charlemagne approached the edge of the roof, he pointed to small cylinders with small metal handles, and said, "Fasten those elastics around this pole. We'll use them as the sturdier part of the roof."

The team took out intricate mechanisms from plastic bags and placed them directly behind the anchors. They were fastened with bolts that went into the concrete drilled in with handheld machines. These mechanisms were hollow cylinders that could move on an axis in any direction. Through the sides of cylinder were two holes. Once those were installed, they were titled back towards the roof. The small poles that were carried up were inserted through each of them, tilted inwards to cross with one another, and fastened with small rods that went through both the mechanism (known as a landmine attachment), and the poles. Each pole was fastened together with a small pipe, and another pole brought closer to the bottom stabilized the device into an A-shape. At the very top of the A-shaped device was a pulley connected to the pipe from where a rope was loaded through and a part of that rope with a coil tied to an anchor at the other side of the roof. An elastic wire was attached to each pole and fastened to the anchors on the roof. When the device was ready, the device was folded over so that the poles were over the side of the roof and rope could be lowered down.

Charlemagne waited and when he heard the sound of a whistle from below, he blew his whistle to signal the others to proceed with the next phase. Barry led his team to begin to pull on the wire, one by one, five in total, pulling while two supervised as they watched from over the edge of the roof as a platform with longer equipment was raised up. Once that equipment was received and it gently landed onto the roof, the team let go and the A-shaped device fell over to rest. Charlemagne blew his whistle, and the team set off to the next phase as they dismantled the A-shape device entirely. A third landmine attachment was installed at double the distance, and the larger poles were swapped in and fastened with steel rods. These two poles came together to form a triangle as well, and they were fitted with a pipe and pulley, and rope loaded in before it was tied to the same steel wire coil and then gently lowered over the rooftop. They lowered the rest of the wire down to the very bottom, and then stayed put. Charlemagne waited as he looked down over the side of the building, and within a few minutes, he saw a square SUV-like vehicle pull up below and the passengers exit out and began to pull a harness from the trunk.

"Get ready," Charlemagne remarked, "they're setting up now." He then turned around and observed the team below attach the harness. A student climbed onto the roof of the vehicle to tie the harness to the top of the navy-blue Moore Yankee and then climb down. He heard the sound of the whistle and then blew his. "Alright, let's go, go, go!"

Team Two began to pull at the wire, struggling to make the A-shaped crane, lift upwards. Charlemagne looked over to the landmine attachments and rest of the device as he could hear the stress in the metal.

"We need more muscle!" Charlemagne acknowledged. Two other students quickly went to join in pulling the wire with their gloved hands. He then looked down and saw the crane move up and the jeep lift up from the concrete below. Team One quickly moved out of harm's way as they dispersed and observed. "It's moving! Keep going!"

The team slowly began to lift the jeep up, raising it above a few yards, and then a few yards more. It went past the first floor, the second floor, and the third floor to Charlemagne's glee. He turned to the team and went to go and join them as another student supervised.

"One, two, one, two," Charlemagne encouraged, bringing his gloved hands to the rope and joining in them. "One, two, one two."

The jeep was lifted up along the side of the building in a careful manner. After a few minutes, Charlemagne observed ahead as he saw the jeep rise up from the edge of the rooftop and be directly ahead of them.

"Don't let go, we're almost there!"

Charlemagne and the others gave in their last pulls as the A-shaped crane tilted back and the jeep was brought over the edge and onto the roof. The crane fell forward, towards the vehicle, but it was safely over the edge enough to land atop. He and the others laughed as they celebrated. He shook hands with his peers and hugged Barry, but before they could celebrate a second more, Charlemagne heard a dreadful lengthy whistle from below.

"What?!" Charlemagne questioned. He hurried over to the edge and couldn't see the others, but he could see down along University Promenade, the sight of two cars approach. "Bollocks, everyone get out! It's the fuzz!"

The team quickly began to pack up their tools and carry them with them as they made their escape. Charlemagne and Barry meanwhile took part the crane and removed the harness. They carried the equipment and hid them behind the rooftop exit shelter, and then they took their toolkits and fled into the building.

"Ah, man," Barry complained, "who the hell ratted on us? There's no way they could have seen us working."

"Nevermind that," Charlemagne responded, "we need to get out of here."

The pair went down the stairs as fast as safely could, reaching the lobby and then hurrying out the rear door as they saw campus security vehicles at the front door. They exited out the back and came around to where they parked the vehicles, but the vehicles were gone.

"Son of a…" Charlemagne cursed, looking about. "we'll need to run for it… just not with these…"

"Where do we run to, Charles?"

"Let me think…" Charlemagne thought aloud. "I've got it – there's a system of steam tunnels under the campus. We'll hide out there."

"Freeze!" a voice shouted. "Stop right there!"

Barry and Charlemagne turned to see a few campus guards face them. They each looked at them; they wore flat caps and dark blue collared shirts and cargo pants. They held flashlights that pointed at them, and neither Barry nor Charlemagne could see the faces of the guards who faced them. Barry panicked, ran southbound with his toolkit, prompting half of the guards to run after him. Meanwhile, Charlemagne froze in place as he shielded his eyes and looked at the guards that faced him.

"Don't do anything stupid," the guard warned.

Charlemagne's ears twitched as he then heard the sound of sirens. He quickly pivoted his foot and made a run for it. He went northbound, coming around to some forested trees where he ran into, but not before nearly tripping on something.

"Bloody hell…" Charlemagne remarked.

"Charles? Charles is that you?" a Londoner accented voice questioned.

"Judith?" Charlemagne questioned. He turned and saw Judith hidden behind a bush. "Judith, we've got to run, the fuzz are after us!"

"They went in here!" a guard shouted.

Judith immediately joined Charlemagne, running through the forest patch and out the other side as they ran towards Harlech Manor. They pushed through a side gate and then came around the rear lawn as they continued to evade campus security. They stopped for a moment at the corner of the building as Charlemagne looked around.

"What happened to you? I thought you fled with the others?"

"Are you kidding me? They left half of us on the ground while they drove off."

"Ugh, you never know who your friends are until a situation like this one, do you…" Charlemagne remarked. "Right then, I have a plan to escape the Law. I've heard about some tunnels underneath the campus, never explored them myself, but reckon that now's the time."

"How do we come to these tunnels?"

"I've noticed a grate near the physics building," Charlemagne replied. "Follow me."

Charlemagne took Judith's hand, and they began to go down the side of the manor to the front. He could see police arrive and park around the center plaza. He then led Judith towards the hedges where they stayed put as guards passed searching for them from behind. Once those guards were gone, they went down along the hedges and towards a gate that exited out near the Anthropology Center. A campus security vehicle parked on Marshall Drive near the entrance of the anthropology building, prompting Charlemagne and Judith to come around to the Science Center. They went around the rear and hid behind a dumpster, allowing the security guards to disperse before they then continued down the rear of the science center to stare down the physics and astronomy building. Charlemagne took Judith's hand, and they went down the alleyway between the two buildings and stopped at a grate in the floor.

"Let's see now," Charlemagne muttered, taking out a tool from his box and beginning to unfasten the bolts. He quickly worked and removed the few bolts, and then he placed his tools back in and kicked them over to a dumpster nearby. "Slowing me down anyways…" He lifted the grate up and then looked down at a fair drop into a shallow stream. He brough his feet around.

"Is it safe to go inside?" Judith questioned, kneeling beside him. "Oh, Charles, why don't we just give ourselves in?"

"Nonsense, my dear," Charlemagne replied, "Charlemagne never gives himself up, and has never been caught in the moment of mischief..."

"There they are!" a voice shouted.

Charlemagne looked over and could see a guard had found them from the plaza. A police officer quickly came around to join him.

"Now's the time. Ladies first, my love," Charlemagne encouraged, taking her hand. Judith quickly jumped down and splashed into the water. He then looked over to the cops, pointed two fingers up and gestured to the law enforcers before he too jumped down to join her. "Let's go! This way!"

Charlemagne took Judith's hand, and the pair went down the warm tunnel, going eastbound to a junction, and then turning right as they made their escape. As they ran down the tunnel, Charlemagne heard from behind the splash of water and the shouts of voices in pursuit of them.

"Not good..." Charlemagne remarked, continuing to run. "We'll have to lose them somehow...."

The pair ran around a curve and then reached a three-way junction left and right. Charlemagne went right and they continued southbound until he came to a dead-end. He backtracked and then went around the right and eastbound, before going around another junction and continuing northbound.

"Oh, isn't this a bit of a labyrinth, eh?"

Charlemagne and Judith continued to run around the tunnels, passing grates above them from where light from the streetlamps poured forth. Charlemagne stopped and then paused for a moment. He could hear the steps of the law enforcers around.

"We're just going around in circles here," Charlemagne acknowledged. "There has to be a way out somehow that doesn't involve climbing out..." He stopped and then looked at his feet. The water was currenting in a certain direction. "Of course..."

Charlemagne and Judith jogged along as they followed the flow of water, stopping every so often to see where it went, and then turning as need be, going right and then left. They reached a long corridor and then continued straight on, coming around to a lengthier segment and then turning right again. Charlemagne and Judith jogged along the final stretch where they jumped down and came into a simple cylindrical pipe.

At the end of the pipe, Charlemagne and Judith found themselves in a creek in the midst of the forest. The pair walked down the stream and eventually found themselves at a cascade. They climbed upwards and rested along the cliffside, looking down. As they caught their breath, Charlemagne began to laugh and smile. He turned to Judith who also began to let out a little laugh.

"How about that, eh? You were right – trouble was afoot..." Charlemagne admitted. "We pulled it off though, didn't we? I can't wait to see what it looks like from below... I bet you can see it from the apartment. I'm sorry this hasn't gone quite as planned, but..."

"No," Judith denied, "no apology necessary, Charles. Although I had my doubts, I knew what I signed up for, and you know what? I don't regret an instant of it..." She leaned over to kiss Charlemagne on the cheek. He turned to her and gazed at her lovingly, and then he leaned and kissed her on the lips.

After a moment together, Charlemagne and Judith stood up and hiked out of the forest. They came out into a suburb, and he walked her across campus to the apartment.

"Allow me to walk you home, my dear," Charlemagne offered. "I want to ensure you arrive safe."

"Nevermind that, you gentleman," Judith responded. "You're safe here now, so you go in and lay low. My dorm is not too far. I'll make it."

Charlemagne nodded as he conformed. She kissed him on the lips again and then the two parted. He entered into the apartment building, climbing up to the top floor and then taking his key out to open the apartment. The door soon opened, and Charlemagne looked in to see Barry standing on the other side. Barry nodded to him, quickly let him in, and then then closed the door.

"What a close one…" Barry admitted. "Boy, I'm glad you got out of that mess."

"Yes, but let's see our end result," Charlemagne said, walking towards the window and picking up a pair of binoculars. He smiled as he saw the Moore Yankee parked on the roof. "What a devilish sight – yes, I'd like to see them figure out how to get it down now."

"I haven't heard from Felicity; I hope she's alright."

"I'm sure she's fine, I ran into Judith, and she said that part of her team split up from her."

"Really?"

"Yes, a bit of a cold play, but it is what it is, I suppose. Judith is safe. I ran into her and escaped together through the steam tunnels. How did you get out?"

"I just ran and ran," Barry admitted. "Eventually they lost track of me, and I came straight here. Felicity just abandoned Judith – what was she thinking…"

"It's alright."

"No, it's not alright, because… because Felicity told me she had some concerns about Judith. She left Judith behind because she didn't trust her…"

"You think that Judith betrayed us?"

"No, it's not my opinion, of course, I think Judith is great, and it isn't any judgement about this op either. Felicity said though…

that she thinks Judith only likes you because she wants to use you..."

"How preposterous," Charlemagne remarked. "I'm not one to be used- I... how dare she..."

"Look, I know it's not what you want to hear, and I didn't like it either, so just keep it to yourself okay?"

Charlemagne didn't reply. He picked up the binocular set again and looked towards the building. His smile turned to a frown, but he said nothing else.

Act 6, Scene 1

"Ah, there she is," Charlemagne expressed, looking ahead, "at one time, she was the most populous city in all of Western Civilization, the Second Rome, the portal from Europe into Asia… It's been quite some time since we were in Turkey. Back when we were focusing on Greek antiquities did we stop by here."

"Yes, a few years ago," Manon responded.

The pair stood at the top deck bow of a large vessel that transported them through the Bosporus Strait. The strait was a large, wide rugged natural canal with dark blue waters that curved through the continents in a jagged formation. To the left of the boat on the coastline were low hills covered with trees, and likewise on the right low hills with trees, though more signs of civilization than the other end with buildings scattered about, especially on the shore. There were numerous other ships along the strait: fishing boats, tugboats, and cargo frigates all passing through, though each vessel kept to the right. Further ahead on the left, directly ahead, were signs of increased civilization, the hills ahead covered especially in buildings, most of which were white and beige in appearance. The skies above were partly cloudy with stratus clouds and otherwise was light blue. The pair held on to the railing of the vessel as they continued to observe outwards.

"The air here is warmer than in Odessa," Charlemagne remarked, taking in a deep breath, "even the breeze pegs me as warmer than at Ivanov's home."

The vessel peeled right and came closer to the coastline from where Charlemagne could observe large homes built on the cliffsides of a low hill. The trees were green, distinct than the ones from elsewhere in their voyage. These trees were fragile, sporadic and somewhat dry. As the vessel continued to slowly pass through the strait, Charlemagne saw a seawall ahead with a road and buildings on the other end. From where he stood, he could see people walking on the seawall in either direction. Seagulls passed overhead, flying towards Asia from Europe. The seawall was soon cut short by a marina and more sea-side homes. The vessel continued along the strait and after a few minutes the outlines of a suspension bridge between the two sides could be seen ahead, measuring close to one-thousand six hundred yards with two towers on either side and steel wires that curved downwards on both ends.

Charlemagne and Manon stood in place as the ferry passed underneath the bridge. The Bosporus Strait narrowed out afterwards and there were greater signs of civilized life on either ends of the strait as the buildings increased along the hills of the city. After another few minutes, the ferry approached another bridge similar in design, though at least one hundred yards longer and more than fifty yards taller. As the ferry was about to pass underneath the bridge, Charlemagne observed the minarets and domed roof of a building on the west side of the strait ahead. The vessel passed close to this structure as it was located behind a seawall with numerous people gathered around. A ferry was moored next to the seawall, directly behind the building.

"Isn't that interesting," Charlemagne pointed out, "aside from the minarets which are distinctly Muslim, the architecture of that building is noticeably Baroque revival in the domed roof, columns on the rear façade and turrets at the corners. You just need to take away the minarets, and you can see what was once a Byzantine church belonging to what was once known as Constantinople."

"You sound like my father when we visited here years ago," Manon simply replied. "He always sounded so nostalgic for a period of time not known for half a millennium."

"Me? Nostalgic for what? For when these buildings were fitted with one set of superstitious beliefs over another group? I don't lament the fall of Constantinople, especially when the

Ottomans preserved much, which I am grateful for unlike early Christians who had their way through Anatolia and Greece destroying temples they considered pagan. The Ottomans were respectful towards the culture they had conquered. I'm simply pointing out that fact in how they maintained a once Christian temple into a Muslim place of worship. You wouldn't see that with Christians, turning pagan temples into their churches."

"No?" Manon questioned. "Are you so filled with hatred towards that which is Christian, *Charles*, that you yourself forget that the Pantheon and Parthenon were once places of Christian worship too? Even in the rest of Europe too, there are many christianized sites that were once pagan places of worship. How can you say such a thing – to let your bias come out like that?"

"Do I detect a hint of bias towards Christians in yourself, Manon?"

"Me? No, I mean… I have not been to church in years, and I do not consider myself Christian, but I can have some respect for the beliefs of others, no?"

"Are you spiritual?"

"I can only say that I am certain that there must be something more than what we live and see, *Charles*," Manon replied. "I have lived a good life. I have not suffered as other people have suffered. I am grateful for the life that I have lived, though I have seen and been present to the sufferings of others and identified them. I sometimes question, 'why,' but I do not resent, and I do not bicker that my life should be anything else, or I anything more, than what I really am."

"Hmph," Charlemagne responded, looking forward as the vessel continued to sail. "And what are you? Everyone has an opinion about oneself, knowing oneself in a way that others do not know them, and likewise other people hold an opinion about another knowing what they, though limited, know about them. What is your opinion about yourself?"

Manon thought for a moment as she looked out and then answered, "Me? I am everything that you have seen about me, from when I was born in Orléans plus the secrets about me that are mine and my heart's."

"Oh, and what secrets are those?"

"They would not be secrets if they were known, would they? I do not believe myself to be too different from when I was a little girl though," Manon replied. "Though when in university, I did have to become a bit more tough than I was, to compete with others."

"I can hardly remember what you were like as a girl," Charlemagne responded. "Perhaps annoying is the word to use."

Manon frowned at him. She then said, "I have always been honest with myself to others."

"Very well then, knowing what you may have as answer to most likely not only be incomplete but incredibly wrong, what is your opinion of me?"

Manon began to laugh as she answered, "Ohoh, I do not think that is a question you want to ask from me, Charlemagne."

"Why not?"

"Ah, because the answer may not be the one that you want to hear."

"What is that supposed to mean?"

"Let me put it this way and then I will say no more: the answer I have to give is different from the answer you yourself believe, because I am certain that you do not even know who you yourself are."

Charlemagne looked at her with a puzzled reaction. She simply raised her eyebrow as she left him with those words to chew on and then left. She returned inside while Charlemagne frowned and looked ahead. He stayed outside as the ferry as they passed large white apartments on the west side of the strait. The ferry then passed a regal structure that had two tall stories with rectangular black windows and thin columns in the middle. The building was beige and consisted of three partitions, square and equal to one another, side-by-side, with an alcove dividing them. This alcove had a balcony on the second floor. Below the building was a promenade connecting with apartments on the right with a garden full of palm trees and green shrubs. From the ferry, Charlemagne could look into the building and see white curtains that decorated inwards. The rooftop of the building consisted of a thick frieze. On the left of the building was another garden, though enclosed with rectangular arches. Further ahead, Charlemagne looked to the west and observed a wider building on the coastline with white metal fences around the perimeter.

This building consisted of three partitions, a center one larger and taller than the ones on the side. The side partitions were very wide and consisted of two stories. The building had a greyish-beige sloped rooftop with balustrades around the friezes above. Around the perimeter of the mansion was a large green garden with palm trees and shrubs. The perimeter fence extended far outwards from the side partition. Behind the southern gardens were numerous trees in a row. The building was constructed out of beige and white stone.

Not too far on the west coast, Charlemagne observed another mosque. He then saw numerous buildings around next door, including apartments and marinas. There were numerous ports ahead with cruises and other passenger vessels moored, but the vessel they were on continued straight. Off the eastern coast, Charlemagne observed a lone tower in the midst of the strait. This tower was short and thick with a building below that had a red rooftop. There was a small pier besides the building from the island it was on and from where there was a small ferry. He could see a few civilians scattered around. The tower had round top to its squared base with railings around the side like a lighthouse. The rooftop of the tower was domed and had yet another round observation platform above it with a spiked flagpole from where the red, white crescent Turkish flag waved.

As the ferry passed this tower, the strait diverged to the west to an inlet that divided the western coast north and south. A low bridge connected the two sides. The bridge was so low that it had a pier on its side with a very low and small tunnel running through the middle from where short vessels could pass though. On the north side of the west coast, Charlemagne could observe a cone-shaped roof of a tower in the midst of this part of the city. Below the roof were short arches along the stone cylindrical shaft of the tower, from where there were larger arches below with arched windows, and smaller windows along the shaft. An observation deck could be seen around these larger arches with a black railing. As the ferry passed through, Charlemagne observed the breadth of the sea ahead as they were reaching the end of the strait.

Charlemagne looked to his right as they were exiting the Bosporus, and he took note of two domed structures elevated above the rest of the buildings on the west coast. Behind these buildings to the north he could also see the peaked walls of a white structure behind some trees. The domed structures were nearly identical, though one was blue, and they were large and had four minarets at either corner of them. The central building had a bluish-green roof with a golden top. The base of the structure was pinkish beige, with some parts orange to orange-beige. The minarets were grey with long cone tops. The building southward had darker bluish-grey rooftops. The walls of the multi-layered base were light grey to nearly white. The minarets were a darker grey. Each building had smaller domes, some semi-circle, along the face that looked towards the strait. Though similar in appearance, the dome of the center structure was larger than the one to the south. Charlemagne looked with astounded eyes at the massive monuments, and as his eyes took in the view, the ferry began to turn towards the east coast.

A P.A. spoke in Turkish through the boat, prompting Charlemagne to believe as they approached the port and that they were arriving at their destination. He met with Manon indoors where they began to walk down to the lower deck where the UAZ was parked. They each got inside and waited as the vessel slowed down, docked, and then vehicles slowly began to exit out. The jeep drove through the ferry terminal and made its way along an uphill road, and as they went along, they passed a wide structure to their left that had an orange rooftop and large garden with a helicopter landing pad. After less than a few yards they reached an interchange and rather than continue east, they began to go west along the eastern coast.

Charlemagne drove along a clean road with tall hedge trees on either side, as well as low balustrade walls and mowed lawns. The road soon curved east again as they reached a commercial zone with small apartments above some shops. The road soon curved north again, and they continued straight passing similar structures, all of whom shared similar orange rooftops. The road curved east again as they passed a large plaza and a shopping center before continuing to reach a freeway perpendicular to the way they were going. Charlemagne drove onto the interchange ramp and then merged onto the freeway to go west.

The jeep drove along the freeway as they approached the Bosporus Strait again, but before they were drove over the bridge, they pulled out and came out into a residential area south before going along a straight road through a commercial area before the water. The car slowed down as they approached a tall building on the coast.

"Well, it's not the Equinox or a Windsor Hotel, but it'll do," Charlemagne remarked. "Perhaps if we broker a deal with Rubashkin, we can stay somewhere nicer."

Charlemagne and Manon exited out from the jeep, retrieved their belongings, and then went to check-in to the small hotel.

A few hours later, Charlemagne changed out into a beige suit and likewise Manon changed out into a pair of denim jeans and striped sweatshirt. She put on a beret and then met with

Charlemagne at a patio that overlooked the Bosporus Strait. The hotel veranda looked directly towards the large and wide structure with the exceptional perimeter. They were provided with menus for the in-house restaurant and placed an order for something to eat. A few minutes later, the pair were joined by Rubashkin, dressed in a greenish-brown blazer coat and dark khaki open button shirt, and Irina Pachayevskovna, dressed in a black dress and her dark hair brought around her shoulder.

Charlemagne immediately stood up, prompting Manon to do the same. As he stood up, Charlemagne observed that Rubashkin travelled with company behind him; men dressed in suits who stayed back and acted casually.

"Greetings," Rubashkin said, offering his hand.

"Hello again," Charlemagne said with a smile, "sorry about the, uh… misunderstanding at your home at few weeks ago."

"Not to worry," Rubashkin replied, "it's all water under the bridge, so to speak. Irina tells me that you have a proposition, that you require my assistance."

"Yes, a bit of assistance," Charlemagne admitted, "you see, we've gone ahead with our exploration in search of the Frankish Crown, but it seems like our next destination has brought us here to the lovely former land of the Ottomans and Eastern Romans. The only problem though before we begin to settle in to this country is a matter of… personal safety…"

"Yes, go on…"

"Since our departure from Berlin, Manon and I have been the target of some Turkish gangsters, and we believed that it was in our interest to hire some protection as we travel through this land to ensure that we are not ambushed again. I'm short on contacts in this part of the world, so I thought it would be a good idea now to negotiate that alliance we were discussing at your home. You are a man of immense connection in this part of the world, so we thought if anyone could hire some protection for us, it would be you. Of course, I understand that your assistance comes with a price, and in exchange for our protection, it is a price we are willing to now pay."

Rubashkin nodded as he held his hands directly in front of him. Charlemagne observed he wore leather gloves despite the mild weather.

"Good," Rubashkin simply affirmed, "you are correct. I would be able to hire some professional protection services to be of some aid. My offer stands the same from when we last spoke, Mr. Cabernet, though with less patience for any treachery."

"Not to worry, you had us well understood to the point at your home. It was a mistake, my bad, and it won't happen again. You can have whatever we uncover from here on out – how is that for a deal we can shake on? In exchange, you hire mercenaries to provide me and Manon with protection, and we'll be on our way to locate that treasure with your men watching over us."

"A fair deal," Rubashkin responded, "I am in contact with a private military company I rely on. They are a small group of soldiers, all former servicemen with the Soviet Armed Forces, some of whom were Spetsnaz GRU."

"Ah, very good. How soon can they be in Istanbul?"

"Very soon," Rubashkin assured him. "In the meantime, my personal guards are at your service. However, before we shake on this deal, I want to amendment it slightly."

"Yes, whatever you want or need."

"Irina and I will join you in your travels," Rubashkin said. "It's been my interest, and Irina shares this interest, to see how you work. Is that any problem to you?"

"No, none at all."

"Good," Rubashkin replied, "and so, what is the level of progress you have made so far and what is your next destination."

Charlemagne proceeded to explain to him the progress he had made since Romania, omitting his traversal through Moldova and Ukraine, or the encounter with Krum. He spoke about the gravesite near the monastery, the corpse of the Cossack warrior, and the registry in Odessa that suggested the crown sold to an Ottoman diplomat.

"In short, we are looking for a diplomatic official who would have worked sometime around 1830 and would have been travelling to Russia… I believe I explained all this to Irina as we spoke on the phone…"

"Yes," Irina confirmed.

"Yes, you did, and Irina shared it with me and I thought it a good idea to bring something from my records," Rubashkin replied, snapping a finger. A bodyguard brought a briefcase and placed it between them. He then opened it and revealed a decaying book. "This manuscript is a preserved almanac from the days of the Ottoman Empire around the time frame you provided. We can have it double-checked, but a friend of mine already reviewed it and it should have the names of the officials you are looking for."

"Oh, is that so? Seems like you've done your homework then," Charlemagne said with a nervous laugh. "You may not even have needed my help then… You should be well off to go on your own."

"We've retrieved a few names," Rubashkin remarked, snapping his fingers again. A bodyguard produced a short list and provided it to him. He then passed it to Charlemagne. "There are five names of possible officials from that time period."

"Hm…" Charlemagne responded, looking at the list, "any of these people immensely wealthy? Whoever bought the crown had enough money to casually spend ten thousand rubles, quite a lot of money in those times."

"According to my friend's work, three of these people should have held important positions in the empire at the time. He crossed two names and then showed Charlemagne."

"Ah, that makes it easier. We should check in with the local university, see if there are any more records for these three people, and do a background check on them to determine what there fate was."

"Very good," Rubashkin responded, "lead the way."

Act 6, Scene 2

Charlemagne looked out from the window at his right side as they flew over a sprawling urban landscape situated in the midst of a desert. The buildings all consisted of a similar color scheme: terracotta rooftops and light-colored stucco facades, either beige or white. Around the curved roads of suburbs around the city center, the single to double story residential homes had a terracotta orange sloped rooftop to them, whereas in the area around the city center, the tall apartment blocks were either flat roofed or had darker brown terracotta sloped roofs. Amidst these numerous buildings were some distinct ones, small white or greyish-white structures with minarets, like the ones seen in Istanbul. In the midst of the city, there was a larger one too, white with light blue domed rooftops. The landscape was hilled at some parts, and flat along others. In the midst of the landscape was one particular large sandy brown hill. There was also a particular patch of land that was light beige and had a rectangular monument and what appeared to be barren trees that surrounded it on dried grass. The settlement took up all space that could be seen up to the horizon, with only the hill in the middle being of empty sandy space and the background beyond of additional low sand brown mountains also. The skies beyond were a greenish-grey, no cloud in sight but also the sun invisible, and despite the hue in the sky there was not a sight of any tree or grassland below. Charlemagne looked towards Manon on his right, a seat between them, as they sat in the small cabin of seats in an airplane.

"It's impressive that a city like Ankara, being a small settlement at the start of this century of little significance, in the course of the birth of the Turkish state, has now become this massive capital city a little less larger than Istanbul," Charlemagne remarked. "Though still, such a large city in the absence of a primary water source, but still a city of its Greek name, *Ankyra*, anchor."

"Like Saint Petersburg and Moscow, Ankara became an important government and industrial center after the birth of their new state," Manon answered. "On the other hand, Ankara has always had an important cultural tie to a people that lived in this land long ago. If I am not mistaken, the Hittite capital Hattusa is not too far from Ankara."

The pair both sat in the small passenger cabin which composed less than twelve seats in total. The seats were arranged in the cabin with four rows of three seats, one seat along on the left and two seats on the right. Manon sat alone on the left, and Charlemagne on the right, using the larger seat to carry his backpack. Behind them were some Soviet mercenaries and other private guards, and at the very back sat Irina and Rubashkin together. The airplane proceeded to descend towards an airstrip on the outskirts of the city where they landed and then walked out of the plane.

Charlemagne looked out towards the tarmac and saw that it was a small airport, though busy, and it was outside of the city limits. They stepped out of the plane and came down a ladder to the dusty tarmac and then they proceeded to walk towards the rear of the craft as the hull lowered to reveal a ramp and cargo materials on the other side, including the UAZ.

Rubashkin approached Charlemagne as the UAZ and other GAZ jeeps were brought out with other equipment.

"Alright, Charlemagne, where to from here?"

"Yes," Charlemagne answered, taking out a map of the city, "I would like to visit the National Library here. It's said to be one of the largest libraries in the world, with many sources that could pin-point to us our next steps regarding these three candidates. The information that we've gathered so far states that one of these was a governor and a diplomat to the British who operated in this region; the second suggests a governor to a neighboring region up north on the coastline, and the third a governor to the east on the Caucasus border. All three of these individuals have been ruled out as being wealthy viziers who dabbled in diplomacy. The National Library will give us more information about their lives."

"Very well," Rubashkin responded, "then let us go there."

Charlemagne and the rest of the crew got into a vehicle which was chauffeured and protected by one mercenary each. The Soviet mercenaries that Rubashkin had hired did not speak English, only Russian, and thus did not talk to either of them. They wore tactical khaki clothes: cargo pants, t-shirts, and caps. They had various equipment on them, but no visible weapons. They drove out from the airport and into the city, coming onto a highway that brought them through the desert and past some dry farmlands to enter into the city at an interstate that brought them into some suburbs. They then proceeded along a road that took them into the city center as they reached a smaller interstate and then came back onto a freeway through the city. Once at the city center, they merged off the freeway and came onto a major road that led up to the National Library. The National Library, also known as the Library of the Grand National Assembly, was a large building on the right side from where they entered into its parking lot. The library consisted of beige smooth bricks and was rectangular in shape. It consisted of numerous partitions and annexes, and before it was a large dry lawn with flowers in the middle. There were numerous Turkish flags around the façade. The center partition where the main entrance was had three stories, rectangular black windows, and ten rectangular pillars in front of. Charlemagne and the rest of the crew exited out, while only Charlemagne, Manon, and a few guards, those who spoke and read Turkish, came with them.

The foyer of the Grand National Assembly was two-stories tall, had beige walls, and blue carpets on either side with a veranda around the side. A sign pointed them towards the library amidst this government building. The library attached was large and spacious, similar to the rest of the building in its design, and with numerous rows upon rows of shelves, and an extensive basement of archives. From within the library walls, Charlemagne and Manon proceeded to work while the rest of the convoy left to a nearby hotel. They stayed in the library and worked for a few days, pulling resources, compiling texts and translating some knowledge lost to time with the mercenaries as they compiled information about the three figures in question. By the third day, Charlemagne felt comfortable to confront Rubashkin with his information.

"We were unable to rule out of either of these three figures," Charlemagne stated, "but we have reason to believe that a visit to their homes is necessary. According to the sources in this library, the palace of the governor of this region from those times has a home not too far which has become a museum on the banks of a lake. The palace of the governor to the north of us is situated upon a rocky hill looking down upon the city of Kastamonu. Lastly, the palace of the governor to the east is mostly destroyed, like the town it is in, but is in the midst of the desert on the border with Armenia. We will need to further our search in visiting each figure, one by one until we can be certain which purchased the crown from the merchant in Odessa."

"Hm," Rubashkin replied, thinking, "and based on your research, which of these three do you believe to be the likely one?"

"In all honesty, it could be any of them," Charlemagne admitted, "but among them, I would say the one to the east to be the most unlikely due to the geographic position. Both the one to the south of the city and to the north seem like good options. I could see either of these as being figures to travel to Odessa based on their wealth and livelihoods."

"Is this man to the east not a wealthy man?"

"He is, accordingly, but it would not make much sense for a man in his position, no less a militaristic man, to travel to Odessa and purchase the crown. I feel very well about these other two candidates."

"Which would you want to go to first?"

"I would rather visit the one nearby in Ankara since it is close by, and then the one up north if it is the other. To be quite honest, I wish I could be in two places at once on this one."

"Ah, so why not then?" Rubashkin suggested. "There are two of you, so why not split up? From what I've seen so far, you are both capable enough to be on your own, and Irina and I could do the same."

"What? You mean I go with one of you, and the other with Manon to Kastamonu?"

"Yes, how is that for an idea? We can each take some protection with us as we go along."

Charlemagne paused for a moment, looked to Manon who shrugged her shoulders, and then over to Rubashkin. He agreed and said, "Very well, it could save us some time, so why not."

"Very well," Rubashkin remarked, "then I will travel with Dr. Dumas and you can travel with Irina south. We will keep each other updated with our findings, and meet back here when possible."

"Good," Charlemagne affirmed.

• • • •

Charlemagne waved goodbye to Manon and then entered into the back of the UAZ with Irina. Irina looked over to him. She wore capris trousers and a khaki blouse. He awkwardly smiled to her while the mercenaries spoke Russian as they sat down and set off. The jeep drove through the south end of the city and began to make its way into the desert. As they entered into the desert, Charlemagne turned to Irina.

"I suppose having to travel with us must not be your cup of tea," Charlemagne remarked.

"In what way do you mean?" Irina questioned.

"Sorry, I should rather say, it is not something you are used to nor would rather do," Charlemagne responded. "I'm sure a woman of your stature would rather be elsewhere."

"And you know what I do?"

"I suppose not," Charlemagne replied. "What do you do?"

"I go wherever Avdiyi goes," Irina answered, "and I take interest in whatever Avdiyi takes interest in."

"How did you two meet?"

"At a party in Moscow, one year ago," Irina stated. "We were both guests at a symposium at the State Hermitage."

"Ah, so I suppose this collection of his is something that you support and bond over," Charlemagne replied. "To have artefacts of cultural significance that should be shared with the world locked up for private eyes. You know, I once had a favorite painting – a beautiful panting, by Riccardo Gasparonni. The painting was of the Prophet Elijah in the desert. Are you familiar with that story?"

"No."

"In the Bible, there was a prophet named Elijah who performed miracles unlike any of those of past prophets, perhaps since Moses. The historical context for this story has the King David's kingdom divided into two, the Kingdom of Israel to the north and the Kingdom of Judah to the south. Both, I believe, were ruled by bad kings at this time, but one of them was married to a nefarious woman named Jezebel who sent priests of the cult of Baal after Elijah. To make a long story short, Elijah triumphed over the cult priests because he was favored by the God of his ancestors, but after his success, fled for his life and came into a desert where he grew depressed and suicidal. Unwilling to carry forward with what God entrusted in him, he wept and God heard his cries to send an angel to feed him. This painting depicts that

Biblical scene of a depressed Elijah in the desert, on his side, with ravens bringing him food so that he can eat. I remember seeing this painting when I was in my twenties at the home of a man, not particularly a friend. He told me that this painting was one of a kind, and that there was none like it in anyplace in the world. Perhaps it was a bit of jealousy within me that he should have this beautiful object all to himself when I desired it, but too there was a sense of justice within me that no, it should be accessible to all people. Any historical or cultural object of immense beauty and significance should be available to all people, in my opinion – why should something like that be in the hands of one or few?"

"I believe you English have a phrase for the answer to that question," Irina responded, *"finders keepers,* if I'm not mistaken. Avdiyi takes pride in his collection, and surely this quest must tell you the importance in preservation of these items."

"This quest has taught me that personal ownership has resulted in this goose chase from country to country," Charlemagne replied. "If the crown had merely been left in a museum, or even the basilica it came from, it would have been where it had been for years beforehand. The vices of other human beings to take and steal has resulted in this quest."

"Rest assured, Rubashkin wants to preserve his collection," Irina said. "His vault will be a safe haven for all his treasures to be preserved forever."

"What good is preservation, to hide something away like a bone for a dog in a hole, if it cannot be enjoyed?"

"A collection is meant to be right where you left an object, so that when you should want to admire and look at it, there it will be," Irina remarked. "You visited his home; he enjoys showing his collection to others. His immense wealth in Russia is nothing compared to all the goods he has stored, and he takes greater pride in them than in corporations."

"Your Avdiyi is nothing more than a collector," Charlemagne rebuked, "and never has a collector been a good thing. How can you exalt him?"

"I do not," Irina replied, "but what else can I do?" she said, looking out the window. "You tell us that men has been chasing after you from Serbia, but yet we have not seen anyone and it has been a week. Who are these men that pursue you?"

"It's a long story," Charlemagne responded, "but nothing spectacular. I'm nothing like Avdiyi – I hunt for treasures to bring them into the public light, not take them home as nice it would be to do so. I've taken upon treasure hunting as a hobby for almost ten years now, and in doing so I've made some bad friends – enemies who wish to harm me and take what I search for. One of these enemies is a spoiled brat named Ali Al-Suli. I'm under the assumption that because his father admires what I do and the corporate relationship we've built that he's become envious of all that I have, and as such, has hired Turkish gangsters to hunt me down and steal what I find. I was kidnapped in Budapest during this quest, taken to Serbia, but escaped – these Turkish gangsters, they suffered a bit of a setback in that moment and now I wouldn't be surprised if these Bulgarian mercenaries, led by some loon named Krum Berezovsky, were themselves hired by Al-Suli to continue the job. Their leader seems like he's interested in the treasure, though to simply sell it, but I wouldn't be surprised if he's being paid to hunt me down."

Irina did not respond. Charlemagne elaborated further on his encounter with Krum's men in Serbia, Moldovia, and their escape from Moldova. She still did not say anything else.

"Yes, it is a funny world, this former land of communist oppression," Charlemagne remarked. "How do these folk ever survive?"

"We toil and endure," Irina answered, "that is how."

"Oh?" Charlemagne questioned. "Up to now, I've assumed you to be of some sort of ancestry to these people of these lands, but Soviet?"

"Russian," Irina clarified, "from Yekaterinburg to be precise, though raised and lived in Moscow most of my life. I am the child of a government official, like Rubashkin."

"Ah, I see," Charlemagne responded, "I suppose that answers my earlier question then."

After another hour, the UAZ jeep arrived to a small village in the desert. The landscape around where they consisted of rugged sandy wasteland with hills in the horizon. This village sat in the midst of that land with a peculiarly shaped but large rock in the middle. The rock was shaped almost like that of an anvil, or perch. They continued through the village and came along the coastline of an immense lake where on the other side was a large palace. The palace was similar to the Hagia Sofia and Blue Mosque in Istanbul in the sense that it consisted of numerous layers. The exterior walls of the castle was beige, and it was surrounded with a circular wall as it was built on a small peninsula along the lakefront. The structure consisted of numerous towers, almost all of which had gold-colored dome roofs or otherwise terracotta-colored roofs.

"Well, that's certainly larger than I anticipated this museum to be," Charlemagne remarked, looking ahead. "Luckily for us, today is Sunday, and in Turkey, most businesses are closed on Sunday."

"Do you suggest that you will have us break in to explore the palace?"

"I highly advise it," Charlemagne responded. "Tourists can only just get in the way."

The jeep continued to drive down the coast as they came around to a neighboring village. This village consisted of sandstone structures and similarly colored terracotta sloped rooftops. They drove towards the front of the museum palace where they found themselves in a small parking lot before the front doors with palm trees in a row up to the main entrance. The parking lot was accessible through an arch through the exterior walls on the peninsula, which itself connected to the inner walls, while leaving a space out to look towards the lake. There were no other vehicles in the parking lot and this part of the village was also very quiet.

Charlemagne stepped towards the front doors of the castle, which were rectangular and loomed over him from an arched nook. He pointed up to a balcony above and Irina requested that the mercenaries throw hooks on ropes to grab on for them to climb up. From the balcony, the pair were able to step toward a doorway that came into a large room.

"Here we are," Charlemagne remarked, looking about. "I don't anticipate the crown to be in this palace, but I need more information about our candidate for us to learn more about them and their travels. If this person had as much of a relationship with the British consulate and trading companies in Ankara as I've read, then he would be a busy man and travelled lots. Help me find any place in which those sorts of records could be kept."

Irina nodded and then spoke to the mercenaries in Russian, and they proceeded to split up and assist in the search with Charlemagne. Charlemagne and Irina teamed up and began to search through the palace together as each team went to one corner of the property. The pair came downstairs to the foyer entrance which led down a corridor with polished floor and slim columns to a set of rectangular golden-colored doors. These doors then led into a small room with a throne ahead.

"The governor of each region in the Ottoman Empire was a powerful man, more powerful than the Sultan, less powerful than the Grand Vizier who effectively ruled the empire until its dissolution. The Ottoman Empire lived as a monarchy, oligarchy, to democracy in the course of its existence, much like Rome. During its time as an oligarchy, from the late sixteenth century to early twentieth century, the Grand Vizier ruled with the regional governors, and at times these governors acted as vizier for the entire empire. No doubt, the family of this palace were very powerful individuals to have their own throne room."

The pair continued to search through the rest of their side of the palace. The interior architecture varied from medieval Ottoman-style to modern regal European-style in some parts. Nonetheless, the design was oriental and royal to say the least with a variety of Asiatic furniture and colorful rugs and tapestries, and Islamic influenced calligraphy in the ornaments of the walls.

During their search, Charlemagne observed numerous parts of the castle were divided as though there were suites within the castle with bedrooms, kitchens, and dining halls repeating themselves. The pair found themselves at a regal bathroom with a large bathtub in the center and balcony that viewed out towards the lake.

"I do have to hand it to the Turks, they certainly know how to build a castle," Charlemagne remarked. "No less one to lose oneself in. This place is a labyrinth, worse than the salt mines in Ukraine."

"Salt mines?"

"Nevermind that," Charlemagne responded. "Shall we?"

"What are you hiding, Mr. Cabernet?"

Irina questioned, stepping towards him.

"N-nothing," Charlemagne replied. "I'm a man of many adventures, and I've ventured to Ukraine before…"

"I had the impression you had never been across the Iron Curtain before."

"No, that's not entirely true…" Charlemagne admitted. "I've been to Poland, Finland… the Baltic States and Russia before."

Irina looked at him as she stood in the sunlight, and Charlemagne in the shadows. As Charlemagne looked at Irina, the darkness of her hair glowed and the color in her eyes were saturated in hue. Her fair skin, pure, was warm. His face grew pale as he looked at her, and his cheeks turned red. Her eyes looked at him straight on, but not with suspicious. Her pupils were wide and she looked at him with a different gaze.

"I suppose with this much space, these number of harems, or separate living spaces for mistresses, would be given," Charlemagne remarked, sheepishly looking to the side. "I forgot that polygamy and harems were staple in Ottoman society."

"Hm..." Irina responded with a frown, retracting her arm to cross them. "Pigs... these men." She then left the room and Charlemagne followed.

"Not all men are like that, I swear..." Charlemagne assured her.

Eventually, the pair came to a large and tall room with bookshelves on the left and right. The room was round with a viewing gallery surrounding it on the upper floors up to five stories and a domed ceiling with windows around the upper perimeter. Between each bookshelf was a display case that showed an item, and on this floor there were open books on display. Each of these books were written in Turkish. The descriptive plaques beside the books were in different languages.

"A very detailed people," Charlemagne expressed, "these books are biographies of the lives of each noble descendant, but that won't be good enough. Ideally, I would need a journal with dates to see if the date on the shipping log matches with them being in Odessa. I've written down what that date was in the Gregorian calendar and the Islamic calendar."

Charlemagne and Irina began to go through the books in the library shelves, eventually pulling together some potential resources. Irina took a radio from his belt and contacted the Soviet mercenary who can read and write Turkish to come up and join them. Charlemagne then began to set out on examining the contents of this room from floor to floor, assisting him translate the subject matter as they hunted for biographies and books.

"Oh, this would be so much simpler if they followed a classification system as in the West," Charlemagne remarked. "Why couldn't they have imported that from Europe?"

Eventually, Charlemagne found a journal, but it was not the journal he needed. He put it aside and with the mercenary's help, began to translate the names of each journal until he eventually found the one he needed. He then narrowed down the date of the journal to find one from the 1830s. He flipped through the pages, coming around to the date of the sale of the crown.

"Really?" Charlemagne reacted. "He was in London at the time... that's no good for us..." He paused for a moment. "What if I've gotten the date incorrect? I may have made a mistake..."

Irina looked over from behind as the radio went off. She picked it up and spoke in Russian. She then waited for a response. She spoke back and then faced the soldier with them. She spoke to him in Russian and he left.

"What's going on?"

"A suspicious vehicle parked out front, possibly local authorities," Irina remarked. "They will monitor and let us know if it is time to leave..."

"I need that man's help to read these books," Charlemagne expressed. "I have to re-check the date, perhaps this writer is using a Gregorian calendar rather than a Julian calendar. He's certainly not using an Islamic calendar."

The pair froze as they heard the rattle of gunfire from afar.

"Oh no..." Charlemagne remarked, standing up.

"Put those books away to take with you," Irina ordered. "We need to leave."

Charlemagne quickly put the books into his bag and then the pair went around the balcony from the table they were at and took position around the archway. Irina had produced a small firearm, a very small pistol, into her hands and carried it at her side. She led the way around as she checked corners and then went out into the corridor. The sound of gunfire could be heard loudly and shouts in Russian came through the radio. The pair eventually came to the long corridor up to the throne room, though from the upper floor as they looked down from the veranda. The gunfire was loud as it echoed through the hall, but before they could move again, they heard the rev of an engine and crash upon a door. The main entrance doors below flew open and an armored truck drove in and crashed into a pillar below them. The bandits poured out from the truck and also through the doors. Irina picked up the radio and spoke in a quiet voice in Russian, and then she took Charlemagne's hand and began to guide him away, but not before recognizing the uniform of the bandits.

"These are Krum's men," Charlemagne told her. "I know that dress well. It's his people."

"We can discuss later," Irina replied, "but now we need to get out of here."

"Can we not go the way we came in?"

"Only if you want to go in a body bag..."

Irina took him around a curved corridor, but then stopped as she saw a shadow come up from the right. She swore in Russian and immediately took Charlemagne with her to hide in the arched nook in the hallway. The pair heard the men speak in Bulgarian.

"We-"

Irina put a hand over Charlemagne's mouth with one hand and looked at him sternly. He looked at her with intrigue. She turned her eyes away from him and to the door at their side.

"Go..." Irina muttered in his ear.

Charlemagne immediately took his hand and opened the door. The pair entered through quietly and closed the door behind them. They entered into a large bedroom with an Ottoman-style bed in the center and divan on the other end.

"We're done for..." Charlemagne expressed, helping her move a wardrobe to block the door. "This won't stop them..."

"Shut up," Irina snapped. "Come now."

Irina brought Charlemagne around to the door to the balcony, but before they could exit there was a thump at the door. They heard some murmurs in Bulgarian from the other side. Irina quickly opened the balcony door and stepped out with Charlemagne. They closed it behind them and then hid around the side of the door. Meanwhile, Irina looked around. They were a story above and the cliffs and lake waters stared them down from below. She hopped down onto a ledge and then jumped across to the adjacent balcony.

"Come on," Irina encouraged. Charlemagne followed.

Rather than continue into the next-door room, they hid around the corner as that room was searched and then crossed over to the next balcony. She opened the balcony doors and then they quietly entered through to the next room just as the bandits came out to the balcony. Irina went towards the open door at the end of the bedroom inside and then peaked out. Charlemagne caught up with her and stood at her side. She stood close to her, less than an inch between them. After a wait, Irina led them across the corridor and down a perpendicular hallway where they quickly dashed across to come to a large sitting room with arched windows. She closed the door behind them and then they continued straight through to an adjacent parlor. They could still hear gunfire in the background, though it minimized.

"Why don't you call for help? Let's link up with the others?" Charlemagne suggested.

"Shut up," Irina snapped once more. "I need to think..." She spoke in Russian again, to herself, though Charlemagne's ears twitched as he could hear a word similar to 'Avdiyi' in her sentences. She then marched to the end of the room where there was a set of closed doors.

"When we drove in, I saw a dock around the edge of the castle," Charlemagne remarked. "We could row our way to the nearby beach and slip away."

"We are not running away like cowards," Irina denied. "We are going to hold our ground." She picked up the radio and spoke in Russian. She then looked over to Charlemagne to get him to follow her again. "Our men are keeping them busy, but we need to join them at the other side of the property."

The pair came out to a curved corridor that brought them around to the library again. They slipped inside and made their way around to the stairwell that came down to the main floor. They then went towards an exit out onto a wide corridor, and then went down and around to a corner with a junction that went two ways. They went straight forward as they went around a curved corridor, but as they went along, Irina could see someone ahead and jumped back. The Bulgarian bandit shouted towards them, and she took Charlemagne's hand and they hid behind a bookshelf. She opened fire with the pistol towards the bandits who returned more deadlier firepower from their AK-47 rifles. The pair quickly retreated and came back to the intersection where they took cover for a moment so Irina could fire back and then retreat again. They came back into the library where she made a dash to the stairwell. The bandits then flooded in to the ground floor, prompting her to take him upstairs and hide behind a column. From above, Irina opened fire and landed a clean shot against a bandit, wounding him and causing him to fall over. The bandits spread out along the perimeter walls below them.

"Stay back," Irina said, going over to the stairwell. She hid in place and Charlemagne watched as she ambushed two bandits who came after her. She grappled one of them, shot the other, and then hit her pistol into the side of the head of the other to knock him over. She then kicked him across the face. She made a remark in Russian, put her pistol away and picked up the AK-

47 to hold. She checked it and then looked over to Charlemagne. "Don't just stand there, grab a rifle."

"Oh, yes…"

Charlemagne picked up the other AK-47 and then followed Irina around to the columns as they took cover around the other side. Some additional bandits came in, one went to the wounded bandit on the floor who immediately warned his brethren. At that sound, Irina turned the corner and rained down fire towards them, causing one to fall down and the others to split up.

"Watch those stairs!" Irina shouted to Charlemagne.

Charlemagne opened fire, but his gun immediately jammed. He attempted to fix it, but Irina went forward to take cover as the bandits flushed in. Charlemagne immediately hid around the perimeter as he continued to attempt to unload the gun. His magazine then slipped and hit him in the foot.

"Woops…" Charlemagne remarked. "I swear, I've handled a rifle before…" He picked up the magazine, released the jammed cartridge, and then re-checked the gun. However, as he moved around the corner, the other mercenaries were already taken care of.

"Come on," Irina shouted.

"Hm… you've got quite some skill in gunfighting," Charlemagne acknowledged. "Bravo."

Irina ignored him and they came back downstairs, and fled through the corridor. They stopped for a moment as she spoke through the radio.

"They're holding out in the throne room with what must be left…" Irina remarked. "We'll ambush them from the side."

Irina led Charlemagne down a narrow corridor and they came out near the main entrance corridor where bandits took position ahead behind the columns and doors. Irina snuck up behind them and before they came right up to them. She pulled Charlemagne closer to her so that their faces were an inch apart.

"I will move ahead on the other side," Irina whispered to him. "We will force them to surrender."

"Certainly…"

Charlemagne went ahead while Irina quietly dashed across and then the pair continued. He moved forward, stopping from column to column. Irina moved in the dark. Windows above poured light into the corridor, but on Irina's side was darkness, while on Charlemagne's it was light. Charlemagne knelt down as he breathed sharply and then stood up to come up to the second last column. However, as he ran, his foot squeaked into the polished floor, prompting the bandits to turn and face him.

"Bollocks…" Charlemagne remarked, taking cover. They opened fire at him and immediately spread into cover. However, they had not seen Irina, so she opened fire back at them prompting them to spread out again and for one of them to become seriously wounded. Charlemagne fired back at the soldiers, but he did not hit any of them, nor did he really aim. He sprayed gunfire at random in their general direction, while Irina attempted to hit at them in their cover. Meanwhile, the mercenaries from the throne room adjusted themselves and took cover at the doorway. The bandits attempted to readjust once more and run away, but they were shot down and the room was cleared. "Sorry about that…" Charlemagne expressed, running up to join Irina at the throne room door. "I'm a little rusty in this… How's everyone doing?"

Irina glared at him and then met with the mercenary leader. He spoke in Russian to her. She then translated for Charlemagne and said, "We should have run into most of them, but to be sure let us make our way to the exit."

They crew split up from the throne room and travelled down the columns on either side, making their way down to the exit where additional mercenaries came through the door and took point at the main entrance. Additionally, a fireteam approached from the left as well. Again, they found themselves in a firefight in the palace, but Charlemagne noticed a few of their mercenaries split up and travel upstairs to gain a height advantage. At the elimination of the fireteam to the left, and their subsequent retreat where the rest of the mercenaries on the ground floor went to pursue, those bandits at the main entrance fled out into the courtyard. Irina and Charlemagne took point at the main entrance and continued to open fire at them, but they took cover behind the jeeps. The mercenaries came down from the second floor to takeover for where Charlemagne stood, and then they continued to put the pressure on those outside.

"Here, this will probably do more for you than me," Charlemagne said, passing his rifle to a mercenary as he ran out of ammunition and rather than reload.

The bandits that remained got into their jeep and left the courtyard. The rest of the mercenaries flooded out into the courtyard to fire back at them, but they were gone.

"Ahah," Charlemagne remarked with a smile, "how's that for good company?" He smiled at the others who looked at him plainly, some with serious glances and others sweating and exhausted. He lowered his smile and turned to Irina. "I told you they were after me…"

"I did not doubt you," Irina replied, "but it's not safe here. If you have what you need, then we need to leave."

"I believe I do – I can examine the books in a safe place," Charlemagne replied. "Let's return to Ankara."

Act 6, Scene 3

"I'm astonished that neither of our candidates were evidently the ones we should have been looking at," Charlemagne expressed as he sat in the back of the UAZ as they drove through the desert. "A part of me is a bit concerned that this last candidate could not be the one we are looking at either, and another part of me questions why we have even bothered to travel out this far."

Manon sat next to him as she read from a book. Charlemagne had his journal in front of him as he wrote.

"According to several sources, although the palace was heavily ransacked and destroyed, the *beylerbey* kept his most cherished possessions hidden away almost a kilometer from the east tower. There were no other sources to suggest that this cellar was also ransacked..."

"Yes, but remember..." Charlemagne said, looking to the mercenaries in front of them before he leaned over to Manon, "we're acting under the assumption that the crown we've acquired in Ukraine is the prize we're looking for. We'll poke around for this pit for the sake of keeping Rubashkin happy, but to be quite honest, I've had it planned out in my mind – I've grown a bit tired of this quest and want to call it quits here."

"Ah, what happened?" Manon questioned, condescendingly. "What happened to the desire for adventure from the Charlemagne that I know?" she teased.

"You and Rubashkin may have had a gay old time at your site, but Irina and I did not. We were ambushed... and I very much embarrassed myself in front of her..."

Manon rolled her eyes and continued to read through her book.

"After our failures at our respective sites, and after reading that this third candidate stored treasure in the desert – implying that they for one had treasure, I'm willing to use that as enough evidence to appease your father in this mess."

"Oh?"

"Yes," Charlemagne remarked, "but we've still got to deceive Rubashkin to have him believe that we're intentionally hunting for the crown and not just evidence for support our acquisition of the crown from Ukraine."

"You are so confident in that crown that you keep in your backpack? Weighing you down as you walk..." Manon remarked. "That crown is not the one you believe to be, *Charles*. I am certain it is the Polish crown, the crown of Boleslaw the Brave, the *Corona Privilegiata*."

"The Polish crown? Fat chance..." Charlemagne rebuked. "Look at this design..." he showed her a drawing of the crown they found in Ukraine in his journal. "Just like the one lost in Saint Denis..." He flipped to a page where he drew an approximate of the Frankish Crown. "At any rate, the crown isn't in me backpack. It's in my luggage."

"Ah, you mean in your luggage in the other car?"

"What?" Charlemagne questioned, looking behind him into the trunk. "Oh damn... all these cars look so similar... Oh, whatever... it's safe and sound in any car. These people don't know we're harboring the crown with us."

Manon shook her head in disbelief at him.

"At any rate, the village we are travelling to is a contentious town," Charlemagne explained. "As we technically travel through West Amenia, though there aren't any Armenians left in this part of the country, this castle was a fortress used against the Russians in the numerous wars they fought against the Turks. Interestingly, in 1855, during the Crimean War, this town was under siege and the Turks and British surrendered to the Russians – that was the battle talked about in our secondary sources. My explanation therefore is that the Frankish Crown was in the hands of this governor, the *beylerbey*, and he put it in his treasury. When the Russians won the siege, they pillaged and razed the castle, taking the crown with them to the Russian

Empire. From there, it was likely kept in the hands of a noble, or whomever, before it was pilfered and thrown into some Soviet institute where it was kept until the Germans discovered it. The reason why the Germans did not say anything about it, no doubt, is because they had no idea the Frankish Crown had made this retarded U-turn through the Balkans, Turkey, and up the Caucasus to come back to them. You'll see – when we find that cache wherever it may be, if still there, we'll find it empty and devoid of any goods."

"Ah, and what will the look on your face be when we find this crown and have two crowns?" Manon jested. "To know that your precious crown was all this time in the middle of the desert, and that you now must share it with Rubashkin."

"An improbable situation, my dear," Charlemagne plainly asserted. "I'll prove you wrong – I'm confident in my hypothesis. After a hundred and fifty years, I doubt this pit may even still exist; I'm so confident that I am right that I see no need to waste our time searching for lost history. We ought to just back up and call it quits..."

"Are you scared that I may be right?"

"No, I'm tired, and I don't want to run into anymore Bulgarian psychopaths in the middle of the desert. Rubashkin seemingly has taken the situation seriously as he's removed himself from the field to the command post, and Irina out with him. They've left us with the grunts to do the legwork..."

"Even if I am wrong, *Charles*, which I will admit, is possible but even if I am wrong, it does not mean that you are right and that your crown is the crown you believe it to be. Even if we do not find this cache, or if we do find it and it is empty, we need to gather evidence. I have a strong belief that this man, Tolcan Göran, is who we believe him to be, the one who bought the crown from Odessa, but where it has gone from his hands...?"

"The library did say he died in the battle," Charlemagne expressed, "part of the reason why they surrendered... If we should fail here, I believe it would be beneficial to engage Dr. Ivanov again." He then sighed and spoke, "Our adventure is far from over, Manon. We will likely need to travel to Russia from here and engage those Soviet archives to learn what it is that we picked up from that salt mine for certain and backtrack from there."

"Ah, I am a step ahead of you, it seems," Manon remarked. "My father and Dr. Ivanov are in conversation, and he and Konstantin are working on it already."

"You really shouldn't be phoning your father from these lands, Manon," Charlemagne admonished. "Who knows who is listening into to those phone lines, if it is the Turkish gangsters tipping the Bulgarians off, or what."

"Ah, but I did not tell my father that we would be going to Ankara," Manon said. "I had last spoken to him in Istanbul when we arrived, and then after I returned from Kastamonu."

Charlemagne didn't respond. The jeep continued to drive through the desert as they went along the freeway. After another hour on the road, the land began to diversify as to their left was a short dry grass while on the left a rocky sand. All around them, the faint horizon of some hills could be seen in what was otherwise a flat and arid land. The road they travelled on was narrow and single lane on either side. The road was also rugged. After a few more minutes, there was a bit more grass on either side, and eventually the sight of some large and extensive farms could be seen all around the left side. The road curved around a hill on the right side that was somewhat rocky, and then continued straight towards a village. The jeep continued through the village and then carried on as they went away and back into the drylands of grass and sand.

After another hour, the jeep went off-road and began to travel along a rocky road. The mercenaries used Charlemagne's GPS to navigate to the point that they needed to travel. They passed the pastures on the side of the road and ventured deep into the desert, going around cliffsides and gulches in the land until they could see a noticeable low rock that held onto the ruins of the fortress. After yet another hour, the jeep went up to the base of the rock and parked.

"We'll need to take a look at the ruins to determine which of these is the north tower, and then we can hike down to the approximate area," Charlemagne said, opening the door. "Let's get this over with."

Charlemagne and Manon retrieved their backpacks from the trunk and then proceeded to walk along a trail that came up to the fortress steps. The fortress was a large and narrow structure upon a very low hill, consisting of three partitions of walls, each connected via circular towers. The entire structure formed a ninety-degree curve. The elevated ascent up to the entrance of the fortress was reinforced with stone walls. As they arrived to the top of this slope, and passed through the half-broken archway inside, Charlemagne observed that the stone walls on the outside were outer walls that were partially broken and decayed. The interior structures of the fortress were entirely gone and all that was inside was dry overgrown grass. They proceeded to walk around to a set of stairs that brought them up along the stairwell. With a compass in hand, the pair walked around the perimeter walls as best they could, traversing over gaps and going around ledges in the pathway to reach a circular tower at the north end. Once at this point, Charlemagne retrieved from his backpack a set of binoculars and looked outwards to the plain desert sands.

"I don't see anything that strikes out as out of the ordinary," Charlemagne admitted. "No ditches, no pits, and no exposed abscesses…" He sighed and lowered his binoculars. "Right then, looks like we'll have to do this the hard way."

Charlemagne and Manon hiked down to the lower levels of the fortress. Before they returned to the ground floor, Charlemagne searched around the inner perimeter, through the tall grass, and then returned back down to where the jeep was parked. He opened the trunk and removed a vertical device from a polyester case and then lifted it out and held it with both hands.

"Let's be sure the dowsing machine is calibrated correctly," Charlemagne remarked, turning on the machine and adjusting the knobs. The device that Charlemagne held as he knelt down was a rectangular metal box with a handle, attached to a pole which in itself had a flat metal circular pad at the end. "I remember using one of these back in the day in Europe, quite interesting devices, but with limited uses. I knew a mate that lived in the southern parts of the United States, would always find remnants from the American Civil War with one of these."

"Ah, the envy of your childhood," Manon simply replied. "Do you remember when we found the little blade by the creeks near the family home?"

"Yes, I was so excited – I thought for sure we had really found something. My grandfather told me it was likely Roman, but your father said it was most likely Germanic. They were both surprised to learn it was the remains of a Celtic blade."

"I still have that blade..." Manon admitted. "I keep it in my office at the university, by my desk. I'm always reminded by that day and how excited we were to come across such history so close to where we lived..."

Charlemagne didn't respond and instead picked up the metal detector. He passed it to Manon, and then took out another one for him to use. He calibrated the machine, took it into his hands, and the pair then set forth. They proceeded to walk down and around the fortress grounds to come out to the desert. Once the two of them were vertically away from the north tower, Charlemagne began to walk forward in a straight line while Manon measured their distance with a GPS device. After less than half a mile, they walked slowly as Charlemagne scanned the ground at one angle, while Manon scanned perpendicular to their location. From these points, the pair scanned the ground at their feet, waving the metal detector in a windshield wiper motion, back and forth, back and forth, while the machine hummed a straight hum. Charlemagne walked close to another mile as he went forward, while Manon walked half that distance and then proceeded to return the opposite direction. Luckily for both of them, the skies were grey and the sun nowhere to be seen through the clouds and the temperature average with a light wind. The day was early, but just beginning. After a full mile, Charlemagne's device didn't pick up any detections and so he began to turn around and return the way he came.

The pair scanned the ground around them along the same axis they started, going back and forth, back and forth. Eventually, during their routes, they came up to each other and paused.

"I don't think we've got a bloody clue what we're doing here," Charlemagne remarked. "I don't see any potential hideaways anywhere along this field."

"Keep searching," Manon encouraged, "we need to at least exhaust this area before we go anywhere else. Please, *Charles*, just to satisfy my father if we are to present that crown to him."

Charlemagne rolled his eyes and then continued to scan as he went down, and then up, down and then up. At around noon, Charlemagne waved the metal detector and his machine began to beep.

"Oh! Oh!" Charlemagne reacted, honing in on the object as he carefully waved his device more closely around the immediate area. The device grew louder in one particular spot, and Charlemagne looked over and began to claw his gloved hands into the sand. He made a small hole in the sand from which he retrieved a very small iron ball. "Oh, you've got to be kidding me... a bloody musket ball..." He placed the ball into his shirt pocket and then continued to scan with annoyance. The area was clear, but after he was sure there was nothing else, he looked around and grumbled. "Which bloody direction was I going...?"

Manon walked in straight directions, to and fro, stopping too a few minutes later and dropping down to her knees at a specific spot. She retrieved a small spade from her backpack and then began to dig in the precise location, pouring the sand besides the hole she was making and seeing if anything came out. She eventually saw a shiny object in the dirt and picked it up, but it was just a piece of scrap metal no larger than a two inches. She took in a deep breath and let out an exhale of disappointment, but said nothing and instead continued to walk in the correct direction.

The pair wandered the desert into the high noon when Charlemagne waved the metal detector around in the sand and began to pick up a detection. He raised an eyebrow and looked around the immediate area.

"What's this? Another musket ball?"

Charlemagne carefully waved the metal detector, going diagonal and away from the path he was walking to finally reach a hot spot, though weak. He turned off the device after found the strongest spot the signal came through and retrieved his own spade to begin to dig into the dirt. He removed the sandy dirt and poured it aside, but as he threw his spade in, he hit a hard object. "Hm?" he thought aloud. He threw the spade in some more and began to clear out some more of the dirt. However, the more Charlemagne dug, the more surrounding loose sandy dirt began to cave in, delaying progress. He dug a foot in to hold up one side of the slopes and threw the spade in to see if he could see what was being hit. He saw something greyish-brown through that was not clearly identifiable. "What the devil is this…?" he said aloud. Charlemagne continued to clear dirty sand, creating a large pile beside him as he continued to dig to the point that he could see something rugged at the bottom of the hole. He tapped it with his spade. "Hollow," Charlemagne noted aloud. "Wood…" He looked up and turned towards where Manon was walking. "Oy! Come here! I think I've found something!"

Manon turned her neck and looked over to where Charlemagne was. She drew a mark in the sand where she was and then went over to join him.

"What are you doing?" Manon questioned.

"What does it look like I'm doing?" he sarcastically replied. "Lend me a hand here, I've found something good."

"What did you find?"

"Listen," Charlemagne said, tapping his shovel into the wood. "You hear that? That's something hollow on the other side, a board covering something up like a well. I want to see how much of this sand is covering and need another hand to move this bloody sand."

Manon didn't respond, put metal detector aside with Charlemagne's, and then joined him to begin to clear some sand. They revealed a significant portion was covered by wooden boards as they moved large amounts of sand from the ground. The pile that Charlemagne had created loomed over a portion of the wooden board, so they had to move their pile further away, digging into the evening as they revealed a group of wooden boards stuck together by metal nails that covered a hole of some kind below. A crack in the floorboards showed that the pit was deep. After a fair amount of dirt was moved, Charlemagne took his shovel and began to remove some of the wood. He took a spotlight from his backpack out and shined it down. The pit was at least two yards deep as he could see the ground below. Charlemagne continued to dig around so that he could expose more floorboards for removal. Manon didn't help as she let him clear the rest of the sand and rested.

Once enough sand was removed, Charlemagne continued to remove the floorboards one by one. Doing so caused remaining sand from around to pour in to the ground. He peeled back the boards enough so that he created a gap large enough for a person to slip through. He shined his light down and saw that a slope of sand came down to a ground that consisted of stone brick floors and walls. He could see some barrels against the walls, and a chest of some sort. Charlemagne continued to remove some more floorboards with care to prevent anymore sand from going into the pit.

"Right, I think that's enough," Charlemagne noted. "I'm going in…"

Charlemagne stuck his foot in and then slid down into the pit. He shined his light around and found himself in a small room supported by additional floorboards above. The room was at least ten feet by eight feet in size. He walked up to the barrel and saw that the plugs were removed and contents empty. He then went to the chest inside and began to wrestle with the latch. Manon, meanwhile, stood from above as she shined her own spotlight down. Once the latch was removed, Charlemagne lifted the lid and found that the contents of the chest were empty.

"As I thought…" Charlemagne acknowledged, slowly standing up as he crouched down. He turned to face Manon. "It's empty… this space has been pillaged, we've wasted our time here on the obvious. I want to meet Dr. Ivanov and discuss with him further."

"Ah, and what will you tell him?" Manon questioned. "You came to a fortress and saw that the cache was empty?"

"Well, yes, of course," Charlemagne replied. "That's what I've discovered."

"*Charles*, we are standing upon a pit that has one-hundred and fifty years between the siege on the fortress and now," Manon explained. "We cannot say for certain that whoever stole from this cache was Russian."

"What do you want me to say Manon? We have to make assumptions at some point?"

"Ah, do you want to make history, or convenient lies to explain how you came across that phony crown of yours?"

"The crown is the crown," Charlemagne assured her. "Besides, I just want to get out of Rubashkin's hair and away from this accursed land once and for all. I'll pay those mercenaries myself now that we're familiar with them if we need the protection in Russia, but I want out…"

"You've only explored half of that room," Manon pointed out. "What of the sand below? Surely there may be something on that side – You must be certain that there are no more clues…"

Charlemagne groaned and picked up his spotlight. He looked around the room he was in and found something shiny on the floor. He picked it up and sat down on the chest to examine it. He swatted at some of the dust with his finger and then showed it to Manon.

"It's a cartridge…" Charlemagne pointed out. "Funny enough, I found a musket ball while looking around the dirt. I thought it could have been related to the battle, only problem is for a battle held during the Crimean War, I'm not sure if they'd use muskets or cartridges. I can't remember when those were phased out in their respective armies. This cartridge could be quite recent from the past hundred years, or from that same war." He continued to look at the cartridge as he nodded. "You know what, you make a good point, my dear. I should scan the rest of the room for clues and perhaps I can deduce who was last in this space before it was closed."

Charlemagne looked around the latter side of the pit but did not see anything of note. He then took his shovel and began to haul dirt from one side to the other. He was eventually able to reveal another chest, but this one like the other was empty. He threw the chest to the other side of the room and continued to remove clumps of dirt. He found a second object in the dirt, a metal object, and it was an opened tin can with the lid half on. Around the sides of the can was a faint label. Charlemagne examined it with care and then showed Manon.

"Any idea when canned goods became standard?" Charlemagne questioned. "I seem to recall they were a result of industrialization…as early as Napoleon's time, perhaps?"

"A French invention, but did not become common until the mid-nineteenth century."

Charlemagne continued to look around, removing sand until he found an object in the corner and picked it up. The object was a tinted empty glass bottle. He picked it up and came around as he placed a hand on the label. "I can't see…" Charlemagne remarked, bringing it into the light.

"Is it a part of the cache?" Manon questioned. "Perhaps it was stored and someone drank it…"

"No, I don't think so… these letters aren't Turkish, and at any rate, Muslims aren't supposed to have alcohol, I believe. Any time I invite Harun Al-Suli to have a drink with me, he refuses. No…" Charlemagne squinted, "these letters appear Russian, but I wouldn't know when to pinpoint this object and the other one. Do you see anything on the label of that tin can?"

"No… not in this light…" Manon responded. "Is there anything else?"

"Not that I can see, but I'll do a final sweep." He provided the bottle to Manon to store, and then did a final check before he climbed out of the pit. "We'll have to check on the label and brand of that bottle of alcohol, but they may tell us who was last down here. We can also check the ammunition cartridge we found. How's that for evidence?"

Act 6, Scene 4

Charlemagne examined the items in closer detail at the hood of the UAZ. The sun began to set, turning the grey skies into a mesh of orange-red. Manon looked at the items with them when in the horizon they noticed a convoy of jeeps on approach.

"Who's that?" Charlemagne remarked, looking ahead. He picked up his binoculars from his pocket and looked forward. He observed that these jeeps were the same green ones that the Soviets were using but also which he was familiar for Krum's men to use. "Trouble?" He lowered the binoculars and looked over to one of the Soviet mercenaries. "Oy, we've got company…"

The Soviet mercenaries turned to face the approaching vehicle. One of them took their radios out while they got into positions. As the convoy continued to approach, Charlemagne looked forward with anxiety as he saw them crouch behind their other jeep and others get into prone positions. He turned to Manon who looked at him with worry.

"Quite the solid lads these mercenaries," Charlemagne noted. "If it's those hooligans again, they've clearly left Ankara forgetting the blow we dealt them."

"We should hide," Manon suggested.

"Hide? Hide?" Charlemagne questioned, as though insulted. "I do not hide, my dear, I fight. He retrieved an assault rifle from within the UAZ, readied it and then turned to Manon. "You should hide, Manon, but I will choose to fight this one."

"Fight? You've never held a weapon like that in your life, *Charles*," Manon rebuked. "You believe that because you completed basic training in Canada but never saw any combat that you can withstand these hard-trained men? These are ex-Soviet soldiers fighting against Bulgarians, members of the former Warsaw Pact, some of whom had deployment in

Afghanistan, the Gulf War, and Yugoslavia. Put that away, *Charles*, and come out of trouble."

Charlemagne looked back at Manon, as though insulted. "Who do you think I really am, my dear? Go on, you, and leave the fighting to the men…"

Manon rolled her eyes and then decided to go off and take shelter near some stone walls near the base of the fortress. Meanwhile, Charlemagne gathered the artefacts and placed them in his backpack. He then picked up the assault rifle again and took cover behind the jeep.

"Run…" Charlemagne muttered, "as though I were some sort of coward that has never seen the strains or struggles of mortal life…"

The Soviet mercenaries continued to hold their positions while one of them continually attempted to broadcast on a radio. He received no response until the convoys were less than a mile from them. He heard a coarse voice speak in a Slavic language to them, which resulted in the Soviet mercenary saying some brief words and then he stood up.

"What?" Charlemagne questioned, observing them. "What's going on?" he shouted.

The mercenaries ignored him and they grouped together in front of the other jeep, facing the jeeps that were on approach as they turned and parked parallel to them. The cars sent a cloud of dust in the general direction of where Charlemagne stood. He waved his arm and then walked forward, seeing persons enter the jeeps and step forward. Charlemagne looked suspiciously ahead, but then lowered his guard as he identified Rubashkin, Irina, and his bodyguards.

"Ah, it's you," Charlemagne remarked, stepping forward. "You sent us in a bit of a panic there… thought it was more trouble…"

Rubashkin and Irina both looked at Charlemagne as he held the AK-47 in his arms. He noticed their attention and gently placed the rifle on the side of the jeep. He then stepped forward while Manon came out of cover and joined them.

"We've just about finished here," Charlemagne remarked. "We found the cache we were looking for, but did not find much inside other than evidence to suggest that it was looted by some sort of unknown group."

"Oh?" Rubashkin questioned.

"Yes, as I mentioned to you earlier, the evidence seems to suggest that Tulcan had bought the crown. We'll have to visit Ankara again and reach out to some universities in the country to verify information about this governor, but based on the fact that the other two were ruled out, I have a simple hunch that this is our man based on process of elimination. His treasures were said to have been stored in a cache north from the fortress, and we found it, but nothing. I also walked around the inner grounds of the fortress – quite a large lot, but seems as though that fortress was built on solid rock and there is no sublevel. Whatever existed of the structure within is absolutely demolished, as it was said to have been demolished and never rebuilt."

"How very disappointing that the crown was not here," Rubashkin replied. "What is the next step then? You say you are certain that the crown was taken from the cache, but where to?"

"Well, during the Crimean War, the Turks fought against the Russians, so if the Russians looted the caches site, which to be honest, I don't see it being any other way, then it was likely done so sometime after 1850."

"Who could have taken the crown? Where to?"

"I don't precisely know," Charlemagne replied. "The cache was quite well buried, so in my opinion, it could have been anyone with knowledge of the cache, from an Ottoman officer or solider, to a Russian officer or solider. I have a hunch though that it was a Russian, based on the evidence within, which contained items with Cyrillic letters, telling me that whoever was down there was Russian. I just don't know when and it could have honestly been anytime between 1850 to 1918."

"Why's that?"

"Because this land was annexed into Russia after the end of the Tenth Russo Turkish War in 1878, so either it was pillaged at the end of the Crimean War, or after this land was annexed and in Russian hands. Either way, a Russian citizen or subject was down there when they took what was hidden. We also found a bullet and a tin can, both of which we want to study for additional clues into the matter to get a more precise idea."

"What will you do next?"

"I want to speak with the expert on Russian history," Charlemagne stated. "I believe I mentioned him to you, he's a good friend of a friend of mine, Dr. Igor Ivanov. He's currently assisting as it is from within Russia. I believe he's gone to Moscow to access archives. We will attempt to meet with him sometime, once we're out of this bloody desert."

"Dr. Ivanov... is he a professor at the University of Moscow?"

"No, Odessa," Charlemagne corrected. "He has access to all the archives we should need..."

"Very well," Rubashkin responded, looking around. "Good work so far. Let's regroup in Ankara, and we can discuss further with Dr. Ivanov and see about connecting with some local resources."

"Yes..." Charlemagne replied. He looked over to Irina who stood behind Rubashkin with a plain look upon her face. "We'll be right behind you – I suppose we'll be attempting to travel over to Kars for the night."

Rubashkin nodded, spoke to his bodyguards, and then they left in their jeeps. Charlemagne turned to Manon, raised an eyebrow, and then they proceeded to pack up their belongings and put them into the trunk. When they finished, Charlemagne looked towards the sun as it was halfway to set and then got into the jeep. The jeeps pulled out and made their way into the desert. Rubashkin and the other jeep could not be seen ahead of them along the road, but they continued to pass along the desert trail as they ventured along the road between two low slopes of tall grass and desert sands.

Eventually, as the jeeps passed along, Charlemagne took notice of a vehicle travelling behind them. He turned around and saw that it was another GAZ-72, like the ones that he had seen Rubashkin and company driving. The jeep came up behind them and began to follow them through the desert. Charlemagne could not see the driver, but simply made a simple, "Hm…" remark and then sat straight forward. The Soviet mercenaries in the cab in front took notice and simply made light chatter about it to each other.

"Hm, I suppose one of Rubashkin's cars got left behind for some reason," Charlemagne simply remarked, looking back at the jeep once again. He could not see inside, though it did seem like it had a mercenary inside.

The jeeps continued to drive along the road, coming around a wind around when Charlemagne began to notice another jeep proceeding from the opposite direction, combined with an armored vehicle. This vehicle looked like the GAZ-72, but with metal plates around the surface with an open-topped rear and machine gun nest out the top. Charlemagne's face dropped as he saw these two vehicles approach and position themselves side by side on the road ahead. The Soviet mercenaries did not waste time to shout in alarm. The UAZ came to a halt, and the GAZ-72 behind them drove quickly to box them in from reversing out.

The Soviet mercenaries spoke to each other in Russian, picked up their rifles to get out of the vehicle and immediately they and those in the jeep in front sprang into action as they opened their doors and took cover. Charlemagne and Manon both ducked their heads down, and Charlemagne closed his eyes and all he heard was gunfire come forth from either sides, and heavy machine gun fire from the armored car. As Charlemagne kept his eyes closed, he could hear grunts and gasps. He could hear shouts of commands, from both sides. After a brief amount of time, the shouts and gunfire came to an end, and Charlemagne continued to freeze in place before he opened his eyes and turned to Manon in front of him.

"Is it over? Did they get them?" Charlemagne questioned.

Manon did not respond, as though in shock. Charlemagne raised his head up, but did not see anyone around.

Suddenly, the door besides him opened and he turned and came onto his back. Before him was a Bulgarian mercenary bandit, armed with an AK-47 who lurched forward and grabbed Charlemagne by the collar of his shirt.

"No...!" Manon shouted, reaching forward, but the Bulgarian snatched Charlemagne and threw him onto the dirt road.

Charlemagne came onto his back and looked at the bandit who picked him up and dragged him forward so that he was before the armored car as its headlights shined forward. Charlemagne looked around him as he saw the corpses of the killed Soviet mercenaries around him in the positions they assumed cover in.

"Oh no..." Charlemagne remarked. "Oh no, no, no..."

Another Bulgarian bandit came around to the rear of the UAZ, opened it, and began to rummage through Charlemagne's belongings. Charlemagne took notice of the amount of Bulgarian mercenaries that were around. There was little less than a dozen in total, including one at the machine gun nest above the BTR-40 armored vehicle. Manon stayed in place as the bandits rummaged through their backpacks, but after going through all his stuff, he shouted out towards his compatriot who was stood before him with an AK-47 in both hands. Another Bulgarian bandit opened the trunk of the GAZ the Soviet mercenaries were using, but found only military equipment. The Bulgarian bandit reported his findings to his compatriot and then made a gesture with his hand as though asking to terminate Charlemagne.

"What? No... no, no..." Charlemagne remarked. "You can't do this – do you know who I am? What I can do for you? I'm Charlemagne de la Cabernet, if you want money, I can..."

The mercenary hit Charlemagne across the face with the butt of his rifle. Blood immediately came out from his nose as he landed backwards.

"*Charles*!" Manon shouted, exiting the vehicle.

A Bulgarian mercenary took shots into the air, prompting her to cover her head, while another came around to surround her at the car and keep her down. Charlemagne came onto his back and continued to plead with the bandit.

"You don't have to do this – Al-Suli would not want you to do this. I can... I can pay you, if you'd like, double what he's paying you, I..."

The mercenary lowered his rifle to point the barrel towards Charlemagne's face. He cowered as he shielded his head and took a fetal position, and a gunshot fired. Charlemagne felt a splash of blood come across the side of his body, and he opened his eyes and removed his arm from his head to see the Bulgarian mercenary who had pointed his rifle at him became lifeless as he stood before him. The rifle dropped to the ground, a bloodied hole oozed forth from the middle of his chest, below the jugular notch, and the now corpse fell over. The mercenaries readied their arms as they shouted out and took position, and within another split second another gunshot fired and hit the merc at the BTR-40.

Charlemagne covered his head again as the Bulgarian bandits began to fire sporadically at the unknown hostile that came after them. He opened his eyes after a brief moment, realizing that the bandits had forgotten about him. He turned to his side as he saw two bandits ahead, taking cover behind the GAZ jeep as they looked around, unknowing to where the gunfire was coming from ahead. Additional shots came from the desert, hitting the mercenaries with precision as they attempted to hide and take cover. Those in cover opened fire towards the hostile object ahead. The bandit that was near Manon was killed, and she climbed into the jeep and stayed low before the seats. Charlemagne looked around as he kept himself low and began to crawl towards the other side of the UAZ where he then sat up against the wheel.

The hostile object fired at the wheels of the enemy GAZ vehicles, and then the BTR-40, causing them to deflate and become useless to escape from. The gunfire also hit any bandit that came out of cover and who attempted to shift positions, or escape to the wheel of any vehicle. Eventually, even the safety of the cover they hid behind was not enough to protect them as gunshots tore through the metal and hit one nearby who hid behind the side hood of a jeep. The bandits continued to open fire into the open, but Charlemagne could not see what they were aiming at as the hostile object that fired forth could not be seen. Eventually, out of realization of this truth too from the bandits, they reduced their fire and instead sheepishly stayed hidden, attempting to gain sight, but losing their life in the process as the hostile object in the desert opened fire at them and cut them loose.

Charlemagne stayed put and saw that there was one more Bulgarian ahead near the GAZ in front of the UAZ. He kept low and breathed quickly, but as he looked up and over the glass to see through the GAZ and out towards the desert, a gunshot ripped through the side of the car and sent them backwards. The bandit held down the trigger of his rifle as he did so, causing some gunshots to hit the side of the UAZ and ground near Charlemagne. He cringed and covered his head as it did so, but then it stopped and he slowly raised his head. Charlemagne breathed quickly and looked around as he sat back. He spoke no words, and he simply hyperventilated as he looked at the dead bodies, the bullet riddled vehicles, and the sound of the engine from the BTR-40 continue to purr. He stayed put and then after a few minutes, looked underneath the UAZ to see the limp dead foot and legs of the bandit that watched over Manon. Charlemagne began to hear another vehicle approach. He turned and came onto his knees, looking out above the glass to see a pickup truck pull in from the other side of where he stood. His eyes turned to the AK-47 nearby on the ground and he stared at it as he heard the screech of the pickup coming to a halt. Suddenly, Charlemagne stayed put and seized his body in place as he heard rapid gunfire come from near the BTR-40, though not from the machine gun.

Loud gunshots came from the pickup truck towards the BTR-40, plinking off the armor of the car. Charlemagne looked over and could see someone behind the BTR-40. They quickly got into the car and took control of the steering wheel. The car rolled forward, passing by and running over the corpse on the other side of the UAZ, the crushing of the corpse audible as Charlemagne cringed, and the armored car escaped the scene. He then heard the slam of a door from the pickup truck as it shut, and then the footsteps that came forward and behind the UAZ. Charlemagne looked over and the man stepped forward.

Cael looked at Charlemagne and quickly turned and knelt down beside him.

"I suppose you didn't think you'd see me again, did you?" Cael remarked.

Cael was dressed in khaki cargo pants tucked into boots, and a short-sleeved collared shirt with many pockets. He wore a tactical vest around his collared shirt and also a khaki Australian outback hat. Around his shoulder he held a long black rifle on a sling.

Charlemagne was silent as he looked at him. His hands trembled and his shirt was covered in blood. His face was wet with perspiration and he continued to breath quickly.

"Take in some deep breaths," Cael quietly spoke. "It's over now. Nobody is going to hurt you. You're safe with me, Charlesman. Where's your bird? Where's Manon?"

Charlemagne looked over to the car door beside him, prompting Cael to stand up and look inside. He opened the car door and Manon looked up from between the car seats to see Cael standing tall and looking down at her.

"Are you alright there, miss?" Cael asked. "It's just me again. Seems like you've found yourselves in a bit of a pickle here..."

Charlemagne slowly began to stand up and turn around. He looked around the sight of many dead and bloodied bodies. He then jumped as Cael placed a hand on his shoulder.

"Fancied you needed a bit of extra help," Cael remarked. "These goons almost had it out for you two."

"H-how is it that you are here...?" Charlemagne questioned. "Have you been following us...? This entire time...?"

"No, not this entire time," Cael cheerfully answered. "I did lose you as you went into Ukraine on your own, but I've been keeping tabs on these Bulgars and sure enough they caught wind of you as we both came into Turkey."

"W-were you there at the palace...? In Ankara?"

"Not too far, but I've been around," Cael simply stated, looking past Charlemagne and around their surrounding area. "Seems like these men have been very interested in you – after we lost track of each other, they went around looking for you in Ukraine. Sadly, they missed you by a few days it seems. Sad to say as well, but seems like their interest in you is both in what you're looking for and also in what they're to be paid."

"Paid?"

"Yup, seems like they've been hired to come after you this way..." Cael remarked, looking about. He looked to his side as he saw a bandit on the ground, twitching. "Hang on, seems like we've got a live one left..."

Cael placed his rifle against the side of the vehicle. He then took out a handgun from his belt and came around. He kicked the rifle away from the soldier and then placed a boot upon his chest. The Bulgarian spoke to him in a Slavic tongue, and Cael responded in the same language.

Charlemagne looked aside as he expected the inevitable, but then his ear twitched at the sound of the name, 'Rubashkin.' He turned and staggered over to stand beside Cael.

"What did he say? Why did he say that name?" Charlemagne questioned. "Did they get him too?"

Cael's eyes looked over to Charlemagne as he stayed in place, and then he spoke to the soldier again. The mercenary said the name again in the sentence that he spoke.

"What did he say now?"

"He's said that he and his men have been sent to kill you," Cael answered. "He said they were to take whatever you had, and then dispose of you both in the desert here."

"Yes, but what about that name, Rubashkin?"

"He says that Rubashkin is their client. He's the one that hired them to kill you."

The Bulgarian began to shout at them, prompting Cael to shout at him and drop his knee into his chest. The wounded soldier cried out in pain. Charlemagne pivoted and turned. He brought a hand to his forehead.

"No... I thought Al-Suli hired these men – how can it have been Rubashkin? He's our ally in this – we had an agreement. I would find the crown for him and he would get to keep it, although we did already find the crown in Ukraine, but he's not supposed to know it."

Cael shouted at the Bulgarian as he began to beat at Cael's thigh with his fists. The bandit began to weep as he pleaded for his life and replied.

"No," Cael replied, "he says he knows who paid them. He had met Rubashkin just recently, and weeks before as well."

374

"I don't believe it…" Charlemagne simply replied. He then jumped as he heard a gunshot. Charlemagne looked over as Cael stood up. The Bulgarian before him was dead, body lifeless and arms spread apart. "Rubashkin sent these men to kill me, but why…?"

"Perhaps, it is because he has all that he needs," Manon admitted. "He will meet with Ivanov, discuss with him, and from there it will only be a matter of linking Russian documents with what we've learned so far. He has no use for us…"

"Cheer up though, ladies and gents," Cael remarked, patting Charlemagne on the shoulder. "You've both escaped your near assassination this day thanks to me, so rejoice and be glad. What's this you say though about already finding the crown?"

"In Ukraine, in the salt mine – there it was…"

"Allegedly," Manon interjected.

"Ignore her," Charlemagne rebuked. "It is the crown, looks just like it…"

"Except you left it in Rubashkin's car from when you went to Ankara with that woman."

"Irina…" Charlemagne replied, shaking his head. "Does she know?"

"What a thing to be thinking about right now…"

"You left the crown in their car?" Cael questioned. "How'd that happen?"

"We split up, were travelling in different vehicles, and I suppose I did leave part of my luggage in their car…" Charlemagne admitted. "Damn… we've got to get it back."

"We need to get somewhere safe," Manon corrected.

"What does this luggage look like?"

"It's not very large, just large enough for the crown. It's brown, has many name on it… You can't miss it…"

"Say no more then, Charles-man," Cael remarked. "I'll get you your crown back, but here's what you got to do for me. You got to do what your miss lady says and get out of dodge."

"We were meant to meet with Rubashkin in Kars," Charlemagne suggested. "He was not too far ahead of us. You may just see meet up with him."

"Aye, I will," Cael affirmed, "but here's where you're going – this country is not safe and because one got away, they'll be sending more. You need to leave before more do – you've severed ties with Rubashkin, so he can't know where you're going, so go east to Armenia and wait for me there. I'll get you your crown back, don't you worry…"

"Why?"

"Ah, call it just some special service from Her Majesty's government," Cael replied. "You've led me to Krum Berezovsky, one of the most infamous arms dealers, and now you've led me to believe that Rubashkin may not be such a nice man either. I'll be keeping up my investigation on them both."

"Okay…"

Cael walked over and picked up and AK-47, some magazines, and then passed it to Charlemagne.

"Drive east, and don't look back," Cael affirmed to him.

"Yes," Charlemagne agreed, taking the rifle into his hand.

"And one more thing, Charles-man…"

"Yes?"

"Don't trust anyone from here on out."

Act 7, Prologue

"Mr. Cabernet, you stand before this panel, accused of numerous criminal charges and campus code violations, including extensive property damage, trespassing, and mishandling of university equipment and infrastructure. Do you understand the seriousness of the charges and violations brought before you at this time?"

Charlemagne held his arms crossed as he looked towards the panel across from him. He wore a brown suit and crossed yellow-blue tie. He sat in a small room with arched windows at his side, curtains closed. The room had a small chandelier above and between him and the panel. He sat at a table in the center rear of the room, while the panel stood across from him. Behind him were some chairs propped against the wall, only one of them was occupied with Judith Cook who sat dressed in a white blazer suit jacket and skirt. There were three persons across from him in the panel, a male in the center with fair skin and greyish-white hair with glasses, an older female with darker greyish-black hair next to him on his left, and a middle-aged East Asian male beside him. Beside Charlemagne was a podium, and beside the panel opposite from where Charlemagne stood there was a small table with a court reporter and RCMP constable.

"Do I understand the seriousness of the charges and violations? I do understand that criminal code and university campus rule sections, if that's what you've meant to ask…"

"It's a simple question, Mr. Cabernet," the male at the center asked once again. "Do you understand how serious these violations are?"

"Well, I could certainly say that they're important sections," Charlemagne noted aloud. "I also know that I'm here, and I want it on record, because this man," he said, pointing to the male at the center, "has had it out for me ever since I stepped forth onto this campus three years ago. I also want it noted that he's an idiot."

The man at the center simply looked back at him with a serious face. He did not say anything in response.

"At this time, you've chosen to not have an attorney present, despite the option to do so," the female stated. "You are now being provided the option to reconsider."

"I wave that right," Charlemagne replied. "I will happily defend myself."

"Mr. Cabernet," the East Asian male said, "you are before us because on the date of Friday, April 2nd, 1982, as a result of tampering of the campus water system, significant damage was reported to numerous buildings across campus. Closed-circuited surveillance cameras provided through Campus Security allegedly show yourself turning valves and operating machinery on the night preceding the reported damages. The damage resulted in the flooding of the Campbell Building, Prescott Building, Psychological Center, and Chemistry Building. The overbuild up of pressure and resulting water sprouts of high-pressure water through grates and manholes has resulted in the injury of 53 students known at this time, the evacuation of the aforementioned buildings, as well as the Alfred Harlech Manor, the Science Center, and Physics Building and Geo-Sciences Building as a precaution, resulting in cancellation of classes on the final day of school before final exams. The cost of damages had totaled more than ten-million dollars to these affected buildings, and the damages to the water infrastructure at another ten-million dollars. On a separate note, in addition to those injured, approximately one-thousand students and two-hundred faculty members were doused in water from the events that transpired on April 2nd. After a brief investigation between RCMP and Campus Security, you were arrested at your apartment under the following violations of the Criminal Code of Canada: criminal negligence, criminal negligence resulting in bodily harm, trespassing at night, nuisance, and mischief. You were promptly released later that same day, and on April 22nd, 1982, had a court appearance at the provincial court in Attlewood where you plead not guilty. Do you understand?"

"I understand, but frankly I don't agree with some of those points you made. I also maintain my innocence in the matter, as I did at the court hearing, that I am not guilty."

"In addition to the criminal charges," the East Asian male continued to state, "you have also violated the following sections of the student code of conduct: endangering the health and safety of others; stealing, misusing, destroying, defacing or damaging University of Harlech property or property belonging to someone else on campus; disrupting university activities; using university facilities, equipment or services without authorization..."

"You can also add making false accusations against any member of the university," the female noted, "and failing to comply with a disciplinary measure or disciplinary measures imposed under the procedures of the Code."

"How so?" Charlemagne questioned, sitting up straight and bringing a fist down on the table. "These are egregious charges and allegations that are being brought before me! I've been more than cooperative."

"Mr. Cabernet, calm down," the Caucasian male replied in a calm tone. "You will have sufficient time to plead your innocence in the matter."

"Mr. Cabernet, you were requested to attend this hearing a week before," the female remarked. "When Campus Security came to your apartment, you, and I quote, 'Yelled at Security and told them to leave at once...' You also 'threatened to call police because you said that Security was trespassing and harassing you...' Additionally numerous letters were sent to your apartment. As a result of your non-compliance, all your university privileges were put on hold, including access to your academic records and housing privileges... When Campus Security and RCMP arrived at your apartment to evict you, you were arrested for attempted assault on a peace officer..."

"Another charge, arguable – that wasn't assault, he placed his hand on me and I refused to move out of the way..."

"As a part of this disciplinary hearing, we must address and ensure you understand the potential consequences if you are found guilty of any of the Code violations: a written warning or reprimand; probation; payment of costs or compensations for any loss, damage, or injury caused by the conduct; issuance of an apology, made publicly or privately; loss of certain privileges; restrictions or prohibition to access university facilities, services or activities; fines or fees; relocation or exclusion from residence; suspension; and finally, expulsion. Do you understand the potential consequences if you are found guilty?"

"I do," Charlemagne replied, "and I also don't know what kind of kangaroo court this is mean to be. Where's the prosecutor? Where's the jury? It seems like you lot are judge, jury, and executioner in the matter..."

"And so here we are," the Caucasian male remarked with a sigh, folding his hands together before him, "I only have to ask, what did you think you were doing in all this?"

"I don't know what you're talking about," Charlemagne replied. "I know you've said you have camera footage, and I've seen it when I was interrogated by the police, but that isn't me."

"Mr. Cabernet," the woman said, "you have been a student at the University of Harlech for three years, correct?"

"Yes."

"Your faculty if the Faculty of Applied Science. Correct?"

"Yes."

"In the past three years, Mr. Cabernet, you've stood before this panel as well as the Dean of Engineering, for numerous disciplinary processes as a result of many incidents over the past three years."

"Well, I would need more details as to what you are referring too..."

"October 14th, 1979, you and a group of other students were caught to have released laughing gas throughout the chemistry building, and you were given a written warning; December 24th, 1979, you and other students were suspected and determined to have changed the outdoor lamps around the Harlech Manor to blink in Morse code, 'Engineering Strikes Again,' no reprimand; February 15th, 1980, you and a group of students were suspected and believed to have raised a carnival tent around the Alfred Harlech Manor and install speakers that played carnival music, written warning; April 15th, 1980, changed all the numbers in your dorm to deliberately confuse tenants, cost of labor provided to you; October 1st, 1980, you and a group of students released a hundred non-venomous snakes through the Biological Sciences Center, fees and written reprimand; October 31st, 1980, placed pumpkins on the spikes of numerous buildings across campus, no reprimand; January 4th, 1981, you and a group of students replaced the furniture of the Dean of Arts with a hay feeder and water trough, and made allegations that he looked like a goat and it was funny... it was not; March 22nd, 1981, hacked into the scoreboard at Harrier Park during the Harlech Harrier versus North Cascadia Kingsmen final; September 29th, 1981, re-programmed elevators across campus to go up two floors more than what they intended; November 25th, 1981, hijacked all P.A. systems across campus so that you could recite poetry; December 9th, 1981, hired snowplows to make it more difficult for students to get into buildings after it had snowed resulting in exam cancellations; January 4th, 1982, you and another student 'accidentally' set off confetti fireworks within the Applied Science Center; January 28th, 1982, you and a group of students installed a jeep atop of the Richard Harlech building; February 14th, 1982, hacked into the university computer system to have the words, 'I love you, Judith,' show up on all university computers; March 3rd, 1982, installed a hot air balloon in the Manor Library, resulting in evacuation; March 19th, 1982, suspended that same jeep from the Simon Grafton Bridge..."

"I don't see how that last one is relevant to the Code," Charlemagne intervened. "It was off-campus, and that was noted during the investigation... not that it was me, as police were unable to determine who it had been... despite the university's suspicions that it was me. At any rate, the jeep atop of Harlech Building, that was never proven to be me, either. What you've done there is list a few items of which I was found to be guilty in, and then many of which I was not..."

"Normally this would be the time in which the defense would get to speak against the violations before them," the Caucasian male stated. "Mr. Cabernet, do you have anything else to say before we take a look at the evidence?"

"We don't need to see the video – it's not definitive proof and there is no way that blackclad figure was me, nor any way you can prove it to be, so if we're done here, I would like to return to my apartment, which I pay my rent to, and access my report card for this past semester."

"Unfortunately, I cannot let you do that, Mr. Cabernet," the Caucasian male stated. "Your campus privileges were frozen until the conclusion of this hearing as you are currently suspended."

"What more is there to discuss?"

"Perhaps the dozens of violations in the past which, yes, half of which you were not found guilty, but still enough times could call into question why you were not expelled outright to save us the trouble of what is clearly escalating behavior..." the Caucasian male remarked. "In all my years, I have never seen quite the rapsheet."

"Dr. Applecroft, you do not like me, and I do not like you," Charlemagne remarked. "You irritate me, you bore me, and you know nothing about what you do or think you know. I've seen more knowledge from a twelfth grader than I have from you. I should praise the fact that you no longer teach since they've made you Chancellor, but through smart connections, no doubt, you now sit in that place in which your predecessor had to soon easily find out that you cannot touch me. My family's business injects funds into this school through our R&D program, money of which the school cannot afford to lose, and since your arrival to this position, I've been continually harassed by your administration for speaking out against you. However, we seem to be in a tight position as it were. I still have one year left of school before I can graduate, and you seemingly have unfortunately landed yourself a job of which you had no preparation for, so it appears that we will just have to learn to endure one another until we part ways never to see each other again."

"Mr. Cabernet, you may have seemingly escaped previous disciplinary processes," the female stated, "but not this time. This time, you've garnered the attention of the media, the city, even the provincial and federal government. We will be expected to take action this time, so a trial is necessary…"

"Dr. Kleinbaum," Charlemagne argued, "what trial? There is no evidence to suggest that I was the one to tamper with the waterworks."

"We do have one piece…" the East Asian male remarked. "A witness…"

"A witness…? A witness…" Charlemagne rebuked. "Who?"

"An anonymous witness," the East Asian male clarified, "who although did not witness you tamper with the pipes and water system, has testified that they knew about your plan, as well as the past practical jokes you've played in the past school year."

Charlemagne froze for a moment and then cleared his throat, "I don't care what you think you have in an anonymous witness, and I hardly believe it is fair to trial me on the basis of someone who I will not be allowed to know, or without hearing more details…"

"Mr. Cabernet…" Kleinbaum interrupted.

"Dr. Kleinbaum, please, you know me. You've worked with me for the past three years, and you understand that although I have a history, this time it was not me, though I could do it. A prank of this caliber is simple to anyone with the knowledge, though it seems as though they made a miscalculation to cause this much damage…"

"The witness, Mr. Cabernet," the East Asian male plainly stated, "and the information pertaining to this witness…"

"I think that in the face of this surprise," Charlemagne remarked, clearing his throat and adjusting his tie, "that a recess is in order. I must also use the washroom."

"Very well," Applecroft stated, "fifteen minute recess."

Charlemagne stood up and left the room. Judith followed. Charlemagne went down the hall and turned the corner at the end. He then turned around to face Judith who followed him. He then approached her and took her into the male washroom.

"What the hell do they think they're doing, bringing a witness into this case?" Charlemagne questioned. "Someone who knew what I was going to do? Why, only you and Barry knew about the plan, so this…? It's all nonsense, they're attempting to expel me unless…"

Charlemagne looked at Judith suspiciously. She looked back at him with red cheeks and looked to the side.

"Barry… he ratted out on me, no doubt. He was all upset over his breakup with Felicity, and jealous of what we have, I'm sure."

"Charles, no…" Judith denied. "No, Barry did not testify against you."

"Are you sure?" Charlemagne questioned. "Of course you're sure. You're always right, Jude, so they must be bluffing to get me to confess… I mean, even if it was Barry, what weight does that hold other than he being my best friend?"

"Charles… it wasn't Barry who told them about what you were planning," Judith stated, taking his hands, "it was me."

"What?" Charlemagne questioned with doubt.

"I told them… I told them all about it, every step of the plan, and I told them why you did it, because of your disdain for Dr. Applecroft, and swore on all that I said to be the truth," Judith stated. "You won't believe why I had to tell them, but I swear to you, Charles, it was for your own good. I only wish you had listened to my warnings…"

"What do you mean my own good?"

"Charles, I have had the time of my life with you…" Judith stated as tears fell from her eyes. "I never believed a man like you was possible to meet, who was both so intelligent and also whimsical. You are so brilliant and ahead of your time to us, and it is a shame that some do not recognize your brilliance, but within you is a broken heart, like a clock that is not properly adjusted, and it accelerates your being so much in such a disordered way. When you set your mind on a matter, you do not turn your focus from anything else. When you want something, you grab it at any cost, including those around you. When you see danger, you do not recognize it, including its danger towards others. I did not know what to make of this compulsive behavior, so I asked my friends, and some of them suggested varying ideas. Some believed you to be a narcissist, others manipulative and self-interested, and then finally some even suggested you to be a psychopath of some kind, totally impulsive, selfish and callous, but I knew that was not true. I know there is something within you that has made you this way, and that this is not you but a response to damage within you, a defense mechanism to stop you from confronting the pain within yourself because anytime that you are successful, you become fearful of your own existence that you must outdo yourself in some degree and make a name for your being. If I did not tell them now, it would have just invited the next attempt that could possibly put lives at risk. I must do what I can, as a person who loves you, even if you do not understand, to clip your wings… so that you can smell the roses and take a breath in…"

Charlemagne looked back at her with a stunned appearance. His face was pale.

"I'm sorry, Charles, but I thought I could keep up with you, but I see the danger you are placing yourself in – no, I see the danger I see us both going along, because I wouldn't want to leave your side, but I don't want this to have been the end of us, even though it will be. Perhaps someday, when you have learned to heal that brokenness within, and we are both older, we can have a life together be possible, but that is not this time…"

Judith began to retract her hands from Charlemagne's hands. Charlemagne's hands simply fell down as he passively allowed her to go.

"I don't believe any of this…" Charlemagne simply denied. "Mr. Applecroft, he's had it out for me since I got here. He hates me…"

"Mr. Applecroft has done nothing of the sort," Judith replied. "If anything, he's the only one on campus who seems to care about you, while all the others, including Ms. Kleinbaum, loathe you. When I confronted him with what I had to say, he agreed to not share this information with the RCMP to avoid criminal charges you may face. He hoped that you would comply and agree, and that it could all be wrapped up with a public apology and a fee paid out in agreement, but I knew it would not be so easy. Kleinbaum insisted you face criminal charges, but Applecroft refused – he fixed them to comply with me. He really did. I knew that despite that… telling you would be the only way I could see you survive this without being expelled, because the other option was if they were to expel you so that you could not be so elated anymore."

"Humph," Charlemagne reacted, "as if…"

"It's done, Charles," Judith remarked, taking a step back. "I'm… I'm sorry, I really am, but I had no choice… please forgive me…" She ran off from the bathroom.

Charlemagne simply stood in silence as he looked down at the ground. He looked at his hands and then turned to face himself in the mirror. He soon left and returned to the panel room. He sat down with a pale face, straight composure, and folded his hands before him.

"Well, Mr. Cabernet," Applecroft remarked, "I hope you've had a productive time to reorganize. If you are ready, we can continue…"

Charlemagne looked up and faced Dr. Applecroft. He looked at Dr. Kleinbaum and then back over to Applecroft.

"I… I do not see a need for us to continue," Charlemagne remarked. "If it'll please the panel, I should like to remove myself from this institute at once as a student. I shan't return, nor do I wish to ever return to a place where I am not respected nor beloved. Do not take my words here as an admission of wrongdoing, it is not, but I will ensure that all the damages suffered in the past month will be paid out to the university in due time, and I also apologize, on behalf of the Cabernet family name, of the trouble I have been to this campus in the past three years in all that I have done. Again, not in admission to fault to what has transpired in the past month." He then stood up and said, "Thank you."

Act 7, Scene 1

Charlemagne looked at his reflection from the water within a steel barrel in a grungy and small alleyway. From another barrel, a warm fire kept him company in the midst of the snow and rubbish that surrounded him from around. From behind, the UAZ was parked with a thin layer of snow atop of it, shielding and hiding it from view. Charlemagne wore the same khaki cargo trousers from the desert, though removed his collared shirt and wore a white sleeveless shirt as he held a knife to his cheeks and brought a thin wet bar of soap to smoothen the touch of the blade as he shaved. The alleyway Charlemagne stood in was small and short, resembling a small court between two-story apartment blocks connected to a four-story building behind. The buildings were built of dark greyish-brown brick. The windows of the building were rectangular, black-framed, and the rooftops of the buildings were sloped and reddish-orange. Within the alleyway was a parked vehicle further ahead, some dumpsters, some sort of yellow construction device, and in the midst of the area was a beheaded statue of some former public figure. The statue was large, at least double in length of the UAZ. Of course, then there was the snow that piled on and was at least a foot in depth. As Charlemagne breathed, his breaths were visible to the cold air and he likewise was pale, skin cold and cheeks flushed. Charlemagne looked at himself with a serious glance as he continued to shave, like the last time, leaving just the moustache that had grown fond of.

"What are you doing here alone? In the cold like that?" Manon questioned, stepping forward into the alleyway.

Charlemagne turned and looked at her. She wore a fur coat and cap, a scarf around her neck and long trousers with boots. Her hands were in her pockets and around her chest was the straps of her handbag. He briefly looked over to her and then continued to focus in on his reflection.

"The pipes were frozen indoors, and I wanted to shave."

"You will catch a cold standing where you are now."

"A cold cannot be caught by simply standing in cold weather," Charlemagne quietly replied, bringing the blade down. "A cold is caught from a pathogen, a virus, that has made its home in the respiratory tract of a person where it multiplies and divides in a feeble attempt to conquer, unrealizing of its puny size compared to man."

"Ah, and you think that standing in the cold does well for your immune system?"

"Look, what do you want?" Charlemagne questioned.

"While you were down here, I received a phone call from my father," Manon expressed. "He tells me that Dr. Ivanov and Konstantin left Odessa, but Rubashkin had spoken to them over the phone."

Charlemagne paused for a moment and then asked, "Go on..."

"Upset, of course, my father has begun to worry... but I did my best to assure him that we were safe and that I was going to return as soon as I could. He tells me that Dr. Ivanov has left Odessa with Konstantin on an airplane to come here and meet us. He says that this was some hours ago, so they could be arriving soon. Ivanov said to meet him at three o'clock at the city square."

"That's a relief that they could get out of Odessa, no doubt Rubashkin was on his way to meet with them," Charlemagne remarked. "Who knows what would have happened then. Did you tell your father Rubashkin tried to assassinate us?"

"No, those words I cannot utter to him," Manon replied. "He knows though that Rubashkin is dangerous and not to trust him."

"Good," Charlemagne affirmed, "so Ivanov will come here, and we meet him at the city square..."

"Republic Square," Manon clarified. "I checked and it is not too far from where we are."

"Good," Charlemagne simply repeated, splashing some water onto his face. He then took a towel behind him and began to dry himself.

"What will you do after Ivanov and Konstantin are with us?" Manon questioned. "Where will we go then?"

"What do you mean?" Charlemagne questioned.

"Rubashkin sent men to kill us," Manon reminded him. "Do you mean for us to travel to Russia? His own homeland so that he can send more men to kill us in that rogue state?"

"Rogue state… my dear, we are presently in a rogue state… a country in which our bloody hotel cannot even provide running water for a shower, or electric heating, or a proper decent meal," Charlemagne remarked. "I've been to many poor countries, but this one is loathsome – I at least expected a little more than this…"

"Ah, but Rubashkin does not own Armenia, the same way he owns the many infrastructures and industries in Russia," Manon pointed out. "If we travel to Russia, we may not come out alive. *Charles*, I know you are not stupid enough to believe it to be safe…"

Charlemagne paused as he held his hands around the rim of the barrel. He looked down at himself and then over to Manon.

"Perhaps there is a risk involved, but Rubashkin has made an attempt once, and we survived. It's been a few days now, and I anticipate Cael to arrive at any moment now with the crown… the real crown… as he promised."

"*Charles*, it has been three days and it took us three hours to drive here," Manon remarked. "Cael is not coming back."

"He's busy, dealing with those fiends," Charlemagne assured her, "which is another point in our favor – he'll probably have taken care of them all for us, like Le Havre's men, to have to worry anymore."

"*Charles*… enough, it is too dangerous to continue," Manon remarked. "The crown is lost, and sooner or later Rubashkin will realize the mistake we made to leave it behind. At any rate, he does not know what we know, nor have the information we have, so give it a rest, huh?"

"I will not rest now," Charlemagne boldly and loudly stated, "not while the crown is missing, and not when we are so far in and close to the end…" He threw the knife into the barrel and turned to Manon. "You may be intimidated by Rubashkin and his thugs, but I am not. I'll travel right through the entirety of Russia if it's necessary to decipher where this crown came from and satisfy the scholars, and I'll do it alone if I have to because by God, Manon, I am growing tired by your whining and complaining."

Manon flinched at his tone and was taken back, but then she frowned and took a step forward towards Charlemagne. He took a step back and pulled his collared shirt from over the hood of the jeep and into his hands.

"You are tired? You are tired?" Manon questioned, angry. "Oh, *je suis desolé, Charles*, for all the hard work that you've placed upon yourself to get to where we are," she said in a condescending tone. "Do you not believe that I have grown tired of you and this… this…"

"What?"

"Insanity," Manon remarked.

"I've said it once, and I'll say it this last time," Charlemagne strictly said, raising a finger to her, "I don't need your company. I don't need your help. I don't need to do this with you because I can very well do it alone."

"Ah, and if I were not here then there would be no *Charles* the Great anymore, would there," Manon spat out, "because he would surely have gotten himself killed near the monastery, or perhaps fallen to his death in that mine. No, I suppose he would have maybe gotten himself shot and killed in the desert if that Irish man had not rescued us."

"I would have managed just fine in all those situations."

"*Mon Dieu*, you are deluded," Manon complained. "You are crazy – how can a man as intelligent as you be so far from reality?"

"Oh, tell it to someone who cares," Charlemagne simply remarked. "If you're done, then go on and get out of here. If you're scared of travelling into Russia, then very well, leave…"

"Ah, I would very much like to, but you know I cannot leave you to die."

"What rubbish," Charlemagne responded, doubtful, "you're nothing more than a junkie for adventure to not want to leave, but allow me to be the man to cut you off. You're at your last warning, Manon, because if I hear one more complaint from you, then I don't want to see you anymore. I'll go to Russia on my own, with Ivanov and Konstantin, and you can frolic back to your desk in France where you belong."

"Hmph," Manon reacted, offended, "perhaps I will leave on my own at that point, because I am at my end, *Charles*. At some point, I have to accept that perhaps I cannot do this anymore… to accept my limits with you and let you come to whatever dark fate awaits you. To believe that you are just so far gone that… that it is futile to go on. To withdraw my hand and leave you to your insanity… out of care to respect your wishes."

With those final words, Manon left to return inside. Charlemagne put on his shirt, buttoned it up and then tucked it into his cargo pants. He then washed his hair, dried himself off with the towel, put on a coat, and then came around to come inside.

The skies were light grey as a few snowflakes fell down from above, and the pair exited out from the hotel and proceeded to walk out into the city. Manon wore the same outfit as the one that she wore to go outside and talk to Charlemagne, while Charlemagne wore a canvas jacket. The pair proceeded to walk down a narrow street adjacent to a major one with high level traffic. They observed some military vehicles parked ahead in the direction they were walking, prompting them to decide to cross the street. They crossed at a crosswalk and then stopped for a moment as Charlemagne looked suspiciously at the parked GAZ vehicles.

"As much as I'd like to stay in public sight in case we were ambushed," Charlemagne expressed, "I don't want to run into potential trouble. Let's cross through this district here and cut through to the square."

Charlemagne led Manon down a narrow lane and away from the major traffic. They began to go down the lane as they passed many poor and rundown single-story homes attached to one another. The neighborhood they entered appeared impoverished, houses made of concrete with steel panel rooftops, or otherwise of deteriorating brick and tiled roofs. There was no traffic through this lane, though the direction of the lane was inconsistent as it curved in one direction and another.

"*Charles,* is this place safe?" Manon questioned, looking about.

"Safer than out there, I do believe," Charlemagne affirmed. "This area is known as the *Kond,* a historic district, despite looking like a Brazilian favela, is much safer than one."

Charlemagne and Manon continued to walk through the district as they passed a two-story structure with no windows, made of mortar and bricks. Another structure had a partially collapsed side as though an explosion had ripped half of it apart. A few other buildings had cobblestone foundations and were partially constructed of stone and cement. Telephone poles and wires were spread out in sporadic directions, and the lane narrowed more and more as they travelled along the winding path. In the foreground they could see a red-bricked church with cone rooftops at the main tower at the transept, and below tower at the narthex entrance. Eventually the pair continued forward and came out to a wide street at a three-way intersection. Around them were tall simple apartment blocks constructed in an orange sandstone. They made their way around the crosswalks and proceeded downhill through to the city center where it was quiet. These same simple, rectangular orange-beige structures flanked them on either side, so unison in appearance, a general sameness in their being. There were a few cars parked on the left and right of the street, but little traffic on the street itself and it was also quiet. Charlemagne and Manon continued to walk through the double-lane street for three narrow blocks before they arrived at Republic Square.

Republic Square was a large plaza that consisted of a small oblong-sized space in the center surrounded by wide street lanes travelling around it and outwards to the connecting roads. Surrounding the plaza were tall and large structures that deviated from the architecture of previous buildings in the city. These buildings were built in accordance to the angle of the perimeters they occupied, so one building was curved while another was straight. The facades of these structures consisted of similar colors, from beige to terracotta orange to terracotta red. The main structure at the top of the square had a very wide fountain that covered the main entrance. Stairs at the side came up to the front which consisted of arched nooks and rectangular columns along a sheltered arcade. This front entrance was tall and behind it was a wide four-story tower in three layers, the bottom layer of which consisted of arched windows, the second of which had two-stories of rectangular windows, and then the top level in an octagon shape had arched windows, each smaller than the other piled up like a cake. The other surroundings structures each exited on a corner of the square and had a similar shape, though different shade. These were curved structures with arched nooks and columns, though no arcade between them and just windows within. These arches were tall and consisted of two tall stories each. Above them were columns and an arcade within forming a sheltered balcony from within that could look down. At the rear of these structures there was a tower, and then a second partition that stretched outwards away from the rest of the building and down the street in a similar architectural style for half a block. In between the two buildings opposite the center structure was a park in between the two avenues.

"Where did Ivanov say he would meet us?" Charlemagne asked.

"Over here along the park," Manon answered, "near the embassies."

"Ah, of course."

Charlemagne and Manon began to walk around to the park, and then cross the street to come to the park entrance. They then proceeded to walk down along a path until they were across from the Embassy of Canada.

"I remember coming here two days ago," Charlemagne said. "Bloody wankers in the government building were of no help to us – because of them I had to sell my watch and we're in that mangy hotel because I can't receive funds from abroad. We're like two tramps out here because of 'em."

Manon rolled her eyes. There were few people walking along the promenade, so the two began to walk around the area as they waited for Ivanov. Eventually, at around three o'clock in the afternoon, the pair spotted a taxicab with one person in a tall wool coat step out with a small briefcase in one hand and a small package in the other. Charlemagne and Manon approached them, and they could see Konstantin in the front seat wave goodbye before the cab drove off.

"Dr. Ivanov," Charlemagne greeted, "thank you for meeting us here... not the most idea meeting locations, but still safer than Odessa."

"Thank you, for warning me about Rubashkin," Ivanov immediately remarked. "Here, Konstantin wanted me to give this to you."

"What's this?" Charlemagne questioned, looking into the package. "Oh... plastic explosives..."

"What?!" Ivanov exclaimed.

"Look, don't worry about it, Dr. Ivanov. Why don't we sit down and have a chat?"

"Here?"

Charlemagne looked around. He spotted some soldiers afar near a parked supply truck. He looked at them suspiciously and then turned to Ivanov.

"You're right," Charlemagne affirmed. "You must be sore from your flight over. Let's go for a walk – where's Konstantin off too?"

"To the hotel," Ivanov answered. "Up town."

"Very well, then let's walk his way. "Let's stay in public spaces, keep to ourselves, and just go for a walk through the city while we talk."

Charlemagne began to walk north with Ivanov at his side. He clutched his briefcase with a look of terror on his face.

"You know, I did not know what I have agreed to in providing you with assistance," Dr. Ivanov remarked. "Why would Rubashkin want to hurt me?"

"Because he's an evil, greedy man," Charlemagne remarked, "but don't you worry. We'll keep you safe…"

Manon looked at him with doubt.

"I'm not sure how much of our exploration through Turkey was communicated to you, but we did manage to somewhat track the crown through Anatolia to come to a fortress near Kars. From that point, it is possible that the crown was kept in a treasure hold near the fortress, based on the evidence within, Russian imperial soldiers looted the hold and who knows where those items have gone."

"Yes," Ivanov confirmed, "I was told of your findings, and that is good because of what I've discovered in my own research. The fortress that you visited was a point of conflict during the Crimean War when Russia sieged and destroyed it, and that battle was led by an officer named Yaroslav Tereschenko, a nobleman and a gentleman, from what I've learned about him, but also a potential enjoyer of rare items. Look at this letter I found in our archives..." He opened his briefcase and provided a photocopy of the letter to Charlemagne. He looked at the letters, but could not make it out as the notes on the side were in Cyrllic. "It is a complaint from the Ottoman Empire to the Russian Empire, from the embassy in Saint Petersburg to the Imperial government. The son of Tolcan Göran demanded the return of precious items to the family, which were taken during the siege and destruction of the fortress and their home."

"Ah, and does it list what those precious items were?"

"Yes, and among the items, is a foreign crown..."

Charlemagne raised an eyebrow and looked to Manon. Manon looked at him with doubt.

"It appears that Göran had somehow acquired a foreign crown of some sort, which could be the crown in question sold in Odessa to him. I communicated with colleagues at the University of Saint Petersburg and Moscow to gather more information, and this Tereshchenko was a public figure. He lived in this region, the Caucasus, near the Black Sea, and he commanded and led a small army garrisoned in Armenia and Azerbaijan. He also wrote much about the crown he had taken from the Ottomans, not believing it to be Ottoman but stolen from Europe during the conquests. He sent the crown to universities, had it studied, and among these scholars... it was generally believed to have come from Western Europe, and among one in particular at this time, to be the stolen French crown jewels."

The pair came to the Republic Square where they proceeded to go around and then down a street northwest.

"Hm," Charlemagne thought aloud, "so it seems like before the Germans caught word of the crown's existence in the 1930s, the Russians were knowledgeable of it around the 1860s?"

"Yes," Ivanov remarked, "and that is not all – Tereshchenko maintained the crown as his own."

"Right, and where did you say this Tereshchenko lived? Nearby?"

"Alexandropol, here in Armenia, today known as Gyumri."

"Gyumri… I believe we passed that town on our way in," Charlemagne remarked. "So we should search there?"

"It is where I believe Rubashkin would be going," Ivanov remarked, "for before I knew otherwise, I told him where Tereschenko lived and worked to suggest you search there. I did not know he and you had severed ties."

"Severed ties, in a most diplomatic way," Charlemagne grumbled, "but why otherwise? Did you find something?"

"Not me, but my colleagues at Moscow who discovered the Will and Testament of Tereschenko. Tereshchenko was a secluded man, a bachelor, without any known children, and he left all his estate to a junior officer who worked alongside him in this country named Vagharshak Karakashian, who he viewed like a son. He was several years younger than him, and everything that the nobleman owned and which he could pass on, he left him, including the crown no doubt."

"Interesting… and what do we know about this man? Karakashian?"

"He was a peasant boy… Tereshchenko writes much about him, with fondness and great detail for years. He was from a peasant family in the Armenian countryside, and he had met Tereshchenko when was just a fifteen-year-old boy. He played music for the forty-some year-old senior officer, and Tereshchenko writes much about the boy, who at the age of 21 was drafted into the army and put under his service, to Tereshchenko's joy who had him put through officer school and ensured he worked alongside him. This was all some years after the Crimean War, in the 1860s. After a few years, the notes about Karakashian become less and less, there is mention that he marries, had children, and his family of whom live at the opposite side of the country from Gyumri in a small village in the mountains close to the border with Azerbaijan."

"Do we believe he moved out to Tereshchenko's estate in Gyumri or stayed in his home village?" Charlemagne questioned as they approached and walked around another plaza, this one surrounding a colosseum-like structure made of grey stone bricks. At either side of the structure were two statues of two figures, each sitting upon seats. Behind the structure was a roundabout leading to another park. There was also a third statue behind the building with a third seated figure. "It very well may be that Rubashkin will be in the right place, but looking for the wrong person."

"No," Ivanov denied, "I do not know why, but it does not seem like Karakashian left his family home. In census records kept in Moscow, he is named in that same village of his. He may have sold the property, the items, but it could be worth a search of his home village to learn more about him. I have only the details of what Tereshchenko said of him to offer to you, which I skimmed through my reading of his personal diaries. Tereshchenko had a particular attachment for the boy that I cannot describe in full detail. He viewed him truly as his own son. When he was young, he spoke much about his appearance. He spoke of his physical beauty... and other males, to an uncomfortable degree that makes me believe that Tereshchenko could have been a... how do you say in English, *pederast*."

"Pederast? Oh my..." Charlemagne questioned. "Hm... how awful but could explain why his chatter about him dimmed down when he grew older. Perhaps Karakashian realized or was resentful of him to avoid him. Do you believe there was ever conflict or abuse?"

"There is no information to believe he ever did anything to harm Karakashian," Ivanov remarked, "no less in the amount of concern that he has for him. By the time Karakashian was in the army, he spoke less of his beauty and more about his fate, believing since his adolescence that he was predestined for greatness and nobility. In later years, he even petitioned the Tsar to title him as nobility over Armenia. Up to Karakashian's marriage at the age of 25, he spoke much about how he hoped that Karakashian could become the king of the Armenians. He did not believe him to be truly Armenian, but because of the faintness in his skin tone, to be of partial European admixture, hypothesizing that he could be a descendant of the House of Luscinia. He even expressed hope that one day, the boy would take the crown, secede from Russia, and unite both East Armenia and West Armenia. The boy completely undermined what was once a stark Russian nationalism and imperialism within to support the freedom of the Armenian people."

"East Armenia and West Armenia?" Charlemagne questioned as they came to the end of the park. The three of them crossed the street and came around to a promenade with a strip of grass in the middle. "I don't follow..."

"But *Charles*," Manon interfered, "how can you not? At this time, 1860 to 1870, Russia is on the front steps of the Ottoman Empire who control half of Armenia, the other half of which they annexed from Persia and we are now in. After the 10th Russo-Turkish War, a portion of West Armenia, including Kars, is annexed. You know that."

"Ah, right..." Charlemagne replied, "sorry, I forgot that this region we were in is called East / West respectively. My mind is in a jumble, at any rate, that war occurred only in 1878-79. If Karakashian was an officer, he may have participated."

Charlemagne and the others arrived at the base of a set of stairs, similar to the ones in Odessa though more than double in length and triple in width. In four spaces throughout the course of the stairway there were four statues, fountains, or patches of flowers in between each squared nook. The staircase was constructed of sandstone bricks.

"What does Tereshchenko say of the boy after he weds and becomes a father?"

"Very little," Ivanov answered. "He speaks of the wedding, which he did not attend due to obligations of his command. He speaks seldom about boy if at all, but does begin to complain about his health and wellbeing. He becomes depressed, but never bitter. What else can I say about the man? He was a man of faith too. He spoke well of Armenia and their personal faith in spite of conquest for hundreds of years under the Persians. He admired Amenia's commitment to the faith through being the first to take Christianity as a state religion. He shared his faith with Karakashian too. By the age of sixty, Tereshchenko grew seriously ill and died. His journals were found in the University of Moscow luckily, as with most of all this other information."

"That's an interesting detail, for those journals to eventually arrive since they would have been inherited through his estate to Karakashian. Who knows, perhaps after all this… the Russian government really had the French Crown, and the Germans took it from them."

"Plausible, but we must keep searching," Manon insisted as they nearly climbed to the top of the stairs. "Is this village far from where we are?"

"Nothing is far from where we are," Charlemagne rebuked. "This country is little less the size of *Vals de Loire*. I'll review its location on the map, but I do believe we should travel there and see for ourselves what legacy this boy left on his home village, if any. I imagine if he seriously liquidated the assets of this man, then he became immensely wealthy, so who knows what sort of impression an inherited wealth of that sort could do to a peasant village if he were to live there, provided he did not squander it all."

"So cynical," Manon remarked, "but so be it, let us travel."

"For your own safety, doctor, I believe it should be good if you stay here and continue your research. Manon and I will make our way to the village and see what we can find, and you and Konstantin stay here. Do not talk to anyone, and do not trust anyone who may come to with aid. Trust only us, and Dr. Dumas, who is in contact with you."

"Yes, of course."

"A bit of caution," Ivanov remarked, stepping closer to Charlemagne, "Rubashkin cannot be too far from you now. He will know I have abandoned my home in Odessa, and when he does, he will surely contact my colleagues in Moscow to learn where you intend to go. You must go quickly to search."

"We will," Charlemagne remarked, "but should we not learn much, we will need to re-examine our position, learn where this crown came from to have been seized and arrived to Ukraine. The Soviets must have found it somewhere."

"If I were to surmise, it was seized during the revolution. Karakashian was fifteen years old in 1865. He would have lived at least to the end of the century, perhaps to the First World War and Revolution. His wealth very well may have been seized by then. You may be near the end of the race."

"So I should hope," Charlemagne said as they arrived at the top of the stairs. From the top of the stairs, the three of them stopped to admire the cityscape of Yerevan, with a looming mountain behind.

Act 7, Scene 2

Charlemagne and Manon drove out from Yerevan into the Armenian countryside late at night. After preparations, and a brief nap for the late-night drive, the pair got into the UAZ and snuck out as all was quiet and calm in the capital city. They drove north where they arrived at a small lakefront town named Sevan, and from Sevan proceeded around the lake to the northeast side before driving inland. They drove through some hills and pastureland, arriving up to a forest at the base of a mountain. They then proceeded through a valley, going from village to village as they slowly went east, driving through a snowy forest between the mountains.

"This village is at the very end of this road," Charlemagne expressed. "I don't like that we'll box ourselves in should trouble follow as Ivanov believes it will."

"I am not sure what we are looking for in this village," Manon expressed. "Neither of us speak Armenian; we won't be able to communicate with the locals."

"We know the lad's name," Charlemagne expressed. "I also wrote it down to show to some people. Besides bumbling around the town like a pair of village idiots, we should be able to make some progress. Worst case, we search the nearest graveyard."

"*Charles*, I do not know about this…" Manon expressed. "Like this road, I feel that we are reaching out end too."

"Nonsense," Charlemagne expressed, "the crown we got has to have made its way through here – if we can't find a lead, then we pull back and do some more research on the lad. We've tracked the crown up to the late nineteenth century now, just at the cusp of tying knots with the early to mid-twentieth century. He should be well pleased with us that we've come this far to offer some sort of explanation for that crown. When we've finished here, we'll get ahold of the British embassy and see what can be done to help Cael if he's in trouble and retrieve that crown."

Manon did not reply as she looked out the window. By the time they could catch sight of the village, the sun was starting to rise up at the start of a new day. The car drove out from the mountain pass and looked down towards the village atop of a hill in the midst of pastures around. The village sat in the midst of a valley with low forested mountains around it on the north, west, and south end. Cliffs to the east showed the extent of the hills and pastures going towards the Azerbaijan border. A very thin snake-like river curved around the hill from the north to south. Amidst the village were at least a few dozen buildings, rectangular huts consisting of tan-colored bricks spread out from each other. At the very rear of the village was a similar-colored church with a round bell tower and cone roof, and rest of the church rectangular, made of brick and with sloped roofs. Behind the village was a forest at the base of the mountain behind. Manon did not say anything as she looked out towards the village.

"Well, isn't that a site – looks like a town left behind in time," Charlemagne remarked. "I suppose not too different from the other ones we've passed, though this one does make me wonder if anyone even still lives here."

Charlemagne drove downhill and then came along the river as he drove along the dirt road to reach the main gates of the village where there was an archway and perimeter fence. He drove through and then came inside, seeing the roads sprawl outwards from the main road. He continued to drive along the coarse road until eventually reaching the city center in front of the church where the road came to an end around the fountain. As they arrived, the bell towers rung and Charlemagne drove around the fountain as though it were a roundabout where he parked the car at the end and put it into park. He observed that the church was beside a cemetery.

"Here we are," Charlemagne remarked, opening the door. "Let's get at it, shall we? Perhaps we could be back in Yerevan before it is dark again."

Manon shook her head, but did not say anything as she opened the door and stepped out.

"Now this is a village," Charlemagne remarked. "All that I could expect – no grocery store, no fast-food joint, and no petrol station… just homes and local small businesses."

Manon looked around as they walked towards the fountain in the center. Water did not run from the sprout in the center, and the water inside was thin and frozen. The fountain was in the center of a cobblestone plaza. The village was quiet and empty as they arrived and came to the fountain.

"Let's make haste and go to the cemetery," Charlemagne remarked. "Let's confirm this bloke was even buried here before we carry on."

Charlemagne walked across the road and went towards the church. The cemetery was on the right-hand side while a small open field with a lone tree at the far end was on the left side. They walked through the stone walls that surrounded the cemetery and saw that it was a large round plot with numerous gravestones. Charlemagne shared with Manon the written name of Vagharshak Karakashian in both Armenian script and Cyrillic, and then the pair set off and began to search tombstones. They searched one after another, going from rock to rock, memorial to memorial, and finally stopping as they came together at the main entrance. Charlemagne walked up to Manon with a hand at his chin.

"You know, I don't see anything even close around here," Charlemagne expressed, looking around again. "Are we even in the right village?"

"What do you mean?" Manon questioned. "Of course we are, no? We checked the map with Dr. Ivanov and were sure this was the same village."

"Hm… Charlemagne expressed, looking about. His eyes caught sight of a local near the fountain. The local wore a tall black wool coat and hat. He looked over to Manon and then stormed forward. The local stopped across from their vehicle. Charlemagne crossed the street and then shouted, "Excuse me, sir!"

The man turned and looked towards Charlemagne. Charlemagne observed that this man was an Orthodox cleric. He had curvy long greyish-white hair that came down from the sides of his wool cap, and he wore round black glasses that were almost like goggles. He had fairish-tanned skin and also a long beard.

"You probably don't speak English, but we're looking for a man that used to live here," Charlemagne remarked, opening his notebook. "You see this? Vagharshak Karakashian."

"*Vagharshak Karakashian…*" the cleric repeated, turning to face the church. He then spread out his hands as he pointed towards the church.

"No, not the church," Charlemagne responded. "A man, an army officer – Vagharshak Karakashian. A man, like me…" he said, pointing his fingers towards himself. "Bloody hell, this man doesn't know a thing I'm saying…"

"Do not be so presumptuous," the cleric spoke to Charlemagne. "You'd be surprised how many know how to speak English even in this small, but humble country."

Charlemagne flinched in surprise and then cleared his throat, as though embarrassed. "Sorry," he said, "at any rate, the person I'm looking for is a man, not a church. He lived and should have died almost a hundred years ago."

"And I say again, with all my heart," the cleric remarked, pointing towards the church, "here is what you seek, the Church of *Saint Vagharshak Karakashian.*"

"Saint?" Charlemagne questioned with slight discomfort. "Hm, so not so much of a humble peasant boy then, is he. What did he do to deserve to be canonized?"

"He died a valiant hero, defender of the faith against Islamic hordes who terrorized and murdered his brothers and sisters," the cleric remarked. "What else do you expect?"

"Well, I suppose it's true what they say, the Orthodox Church really canonizes whomever they feel," Charlemagne remarked, looking towards the church. "So, this is his parish then, in his honor, and I suppose he's buried inside?"

"No," the cleric replied, "not inside the church…"

"Well, we couldn't find him in the cemetery just now," Charlemagne expressed. "So where? And don't tell me in Turkey or anywhere else…"

"Not too far from here," the cleric answered.

"Well, that's a good start," Charlemagne remarked. "So where?"

"You are not a pilgrim to his resting place, are you?"

"If I said we were, would you tell me where he was buried?"

"Of what use it is to you?"

"Perhaps I should explain myself," Charlemagne responded. "My name is Charlemagne de la Cabernet, and my friend here is…"

"What do you hope to change by telling me who you are?"

"I am simply introducing me and my comrade here," Charlemagne answered. "We come a great many miles from the West as historians, and we've come across Saint Vagharshak with intrigue. If you don't want to tell us where he was buried right now, then by all means, but please grant us the indulgence to know a little bit more about him. I understand that he is from the village, was a military officer in the Russian Army, had a wife and children who lived with him in this village… Tell us more about this saintly figure."

"You are correct, Saint Vagharshak was born and raised in this village, and he was an officer in the Russian Army."

"So, what else? Why is he celebrated as a saint? I seem to recall that saints lived magnanimous lives, were of immense virtue, and some were martyred for their faith while others lived whole lives to the faith."

"I already told you," the cleric stated, "he died in defense of the Christian faith in battle against Muslims who threatened his people."

"Then tell us a little bit more about that story," Charlemagne requested, growing annoyed.

"Certainly," the cleric replied, coming around to sit down. "Sit…"

Charlemagne sat near the cleric as he looked towards the church. Manon sat down next to Charlemagne.

"It happened while Russia was at with the Ottoman Empire," the cleric explained.

"What year?"

"The end of the 1870s," the cleric replied. "Now do not interrupt. Save your questions to the end. You expect me to tell you that Vagharshak was a holy, pious man of no error or fault through his life, but that is not what makes a saint, nor is it the man you should expect him to be. We are all sinners in our lives, with an evil that comes from our hearts, seeping outward from us to enter into the world. Vagharshak was no different than you or me, though some say he had a kind heart from his youth, raised here a Christian boy, but in every other sense was an ordinary man who found great opportunity when he was called up to military service and found himself unlike other boys his age in officer training school. The lavish life that he had found himself in made him haughty as it gave him status as someone within the empire, and that status and position paid him handsomely to earn more wealth than he could hope to know or do with.

408

"After some years in this lifestyle, of excitement and adventure afar, it eventually came to a halt as he lost himself. The legend says that he became fearful of losing himself to a hardness of heart, the sin of blasphemy against the Holy Spirit, as he saw the hand of God ever so often, but shunned it so many times until one day it was not there for him and he found himself more alone than ever before, and he felt the fear that plagued him, of his own existence, that he wept for his sins. From what is told, he suffered greatly in his youth as a peasant, and none was kinder in the laps of luxury. Like all great saints, he repented and came to his faith, to stare up towards the bronze serpent of the Cross and find healing of his heart from the poison within. He thus took up his cross and lived his life. He married, had many children, and continued to serve the Russian Army a changed man, though his family lived here and he would be separate from them at times. He lived the difficult life of a father providing for his wife and children, and then war came to this region for the first time since the Crimean War. So, he fought in that war and by his efforts, Russia annexed more land that belonged to the Armenian people, and he was celebrated for his efforts."

"I thought he died at the end of that war," Charlemagne pointed out.

"I told you to not interrupt," the cleric replied. "Vagharshak loved his people greatly. He saw the suffering of his own people at the hands of the Ottoman Empire for the first time through that war, worse than that under Russian rule as they were made subjects, not citizens, of an empire. He wished to elevate his people the same way he was elevated. And then, as the years went on, came the massacres from across the border. At first, there were rumors, and then fleeing refugees, and worse stories as the years went on that Vagharshak could only stand-by and listen, fearing for their existence. He dreamed to unite Armenia, one nation, indivisible, subject to neither the Ottomans nor

Russia, but unlike many dreamers he did not dream himself in that role. He feared the call to believe he was meant to be that person, so while he felt the burden of responsibility, others in his circle begged him to take up the cause of an Armenian nation. In 1895, rumor came to him that there was a great massacre of hundreds-of-thousands of his people, which led to revolt in West Armenia against their captors which would likely be crushed by the Ottoman rulers. Vagharshak came to the aid of his brethren with his army, but not waving a Russian flag, but an Armenian flag. He intervened as he crossed the border, and in a mission to rescue as many of his people as he could to retreat from the Ottomans, they pressed him to continue to fight, but it was not his fight to win. He held the line, fought on the battlefront with his brothers, as women and children were escorted into East Armenia, and it was then that people hailed him as their king, a title of which came back to his fears of a leader to an Armenian people. He would surely return to Armenia as a hero to the nationalist groups, but then he fell in battle.

"If it was not for his valiant efforts, thousands more would have perished as a result of that revolt, but Vagharshak made the self-sacrifice to lead a rescue mission; to ride into battle and defend his people who were persecuted for their faith and ethnicity... Sadly though, his legend would not be shared as widely as it could have hoped to share in that glory he made to God. During the communist regime, the story of Vagharshak was suppressed, a statue of him in this courtyard destroyed, and this church only recently finding attention as his name is remembered once more. In the end, he was made an unlikely leader of Armenian people in a time of oppression, and as a result, the Armenian people posthumously crowned him King of the Armenians."

Charlemagne waited as the cleric paused for a moment before he interrupted and said, "He was crowned? As in, with an actual crown?"

"I do not know," the cleric answered, "but surely he was crowned with glory in the afterlife…"

"Yeah, yeah," Charlemagne dismissed, "so where was he buried? Somewhere around here, and it was exhumed by the Soviets to oppose any veneration?"

"No."

"So where then," Charlemagne desperately asked.

"According to legend, Saint Vagharshak was buried in a tomb made specially for him, by the Armenian people who venerated him at the time. It is a tomb in the mountain… hidden from the communists and those that seek to deface it."

"How do I get there?"

"It is not for visitation," the cleric replied.

"What if I want to pay homage to the saint? Surely you cannot deny me that opportunity as a pilgrim?"

"Are you a pilgrim?"

"Oh yes, I am," Charlemagne remarked. "I heard it said that Vagharshak was rumored to be descended from the House of Lusinia, of French royalty in other words, and predestined glory to be the king of the Armenian people. Where was he buried?"

"Hm…" the cleric responded, bringing a hand to his chin. "If you are truly a pilgrim, then I give you this riddle to locate his tomb. When you've solved the answer to this riddle, then come find me and I will take you there."

"A riddle… very well," Charlemagne replied. "Have at it."

The cleric cleared his throat and then said, "Behind my walls and door, you will find me. Behind me, you will find the way. Who am I but that which gives life; I am small but mighty, savior of millions. Many who receive me will be saved while, Many will lose out as those who I never knew. Without me, none can make the journey, I have been waiting and my offer is here. Hurry and come to me, before it is too late, if you do not want to join the billions."

"Hold up," Charlemagne remarked, jotting down that riddle in his journal. "Right then…" He and Manon re-read it. "I am behind a wall and a door. I save millions. I am the way to salvation… The answer is simple… it's a religious puzzle, the answer is Jesus Christ." He then turned to where the cleric was seated and he shook his head.

"Be more specific," the cleric answered, "I am talking of a specific place where you will find the entrance to the tomb." He then stood up and began to walk away from them.

"Alright…" Charlemagne replied, re-reading the riddle.

"What about a church?" Manon suggested. "It has walls, a door, and it is where one goes to find Jesus Christ."

"Not specific enough," the cleric answered from afar. "Keeping searching, pilgrims. You will find it if you truly believe."

"Ugh, this is folly," Charlemagne remarked, "come on, let's take a look and see if there's a clue inside the church."

Charlemagne quickly walked towards the church, opened the heavy wooden doors and the pair entered through to come inside. The inside of the church was dark with only a bit of light pouring through slots above them. At their left and right were two thick stone brick columns, one of which had an icon of the late Saint Vagharshak, his head surrounded with a gold circle, a halo; another painting had a depiction of the Annunciation: a young Virgin Mary met with the Angel Gabriel. Before each painting was a glass metal table with candles above. From the main entrance of the church was a thin rug up to the sanctuary, the very front of the church where the altar was. Between the thin red rug were small pews. The next set of columns were directly besides the sanctuary with altar rails between them. These each had two paintings, one of which was an icon of the Paraclete, Holy Spirit, and another of the Mother of God, Theotokos. The sanctuary past the altar rails was curved and narrow. A curtain in front of the altar rail was pulled to the right, and behind it was steps up to the altar. Above the altar was a gold-colored arched cabinet nudged within a slight arched nook in the church walls. The nook was little more than double the height of the tabernacle. Above the pews was a circular chandelier with candles. Charlemagne looked about his left and right, where he found a curtain with a lectern stand behind it, and on the other end a steel font with water. He stepped down the rug and continued to look around.

"I don't see anything here..." Charlemagne muttered. He then turned around to face the tabernacle where he observed a painting in front of it that showed a Byzantine depiction of Jesus Christ looking straight at him. "Oh... hang on..."

Charlemagne approached the tabernacle, hopped over the altar rail and then made his way up and around the altar as he looked over to Manon. She stayed back and behind the altar rails as she looked over to him.

"Behind my walls and my door... I give you salvation and reach out in offer to you... To be received as a power to save others... That old fool is referring to what Christians receive during their services, Holy Communion, which in Catholic, and I suppose Orthodox belief too, is that bread that is stored in these cabinets called tabernacles; the body of Jesus Christ," Charlemagne said, turning around. "He gave himself up to save the world, so they say... except I did not ask him to give me his salvation..." He turned a frown and approach the tabernacle that loomed over him. He then climbed the altar, alarming Manon.

"*Charles*, what are you doing?!" Manon remarked. "Get down from there... now is not the time to be making an anti-religious statement."

Charlemagne placed his hands on the side of the tabernacle and then tilted it over, causing it to fall out of place and onto the ground before the altar. The collapse made a loud sound.

"*Charles*! Are you completely out of your mind?!"

"No, my dear, not completely..." Charlemagne remarked, stepping around and looking in the nook behind, "just more clever than I know what to do with..."

Within the nook was a thin passageway with steps downward into the unknown.

Act 7, Scene 3

Charlemagne and Manon both travelled down the steps of the passageway as it brought them around a curve angle. They both carried candles taken from the altar in their hands to give them a bit of light as they looked around and came to an arched corridor that went forward an unknown distance.

"Seems as though beneath the church is a crypt, which seems to me like where they buried this supposed saint," Charlemagne expressed. "Let's see how far this goes…"

Charlemagne and Manon proceeded to walk down the corridor with cautious footsteps. The corridor stretched out for a few yards before it reached a tunnel that stretched out into a room with a staircase that went down a level. This staircase then brought them around and into a tall domed structure with a spiral staircase that went downwards. They proceeded down the staircase, going down at least three more levels to reach another arched passageway. This passage let to some steps that went down and into a wider and more extensive cavernous corridor. They stopped for a moment as they examined the stone brick columns at the sides of the cave walls. Charlemagne and Manon then proceeded forward, walking down along the lone path that went a few yards deeper.

The cave system had loose dirt ground and greyish-brown walls. There were roots hanging down from above and moss and mushrooms growing through the dirt. The cave was also cold as both Charlemagne and Manon could see their breath as they hiked along the winding path to reach a portion that consisted of partial brick floor and walls. At the end of the cave was an arched tunnel that led into a wider aisle than ones before with additional arched nooks on the side, consisting of empty spaces within. These arched nooks were low, at least five feet tall, and there were four of them that followed another passageway.

"Are these crypts? Lots for graves?" Charlemagne questioned. "The architecture and design of this space is certainly bizarre."

Manon did not answer as she crossed her arms. She was visibly upset with him. He fully ignored her and continued to walk down as they came into a rectangular room with stairs that went up to another short passageway, which then led into another cylindrical room and another spiral staircase. This staircase took them up, reaching a landing before the staircase went further up where there were three arched passageways before them. They journeyed forward to see what lied ahead and found a similar squared room with four arched nooks and spaces within. They then returned and likewise the other rooms were the same. They then went up the spiral staircase to continue their ascent back up, reaching a second landing, a third landing, and finally a fourth landing, each of which had the exact same rooms. Finally, they journeyed up and reached a single arched aisle. At the sides in which there were other passageways on the rest of the four levels, there were instead statues, one of the Virgin Mary holding a baby Jesus, and another of a bearded male figure wearing a robe and holding a crook. Each of the statues had stone plaques beneath them.

"I would hazard a guess that this place was looted, a long time ago," Charlemagne remarked. "I would say the Soviets had their way with this burial place, or otherwise, took whatever was in whatever this place is supposed to be."

Charlemagne and Manon went down the archway as it led to yet another spiral staircase that took them upwards. As they went up the staircase, Charlemagne observed natural light pour in as well as a breeze. They came to the top of the staircase and found a short-arched tunnel that led outside. Charlemagne shielded his eyes as the brightness overwhelmed him, and once they were out he blew out the candle, put it in his pocket, and then looked around. The tunnel brought him outside to a sandy gully between two slopes with rocks inserted into the low-sloped cliffs. From above, Charlemagne could partially see some grass and tall trees. The area was snowed in slightly, so they trudged through the snow where ahead a domed structure could be seen, and behind it another larger domed stone structure. Charlemagne and Manon went into the domed structure, through the wide archway that led inside to come into a room with a curved dual staircase that joined up at a landing before yet another arched entryway.

The pair travelled up the stairs and came to the entryway, entering a large circular room with thin columns forming an ambulatory around the center. Open windows above the ambulatory allowed light to pour in, and unfortunately also snow to trickle through. Around the ambulatory walls were murals that depicted scenes of battle. Below the window were carved figures as well, angels in the form of Greek cherubim. At the very top of the ceiling where there was a small inward dome was a depiction of the Holy Spirit above them in white with fire around its being. Looking down from the ceiling, in the very center of the room, was a rectangular marble tomb. The pair stood before the grave site and simply looked at the tomb with plain eyes.

"I don't suppose this would be the resting place of the dear saint, is it?" Charlemagne asked, semi-sarcastically. He took off his backpack and revealed a crowbar.

"*Charles*, what are you going to do with that? Enough vandalism, please," Manon pleaded. "Don't do it, please. You do not know what you will find... you're not going to see what you want to see."

"I have to be sure the crown is not resting upon this so-called king's head," Charlemagne remarked. "I mean, otherwise we'll have to go chasing to see what the fate of his children was, and whether that title of king followed them, along with the crown. However, just to be sure with ourselves, I have to make sure that the dead don't still have what is rightfully mine..."

Manon did not respond as Charlemagne left his backpack on the ground and approached the tomb. He placed the crowbar in and then levied the weight of the tomb lid up, allowing it to pop out and for him to use his hand to slightly pivot it. He then pushed it with all his force, causing it to fall over and hit the floor beside where it fell on its side and then backwards on its back. Manon stepped forward as Charlemagne's devilish smile turned to a deep frown.

Within the tomb was a mummified figure, body and skin shriveled, skin colored and textured like raw clay. He was dressed in a long-sleeved greyish-beige tunic underneath a black short-sleeved robe. The shirt had a crimson red pattern on the chest and around the wrists. The robe had a knitted golden pattern around the edges, and extending from the shoulders were flaps that extended downwards the entire length of the robe in a diamond-like shape. Around the waist of the figure was a silk-like black belt, and attached to it was a black sheath with gold-colored ornate designs that held at least a ten-inch dagger. The figure also wore black baggy pants with hand-made black boots. His feet were put together, and his hands placed atop of his abdomen as though at peace. At his side was a hand-carved rifle. At the head, the eyes of the deceased were closed, as was the mouth, and around the head were thin remains of black hair. Atop of this hair though was a thick golden band with four fleur-de-lis plates on each side curved inwards slightly with smaller arched bands crossed-over, upholding the crown and a velvet cap within. There were no jewels, no pearls, but just the simple appearance of a simple gold crown.

"*Charles...*" Manon uttered.

"No..." Charlemagne denied, shaking his head, "that's not right..."

"*Charles*, I told you," Manon piped up, "I told you that the crown you found in Ukraine was highly unlikely to be the crown. I remember, the image you showed me, the Crown of

Charlemagne had four fleurs-de-lis, while that one you found had eight."

"What is it doing here?!" Charlemagne snarled. "Resting in this tomb, on the head of this peasant no less; this fake king and holy fool..." He lurched his hands forward and grabbed the crown off the head of the corpse. "To think that I've struggled life and limb only for my crown to be resting in a mausoleum to a pretender to the throne, as if he really were of Lusinian blood, this scoundrel... At long last, I have found you, the crown of my dreams... my crown. How I will be glorified before the people of the world with this, Manon. Imagine, me on the front of Time magazine with this on my head. Oh, I can't wait..." he said in a greedy tone. "I am finally... fulfilled."

Manon frowned at him as she looked at him from across the tomb. She looked at the corpse of Vagharshak Karakashian, and then to Charlemagne as he idolized the crown before him.

"I can't believe you..." Manon expressed.

Charlemagne's eyes shot forward.

"Here I was, at your side to search for what I had hoped to be an important artefact," Manon said, "when it doesn't seem like you even care about the history. All you cared about is to put that silly thing on the top of your head, when it doesn't mean anything or anymore to be on your head then it does on the head of this dead body. How can I be certain that you even intend to forfeit that crown now and not put it in a private collection of your own? How do I know you would part with that crown?"

Charlemagne's frowned deepened as he replied, "Am I not allowed to take a bit joy in this moment of victory for myself? Do you not understand that since I was a young child, learning about Charlemagne, the man of my namesake, that I dreamt about wearing his very own crown, and now here I am holding his crown and all it should take is for me to lift up my arms and place it upon my head."

"If you were to do that, you'd be a silly fool yourself," Manon lambasted. "As if that crown held any sort of power to change who you are. You are blind, *Charles*, with a misunderstanding of your own worth and a grandiose delusion that you be something more than you are. I do not think that we should take that crown from this resting place, knowing where it is, let it be, *Charles*."

"Oh, come off it," Charlemagne replied, rolling his eyes, "to let this priceless artefact stay here? How is that any different to what Rubashkin wants to do in throwing this to his vault?"

"Plenty, to your own soul," Manon pointed out, "we've discovered the crown, its existence, so let it stay here and we can write about it, but take that from here and I do not think it will see the light of day. You have no intention to let go of that crown, do you? Where would you take it?"

"Obviously, a crown as majestic as this would need to go somewhere special. Still though, I can only imagine the fight for it from country to country... I would need to take it away from Europe in the least... somewhere safe... like Canada..."

"Or Allabrese? Your home in the countryside?"

"I didn't say or mean to suggest such a place... although..."

"Aside from the greed to keep that to yourself, I see in you that you are no different than Rubashkin," Manon asserted.

"Pardon me?" Charlemagne questioned, unimpressed. "Have I plotted to kill you? To abandon you? To use you?"

"Ah, perhaps not in your own consciousness, but very well have you held a complete disregard for the safety of me and yourself this whole trip."

"Oh, here we go now, at the end of our adventure, and here Manon is, just as she was in Tunis at the end of our last adventure... offering a moral lesson when nobody asked for it."

"How can I not when *Charles* Cabernet is acting like himself? This... this pride and this vainglory, I am coming to conclusion that it is not some defect of yours, but it is very well you. You are just like your namesake, not a very good person."

"Excuse me?"

"You heard me, *Charles*, you are not a very good person, just like Charlemagne, King of the Franks. You and him, you are both… evil."

"You're saying Charlemagne was evil?"

"Are you so blind in idol-worship of him that his crimes have surpassed your mind? Charlemagne was a terrible man; a man who massacred thousands, captors no less. He was a tyrant that punished dissonance and harshly taxed his people. He exploited the poor and made slaves of his enemy's people. He was a terrible father to his children, cheated on his wives with concubines, and bore illegitimate children he ignored and threw out from his sight. You tell me in what way is this man, the Holy Roman Emperor, anything less than evil?"

"All those claims about Charlemagne are greatly exaggerated," Charlemagne dismissed. "I think you're being overly dramatic."

"Ah, but I am not finished yet," Manon remarked. "For you, Charlemagne, are evil too. From what I recall, Derby knew it too – the Cabernet family name, held less than honor in its name."

"What are you on about?"

"You tell me that the Cabernet herald of a wolf is a noble and loyal, when it has been nothing short of ravenous, like a wolf that plunders in the day and divides in the night, so too has the Cabernet ancestors operated in exploitation, taking its first steps in the international market through arms dealing, just like Krum Berezovsky."

"Oh, now you're comparing me to that Bulgarian," Charlemagne groaned. "Come off it, Manon, you're tiresome. You've always been tiresome, even when you were a little girl were you a tiresome brat that followed me around with starry eyes that recognized me for who I truly am. Do you forget that I am a descendant of Queen Victoria through my grandmother Ophelia? That in my blood is the lineage of kings spanning back to Alfred the Great? Do you not understand that within my very-much royal blood is the DNA of kings from all across Continental Europe, perhaps going so far to Charles the Great himself? From the time of my youth have I been recognized for greatness, Manon, everywhere I go, and if I were to dismiss that greatness I would be a coward in doing so – I hone it, I am a great man destined for great things, and this crown is very much mine… mine for the taking to do so with as I please."

"Mon Dieu, cet idiot est totalement aveugle et dissocié de la réalité!" Manon cursed as she threw her hands into the air and then left. *"J'en ai assez, je m'en vais!"*

Charlemagne shook his head and then continued to look at the crown as he raised a smile again. "Hello gorgeous, welcome home…" he muttered to himself. He then began to raise the crown up to his head, but before he could place it down, he heard a terrible shriek. "What?!" The shrieking continued as Charlemagne groaned. "Oh, what now…" He put the crown into his backpack and then went forward. He took a handgun out from his pocket and kept it has his side as he came around to the top of the stairs to look down to the main entrance.

At the main entrance, Charlemagne identified mercenaries dressed in winter clothing pointing up towards him with their rifles. An additional two mercenaries closed in from either side before he could even react, prompting him to raise his hands to the air immediately. A mercenary swung the butt of their assault rifle and struck Charlemagne across the face, causing him to tilt over and stagger sideways, while another caught him by the neck and pushed him forward and down the stairs. He fell down the steps and came to the bottom where he was picked up and thrown outside into the snow. The mercenaries cursed at him in Bulgarian. He was picked up again and brought to his feet. A mercenary cocked his handgun while two others behind him held their assault rifle. Another mercenary came around from behind and knocked him to his knees. Charlemagne kept his hands behind his head.

"*Charles!*" Manon shouted from uphill. "*Charles!*"

The Bulgarian mercenaries shouted at her and she was escorted away. The mercenaries around Charlemagne then began to discuss as one picked up a radio. He lowered his head and gritted his teeth, and then closed his eyes as he heard a gunshot. He then looked up and saw one of the mercenaries fall over, blood splattering the clean white snow beside him. The two other mercenaries looked around, and the second was shot, prompting the third to come up to Charlemagne and take him hostage. He pressed the barrel of his handgun into his temple and then looked around fervently as he held Charlemagne close. They began to spin around, and as they did, Charlemagne looked up the hill and could see only the evergreen spruces above. A third shot took the life of another, leaving only the one that held Charlemagne hostage. In an instance, the Bulgarian mercenary shouted out, his grip left Charlemagne, and he fell over sideways dead.

Charlemagne seized in place and then froze with terror. He then flinched as he began to hear gunshots from afar, jerking his neck up towards the hill where he saw a familiar face in winter camouflage clothes.

"Cael!" Charlemagne remarked, bringing a hand to his heart. "That's three times now you've saved me. How can I ever repay you?"

"We can talk about that later, Charles-man," Cael replied, sliding down to join him. "Sorry I missed you in Yerevan, but I've been on the hunt for your predators as you can see. T'was only natural that we'd run into each other again – I haven't been too far behind them."

"You've been a guardian angel in all this," Charlemagne expressed, picking up a rifle, "but I'm afraid I have one more favor to ask of you before we go this round."

"Aye, your friend, Dr. Dumas," Cael remarked. "Not to worry, I'll get at them for this. Just get yourself out of here, will you?"

"I can't," Charlemagne replied. "I don't know when I'd see you again."

"We'll always see each other again, Charles-man," Cael said. "So long as you keep hunting for that crown and these blokes keep hunting you."

"No, it's not that, though I found it – I found the real crown. The one that Rubashkin stole off me was not the real one – I don't know what that is, but right here, in this tomb, I found the true crown of Charlemagne."

"Did you now?"

"Yes," Charlemagne affirmed, "so I don't know if you were able to salvage the other crown or not, but it's of no importance to me."

"Aye, I did," Cael remarked. "I have it in me car. Good to know though, still could be worth something, I suppose…"

"Most certainly," Charlemagne replied. "My colleague believes it is the long-lost Polish Crown, but it would need to be investigated in greater depth. No, I want to join you to help Manon – I can't let them hurt her."

"Oh?" Cael questioned. "Very well, I suppose I could use a hand. Take one of them guns off them corpses," he instructed, "and load up on some magazines. We're going to need them."

"Do you have any idea where they could be taking Manon?" Charlemagne asked as he did so. He picked up an AK-47 and some magazines. He then equipped himself and the pair began to climb uphill to come into the forest.

"Only a slight idea," Cael answered. "I've been tracking these men through Yerevan as they searched for you. They found your friend, Dr. Ivanov, and beat the truth out of him. He'll be alright and all, but from what I've heard they've got reinforcements touching down in an abandoned airfield at the other side of the border. I wouldn't know where they hope to take your friend, but they're certainly planning on leaving with her."

"We've got their tracks in the snow," Charlemagne remarked, reading his rifle. "They shouldn't get too far if we hurry."

"Aye, let's move on out then lad."

Charlemagne and Cael trudged through the snow together, arriving at a slim and narrow cave entrance. They proceeded forward and came into a narrow tunnel that was divided in the middle by a concrete wall with a doorway through. The door was shut and could not be opened.

"Damn, we'll never get through."

"Not so fast," Charlemagne expressed, taking out some plastic explosives. He placed it at the door and inserted a charge and pulled out the trigger.

"Lovely," Cael expressed. They cleared out of the way before they triggered the explosives, sending the door flying. Cael proceeded to filter through and they continued. The cave then widened out as they came out into a larger grotto with trees spread out.

"Get into cover!" Cael shouted as mercenaries fired back at them. He crouched into a prone position and observed through his sniper rifle while Charlemagne attempted to provide some covering fire.

The grotto they came out into was massively large and between two rocky cliffside walls. Charlemagne could see at the far end of the grotto, the hill came up to a wide but low cave entrance ahead where hostiles were spread apart. Charlemagne continued to provide covering fire while Cael with his sniper rifle cleaned up the hostiles, clearing half of them which prompted the rest to retreat.

"Move up!" Cael shouted.

Charlemagne advanced, and Cael picked up his rifle and went closer towards the cave entrance, dropping down halfway to continue to push the mercenaries back. Charlemagne reloaded his assault rifle and then they made another push towards the cave. The cave entrance was wide, but then narrowed out as it funneled to the right and then went down towards another concrete wall with a doorway. Cael took a grenade from his belt and threw it down, waiting for it to pop off before he advanced in and took cover at the doorway. Charlemagne took cover on the other side and they looked in at the wide cave with many natural columns from where hostiles took cover. Cael threw another disorientation grenade and then pushed into the room where there was another concrete wall ahead with a door. Likewise, they planted an explosive charge, detonated it, and then continued. Charlemagne advanced and they found themselves at the next wall where hostiles continued to retreat.

The cave continued along with an opening in the ceiling ahead as the tunnel was wide with many natural columns to hide behind. Natural light poured through the ceiling with light pouring from the other side as well. Charlemagne helped Cael provide covering fire and then they advanced into the cavern as they continued to follow the mercenaries as they slowed them down. Charlemagne concentrated as he returned gunfire at the hostiles. They then retreated again towards the back of the cave where the walls narrowed out and then widened out again, this time exposing out towards a large canyon on the other side.

Charlemagne observed a helicopter pass the cave walls and fly forward through the canyon. He opened fire at the helicopter and could hear the screams of Manon from not too far away.

"She's nearby," Charlemagne shouted. "We're almost there!"

Cael continued to open fire, but rather than retreat, hostiles began to flood in to the cave and take point around the natural columns. They could continue to hear the rotors of the helicopter from afar before they began to grow faint. At that moment, the hostiles began to retreat again, going the way they came, around a corner on the cliffside. Charlemagne and Cael followed, and Charlemagne took a moment to look down the side of the cliff to see the nearly mile length drop below to a river. The cave exit took them along a narrow cliffside path which then led back into another cave which widened out to a large cavern with old machinery taking up much of the space with pipes and gauges, pistons and scaffolding. At this room, the hostiles thinned out as they retreated quickly. Charlemagne and Cael passed this room to reach a concrete wall and open door, stopping to breach, and then continuing along. The other side led down a set of metal stairs along a steep cave tunnel, coming around to a sprawling network of tunnels, some of which had rusted rails spread through. The tunnel was dark, but light poured forth from the end. The hostiles took position along the far side of the mine and opened fire at them. Cael continued to open fire, and Charlemagne provided covering fire as they pushed them back while the hostiles seemingly attempted to stall them further.

Eventually, the hostiles broke and fell back, allowing Charlemagne and Cael to move before being stopped again.

"I haven't felt this much resistance in a long time," Cael remarked to Charlemagne as he reloaded. "I'm not used to having such a hard time getting out of dodge."

"Perhaps not what you'd come to expect as a field agent," Charlemagne responded. "Certainly not what I've come to expect..."

"Aye, they're pulling back again," Cael remarked. "Let's go."

Charlemagne and Cael approached the end of the cave, reaching another narrow straight path on the cliffside. They took cover against a wall as the hostiles continued to retreat, going up a side path further ahead on the right.

"Yup, looks just about right from where I caught them," Cael said. "There's a road above, and my car is parked not too far. They'll likely be going to join their comrades, so let's give 'em chase and join 'em."

Act 7, Scene 4

Charlemagne and Cael climbed up the narrow path to the very top, several yards high where they reached a narrow lane road. The sight of vehicles driving forward could be seen not too far ahead, but Cael did not stop to watch and instead rushed down the road and around a bend where parked besides a rock, out of view, was his open roof jeep, similar to the ones at the base in Moldova.

"You up to shoot or drive?" Cael questioned.

"I'll drive," Charlemagne offered, catching the keys as they were thrown to him. "I'm not much use of a marksman."

Charlemagne got into the driver's seat and then set forth down the road going after the escaped vehicles. He took notice that this area was a lot more arid than the pastureland by the Armenian village, and there were less trees, although the trees that there were, were thin coniferous trees. As he drove as quickly as he could, Cael prepared his own AK-47 rifle for combat.

"You've got quite the military experience, don't you," Charlemagne suggested. "Is that all from MI6 training?"

"No," Cael denied, "I mean, a lot of is from training and the other half is just life experience, keeping my ass down and my head up."

"Right."

"We'll never catch up to them at this rate, Charles-man," Cael expressed. "Cut through here and we'll reach 'em for sure. Pull left."

"Left?" Charlemagne questioned. To the left of them was a low snowy hill."

"Aye, she can take it," Cael insisted. "Come now, trust me and we'll get to your little friend before they can harm her."

Charlemagne pulled left and began to traverse the hill. He then came out on top and proceeded forward across the snowy hill before coming around to the top and seeing below on the other side the convoy of vehicles as the road span around as it moved away from the cliffside.

"There they're at," Cael said, standing up, "after them!"

Charlemagne drove forward while Cael opened fire and took shots at them. The hostiles in the back of the truck began to return gunfire.

"Hang on!" Charlemagne shouted as he drove downhill and towards the convoy. The jeep swerved as Charlemagne merged onto the highway and continued to keep up at the same speed needed to pursue the GAZ and personnel trucks that attempted to evade them. They drove from behind as the mercenaries attempted to make their escape. The road stretched out and curved, passing a low canyon with rocks and hills on either end, winding around to come back along the cliffside where they began to approach traffic on the road in either direction. The convoy of vehicles drove forcibly forward, going around traffic going in the same direction, sometimes at the detriment of oncoming traffic who steered away and often times crashed or came to a halt. Charlemagne attempted to evade the traffic and the reaction of vehicles as they came up against the mercenaries and Cael in a firefight. He also did his best to keep his head down as bullets passed him from above and around, hitting the windshield to the point that it could just be pushed out.

The vehicles approached a tunnel where they continued to open fire at one another. The tunnel curved in a slight arch and then continued forward along the cliffside for a short distance. A mercenary picked up a rocket launcher and aimed it towards them. The rocket flew forward and hit the cliffside instead, causing rocks to tumble down and hit the road. Another rocket flew upwards and missed by a wide margin.

"Watch those rockets, Charles!" Cael shouted.

The jeeps and trucks drove into another tunnel where a rocket flew past them and hit above. The sound of cars honking could be heard as they evaded traffic. They then came out to another stretch besides a cliffside, and then another tunnel before reaching a segment of the road that arched around from the outside. Another rocket flew over them until Cael was able to neutralize the rocketeer.

Charlemagne watched as this mercenary fell out and hit the road, their corpse left behind as the chase continued. He saw a fuel truck driving towards them from ahead, and then from the skies above, a gunship helicopter that began to open fire not just at them, but at the convoys ahead. The Bulgarian mercenaries shouted out and pointed up to the helicopter as it neutralized a jeep and sent it tumbling into an explosive fireball. Charlemagne covered his forehead at the brightness and heat, and steered clear. The fuel truck that passed them drove into the wreckage, tipping over and detonating into a large fireball that radiated outwards in a tremendous distance in blue flames, nearly catch the tail end of their jeep. Charlemagne watched as the mercenaries changed their fixation away from just them, but to the gunship as it flew past and then made a turn to approach them.

"I don't understand, is that helicopter with you?"

"Me? I don't have any allies out here," Cael replied, observing it as he reloaded. "It certainly is no ally to us, so tread carefully."

"Aye aye," Charlemagne replied, continuing forward.

A mercenary prepared a rocket as they watched the helicopter approach again. It fired missiles towards them, hitting the cliffside walls instead, and then it began to open its machine gun cannons.

"Come to think of it, this Hind may just bugger us in the ass," Cael expressed. "We need these cars to survive 'till we reach the airfield. If it destroys all of these cars, then we're screwed."

"Do you think Krum is eliminating his own men for that reason?"

"Anything is possible."

Charlemagne continued to evade the helicopter as it concentrated fire on both of them. He pulled back to evade the majority of the gunfire as it concentrated on the mercenaries. The mercenaries launched rockets towards the helicopter, greatly missing, while Cael avoided to become a target as he took the opportunity to reload his assault rifle and then pick up his sniper rifle.

"I'm going to take out that bird the only way I know how," Cael expressed.

"Good luck."

"I'm Irish, I don't need luck."

Charlemagne continued to drive forward as they approached a longer tunnel, this one with openings between columns to provide natural light in. The helicopter passed along the open canyon besides the tunnel as it unloaded its machine guns into the columns, chipping away at the integrity of the supports. The helicopter then intensified its gunfire as it began to unload rockets of its own, but they hit above the tunnel though they still did enough damage to cause the collapse behind them. Charlemagne sped up as he rejoined the hostiles, left between one personnel truck and jeep. For the remainder of the tunnel, there were no opens or columns, but thick walls as they approached the end. The tunnel continued to collapse up to this closed section towards the exit.

"Bloody hell!" Cael cursed as they came outdoors. "Right, I'm taking this fecker out!"

The helicopter gunship opened fire at the personnel truck and jeep. A rocket flew forward from the jeep and nearly hit the gunship, causing it to steer out of the way. Likewise, a missile hit towards the jeep and personnel truck, causing the truck to swerve and then tip over as it tumbled directly in front of Charlemagne and Cael. Charlemagne took an evasive maneuver and drove off road to evade the truck, seeing the corpses and bodies of the mercenaries flail lifelessly like dolls. A vehicle driving the oncoming direction crashed directly into the truck, but Charlemagne was able to continue to drive forward.

"Watch it, mate!" Cael cursed as he attempted to stabilize the rifle. "I need a clean shot."

"Sorry," Charlemagne apologized.

The two jeeps proceeded around and came towards a straight path over a bridge. Cael took the shot and was able to hit the engine of the helicopter, causing it to smoke.

"Nearly had it..." Cael expressed. "I'm taking another shot..."

Charlemagne peeled right and began to continue downhill as they drove around the cliffside from the other end. Cael took another shot and pierced the glass.

"Bullseye!"

The helicopter began to spin out of the control and smashed itself into the cliff directly above the jeep, causing rocks to tumble down.

"Slow down here," Cael expressed. "We don't want to lose that truck ahead, but we don't want to give them the impression that we've survived.

Charlemagne drove through the smoke of the wreckage, and slowed down. The pair could see the truck ahead, but then slowly came to a regular speed and kept up with the rest of the of traffic. Cael reloaded his rifle and came around to sit down next to Charlemagne.

"I haven't had this much of a fight since I was Afghanistan."

"You were in Afghanistan?" Charlemagne questioned. "I had heard that the Americans sent the CIA in to Afghanistan to disrupt the Soviets, but MI6 as well?"

"Of course," Cael replied, "why wouldn't they? Perhaps a time for another adventure, but there's said to be a great number of lost treasures in the rest of the Soviet Union, including Afghanistan and Central Asia. Perhaps when you've finished here, you can head on out. Of course, you'll need to work on your sharpshooting if you want to survive in those lands."

"So now Her Majesty's Government is giving me advice on where I should tread to next," Charlemagne pointed out. "I didn't realize how supportive the British government could be towards me. Certainly more supportive than the Canadian government has been, calling me a lunatic."

Cael laughed and replied, "If you haven't been to Afghanistan, then you certainly should at some time. Likewise with all those lands, and even up into Russia too. Beautiful country…"

"Seems as though you've spent too much time in it."

"Not enough," Cael responded, "still lots to see. I've been doing this for only fifteen years or so since the Troubles ended. I could never imagine returning to Ireland or the life I left behind, though it was not much. Awful country, no thanks to the British, but not a place for me."

"Oh? I've been to Ireland, seems peaceful, a lot like where I'm from in Canada."

"You're from Canada?"

"Yes, of all places."

"Never been there, but I've heard the outdoors are similar to around here."

"I couldn't say," Charlemagne responded. "I'm not really one for the outdoors, though I do enjoy a good excursion. I do enjoy Europe though for its richness in culture, and the people too. A lot better than the folk in Canada for one."

"Ah, I wouldn't know if that's true for Ireland."

"No wonder you defected to join MI6," Charlemagne remarked. "You don't seem to like much about the Emerald Isle. I don't see what is that much better in the British Isle, aside the profession of faith."

"I don't think I enjoy the British Isles anymore, lad," Cael expressed. "I enjoy what I do out here, it's refreshing – being out in the field of this lawless world. I really feel like I could make a name for myself out around these parts, you know."

"As a spy?" Charlemagne questioned. "I thought you were supposed to keep a lid on things."

"Ah, I'll be a legend either way," Cael remarked. "Just you wait, Charles-man, and I'll be a better legend than I could have been being strung up like a dog for supporting the IRA, or shot in the head for betraying my country."

The jeep came out to a low clearing as they drove along the side of a river. They came across an arid land with low hills, and eventually the jeep pulled out and began to drive off-road.

"Easy there," Cael remarked, "keep it slow to let them go on their way, and then we'll pull out and follow their trail."

Charlemagne did not respond and instead did what he was told. He slowed down to let the jeep disappear along the other side of the hill, and then he pulled out and slowly began to follow the tire tracks. The snow in these parts was very thin, like thick frost more than it was like snow, with clumps of clear land in certain spots. Eventually, after following along the trail, Charlemagne and Cael observed an immense lot ahead with many airplanes parked around, and otherwise scraps of airplanes and submerged aircraft pointed out like a junkyard.

"Right'o," Cael expressed, taking a pair of binoculars as they drove forward. "I don't see much in the way of defenses…"

Charlemagne then turned his head to the left and saw some transport helicopters approach. The helicopters hovered over the scrapyard ahead and they both saw soldiers rappel down.

"Could it be that the Russians have caught wind of what's going on? We are on their doorstep," Charlemagne pointed.

"The Russians?" Cael questioned. "No, not likely – by my account, we should have crossed into Azerbaijan, not Russia, and the Azerbaijan would not respond to this extent. They could barely stand up and pull their trousers up… Steer clear, if those mercs were hostile to an unknown group, then likely whichever ones here must also be hostile to these men too. We could be walking into a three-way war. Drive up around the rear here where there's a road in. We'll split up and search for that lovely lady of yours, Charles."

"What's the plan once we find Manon?" Charlemagne questioned. "We could never escape in this jeep – our petrol is low and they outnumber us severely."

"Well, it is an airfield," Cael remarked. "We should be able to secure some sort of air transport. We would have to travel only short distance north into Russia."

"I'm all in."

Charlemagne drove into the front of the airfield where there were some abandoned checkpoints. He drove around besides a hangar and then stood up. He picked up his rifle and then came out. Cael stood up and got into the driver's seat. The sound of gunfire and shouting could be well heard from within.

"Keep a low profile and have a look around for that friend of yours," Cael encouraged. "I'll scout around the perimeter to see if I can find a vehicle to jack, and we'll meet up at the runway."

"Affirmative," Charlemagne responded, jumping out. He immediately ran towards the checkpoint barriers while Cael backed up and then drove off in the opposite direction.

Charlemagne climbed over the checkpoint barrier and then went forward along the dirt road past an abandoned structure on his right and left. He saw a junction in the road with the road continuing forward and also to the left. On the right, past the building, there were heaps of shipping containers piled around with piles of metal scrap nearby. Some more helicopters flew overhead to drop off BTR-40 vehicles that revved into action and began to set up a perimeter in this area, while pickup trucks along a junction further ahead and nearby pulled up and began to engage the BTR-40. A cloud of smoke appeared near the armored cars, and the helicopters hovering over began to rappel men in professional greenish-brown uniforms with face masks and helmets. Charlemagne recognized a Soviet emblem on the side of the helicopter and began to go towards a shipping container on the left beside the abandoned building as he took cover.

"The Soviet mercenaries..." Charlemagne muttered. "Are they out for revenge...?"

Charlemagne observed Bulgarian mercenaries engage the former Soviet soldiers in a firefight. The armored car tore the pickup trucks to pieces, but the rest of the bandits spread out around the heaps of trash that was around to act as cover.

"I'll never get past here..."

Charlemagne looked ahead at a dumpster and began to climb it to kick down a window into the abandoned structure. He then entered into an abandoned office and found the corridor. He then went around to move to the other side of the building where he found a lot with wing of an aircraft lodged into the ground, and various bits and pieces of aircrafts left around, with additional planes further ahead in disuse and neglect. Around the planes further ahead was a tall signpost with a simple word marked in Cyrllic, "Лот 1". Charlemagne moved up and took cover atop of an airplane wing surface that was sloped in the ground and provided him with protection as he went into the prone position. He saw further ahead two sides, left and right, exchanging gunfire past another road parallel to the building behind him. The skeletal frame of some aircraft could also be seen around, but the majority of cover ahead was in the entire structure of airplanes bellied upon the earth. Charlemagne looked around as the two sides engaged each other and then moved up to take cover behind the torn wing propped up in the frosty and partially snowy ground.

Once the coast was clear, Charlemagne moved forward some more and came around to the front of a shipping container where beside it was a piece of airplane hull with windows. He took cover behind this piece of aircraft and looked out towards the two sides as he got closer and passed the road. He then moved around and came into the semi-cylindrical hull of a craft partially in the ground and looked out those windows. He caught sight of the Soviet mercenaries fighting against the Bulgarian bandits. The amount of trash ahead formed a perimeter ahead that could not be trampled, no less with a chain link fence and piles upon piles of aircraft scrap that bore Soviet insignias. Likewise, on the left, leaving the compound, was a tall chain-link fence with barbed wire that blocked the exit. The Bulgarian mercenaries had pickup trucks with machine guns strapped to the back that held this position. Rather than go forward, Charlemagne went to the right within the hull he was in, leaving, and going around to a large dumpster besides a detached platform with a cross-section of a hull atop of it. He began to steer right as he went into the depths of the scrapyard. He then jumped as a Bulgarian bandit came behind the dumpster, clutching his neck as blood squirted out and staggering as his dropped his rifle. He fell over backwards in front of Charlemagne, and Charlemagne watched as blood drained from his body and bled into the snow. He likewise watched as the life left the eyes of the soldier, slowing becoming soulless and body like a wax sculpture.

Charlemagne looked away as he knelt down. He shook his head and then ran forward. A large partial aircraft was lodged on the right, blocking the path, but Charlemagne ran into it and took cover around the cockpit while he heard Bulgarians within it open fire at mercenaries ahead. From here, Charlemagne observed that there were many signposts around the scrapyard in every direction, all carrying the same word but with different numbers up to the twenty range. He ran forward and entered into a semi-cylindrical hull and then climbed up into another hull at the end that was raised off the ground. He traversed past another line of defense, stopping to look out the window as he found an open section of the battlefield where he could see a BTR-40 parked at the opposite corner and opening fire towards the line.

A cloud of smoke surrounded the armored car, and gunfire came out from the left side towards the Bulgarians who stood their ground. They were supported by more of them on the right-side. Charlemagne could see all sorts of debris in this junkyard, from cargo palettes to oil drums, to construction vehicles and bulldozers, to shipping crates, dumpsters, and steel trays. Charlemagne looked around the battlefield as the Bulgarians attempted to support their men with white pickup trucks that drove around sporadically in battle, but behind the Bulgarian line was a partially intact cargo airplane with wings span across the one side.

From where Charlemagne took cover, he went forward and hopped down. He quickly went towards the next hull which was entirely intact and went down the bottom of it as he crouched down. He then stopped and could see the cargo airplane ahead, behind some shipping containers and other wrecks that formed the defenses of this craft. A transport helicopter was parked near the cargo plane, and additional transport helicopters moved in to provide reinforcements to the Bulgarian line, as well as an attack helicopter that fired missiles onto the Soviet troops. Charlemagne watched as the Bulgarians ran forward towards the frontline, while he stayed back in the dark and then moved in to come around the opposite side. He climbed into the cargo plane and popped his head over as he could hear some talking in Bulgarian. Charlemagne climbed up and then hid around the side of a wall. He looked in and could see a man in a familiar uniform, pacing about as he stood around a table. Krum smashed a fist into the table and yelled at the men around him. He looked about, but did not see Manon anywhere along the stretches of the cargo hull. After Krum finished yelling, the mercenaries with him left, and he likewise walked down and exited out through a side exit. Charlemagne then looked forward to the cockpit as he could hear some movement. He stood up and then snuck around into the cockpit where he took cover and saw Manon tied to the co-pilot chair. Her mouth was gagged with duct tape and her wrists to the seat. Charlemagne took the ties off and then removed the tape as he raised a finger to his lip to keep her quiet. He then took her hand and they came into the forward compartment. Manon lurched forward and embraced Charlemagne.

"Oh, *Charles*," Manon expressed, "you have no idea how glad I am to see you. How did you get here?"

"With a bit of help," Charlemagne replied. "Cael was on the tail of these mercs, but it seems like the former Soviet war dogs were behind them as they're fighting one another in this boneyard."

"Where is Cael? You did not leave him again, did you?"

"No, he's around, trying to find us some transport out from this land," Charlemagne expressed. "We've got to go meet up with him, so keep your head low and hold my hand."

"Oh, *Charles*," Manon remarked, embracing him again. "Can we finally go home."

Charlemagne did not respond as she placed her head on his chest. He instead maintained a deep strict face as he pulled her off and said, "I thought you hated me. I thought you loathed me. I thought you wanted nothing to do with me."

"Of course, I was mad at you, Charlemagne," Manon replied, "but do you really think that I would stay mad at you?"

"You never were one to hold grudges," Charlemagne pointed out. "Ow!" She brought a fist down like a hammer and hit his shoulder.

"Though I am greatly peeved in your actions," Manon said, "I cannot stay mad at you, *Charles*. We've known each other too long to be upset with one another... it would take a far greater sin to push me away. I know you have many faults, but you must understand that I love you the same." She then embraced him again.

"You... you love me?" Charlemagne questioned.

Manon's eyes opened and then she removed herself from him. She appeared embarrassed at what she said.

"Do you love me, Manon?"

"*Charles*, we have known each other for so long, of course I love you," Manon expressed. "My father too. You are one of us in a certain way…"

"Oh, so like a brother then," Charlemagne dismissed.

Manon tilted her head and questioned, "Did you think I loved you in any other way?"

Charlemagne did not respond and instead said, "Come on, we better get going…"

Manon took his hand and kept him from turning around. She looked at him. He held a frown on his face and avoided eye contact.

"*Charles*… in case we die here," Manon remarked.

"That's not going to happen," Charlemagne affirmed.

"If we do…" Manon repeated, "would it make a difference to you if I said I loved you in another way?"

Charlemagne turned and looked at her. She looked back at him with her medium blue eyes as they sort of glistened at him. His cheeks grew slightly pinkish.

"Don't lie to me, Manon," Charlemagne expressed in a weak tone. "I've seen the way you've treated me, the way you yell at me, and the way you despise me in who I am. You don't need to lie to me that you've looked at me in any other way to make me feel better or fight harder."

"What if it was not a lie, Charlemagne?" Manon asked. "What if… I've liked you for a long time?"

Charlemagne did not answer.

"Would anyone else travel this far to be with you? You tell me that I am here for the adventure, and it is true, but also it is the adventure with you that I have enjoyed, not feeling this joy since we were children exploring every surrounding that our fathers took us to. The days in which we used to pretend and play together. My words have been true though, I did not want to see you kill yourself out here as I had seen the risk unfold alone. *Charles*, you say my actions tell you that I do not love you, but would any other woman you've known come this far with you? Has any other woman ever stood by you this far?"

Charlemagne simply looked at Manon. He swallowed his breath and looked towards the side exit.

"I... I think we can have this conversation later, Manon," Charlemagne expressed, clearing his throat. "Now isn't the appropriate time..."

"No, perhaps not..." Manon remarked, lowering her hand from his chest, "but *Charles*... in case we were to die..." She leaned forward and kissed him on the cheek. "For good luck."

Charlemagne then turned to her and said, "A peck on the cheek as though you were an English woman..." He then leaned in and kissed her on the lips. They held each other closely for several seconds before they parted.

"A kiss as though you truly were a French man," Manon affirmed with a timid smile.

Charlemagne finally raised a smile at her and then took her hand. "Come now, this isn't the end of us, Manon. Let's find Cael and get the hell out of here."

The pair stood up and immediately went to approach the side exit together, but as they did, a foot stepped forward and entered into the hull.

"Ah, here you are," Krum remarked, taking a firearm out from his belt and pointed it at them. "I had hoped I would get the chance to avenge my men that you killed in the desert..."

"How flattering for you to believe that I killed your men," Charlemagne expressed. "In all honesty, I haven't even hurt a fly..."

Krum swore at him in Bulgarian and then stepped forward to jab at Charlemagne's abdomen with his handgun.

"I am going to enjoy seeing you die…" Krum expressed in a quiet tone.

"You won't get to know what I found with you treasure map though…"

Krum raised an eyebrow. Manon's eyes then left his face and towards the appearance of a figure from behind. She raised her own eyebrows as the figure pointed a handgun towards Krum.

"Stop!" Irina shouted.

Krum froze and stepped back.

"I said stop," Irina shouted again. "Hands up and apart – drop the gun…"

Krum did as she asked, placing his hands up and then dropping the handgun.

"So, Rubashkin sent you to finish me off, did he?" Krum questioned, stepping forward.

"Do not take another step, and I will finish you off right here," Irina threatened. "Disobey even one word of mine, and I will tell my people you fought savagely but died like the dog you are."

"I knew Rubashkin should not have trusted you," Krum remarked. "I didn't trust you…"

"You're under arrest, Berezovsky," Irina remarked. "Now come down to your knees and place your hands behind your head."

"Arrest?" Charlemagne questioned as he held Manon with one arm around her back.

Krum fell to his knees and then placed his hands behind his back. Irina skirted around him as she took out a pair of handcuffs from her black poncho. She then moved in and handcuffed the arms dealer.

"Krum Berezovsky, under the authority of the Federal Service Bureau of the Russian Federation, you are under arrest," Irina remarked. "Now stand up, and walk with us."

Krum swore in Bulgarian.

"FSB?" Charlemagne questioned. "Hang on, you aren't who you say you are, are you?"

Irina held on to Krum by his wrist and then turned to them. She pointed her handgun to the air. "I have been everything I've said I was. What I have not revealed to you was never said otherwise"

"You're a Russian spy," Charlemagne concluded. "Does Rubashkin know?"

"Do not worry about Rubashkin," Irina responded. "Right now, I will help you get out of here if you want to live. I have a helicopter not too far, and there is space for both you two and him."

"I... I don't think that'd be very wise," Charlemagne expressed. "Sorry, but I think we'll take our own transit out..."

Irina looked at him with surprise and then said, "And how do you intend to leave this mess? What are you scared of? Do you not trust me?"

"No, sorry, I don't," Charlemagne remarked. "You've been the woman of my worst enemy, and just because you slap a pair of handcuffs onto this bastard, you think you can call yourself FSB. You were with Rubashkin moments before he sent these dogs after us. How can I trust you?"

Irina sighed and then took an official badge out from her poncho to show him. "Satisfied?"

"Not in the slightest," Charlemagne remarked, looking at the badge and then at her. "So we go with you to Russia, but then the Russians steal what is mine. I don't like it..."

"You mean the crown?" Irina questioned. "You found it?"

"Yes, I did," Charlemagne replied. "Do you want to kill me for it?"

"No," Irina responded, "but you know that if I did want that crown, for Rubashkin, I would shoot you right now for it. Trust me, Mr. Cabernet, I can take you and Dr. Dumas to safety. We won't even fly to Russia. I can take you to Baku and to your embassy so you can go to wherever you please. Your treasure is yours. Let us make our escape."

Charlemagne looked to Manon and then over to Irina. "Fine, it's a deal." She then pointed over to a roll of duct tape on the table. "Pass that to me, before this oaf gives away our location as we go out into the battle." Charlemagne went to fetch the duct tape and she taped his mouth thoroughly. "You make any sort of move, I will shoot you. You try to run, I will shoot you. Piss me off, and I will shoot you. Am I understood?"

Krum simply mumbled.

"Good," Irina replied. "Charles, take point. I will keep this human garbage in check."

"Aye, ma'am."

Charlemagne, Manon, and Irina left the plane and came out to a clearing behind where there were various scraps of debris besides another plane, cut in half with either half sloped upwards from the middle except the rear. Charlemagne took point with his rifle, while Manon stayed close to Irina. They hid behind a bulldozer as the battle continued to rage on around them before Charlemagne led them into the commercial airplane in three parts, coming in through the middle and climbing up the slope. He came into the prone position from above, and from either side of the scrapyard did he see forces fighting. A military transport plane lay in the ground in pieces on his left, and many more pieces on his right. Ahead of him was a road with low slopes on either side, and directly beneath him was a steeper slope going down into the rest of the scrapyard. He could see large commercial airplanes and more military transport planes around him, as well as large dumpsters and metal pieces about. On the other side of the hill, like on their side, the planes were lined up, and from this height, Charlemagne could see the extent of what appeared to be hundreds of aircrafts around in more than twenty, but thirty to forty lots in total. From above, smoke filtered upwards from various sections of the rest of the airfield.

Charlemagne left the plane and slid down the slope to come to the bottom where he hid behind a dumpster.

"Which way?" Charlemagne asked Irina.

"The helicopter is to the right, besides the runway," Irina said. "We will need to stay down to survive."

"Of course."

Charlemagne led the team around to the left, behind the transport plane and then behind a dumpster next to it. They came between the transport plane and a large commercial airplane which they then stayed close to. Next to the rear of the airplane was a dumpster they stopped at as a BTR-40 drove forward and opened fire from the Soviet side. A helicopter then flew past and shot a missile that destroyed it in the midst of the road. Charlemagne led the team to the bulldozer and then over behind the BTR-40 wreckage as smoke filled the area.

Further to the right, Charlemagne saw parked helicopters behind a chain-link fence. Through the smoke, Charlemagne could see Soviet mercenaries running towards the front line while helicopters flew above with reinforcements. A separate attack helicopter destroyed the Bulgarian one, and little helicopters flew together as an all-out war continued around them. At the top of the hill, Charlemagne and the others stayed behind two shipping containers that provided cover both ends, and then numerous wrecks around a lot above the field where Soviets skirmished with Bulgarian mercenaries. Charlemagne and the others stayed out of the way, but as they went from the shipping container to behind the wing of a cargo plane raised up, they ran into a Bulgarian soldier who Irina shot point blank. At that moment, Charlemagne felt the target of gunfire on their location.

"I suppose it was too good to believe that we'd be in the clear here," Charlemagne remarked. "We don't' stand a chance against either side."

"We don't have to. Just keep going and keep your heads down," Irina instructed.

Charlemagne went forward and crawled underneath a cross-section of a hull. He shot at some soldiers who were behind them and was able to get them to disperse. Irina came around and opened fire with her handgun. A BTR-40 in the center of this lot opened fire in numerous directions before a rocket came from a random direction and caused it to blow up into a fireball that rose upwards. Charlemagne then went forward and around to a dirt path where it was quieter. Parallel to the dirt path was a chain-link fence with numerous aircrafts parked and in one piece. On the right were parked cars that blocked progress that direction, so they went left and continued down the side of the road as they made their escape from the conflict. Helicopters continued to fly by above of them, and as Charlemagne looked ahead through a dirt cloud, he could see vehicles approaching so he took them behind a fuel truck and they waited them out. He took them around the fuel truck to the front where a little bird helicopter flew in the opposite direction and fired rockets at a BTR-40 on approach to cause it to erupt into flames and block the path continuing forward, so they ventured past a gate into the lot beside them. Charlemagne went forward and hid underneath a modern jet.

The dirt path ahead of them had numerous jets lined up on either side, but each with some sort of defect from the other. There were oil drums, and other loose pieces and machinery spread around this lot. Charlemagne kept them near the wheels of the jets and other machines. The jets were set up in two groups, with a bunch of helicopters, likewise appearing defective and out of service. The conflict was quieter in these parts, though the presence of helicopters above was more than the others as reinforcements landed additional hardware and troops in open spaces about. Charlemagne and the others kept their heads down as they reached jets again, and then went forward to come around a group of commercial airplanes that although decrepit, at least stood on their wheels. Charlemagne began to guide them towards the right towards the approximate location of Irina's helicopter when they began to come around to some attack helicopters and tanks at the bank of the runway.

From where they were, Charlemagne could see the helicopter further ahead atop of a helipad marked besides the start of the runway. He stopped and looked elsewhere as he saw numerous better-looking aircraft on the sidelines of the runway. He looked as far to the left he could see, near a concrete building, to notice a jeep parked out behind. He eyed the jeep with intent, while Irina began to guide Krum and Manon to the right.

"Charles, let's move," Irina stated. "It's time to go."

"Go on, don't feel the need to wait for me," Charlemagne remarked. "I've got a loose end I need to tie."

"What are you talking about, *Charles*?" Manon questioned.

"You know what I mean," Charlemagne responded. "Nobody gets left behind. If I'm not there in ten minutes, then leave without me."

Irina did not respond and instead continued along. Manon looked at him, and he looked back at her, nodded, and then left down the runway. He came around to the jeep, recognized the missing windshield to be the one he drove in with Cael, and then came around to a door to enter into a hangar. He looked around and saw several planes parked with the shutters open, and a fuel truck nearby with a hose.

"Cael!" Charlemagne shouted. "Cael, are you here?!"

"I'm right here, Charles-man," Cael answered, hopping down from the wing of the same plane with the hose. He pulled the hose away and Charlemagne saw fuel ooze from out. "Look at this beauty; a vintage World War II close ground support aircraft, the *Ilyusha* 10. I've just finished readying her for flight. Did you find your girl?"

"Aye, I found her, and she's on her way out with some help."

"Fantastic, lad," Cael remarked. "There's space for two of us in this plane, so hop in the back to man the guns, and I'll man the cannons and pilot."

"I didn't realize flight training was also part of your training."

"I'm trained in all manners, mate," Cael said to him. "Let's get out of here."

"I'm afraid I can't do that... I shouldn't part from Manon, but I don't trust who we're about to leave. I think she may try to steal the crown from me and hand it to the Russians who she works for."

"You're talking about that Irina lass, aren't you?"

"Yes, that'd be her. Did you know she was a Russian spy?"

"Yes," Cael answered, "how did you know?"

"She told us as she arrested Krum."

"She arrested Krum?" Cael remarked with surprise. "Well then, bravo for her."

"Anyways, I want to give you the crown – I need you to take it with you back to the West for me. Can I trust you with that?"

"Aye, of course, Charles-man, you can trust me with anything."

Charlemagne unzipped his backpack and held the crown in his hands.

"I don't want to raise any suspicions about the fate of the crown, so let's trade with the Polish one. I'll meet you in Baku sometime soon, at the British Embassy. Does that work with you?"

"Of course, Charles-man. I needed to return that way some time or another."

The pair walked out to the jeep where Cael opened a reinforced container from where the other crown was kept. He picked it up and they exchanged it for the Frankish crown. Charlemagne put it in his backpack, and then the pair carried the container. He helped Cael raise it up to the rear cockpit seat, and then he hopped down while Cael kneeled on the wing of the airplane.

"I suppose this is where we part," Cael remarked, smiling at Charlemagne. "It's been an honor adventuring with you, Charles-man."

"Likewise to you, I really owe you for keeping me and Manon safe through these times."

"Ah, it was nothing," Cael responded. "Buy me a drink when we see each other again. How about that?"

"Aye, that'll do," Charlemagne remarked, waving to him. "Safe travels, friend. It's been a pleasure to have met you."

"Same to you, Charles-man. Same to you," Cael remarked, waving to him and then climbing into the cockpit. The airplane rotors began to start, and the plane drove forward towards the runway for takeoff.

Charlemagne held the keys to the jeep in his hand, and then went around to drive it to the helipad on the other side. He watched the Il-10 roll down the runway and began to pick up speed before it took off. He stopped to see it fly away before he came around to the helicopter as it likewise began to move its rotors. Irina sat in the helm of the helicopter. He came around to the side door and stepped up. Manon held a saddened face and then looked at him with a smile. She stood up and went to help him up. Krum was knocked out and on his side on their right. Charlemagne held Manon's hand as he was lifted up into the helicopter as it began to ascend.

"*Charles,*" Manon greeted, pulling him in.

However, before the pair could be reunited, Charlemagne's head turned as he heard a loud growl and yell. A man placed his arms around Charlemagne, pulling him backwards, prompting Manon to grab hold and pull Charlemagne in with one hand.

"Irina, it's Rubashkin!" Manon shouted. "He's trying to pull Charlemagne out!"

Irina looked behind, but could not see the chaos. The helicopter hovered a few feet off the ground. Charlemagne held one hand on the sides of the door as he attempted to shake Rubashkin off.

"I can feel it!" Rubashkin cried out. "I can feel the crown in your backpack!"

"It's not the crown you want, you crazed fool!" Charlemagne replied with a struggle. "Let go of me!"

Some Soviet mercenaries that appeared behind Rubashkin began to open fire towards the helicopter.

"I can't stay here!" Irina shouted. "I'm taking off!"

"No!" Manon contested.

The helicopter flew upwards a few more feet and then went forward and away from the mercenaries as they came towards the runway. Rubashkin used one hand to open Charlemagne's backpack as he fished around for the crown.

"Rubashkin!" Charlemagne cried out. "Stop! That's not the Frankish crown! That's the Polish crown!"

"Shut up!" Rubashkin replied. "You stole it off me. You stole the map off me – that was my map, and this was my treasure!"

"It's not the Frankish crown! It's the Polish crown!"

"Polish?! Polish?! You believe this crown is Polish?!" Rubashkin questioned. "The Polish should wish to have a crown as beautiful as this – no, this crown belongs to my ancestors, a people who inhabited this land of the Caucasus more than a thousand years ago – before your Frankish king was even born! A nation earlier than Russia, Ukraine, Poland... a people who inhabited these lands and everything north around the Volga into the Ukraine many years ago. My people...."

"You're absolutely mad!" Charlemagne remarked as he continued to struggle. "You're a worse pain my side than that twat Ali Al-Suli and that moron Musa Le Havre who he hires."

"Who he hires?! Rubashkin questioned as he continued to open Charlemagne's backpack. "Have you thought all this time that Le Havre was responding to the son of Harun Al-Suli?! I'm the one who hired Le Havre, to harass you and claim those treasures, though half-wittingly! When his men were killed in Belgrade, I knew I had to up the ante! I had to hire these useless mercenaries who couldn't even kill you in the desert!"

"Funny enough, I had some protection," Charlemagne remarked, elbowing Rubashkin. He then kicked his heel into his shin, causing him to fall down.

Rubashkin grabbed hold of Charlemagne's legs, pulling him down with him while Manon continued to struggle.

"*Charles*, I do not know how much I can hold you both!" Manon shouted. At that moment, she lost control of him and both Charlemagne and Rubashkin fell down another notch.

Charlemagne grabbed hold of a grip on the side of the plane, while Rubashkin continued to hold onto Charlemagne's legs. The helicopter continued to fly around while vehicles began to position themselves on the runway, including BTR-40s as soldiers and cars alike opened fire at the helicopter, causing it to swerve out of the way and make it even more difficult to stay in place. Charlemagne gripped the bar with both hands.

"Let go of me!" Charlemagne shouted out.

"Did you think that I just happened to take notice of you?!" Rubashkin questioned. "I've been after you from the very beginning, Charlemagne. Since the moment I noticed you and the exquisite treasures you could discover and which I wanted for myself."

"Let go!"

"Land this helicopter, and the two of us won't drop to our deaths."

"Irina, land the helicopter," Manon pleaded. "He's going to kill them both."

"I can't," Irina shouted. "The landing zone is too hot!"

Suddenly, Charlemagne saw an aircraft fly in from ahead, the Il-10 opened fire with its cannons and destroyed the armored cars and trucks parked below, wreaking havoc on the hostiles below. The plane flew swiftly underneath them and then carried on in the opposite direction. The helicopter ascended more and flew down the runway as Charlemagne and Rubashkin continued to struggle.

"Ah!" Charlemagne shouted as Rubashkin released grip from one arm, shifting weight as he pulled harder to sustain himself. He took it into his hands.

"Land this helicopter, or I will take Charlemagne with me!" Rubashkin threatened aloud. "I know you are there, you miserable woman! Land this helicopter now!"

The helicopter stayed put at more than several yards above the ground. At least the equivalency of more than ninety floors.

Charlemagne cried out as he began to lose grip. The Il-10 made a returning pass, this time opening fire in midair directly below Rubashkin.

"Gah!" Rubashkin shouted as a bullet pierced his own ankle. He dropped and took hold of Charlemagne's ankle. The tug caused the crown to fall out from his backpack and land upon his head. Rubashkin took the dagger and then swiped at Charlemagne's thigh with it.

"Agh!" Charlemagne shouted out, losing grip of one hand.

The loss of grip caused Rubashkin to slip down, and the jerk of his leg caused him to kick Rubashkin backwards, throwing the crown off his head and subsequently Rubashkin off his leg. As Charlemagne's fingers began to slide off the rest of the bar, Manon leaned forward and took hold off him.

"I've got you!" Manon shouted. She pulled himself up and he grabbed hold of the bar. He then began to climb up with her help and came into the transport helicopter. "Irina, he's safe! I've got Charlemagne! You can go now!"

"Thank goodness," Irina remarked. "What about Rubashkin?"

"Seems as though he's met his fall," Charlemagne simply said, sitting down as he panted and held his arm. "He's gone, Irina, which is a shame – seems as though he had made himself into a worthy rival. Nevertheless, it's over now... Take us home."

"I'm so glad you are safe," Manon remarked, kissing him on the cheek. "I thought he was going to kill you..."

"Not this time... after all, love. I'm Ch-" he then paused for a moment before he could speak. He then said, "I'm just lucky to be alive... though, I think I dislocated my shoulder in that fight. I think I'm just about ready to retire from this adventure. What do you think?"

"I think so too."

"As soon as we land in Baku, I think I'd like to visit the British Embassy and get the hell out of here."

Act 7, Scene 5

Charlemagne sat in a corner office on the top floor of a building in the midst of a large city. From out the window, Charlemagne could see stretches upon stretches of apartments in all directions except south where the bay at the cusp of the Caspian Sea was a dark blue. Charlemagne appeared clean shaven, moustache still under his lips but face washed and a bruise around his cheeks. His hair was also recently trimmed. He wore a light grey suit with an open collared white shirt. His left arm was in a sling. He sat atop of a table with two chairs on either side. He then stood up and began to pace around the room, walking with a minor limp as he did so. Suddenly, there was a knock on the door and a man entered inside. Charlemagne looked over to the man who had fair skin and balding dark hair. He was dressed in a navy-blue suit with a British flag pin at the lapel. Charlemagne sat down at the side of the chair and looked over to him.

"I have a Ms. Irina Pachayevskovna here to see you, Mr. Cabernet. Shall I let her in?"

Charlemagne nodded and he stood up. The man nodded and then left, and behind him walked in Irina who was dressed in dark blue dress, holding a clutch in her hand and her black hair straightened around on either side. She wore deep red lipstick and her face was serene and clear, and at least compared to Charlemagne, wound-free. Irina offered her hand, and Charlemagne shook it with his right.

"*Zdravstvyutye*, Mr. Cabernet," Irina greeted with a calm smile. "I thought you'd still be in Baku."

"Of course, I'm waiting for Cael still..." Charlemagne remarked. "Nobody here seems to know who I am talking about when I say his name, and I've urged them to contact MI6 to say that their agent is missing. He was supposed to meet me here, but that's beside the point. I would have thought you'd have left and returned to Russia with Krum in custody, and Rubashkin out of commission."

"The news of Rubashkin's death certainly came at a shock, though not that I was involved. His death is being shared as an unfortunate tragedy, an accident while on vacation," Irina remarked. "Meanwhile, Krum has been handed over to my bosses and flown to Moscow where he awaits several dozen charges for his involvement in international arms dealing. I need to hand it to you, as they say, you did your share to bring that man to justice for his crimes, so although you lost your crown in the fight with Rubashkin, I hope you can have that satisfaction."

"I'll be more satisfied when Cael comes around," Charlemagne remarked. "You should meet him – he knew that you were an FSB agent before I did, though I don't know how…"

"Yes…" Irina responded, lowering her smile. She straightened out and placed her hands on the table before her as she raised a straight face, "and in actuality, this Cael is why I took the time to come here and speak with you, Mr. Cabernet."

"When you told me that you were saved and watched over by a man named Cael Monaghan, a British operative, I thought it strange because British intelligence does not act in the way you described, like some James Bond character or British commando."

"I thought it strange too, but what are you saying? Cael isn't who he says he is?"

"He's certainly named Cael," Irina affirmed. "Cael Monaghan – but I checked with my bosses, and we ran his name through to MI6, and although they would be likely to deny that an agent of that name operates in the East, they also denied that an agent of that name even existed."

"So, Cael Monaghan *isn't* his real name. Did you try Kyle? I believe Cael is the old form of what is really a modern name."

"We tried that, yes…"

"I'm not too surprised, though a little disappointed, that he never shared his real name, but still… his accent, his skills and techniques. His story…"

"There is no MI6 agent by the name of Cael Monaghan," Irina clarified, "but… there is a someone else we know by that name who is on our list of wanted criminals. Though, in these parts, he does not go by that name. When we informed MI6 about this man, they asked us more questions and shared with us his history as it seems that he's wanted by them too. This Cael Monaghan is wanted for numerous crimes for his part in the Irish Republican Army insurgency, as a member, which lined up with what we know about him too, but in these parts, he is better known as a professional thief named *Kirill Masurski*."

"A professional thief?" Charlemagne questioned. "I don't believe you."

Irina opened her clutch and then placed down some documents. Here he is listed as the suspect in the robbery of a valuable diamond… here a bank robbery… and here the stealing of some priceless art… It's no wonder he was so close to you, eyeing that crown of yours, and still too, near Rubashkin and his personal collection. I can only imagine now he must be in Romania to pillage what was there."

"I don't believe this…"

"Yes, around fifteen years ago, he migrated from Ireland to the Eastern Bloc, acting as a liaison between the KGB and IRA for several years until the Soviet Union collapsed and from there he took up his career as a thief. He's very good at what he does, but still… it seems like he manipulated you to get that crown from you to steal it."

"How are you so sure?" Charlemagne questioned.

Irina frowned and then took out another folded piece of paper from her clutch. She unfolded it. The piece of paper was a front page of a newspaper that showed a picture of the very same Frankish crown, in a display case.

"Because just yesterday, this article made the headlines – the Frankish Crown in the State Hermitage in Moscow. Some details into the article do not name *Kirill*, I mean Kyle, but do say that the item was located in storage…" Irina remarked. "I did some of my own research, and it appears that the curator, good friends with our cultural minister, retrieved it from him. If I had to guess, your friend made a deal with the minister, possibly money in exchange for the crown. In the end, this man was just that – a thief, interested in his own greed more than anything, like Krum."

"No…" Charlemagne remarked, shaking head.

"Well, believe me if you want, but…"

"Not like Krum," Charlemagne stated, looking out the window. "He was not interested in the money… I think… he was interested in making a name for himself, and perhaps then, as a professional thief."

"What makes you so sure?"

"Because I… I know him, his heart that is," Charlemagne remarked. "He wants to become the best damn professional thief there is, so much so that people will talk of him for generations."

"Well, okay then," Irina remarked. "My bosses will be questioning the Russian minister on his alleged transaction with *Kirill*, but I do not believe anything will come out of it… I just wanted to give you the news…"

Charlemagne did not respond. She walked around to stand beside him and he finally turned his head. She leaned forward and kissed him on the cheek.

"Goodbye, Mr. Cabernet," Irina remarked. "I am sorry your adventure did not come out as you hoped…"

Charlemagne simply looked at her with loving eyes as she then walked off. He then stayed put as he placed a hand before him on the table and looked out the window with a frown. After a few minutes, footsteps approached and Manon entered the room. She likewise appeared healthy. She wore a black t-shirt and denim pants. She also wore a beret.

"Well, I just spoke to my father to give him the news of what's happened, and that we await this Cael here, but he's certainly suspicious of it all. He's upset we lost the Polish- sorry, the Kazar crown, though he could see how those two could be one and the same too, so he's going to investigate further though he did suggest perhaps we could. I told him I was exhausted and so were you, and here we are, waiting…"

"Cael is not coming…" Charlemagne simply stated.

"What?"

Charlemagne explained to her what Irina told him, to which Manon sighed and replied, "Perhaps it was too good to be true, all that he did for us…"

"Alas," Charlemagne simply replied, sighing and then leaning back, "but I suppose as I've waited here for him, I've had a chance to think."

"Oh? What of?" Manon questioned, hand on her hip.

"Of what a wretch I've been," Charlemagne answered. "I've risked it all for this crown, and now here we are empty-handed on both accounts. I don't even suppose that gold in that train is still there; probably been looted as well, as so all that treasure in the salt mine. I'm utterly empty-handed."

"No, not utterly," Manon expressed, walking over to him and placing a hand behind his back. "I found… how even how much of a pain it can be to be with you, the love I have for you keeps me at your side. Can you at least say the same?"

Charlemagne looked up at her and attempted to raise a smile, but then he said as he shook his head, "We've been little more than a month together, and all it'll take is a few more for you to grow bored of me, to see me as too much to handle, or reckless, to then leave me. You've stayed with me through one adventure, but I… I'm not fit for love. My life has taught me that…"

"No, that's not true," Manon sternly said, "*Charles*, I stayed by you to the end. I risked my own life, and I let you risk my life – how can you even suggest or believe that I would abandon you?"

"You will do it though, I know it."

"No, *Charles* – now I am the one that tells you that I will not leave, but if you do not want to be together then you must be the one to leave. Go on, leave me – tell me you do not love me, and I will go."

"Manon, I... I can't do that..." Charlemagne quietly remarked with a minor laugh. "Why would I do that?"

"Because you are Charlemagne," Manon affirmed. "You speak no sense, and I love you for all your craziness and all your ambition. I love you for the great ego you have, because I know the child within you – the child that used to laugh with mine. I know your heart, *Charles*, and it is that which I love most of all, even though your faults, I am – I have been patient with you, and I will continue to be patient with you because you... are patient with me. At any point could you have left me behind – you did not need to take me with you, but you enjoyed my company, and I enjoyed you. We fought, we bickered, but we made it to the end. How can you say that this was not a test of our match for one another?"

"I suppose it was..." Charlemagne admitted with another laugh. "I just... I never thought it would come to this... I remember when I left the farm after my grandfather's funeral, that was it, and then I met your father again after years, and there you were. Not so much the snot-faced girl I knew..." Manon hit him in the shoulder, "but the beautiful woman you had become."

"You are the fool, Charlemagne, if you have not seen my love for you," Manon expressed. "You are a maniac, but I still love you, and I will never leave you... so long as you do not break my heart, I will love you."

"I will love you too, Manon," Charlemagne said, standing up to look at her. The pair kissed and Charlemagne placed his hand around her waist and brought her in. The two then parted afterwards and Charlemagne continued to hold to her as he said, "I think I've had enough adventures, at least for a few weeks, maybe a few months… How about we return to Paris and work on that paper – the discovery of the Frankish Crown, and it's new estate in Hermitage of Russia, for all to see."

"Will we go and see this crown?"

"Perhaps in due time, but right now, I just want to have a lie down and a rest… with you, of course. How does that sound?"

"*Parfait, mon cheri.*"

Epilogue

Charlemagne looked around the plaza he was in. The skies above him were grey, but to his right was a wide structure with thick greyish-white columns above a set of steps supporting a pediment roof. The structure had eight tall rectangular windows on either side, and eight square windows above. The structure also had grey tiles on a sloped roof. The main entrance of the structure an arched white French window, and before the building were parked cars. A driveway came up and merged with the top landing of the steps and then went down the other end to merge with the road. Charlemagne stood at a roundabout where vehicles drove in, and he held a map that showed the approximate location he was at with words in German. The structure ahead of him was the *Neus Kurhaus Aachen*, while the building to his left was the *Eurogress Aachen*. He turned towards the Eurogress, which was a modern building constructed of glass and steel. The center was besides a four-story white structure further to the left with dormer windows within a tall dark grey sloped roof. In front of this structure, and on approach to the roundabout was a double pathway avenue with trees and a grassy field further in front, met with a pond to consist of a wide park. Charlemagne looked about with a young face, clean-shaven entirely, and dressed in a dark suit.

As people got out of cars and walked up the steps, so did Charlemagne as he read signs and was guided up a set of stairs to a top floor. He found a lobby with many tables where people were picking up lanyards with names on them. He stopped for a moment and then found his name, placing it around his neck and then turning around as he continued to look around. There were many people in the lobby, conversing with one another, and many of them were males in suits of all different sorts and kinds. He began to navigate around these people, greeting a few that greeted him, and then stopping as he eyed a person amidst the crowd. This person wore a tweed brown suit and had a jovial look upon his face, a deep greyish-white beard, and thick glasses.

"Dr. Dumas?!" Charlemagne questioned.

The man jerked his head over, doing a double take as he realize who had called his name. He squinted for a moment and then realized. He raised his confused expression up to a joyous one as he exclaimed, "Charlemagne de la Cabernet!"

Dr. Dumas rushed forward, leaving behind the people he was speaking to as he wrapped his arms around and embraced Charlemagne with an affectionate hug.

"*Ah, Dieu soit loué!*" Dr. Dumas praised. "It is you, the prodigal son, no?"

Charlemagne laughed and then parted from Dr. Dumas as he looked at him.

"How many years has it been?" Dr. Dumas questioned. "Many, many years, and yet I knew it- I knew it was you because I saw those eyes and that hair, and it was the same face of a boy that I long knew and had not forgotten." He then slapped a hand behind Charlemagne as he expressed. "How are you? It is good that you are here, perhaps it was natural I should come find you here. What are you doing now? Are you a professor? A researcher? Tell me, what kind of work are you doing to come here? It is only natural that the son of Derby de la Cabernet should follow in those footsteps, no?"

"Oh, I'm not here under any sponsorship of any sort of university," Charlemagne expressed "In fact, I don't even have any academic background in history. I'm just here of my own volition… if not, personal business of mine."

"Ah?"

"Yes, I've longed to engage in the sorts of activities that my grandfather got to, but I want to take it to the next level," Charlemagne expressed. "My father, as you may know, abandoned Cabernet Industries, and after a bit of maneuvering,

I've come out on top of my siblings for full control of the company, but now that's come to an end, and I have trustworthy people piloting the helm, I have more free time than I thought. I thought, why not use company resources to sponsor a historical research project? A team, so to speak? What do you think? Are you up for the grand old adventures that my grandfather used to put you through? I will need an expert in historical research, and I see no greater person for the job than you."

"Ahah," Dr. Dumas laughed, "I appreciate the offer, but I could not possibly. I am not in the same shape I was twenty years ago. My knees have become fragile, and my back aches... all the best to you, and I hope all the best in your research, but if there is anything to do with research in the libraries and such, I would be happy to assist."

"Oh, I'd be happy for you to contribute in any sort of the way."

"Yes," Dr. Dumas remarked, "but tell me about yourself, my son. How are you? How old must you be? Thirty?"

"Just under thirty," Charlemagne expressed.

"Ah, so you must be married, no?"

"No, not married," Charlemagne corrected.

"A girlfriend?"

"No, no girlfriend either," Charlemagne remarked, awkwardly laughing. "No, I've had my romantic interest or two in recent years, but nothing long-term for me anymore. I've sworn that off completely since university for it was too burdensome and troubling to cope with. I'm happy as I am, a bachelor with no strings attached."

"Is that so?"

"Yes, it is so," Charlemagne replied, "but what about you? How is Marie? How is Jacques... and Manon, what about her? What is she doing now?"

"Why not ask her yourself? She is travelling with me," Dr. Dumas clarified.

"She is?" Charlemagne questioned, facing going pale.

"Yes," Dr. Dumas affirmed, *"ma petite chérie* just recently earned her doctorate degree in European History, and she is eager to begin her own research away from my nest. Where is that girl?" Dr. Dumas looked around and then pointed forward. "Ah, there she is!"

Charlemagne looked and saw a woman with brown hair, slightly obese and in a long dress. She had fair skin and a hooked nose.

"Oh, is that her?" Charlemagne questioned in total lack of appeal.

"Nonsense," Dr. Dumas remarked, "that is not her. Look past, and around..."

Charlemagne looked around and at a table, writing her name on a name tag, he saw a woman in a blazer and skirt. She had luscious medium brown hair, and fair pinkish skin. Her cheeks were rosy and lips red. She held a handbag around her shoulders and at her feet were high heels. She held a smile on her face and after writing her name, placed the name tag over her collar and then came forward as Dr. Dumas waved to her with one hand and placed an arm over Charlemagne's shoulder with the other.

"Manon! *Viens ici, ma chérie!*" Dr. Dumas shouted out.

"*Père, c'est quoi toute cette agitation?*" Manon questioned, looking at him and then over to Charlemagne. Charlemagne looked stupefied and terrified as he looked at her smile.

"*Ma chérie*, you will never believe..." Dr. Dumas remarked, looking who I've found, "it is your old friend, *Charlemagne de la Cabernet!*"

"*Charles?*" Manon questioned in surprise, looking at him and then at Charlemagne. "Is that so?"

"Yes..." Charlemagne affirmed, breaking tone. He cleared his throat and then expressed, "Hello, Manon. How are you?"

"Fine," Manon replied, "isn't this a surprise? *Charles*, look at you, you've grown so much..."

"Same with you…" Charlemagne remarked, looking at Manon intently. He cleared his throat again.

"Hasn't this become a lovely reunion?" Dr. Dumas expressed. "What a joy, an utter joy. You must stay with us, *Charles*. Walk with us. If you want to find a team, I will show you the best of the best…"

"Team?" Manon questioned.

"Yes," Charlemagne quickly affirmed, "Manon? How would you like to join my expedition team?"

"Humility... is not identified with humiliation or resignation. It is not accompanied by faint-heartedness. On the contrary. Humility is creative submission to the power of truth and love. Humility is rejection of appearances and superficiality; it is the expression of the depth of the human spirit; it is the condition of its greatness."

– Pope Saint John Paul II